PENGUIN BOOKS

Orders for New York

Leslie Thomas is one of Britain's most popular writers: a bestselling novelist, a travel writer and a television and radio personality.

He was born in 1931 of a South Wales seafaring family. At the age of twelve he found himself in an orphanage following his father's drowning in the South Atlantic during a U-boat attack on a wartime convoy and his mother's subsequent death within six months. His experiences were recorded years later in his first book, *This Time Next Week*, quickly followed by his first bestselling novel *The Virgin Soldiers*, which became a highly successful film.

Leslie Thomas has written eighteen novels, including his bestsellers *The Magic Army*, *The Dearest and the Best* and *The Adventures of Goodnight and Loving*, all published by Penguin. His travel books about the lesser-known parts of the British Isles, *The Hidden Places of Britain* and *Some Lovely Islands*, in which he explores islands off the British coast, have also been published by Penguin. *A World of Islands* is another of Leslie Thomas's lyrical travel books. He also wrote and presented a television series *Great British Isles*. There have been television adaptations of his novels *Tropic of Ruislip* and *Dangerous Davies, The Last Detective*. His autobiography, *In My Wildest Dreams*, was published in 1984 by Penguin.

Leslie Thomas lives in London and Romsey, Hampshire, with his wife Diana and son Matthew. He has three children from a previous marriage. His hobbies include cricket, photography, philately, music and antiques.

LESLIE THOMAS

Orders for New York

Penguin Books

PENGUIN BOOKS

Published by the Penguin Group
27 Wrights Lane, London W8 5TZ, England
Viking Penguin Inc., 40 West 23rd Street, New York, New York 10010, USA
Penguin Books Australia Ltd, Ringwood, Victoria, Australia
Penguin Books Canada Ltd, 2801 John Street, Markham, Ontario, Canada L3R 1B4
Penguin Books (NZ) Ltd, 182–190 Wairau Road, Auckland 10, New Zealand

Penguin Books Ltd, Registered Offices: Harmondsworth, Middlesex, England

First published by Methuen London Ltd 1989
Published in Penguin Books 1990
10 9 8 7 6 5 4 3 2 1

Printed and bound in Great Britain by
Richard Clay Ltd, Bungay, Suffolk
Typeset in 10/12pt Lasercomp Baskerville

To Geoffrey Strachan

with my thanks for his patience

Author's Note

The contemporary episodes in this story,
and all the characters described therein,
are fiction.

The landing of four Nazi agents from
a submarine at Long Island, New York,
just before midnight on 12 June 1942
is fact.

Secrets are edged tools

DRYDEN

I

When I think of how, like four consecutive poor jokes, they waded ashore from the submarine, trudged across the sand-dunes, and took the Long Island Railroad to New York; under the stars, they said, but it was foggy, foggy June. And how, almost fifty years on, people have lost their lives because of what happened (or, rather, what did not happen) that night. Old lies die hard.

Even now I find it difficult to imagine myself sitting beside a German river with a naked woman, naked myself but holding a rose. And poor, fat Renate in Chicago (she, whose brother went to the electric chair) lively as a balloon on her finest and final evening; not to mention the cat with its tail afire. The Nazis singing 'Ain't Misbehaving' as they tramped the lanes around Brandenburg. The great fire melting the snow; a go-go dancer who was going no further; the deep lips and pale thighs of my former wife; the exquisite Cara in Mexico; Roosevelt's old trick; the life of Fred Robinson of the FBI. All the lies, known and unknown, lies told through the years that are still lies today. Tomorrow will see the truth. There will be no need for further killing.

It all began quietly. It was a silent and golden morning at Thoughtful Creek, Massachusetts. I had intended it to be the first day of my new life.

At eight-thirty I went down to the water's edge along

the dewy, unkempt grass to the wooden jetty. This was what I had waited for. Everything was glowing and deserted. It was a vacation area and people slept late. On the far bank of the creek was a white timber house, and the night before somebody over there had been playing 'As Time Goes By' on a piano, the notes floating across the flat water.

Now the house and the others along the inlet stood dumb among the summer boxwoods, boats balanced on their own perfect images. Across the olive water the early sun shone like a light on an empty stage.

A fish jumping two hundred feet away startled me. I had knelt on the jetty to look down into the deepness of the creek. The fish made the dull plop of a silenced rifle. Out of habit I ducked. Then the telephone began to ring casually in the house. My first inclination was to let it ring and afterwards I often wished I had. I've spent my life running to telephones. It kept ringing. I walked back without hurry. Since I had arrived only the evening before I thought it had to be for the previous tenants. But it was for me.

Her remembered voice said: 'Michael?'

It had been more than ten years. 'Madelaine,' I answered.

'That's amazing. You knew.'

I grimaced in the mirror above the telephone table. 'I always recognize the voice of a former wife,' I said. 'Where are you? Not around here?'

'Don't panic. I'm in London. I called the paper.'

'Where I no longer work.'

'Right. Then I called your house . . .'

'Where I no longer live.'

'Right. She sounds nice. How come?'

'The usual reasons. You know them.'

'I get it. It's really weird. I'm here in London and you're in . . . where is it . . .?'

'Thoughtful Creek,' I said carefully. 'Massachusetts.'

She understood my tone and said: 'Really . . . well, Michael this is not a social call. I've traced you for a reason. Your daughter wants to see you. Susan . . . remember?'

'Of course I remember.'

'Well, she doesn't. She was a baby. But she wants to see you. She took a fall from her horse and when she woke up that's what she wanted.'

I tried to picture Susan. I wondered what Madelaine looked like now. 'Is she all right?' I said.

'Don't be too concerned. The fall was last year. In California. But my husband, Sam, had to come to England. He met the Prime Minister yesterday.'

I made no comment although she waited. Eventually she continued. 'I thought it would be a good time for you to meet . . . see Susan.'

I said: 'It's odd, isn't it. You're over there and I'm over here.'

'An ocean between us,' she agreed. 'Nothing changes.'

'Your husband. He's a senator, isn't he?'

'Senator Sam Keenor,' she said firmly. 'One day, he'll be President.' The tone altered. 'But what are you doing, for God's sake, at Thoughtful Creek? Where the hell is it, anyway, apart from Massachusetts?'

'It's New Bedford,' I told her. 'I only got here last night. I'm going to do what I've wanted to do for years, Madelaine. My book about whales and whaling.'

She laughed outright. 'Shit! Not the whales and whaling book still!'

'Yes. Shit, the whales and whaling book still.'

'Sorry . . . but it's been so long.'

3

'I'm not tied to anything now.'

'Why did you quit the newspaper?'

'I got pissed off with Beirut and places like that. I'd like to live to see forty. I've rented this house for six months. It's all here. New Bedford was the biggest whaling port in America. And I'm going over to Nantucket.'

She said: 'You know what I always said about Nantucket.'

'I do. And it still rhymes,' I answered. 'What are we going to do about Susan?'

'Fix to meet sometime. We'll be flying back to New York before going home to Los Angeles. It will be a week or so. It depends on Sam's plans. I'll contact you. Give my love to the whales.'

Madelaine had married her senator four years previously, five years to the day after our divorce became final. I would not have made a note of anything so esoteric except that my circumstances, at that moment, gave me the opportunity and the time to think about it.

I had picked up a copy of *The New York Times*, some weeks old, in Borkov-Ennedi, an ugly, hot and dangerous place in Chad in Central Africa. In the social pages was an announcement of their marriage. Normally I did not read the social pages, and especially not the weddings, but there was little else to do since we were being pinned down by rocket fire from Libyan troops, and for thirty-three hours there was no way out. The newspaper had been the wrapping on a packed lunch provided the day before by the Luxarama Hotel, Najamena.

More recently I had seen Keenor's photograph, once in *Time* magazine, when it published a piece of stargazing on Presidents-of-the-future. He was mid-forties then, faultless eyes, strong jaw, easy looking, the sort bred for American politics. The background to the picture was a cascade of ivy on a wall, intended to make a point. He was wealthy, but not mega-wealthy, smart, and ambitious; made for my former wife. She was described as his greatest asset.

When I went out to Nantucket the island's blissful mist dropped, and I was marooned there for four days before the boat could sail back to New Bedford. I spent hours in the whaling museum and the old library, reading log books and manuscripts, tracing charts, making notes, listening to the Nantucket fog-horn sounding over the blind sea. I doubted that I had ever been so quiet, so content, like a sailor home from a long voyage.

The evening of my return to Thoughtful Creek she telephoned again.

'How are the whales?'

'Endangered. Perhaps you could get your husband to put a word in for them.'

'I will,' she said. 'Although I expect he has thought of it already.'

'How is Susan?'

'She's just fine. I called to say that Sam's finished with all his meetings here in London. We're flying back to New York on Wednesday before going on to Los Angeles.'

'Where do I see Susan?'

'Do you think you could make it to Long Island, the Hamptons?' she inquired politely. 'You can get a ferry from somewhere and it cuts out having to go into New York City. Sam says so.'

'Sam's right,' I said, thinking that probably he always was. 'How does he feel about this?'

She sounded surprised. 'Feel about it? Oh, about Susan seeing you. Oh, well, he's okay. Sam's very flexible.'

'Politicians are,' I agreed. I could tell that she smothered a retort. Instead she said quietly: 'Don't give me a hard time, Michael.'

'I'm sorry,' I said, meaning it.

'Thank you. We'll be at Middlehampton on Friday. Sam's father has a house there. You may recall him, Herbert Forrest Keenor. He was a senator. Susan's very fond of him and she loves being there.'

'I won't be intruding?' The tone was more sarcastic than I had intended.

'Mike, *don't*. Susan wants to see you but it's up to you if *you* want to see *her*. It's been a long time.' Then her sharpness softened as though someone had put a hand on her shoulder. 'And there *is* something else I have to ask you.'

'Really? What's that?'

'Not now, Michael. When I see you.'

'Where do we meet?' I asked. 'Do I stroll up to the Keenor front door?'

'I don't think that would be a good idea. It could make things difficult for Susan and we wouldn't want that. You and I ought to rendezvous first. How about the American Hotel in Sag Harbour? It's on Main Street.'

'I know the hotel,' I said. 'How will I know you?' I heard her draw in breath across the Atlantic. 'As you said, it's been a long time.'

'I'll be there at noon on Friday,' she said patiently. 'There's an animal's head sticking out of the wall, a bison, I think. If you don't recognize me, you'll know what a bison looks like. And there's only one.'

A merciful amnesia sometimes grows over the residue of finished marriages, so that the participants fail to remember a single intimate detail and are glad of it. But, with Madelaine, even though our later times together are obscured, I can recall our first time with ease; a one-night stand that lingered for two years. One night would have been excellent.

I was working in New York and I had been at the United Nations interviewing a British diplomat on a subject which seemed important at the time. It was one of those gritty Manhattan evenings around the beginning of November, the city grey and mild. When I left the UN there seemed nowhere special to go. I had only been in the New York office a month. I was twenty-five and I did not care to go home early, especially as home was a one-bedroomed apartment on the West Side, with a bad but relentless trombone player next door. I walked past the window of a restaurant called Bronte's, on Lexington.

A couple came out, laughing, walking unheedingly past me, making me feel more solitary. In those days I had not cultivated my own company. As the door opened I could hear talk and fragments of laughter. I paused and looked through the paned window. A group of people were having drinks, formally, restrained, as if they did not know each other well. I opened the door. The restaurant was busy. There were three long, large tables, vacant but set and decorated for dinner.

Some of the party were not at all acquainted because as they circulated there were introductions, smiles and handshakes. Madelaine, wearing a short, black, puffy dress, had her back to me.

It was my first sight of her . . .

The requirements of my professional life, putting the foot in the sorrowing widow's door, questioning the dying soldier, laughing with charlatans, posing with politicians, had left me with scant appreciation of social niceties. Neither has caution been one of my strong points. I stepped into the restaurant and joined the party.

It was simple, merely a matter of strolling into the general area, accepting a drink from a floating tray, and peering amiably around, as if I belonged. I asked the waiter if I could have the Martini just a trifle drier. Two minutes later I was talking to her.

'I'm Michael Findlater,' I said. There seemed no immediate advantage in lying. People were still being introduced all around. She was dark and beautiful. Her accent was English.

'And I'm Madelaine Cousins,' she said. Deliberately her eyes rose over her glass. 'It's very nice for everyone to meet like this, isn't it. And you're from England. I've been in this city for years but I was born in Kent.'

'Oxford,' I lied.

'Who are you with?' she asked.

'Myself,' I smiled blatantly.

She laughed refreshingly. 'Stop it,' she said. 'I mean which company?'

'Guess,' I suggested.

She agreed to play the game. 'English,' she echoed to herself. 'Qualtrick's . . .?'

'No, but you're close,' I encouraged. Who the hell was Qualtrick's?

'Bertenshaw's?' She regarded me brightly. I was about to congratulate her on being right when she added: 'With Rodney.' She nodded across the room.

'Purdey's,' I gambled blatantly. 'I'm with Purdey's.'

Light was catching her glass and making a fallen halo across her forehead. She frowned, denting the halo. 'Purdey's? I don't think I know them,' she puzzled. 'I thought I knew all the antiquarian booksellers in London.'

'Ah,' I breathed. 'Basingstoke, actually.' It was a bad choice. 'Just outside,' I faltered.

Her quizzical stare was interrupted by the announcement that dinner was about to be served. There would be one space too few at the table. Quickly I said to her: 'Do you mind if I sit beside you? I'm so enjoying our conversation.'

She regarded me sideways. 'Please,' she said and I sat down. The other guests arranged themselves around the three tables leaving a slow-faced man standing alone and perplexed. The head waiter looked peeved and beckoned a waiter who immediately laid an additional place, fortunately at another table because ours was fairly tight as it was.

Antiquarian booksellers do well for themselves. The dinner was excellent. 'It's astonishing, isn't it,' I ventured close to her ear. 'How outsiders always think this trade is populated by dusty old chaps wearing coats with baggy pockets.'

'In cobweb-hung shops,' she agreed. She examined the company. 'Yes, we all look pretty sharp. This is the one night we impress each other.'

She was impressing me. I was impressing her too, or something, because she kept slyly looking at me, her eyes flickering sideways.

Eventually she said: 'What price did the Spenser fetch in London last week? I've forgotten.'

'Ah, the Spenser,' I repeated. It was not a question but she answered it. '*The Faerie Queene*,' she muttered. 'First folio.'

'God, I've forgotten too,' I said airily. 'It must have been a lot.'

'Lot 54,' she muttered again. 'At Christie's.' I was relieved when she began to laugh.

When we were strolling along Lexington two hours later, having said goodnight to our antiquarian friends, and I was searching up and down for a taxi, she said very casually: 'There is no-one in the trade called Purdey's. Purdey's are gunsmiths.'

I did not look at her. 'It's close,' I said.

We got a taxi to the West Side of the Park. Until we were in her apartment, she made no further reference to it. On the journey she even pointed out to me the shop where she worked. But when she was in the kitchen making coffee, she called out: 'That's the biggest fucking cheek I've ever known.'

'It was all I could think of at the time,' I called back.

'You're an asshole,' she added as if she had finally made up her mind. She brought the coffee in. I owned up who I was and told her that I had been in Beirut, Vietnam and Northern Ireland and had suffered terribly, but that basically I had gone into the restaurant because that's where she happened to be. The following moment I was kissing her eagerly and she was responding. My hands went down to her hip-bones. They were very fine, like the handlebars of a racing bike. I was in love.

Madelaine was wonderfully unfussy. She took her clothes off as if we had been familiars for years. Even though I became used to it eventually, I have always remembered her body with affection and admiration, slim and pale, with her dozy breasts, her hip-bones and her pubis like an exclamation mark.

'Have you really been in all those places, Beirut and wherever?' she asked. She was standing in front of a long mirror, naked except for her watch. Briskly, but without hurry, she brushed her hair. 'Or is that another instant fantasy?'

By this time I was sitting up in her bed waiting for her and feeling at home. I said: 'The newspaper I work for keeps trying to kill me. Every time there's an explosion, anywhere in the world, they send me. New York is a doddle.'

'Rest and Recuperation,' she suggested. She turned from the mirror and slid into bed beside me. 'I've been waiting for you.' It was determined, almost a challenge. 'All week.' We stretched down the sheets. Her skin was sublime. Her toes pushed my shins.

'There's a book in the bed,' I said. I reached down and took the book from beneath the sheets.

'Mary Shelley's Diary,' she agreed. 'I read it every night.' She reached blindly for it. 'Some of it is very sad. Her baby dies. And there's a man called Hogg who keeps appearing. He just comes and goes. So far I haven't discovered who he is.'

You have to be very sure of yourself to discuss Mary Shelley and a stranger called Hogg at a time like that. Madelaine was absently stroking my groin. I opened the book: 'Third March, 1815,' I recited. 'Nurse the baby; talk and read *Corinne*. Hogg comes in the evening.'

'Read some more,' she suggested softly. Her hands continued to caress me.

'Fourth March, 1815. Read, talk and nurse. Shelley reads *The Life of Chaucer*. Hogg comes in the evening and sleeps.' Reading aloud is difficult at such times. Our bodies were against each other. Her watch was ticking against my groin. 'Hogg turns up most days,' I said unsteadily. I was still holding the book. 'Sixth March. Rained all day. Hogg came in the evening . . . two days later. Shelley wrote . . . Hogg came and stayed.'

Madelaine leaned across me, her hair overwhelming my face, her naked breast touching the page. 'March tenth,' she said. 'Hogg came at seven.'

There are limits to this sort of game. Quietly I put the book down and turned her onto her back. Kneeling above her I took one splendid hip-bone in each of my hands. Truthfully, but not surprisingly after all this time (and being married to her for two years of it), I remember few other details. But I do recall she awoke twice in the night. At the third time I protested, and she said she would let me sleep and promised to sleep also. She asked drowsily: 'Did you come that last time?'

'It wasn't Hogg,' I said.

Over the years I have suffered a movable nightmare. Sometimes its setting is the Falls Road, Belfast, at others the Rue Abdul Azeez, Beirut (I am familiar with most of the world's sadder streets), and occasionally, for some reason that only the makers of dreams know, it has happened in Madrid, where I have been only fleetingly and nothing terrible occurred. I used to think the Spanish version might be a warning of something unpleasant in the future, or perhaps a throwback to the Civil War, which in 1937 my father reported for Reuter.

The story of the dream is constant. There is a seeping smell of burning and I find I am in a room where the walls are running blood, or wine, whichever edition is showing that night. An agitated member of the Royal Ulster Constabulary arrives in the Belfast scene and shouts: 'It's not wine, you fool, it's blood!' In the Beirut version he has transferred to the Militia but he is crying the same thing. Confusingly the RUC man sometimes materializes in Rue Abdul Azeez, while the incongruous Militiaman occasionally staggers down the Falls Road.

In the rare Madrid scenario it is a member of the Guardia Civil wearing one of those operatic upturned hats that looks as if it has collided with a wall. In this one the message is reversed: 'It's not blood, you fool,' he shouts. 'It's wine!' The stench of burning remains.

The dream recurred at the Ferryboat Motel, New London, Connecticut, where I spent the night before going across to Long Island. A benignly fat lady with a cat rolled at her elbow was at the desk when I arrived. I went out to eat at a diner across the road, played pool for an hour and went to bed. In the middle of the night the cat jumped on my bed. How it got into the room, I do not know, but it startled me from the blood and wine dream, and I was grateful to it.

The morning was bright and I took my time. I caught the ferry to Orient Point, Eastern Long Island, drove across the North Fork and took another ferry from Greenport to Shelter Island and a brief third voyage from Shelter Island to Sag Harbour. There was plenty of time to take a look around the whaling museum at Sag Harbour before going to the American Hotel. In the museum a man told me where he thought an old harpoon was to be bought; not one of the wooden harpoons which the Wampanoag Indians on Nantucket and the Shinnecocks there on Long Island used, but one which had its last fling, so to speak, in the late nineteenth century when the East Coast whaling industry was coming to an end. Down at the harbour, I found the owner of the harpoon and bought it from him. It turned out to be useful.

The man liked to talk of the whaling days and told me he often used to converse with John Steinbeck about them. I was five minutes late at the old American Hotel, and saw Madelaine standing with her back to me, under the head of the bison in the dim lobby. 'Excuse me,' I inquired quietly. 'Could you tell me if this is a bison?'

Another woman might have turned quickly. After all, it was ten years. But Madelaine continued looking away and muttered: 'It was once.' Only then did she casually turn, her smile forming as we came face to face. She looked terrific. And rich.

'Hello, Michael,' she said. She looked down at the harpoon. 'What's that for?'

'Killing whales,' I said. 'It was once.'

When she smiled I saw her teeth were different. Other things about her had been changed also, the colour of her hair, and the deeper setting of her eyes. Naturally the clothes were expensive. When you marry a senator things are certain to alter.

'It's funny,' she said. 'But you look shorter, Michael. Terrific but shorter.'

I had always accused her of trying to diminish me. 'How about a drink?' I said.

As if she were annoyed with herself, she said: 'Now I've upset you again. You can't be *much* shorter.' She smiled fully, meaning it.

'I've done a lot of ducking,' I said, 'and crouching.' Once her teeth had been wilder but more natural.

'I'll have a Vodka,' she said. 'Collins.' We moved towards the bar, an extension of the lobby. Earnestly she asked: 'Shouldn't we shake hands? Or even kiss?'

'Which would you prefer?'

Her eyes dropped and then came up. 'In the circumstances, a handshake seems inadequate,' she said.

I asked the barman for the drinks. I had not had a Vodka Collins in years. 'A handshake usually *is* inadequate,' I agreed. She leaned forward and I was treated to a perfumed brush of her cheek. She touched me on the front of my shirt with a touch I had once missed dearly but had since forgotten. Her rings felt as heavy as they looked. We kissed.

'You taste different,' I said.

'A change of lipstick,' she answered.

Below the drooping lip of the bison we sat and the barman brought the drinks. Madelaine was wearing a light linen suit with a wide jacket. Something heavy, pendulous and valuable, lay against the fawn skin of her neck. She kept touching it as though concerned it might go missing.

'God, I was so nervous,' she breathed, treating me to her frank look across the little table. I tried to spot our wedding ring perhaps cringing somewhere among the welter of gold and diamonds on her fingers. I could not see it.

'So was I,' I said. 'Nervous. That's why I went and bought the harpoon.'

'Protection?' She laughed.

'It was something to do. To occupy my mind. What's Susan like? I should have seen her before, I know, but I've been like a hobo, travelling . . . you know how . . . '

'She's beautiful,' interrupted Madelaine. 'She's going to be tall.' She said: 'She keeps asking me what you're like.'

'You told her?'

'I lied,' she said mischievously. Her vodka was almost finished. 'Play it quiet, will you, Mike?' she asked. 'Just make it as natural as you can. Please. For her.' She touched her handbag. 'I'd show you some photographs but it seems too late for that. You'll be able to see the real girl.'

We finished our drinks and she declined a second

although I could have used one. 'You mentioned something else,' I said. 'On the phone. Something you wanted.'

'I'll tell you later,' she said. 'We ought to leave.'

She rose and said: 'We'll go up to the house right away. The old man, my father-in-law, thinks we should go out in his boat. It's a beautiful boat. It will be easier, more natural, like that. Susan loves going on boat trips.'

'Fine,' I said. 'Perhaps we'll see some whales.'

'Bring your harpoon,' she said.

Once we used to ride the New York morning subway but now she had a long, icy blue Cadillac. She eased it down to the car park on the Sag Harbour jetty so that I could stow the harpoon in my rented Ford. As we sat in the car I took the opportunity to study her in profile. She had put on a little weight in the face. Good feeding I suppose. We did not take the harpoon in the end. It would have been a conversation piece certainly, literally an ice-breaker, but perhaps unduly aggressive when you were going to meet a daughter you had not seen in ten years.

'How long will your whale book take?' she asked as we were driving out of the harbour town and towards the Montauk Highway along the South Fork of Eastern Long Island. The sun glistened on her fingers.

'Two years,' I guessed. 'A year's research and another year writing.'

'Who's the publisher?'

'There isn't one yet,' I said. 'I'll wait until it's finished.' The big downy car had ample space between the front seats and there was a thick dividing arm rest, but I was conscious of the intimacy of being with her. I glanced quickly at her breasts under the blouse.

'You can wait?' she said. 'For a publisher?' She half-turned and caught me in the middle of my sensual thoughts. She gave a sly smile.

I said: 'I can keep body and soul together for a year.'

'They must have been crazy,' she said turning her eyes back to the road. 'Letting you go.'

'Tycoons run newspapers now, not editors.' I shrugged. 'Our tycoon probably had no idea who I was. He didn't care either. I was just another hack. But I wasn't sorry. It's become a shitty trade. It probably always was. They offered me a pay-off so I took it.'

'What about Alice?' she asked. Estranged wives always seem concerned about other estranged wives. We came to traffic lights and she leaned back and regarded me. There was no doubt. She was certainly rounder in the face.

'I think it's finished, cooked,' I told her. 'She doesn't need or want me to keep her. She earns her own living.' The lights changed and Madelaine turned the car on to the main road at Bridgehampton. It was a warm day, busy with people going to the beaches. 'No children, no worries,' I said watching the people. 'Only the few, usual, regrets.'

'How long did it last?' We were travelling east now, towards Montauk.

'Four years or so,' I said. 'Mostly by telephone.'

'Your marriages usually are,' she said. She regretted saying it because she quickly softened.

'And now you've stopped running, you're by yourself,' she observed quietly. 'That's a big shame.'

'It's no shame,' I replied. 'I've always got the whales.'

She grimaced, to herself rather than to me, and said: 'Mike, you'll always find company.'

'I just walk into other people's parties,' I said looking at her sideways.

She laughed outright. 'That,' she said, 'was the greatest goddam nerve. I should have had them throw you out.'

'You didn't,' I said.

'I still should have,' she replied thoughtfully.

We were driving along the precise Hamptons; tidy green spaces, duck ponds, restored windmills, the nicely petrified past.

'How's it with you?' I asked her.

'Just fine,' she said. She meant it. 'I couldn't be happier. I've got a famous and wealthy husband. And Susan. One day we'll be living in the White House.'

She took one of the incised lanes that go down to the Hamptons beaches, past the Chapel-by-the-Ocean and the yacht club; gardens and lawns, walled swimming pools and tailored tennis courts, arranged around homes that contrived to combine modesty and exhibitionism. We turned onto a drive leading to an iron gate which, at a word from Madelaine, tilted up. 'You have to know the right word,' she observed. 'As you know, Michael. Knowing the right thing to say at the right time is always important here.'

As the drive went up a steady gradient, a huge Stars and Stripes rose over the lawned horizon; its pole the girth of a schooner's mainmast. The flag rolled languidly in the summer wind.

'In America,' Madelaine said, 'it's patriotism not cleanliness that's next to godliness. Patriotism – and especially in politics.'

'Is your husband going to be here?' I asked.

'He's in Washington. He'll get here this evening.'

'He finds time for his family?'

'Prospective presidents have to,' she said. She looked up quickly and said: 'There's Susan. She's come to meet you.'

A slight, tall child in a pale blue dress was standing on the path ahead. As we drove up an easy hill with white stones at its edge the house grew around her. '*Now* I'm nervous,' I said.

'So is she,' said Madelaine.

'Do I kiss her?' I asked desperately. 'Or shake hands?'

'Let her make the running,' Madelaine suggested.

There was a frail smile on the girl's face as we neared, the car slowing. She was alone, standing with her hands held in front of her. Her blowing hair was fair, her skin fawn. I let Madelaine get out of the car first.

'You found him,' smiled Susan. For some reason I was unprepared for the American accent. I stood, grinning awkwardly. She came forward and solemnly shook my hand and then to my relief kissed me on the cheek.

'I'm Susan,' she said.

'And I'm your father,' I said, suddenly ashamed.

From the flying flag overlooking the ocean, settled and pale blue on this day, the trimmed and ordered lawns ascended in a series of stages to the wide, white and magnificent mansion, with its great windows and its colonnade. It was called 'Flagstaff'.

We had lunch sitting in cushioned wicker chairs on the terrace, striped by the thick shadows of columns dividing the Atlantic sunshine. I felt like a last-minute character in a play, unsure of his lines. When the old man, Herbert Forrest Keenor, cream-suited, arrived, strolled in, my daughter jumped to her feet and elaborately introduced us. It was a curious moment. 'Grandpa!' Susan exclaimed. 'This is Michael Findlater, Esquire – my father!'

Everybody laughed. Herbert Keenor's heavy white teeth beamed in the sun. He was handsome; tanned, well-tended, well-nourished, his wrinkles in the right places. He looked as if he had known few worries in his life and had none to speak of now. Everything about him was generous, his deep voice, his laugh, his handshake, and his lunch.

Susan was eager to talk to me. As she sagely pointed out, we were catching up on ten years. She sat next to me, studying the side of my face when I entered the general conversation, putting more smoked salmon on my plate and even beating the cruising servant to the wine in order to pour me another glass. She fixed him with her mother's eye and he let her do it. I felt shamed that I had missed out on her for so long, but there was no resentment in her.

Madelaine sat near the balustrading which scalloped the elongated lawn, two gardeners recumbent in the distance, like figures in a painting.

'Old Glory has flown here every day since Flagstaff was built in 1923,' said Herbert Keenor leaning back and nodding towards the huge rolling flag. 'It's a requirement in the deeds, believe it or not. The man who owned the house previously, Franklyn Smith, was a patriot, although he went broke.' He peered with odd but undisguised fondness at the banner, his bulky white eyebrows clamping down like shutters as he looked against the sun.

'Mind you,' he added with gruff and disarming frankness, 'when the wind gets up the flag flies out straight and blocks the finest sea view in Eastern Long Island. You can't see a darned thing but Stars and Stripes!'

After lunch we went out on Herbert's shining boat. Susan changed from her blue dress into a pair of jeans and a shirt. So did her mother. Madelaine's breasts were tight under the shirt as the breeze dented her. There was spray on her cheeks. She looked almost hard, almost masculine. We went driving out of the creek and into the long, pale, open sea before turning into another of the green inlets with which the coast is serrated.

Against the wheel stood Herbert, his stomach scarcely protruding. Once we entered the second creek, he casually turned the powerful boat towards a jetty which fronted another widespread white house. 'Here's a man I'd like you to meet,' called Herbert to me over the growl of the engine. 'Brant Irving. He's a lawyer. A great man. You'll like him.'

He said it as if he expected this to be an extended association, like someone being introduced to a new colleague. A lifetime of politicians has taught me that nothing is for nothing. I glanced at Susan. She was waving towards the shore where a man had now appeared on the jetty. The breeze was rolling Madelaine's hair. The man on the jetty began to wave. 'Wave,' urged Susan in her American voice and without turning. 'He's an important man.'

I waved.

We neared the jetty and further animated greetings were called as though this person had come from the dead, not merely from his house. Irving, the lawyer, however, confined himself to reciprocal smiles. He was a tall sparse man; you could see him playing college basketball thirty years before. A few fair hairs bent like dried pampas on top of his head, but the otherwise bald pate was heavily tanned. He boarded the boat with the ease of a man who has kept himself fit. He was quietly humorous, exchanging jokey remarks with Susan, kissing Madelaine with difficulty over the front seats of the boat, and attempting to reach Herbert to pat him on the shoulder. As we were introduced he treated me to a quiet examination accompanied by a short but reassuring smile.

'All aboard?' called Herbert over his shoulder.

'As much as I'll ever be,' responded Irving. 'Let her go, Herbert. Let's get some salt!'

Until that time we had proceeded at a donkey pace, plodding over the small waves, hugging the shore, but I had eyed the powerful front of the boat with misgiving. I'm an unhappy sailor.

The engine was now given half, three-quarter, and finally full throttle and we tore off through our own white cleft in the sea, spray splattering over the side and the bow hitting the waves like a club. Susan and Madelaine were strapped in. I looked for my straps but there weren't any. Madelaine's smile was pinned on her face by the wind. Susan called out. I hung on, kept shutting my eyes, and gulped. It seemed to be a long time before they noticed my discomfort and cut the speed back, but we were then far out and we had to return against long, sluggish rollers, which was more protracted and almost as bad. I lay back against the cushioned seat and tried to wear a smile, but it refused to stay.

II

A silent chauffeur took me back to the American Hotel at Sag Harbour, in one of the Keenor limousines, returning me to Flagstaff that evening in time for drinks. There were six of us to dinner: Herbert Keenor, who was a widower, an athletic-looking middle-aged blonde called Lucette Harvey who was his secretary, Brant Irving and a wordless wife, her veined, knuckled and grossly bejewelled hands hardly able, it seemed, to lift her fork. On occasion her wan eyes were raised and I thought she might be going to speak, but she thought better of it and they dropped again. Then there was me and there was Madelaine. Her husband was expected but did not arrive until we were sitting on the terrace after dinner. Following a flight from Washington he had rented a private plane to the Hamptons. We saw him come busily in, the wing-tip lights low over the creek. 'That's Sam,' said Madelaine as if he were himself flying, arms outstretched. 'That's your daddy,' she said to Susan who had stayed up but had not eaten with us. 'I know,' said the girl. She seemed tired. It had probably been a difficult day.

Fifteen minutes later, creaseless, Sam Keenor, smiling well within himself and taking account of everyone, strode in. The man who had married my former wife came as a considerable disappointment to me. He was everything she had made him out to be. Sam Keenor's breadth and height, his loping smile, young-grey hair, and adjustable brow furrows; his wanting-to-know-all-

about-you eyes, and his inherited timbered voice, marked
him as a thoroughbred. Sincerity shone from his shoes.
As he spoke, he looked fully and warmly into your face
as if he had once saved your life and was glad of it. A
man who could diminish you with one handshake.

For all his general geniality there was a purposefulness
about him, a sense that there were pressing matters
elsewhere to be attacked. He kissed Susan, at once a
greeting and a goodnight, with a single word: 'Honey'.
His pause to glance at me after the action was deliberate,
and probably deliberated. You could tell he enjoyed
provoking tense moments. He suggested that she came
and kissed me goodnight ('Our visitor – your father') just
as she was about to do exactly that. He successfully
fucked up that moment. She gave me a perfunctory kiss
and left.

It was not until this cameo had been acted out and
Susan had left for bed that Sam allowed us to be formally
introduced, although he eyed me, as I stood awkwardly,
his lips greeting Madelaine's cheek, with a glance that
said: 'Sure, I know you're here. I'll get *to you* in a
moment.'

Eventually, with the air of one who has cleared the
family decks, he advanced and his large warm hand
enfolded mine that seemed to have become suddenly
small and cold. 'You must be the husband,' I said.

His bellowing laugh almost rattled the glasses. 'Good,'
he said shaking his head and my hand again at the
wonder of it. 'So good.'

They had left some cold dishes for him and he sat at
the table and pulled a friendly chair out for me, pushing
away crockery and cutlery. He did not seem to see or
care what he ate. He ignored the wine and poured
himself a glass of apple juice, dismissing wordlessly with

the same glass the servant who offered to do it for him. I had imagined he would want to discuss Susan, or at least tell me about her, but instead he plunged into a series of inquiries about my attitudes to Beirut, British politics, Northern Ireland, AIDS, and unleaded petrol. At one point, in response to some commonplace aside of mine, he looked at me with deep approval, put his hand on my thigh and gravely announced, as if I had successfully passed an audition: 'You're a *funny* man.'

Herbert Keenor, largely occupying one of the rattan chairs at the end of the dim terrace, had become engrossed in a low conversation with Irving. He glanced sideways once or twice and I saw him nod as if gratified that his son and I were getting acquainted. Unspeaking, Mrs Irving sat staring at the rings on her fingers like someone required to make a difficult choice. Madelaine left to say goodnight to Susan and returned just in time to collide with a departing kiss from her husband, who abandoned me and the table with excuses shot like arrows, and was heading for 'his room' to work on papers. Lucette, the secretary, who had throughout politely contributed to the conversation and had asked me about Wimbledon tennis, stood up and said she was going to take a walk by the water. I thought she had been drinking more than she was accustomed to, but I may have been mistaken.

Mrs Irving then bowed from the company muttering an excuse or perhaps a prayer. She never returned to the room. She was one of those people you don't miss. Once that evening I had caught Irving regarding her with an expression which suggested he was wondering where he had seen her before.

When the two elder men were left with me, and Madelaine had gone out again, this time to see how her husband was coping with his papers, they moved towards me and Herbert Keenor poured me another drink.

They came and sat one each side of me, converged almost, like old cronies and as though they needed to tell me things they knew too well themselves.

'It's a crazy part of the world, the South Fork,' said Herbert. 'It's an old, old place, you know. Families who settled here first are still in the telephone book now.'

'The Gardiners,' added Irving. 'They bought Gardiner's Island in the very beginning, seventeenth century, and they're still around.'

'Plenty of them,' put in Herbert. 'They exhumed the body of old Lion Gardiner a few years back. He was a man familiar with pirates and kings. His hair was still long and golden in his coffin, and each of the family was given a snippet of it to wear in a locket.'

They began talking about some of the great houses of the South Fork.

'Lightning House,' said Herbert, 'Montauk. They had a big society wedding there, old Billy Widlake's daughter, and while they were dancing and drinking on the lawn the house burned down. That didn't stop Billy Widlake. No sir. He told everybody to carry on dancing and enjoying themselves, and they did just that, while the house burned to the ground. Some sight.'

Madelaine returned, smiled at us, and said she was going to bed. I felt a brief pang because I could imagine her going up to Sam, touching him, and asking him if he would like to go to bed and he, shuffling his papers, standing and kissing her as I once did. Now she came and kissed me on the cheek, after she had done the same with the two older men, and then she left. I imagined her undressing in one of the rooms overhead. I could easily remember what her breasts had been like when she was going to bed. Herbert was regarding me with a wise smile when I looked towards him. 'Regrets?' he said.

'Not really,' I answered when I realized what he had meant. 'These things go away. But you feel a sense of ... well, carelessness.'

'Sure, sure,' he nodded, pouring me another drink and then adding one for Brant Irving. 'She's a sweet lady. And you're a good man, I can tell that, Michael. But it's too late. Some things get too late. Sam's very good for her and she is for him. One day ... ' His voice diminished. 'I pray I'm still around to see them in the White House together.'

I said I thought I ought to get back to the hotel. Herbert picked up a telephone and instructed someone to fetch a car.

We finished our drinks and walked out onto the terrace from where you could see the approach road. 'Ever had any experience with espionage?' Herbert asked, casually adding 'spies', as if I might not understand.

'Only on aeroplanes,' I laughed. 'Reading about them. I've come across characters who have turned out to be spies but at the time I thought they were cultural attachés.'

'In your professional life, I thought maybe. Cloak and dagger ... '

'There's been very little cloak but a fair amount of dagger,' I said. I thought he was making conversation until the car came. Both men laughed. The headlights of the car began to grow like a swiftly-climbing moon over the dark of the mounded lawns. 'We had some spies here, right here on Long Island ... ' said Irving.

'On the South Fork,' put in Herbert. 'Came ashore from a submarine.'

'That sounds like a good story,' I said. The car drew up to the side of the house and all three of us walked along the terrace towards it.

'It is,' said Irving. 'You must hear it some time.'

Madelaine telephoned me at the American Hotel while I was eating breakfast, and told me that she and Sam had to take Susan to Washington that afternoon. Something unexpected had surfaced. We arranged to meet at mid-morning, and I suggested we went to the Sag Harbour Whaling Museum. Even on the phone I realized she would smile. She said she would ask Susan. 'Girls don't always like whales,' she pointed out.

But Susan wanted to go. We walked around the exhibits. Me and Susan, Madelaine lagging a little, looking vaguely around her. 'Hermann Melville wrote *Moby Dick* after one trip in a whaler from Martha's Vineyard,' I said to Susan. '*And* he was seasick.'

'How come he knew it all?' she asked. 'So he could write it?' Her face was fresh and her eyes soft but interested. I was glad she liked me.

'It all came from another man's log book,' I said. 'A whaling man from Nantucket.'

'What you used to call "lifting a story",' commented Madelaine. She had never been taken with the things which engrossed me, and she continued to look at the relics of the sea-town without comment. Susan went to look at a model interior of a whaler's house. 'There was something else,' I mentioned quietly to Madelaine. 'Something you wanted to ask.'

She smiled a little. 'Yes, there was,' she said. 'I'm glad you remembered.'

'I haven't been able to sleep,' I said.

She touched my arm, smiled and whispered: 'Liar.' It

was the first moment I had felt that there was still anything left between us. There was a polished oak bench in the lobby of the museum, and she sat on it and I sat beside her. Her manner changed as if she regretted the smile and the touch. 'This is a little difficult,' she hesitated. 'But I have to know.'

'Try me,' I said.

Her eyes drifted to me. I wanted to put my fingers on her cheek. As though she knew and wanted to prevent me, she put her hand, not familiarly, across the top of my knuckles on the bench. 'The way Sam's career is going,' she said carefully, 'I'm going to be, to a certain extent anyway, I can only guess how much, in the public eye. I'll probably be getting increasing publicity. It's the way it happens.'

'Prospective President's charming and clever and *English* wife,' I recited.

'The reporter never dies,' she observed. 'That's exactly what I mean, Michael. Although I *am* an American citizen now. I took citizenship just after I met Sam.'

'A good move,' I said.

'We thought so. But whatever, I'm going to be interviewed by the media and asked about my past life . . .'

'And up I swim from the murky depths.'

'Don't put it like that.'

'That's what you mean.'

She would not answer. Instead she said: 'And when the media get to know that my ex-husband is a hermit at . . . where was it . . . ?'

'Thoughtful Creek,' I reminded her. 'Massachusetts.'

Her glance was almost icy but again she touched my hand. 'Thoughtful Creek,' she said. 'Massachusetts. And that's where they'll be heading. The war correspondent, the world-weary traveller, who's gone to ground to study whales.'

'A nice mixture of metaphors,' I said. A resentment grew inside me. 'This is why you got me down here?'

'One of the reasons. But I wanted you to see Susan. She wanted to see you.'

'And conveniently it all happened at this time – when you and Sam are going to need me.'

She looked as though she was going to be angry. 'You don't *have* to do anything, Michael. You haven't been set up for this, I assure you. It might even be a good opportunity to tell the media about the whales . . .'

'Now you're being shitty,' I muttered. Susan had moved on to another exhibit. 'Daddy,' she called over her shoulder. 'This is a harpoon gun.'

'They're deadly,' I called back. I looked at Madelaine again. 'Okay,' I said evenly. 'So I get interviewed.'

She shrugged. 'You only have to tell the truth. They'll want to know about our marriage and why we broke up. How much you say is up to you. This is not so much a plea, Michael, as a warning of what might occur. You and I have nothing to hide. It was an everyday divorce.'

'And now I've been reunited with my daughter and met Sam,' I breathed. 'The one-day-to-be-President has a lovely wife who has a lovely ex-husband.'

She laughed outright. She knew it would disarm me. 'All right,' I said. 'I might even give a press conference.'

'That would be neat,' she said. She was relaxed now.

'I never could stand reporters,' I said. 'Even me.'

The three of us, like husband, wife and child, walked down the main street of Sag Harbour towards the jetty where I had left the car. It was my intention to check out of the American Hotel and drive north that afternoon. I would be at Thoughtful Creek by the evening.

As we reached the waterfront by the old windmill, a car with misted windows drew alongside, the rear window slid down with a hush and Madelaine's husband looked out. He looked as relaxed and purposeful as the previous evening. Madelaine put her hand into the car and he kissed it casually, and just as casually murmured, 'Honey.'

'Why don't you join us for lunch?' he called to me. Susan put her face near the window and he tapped her on the nose. 'We've been to the Whaling Museum,' she said.

For a moment I thought he was going to frown but he stemmed it with a smile. 'So it's been an educational morning,' he said. 'That's good.'

'I won't come to lunch, thanks,' I said. 'I'm just going to check out of the hotel.'

'Please,' said Madelaine touching my sleeve in full view of Sam. 'Stay for a drink anyway.' She turned to Sam's face. 'Michael's been very understanding,' she reported.

'Oh good, great,' said her husband. 'In that case we have to drink to it.' The chauffeur, a young man in a crackling white shirt, had left his seat and now opened the rear door. Unhurriedly, Sam got out. He wore a sky-blue shirt, the sleeves turned up to show his strong brown wrists and expensive but restrained watch. He shook my hand deeply. 'You have time for a cocktail,' he said.

We walked to a restaurant overlooking the harbour and sat down at a table on the wooden deck. I felt unhappily isolated from them now, awkward and anxious to be gone.

'I can't tell you how much I appreciate your co-operation,' said Sam as we sat with our drinks. Seagulls screamed and a couple at another table came over and asked for his autograph. Susan looked impressed. He complied as though it were just one of many he had signed that morning, but after signing he regarded them seriously and said: 'When the time comes don't forget to vote.' They promised and went away.

He saw me studying him. 'In the United States people like *good* guys,' he said without embarrassment. He returned my studied look. 'That's why I'm grateful to you, Michael.'

'There's no reason to be,' I answered. 'It's simple. I'll tell the truth. Madelaine and I got married, we had a daughter and we divorced. End of story.'

He smiled and said: 'Happy families is the name of the big game, Michael.'

'It's no trouble,' I told him. I wanted to leave. Madelaine always watched him so carefully when he spoke. It seemed hard for her to turn away.

'You may get some disturbance, some interruptions,' continued Sam solicitously. 'And that concerns me. The media may well intrude into the work you're doing.'

'The Man from Thoughtful Creek,' I recited.

'You still think in headlines,' said Madelaine.

'Don't worry about the press,' I said. 'I know how to deal with them.'

'You're a good man,' said Sam Keenor. He looked at me for all the world as if he meant it.

When I returned to the American Hotel, there was a message asking me to telephone Brant Irving. He was not to be one of those people you meet and never see again.

He was diffident. 'Michael, are you checking out of the hotel today?'

'I was just about to do it.'

'I see. Would I be able to prevail on you to postpone your departure for twenty-four hours? There is something that Herbert Keenor and I would like to discuss with you.'

'What would that be?'

'Well ... it's a proposition, a professional proposition, you could call it. If you say "no" then okay. There's nothing so final as "no" for some people, and I'd say you were one of them. But we'd be grateful if you could hear us out.' He hesitated further. 'We would, naturally, meet your additional expenses.'

'That's all right,' I said. 'It's nothing.'

'Herbert is very anxious.'

'All right,' I answered. 'The whales won't be gone by tomorrow.'

'Thanks, Michael.' He sounded genuinely glad. 'Herbert wants you to come and have dinner this evening. If that's all right. It will be very casual, a kind of working dinner. Just three of us. He'll send a car for you at seven.'

That afternoon the weather turned. Wind began to seep from the sea. When the car arrived the little town was shiny with rain. Keenor's chauffeurs were non-talkers. The only sound as we drove out to the ocean shore was the undertone of the wheels on the wet road.

The lights of 'Flagstaff' were curtained by rain. I could hear the grumbling sea. Brant Irving was already there. As if to signal the informality of the occasion, Herbert was wearing an old-fashioned smoking jacket.

'Let's go through to the library,' he said taking my arm. 'It's a good place on a rainy night.' He led me along the panelled corridor. Brant Irving said: 'In summer everybody out here welcomes an evening like this. You can have too much of the great outdoors.'

Herbert turned through a heavy doorway. 'This is called the Armoury,' he said. The room was dim. It was stacked, hung, almost festooned, with rifles, pistols, and sub-machine-guns.

'It's one of my interests,' said Keenor. His fingers tapped along the barrel of a machine-pistol. 'This I just obtained.'

'It looks like it's still warm,' I said.

'You're familiar with the weapon?' he asked.

'Every time I see one I want to duck,' I told him.

He said: 'Most of the small arms are in working order.' He smiled: 'But we're out of ammunition.' Irving laughed. 'This item,' said Keenor moving towards the wall; he ran his thumbnail down a belt of machine gun bullets: 'This came from one of the few Japanese planes shot down at Pearl Harbour. It crash-landed on the island of Nihau, almost a hundred and fifty miles away, where the natives knew nothing of the raid. They didn't even have a radio. They went to help the pilot and he began shooting at them. The Nihau policeman had to break the Jap's neck.'

He began to walk through into a further room from which a firmer light was coming. As he went past a Colt in a case he said: 'That was Bill Cody's – Buffalo Bill.' He led the way into the adjoining room. Irving followed me and closed the door behind us. It was a fine library banked with books, some reflecting the light in their lettering, others high on the shelves, remote and brooding. There was an impressive desk, leather surfaced, and appearing as if it was often used. Papers were arranged at one side, and in two mahogany trays. A single red file rested on the pad in front of the chair.

Facing the desk were two thick leather chairs. Irving motioned me to one. Herbert sat behind the desk and

Irving went to a cabinet in a dim corner of the room and poured us all drinks.

'It's very good of you to postpone your departure,' said Herbert Keenor. He leaned forward with his hands on the red file. Suddenly he looked like a man with a lot on his mind.

'Not at all,' I assured him. 'Since I've retired from newspapers I've tried to suppress my overactive curiosity, but sometimes it refuses to be suppressed. If I hadn't stayed, I would have been left wondering.'

'Thank you,' said the old man. The light of the room had produced deep indents in his face. He looked older than in daylight, but his eyes were stronger. 'I hope we have something to interest you.'

Irving had settled in the other chair. They seemed to have decided in what order they were going to speak, and it was the lawyer who began. 'Yesterday, when we met you for the first time,' he said slowly, 'it occurred to Herbert, and later also to me, when we were here in the house, that you might be someone whom we could trust with a certain undertaking. In a sense, we had been waiting for you.'

Herbert followed him: 'We need someone with your sort of experience and background, Michael, and someone who knows how to be silent. The reason we did not consider an American investigator is that we needed someone from outside, someone fresh, someone who could keep quiet.'

'Investigator?' I asked cautiously. 'An investigator?'

'An investigator,' he answered, his eyes firmly on me. 'It's not a criminal matter,' put in Irving. He looked at Herbert.

'No, no,' agreed the old man. 'Maybe investigator is the wrong word. A researcher might be better, especially since we're dealing with history . . . a resourceful researcher . . . and, of course, a writer.'

They both smiled. 'It might be that what we have in mind would finance several years of your own work,' said Irving. Herbert said: 'Will you at least hear us out? If you're not interested, then that's fine. Although we would be grateful for your word to keep the matter confidential.'

'You have it,' I said.

'Good, then you'll at least listen.'

'Of course. I love stories. I've lived by them.' I thought Herbert glanced at Irving before he began. Then he opened the file on the desk. I had thought that it was not there for nothing. From the file he took a folder, and from the folder a photograph. He handed it to me.

'I would like you to find this man,' he said.

'Peter Karl Hine,' said Herbert. The photograph was of a smirking man in his thirties, hair plastered down, looking almost insolently at the camera.

'Who was he?' I asked. It was an old photograph.

'Is,' corrected Herbert. 'He remains with us, I believe.'

'When was the picture taken?'

'Nineteen forty-two.'

Irving, fingertips touching in front of his chin, said: 'He was a spy and a traitor – in an odd way, twice over. He came ashore just along the coast here on a night in June, 1942, six months after Pearl Harbour.'

'You mentioned it last night,' I said to Herbert Keenor. 'As I was about to leave.'

'A hint,' said the old man. 'I'm glad you caught it.'

Irving continued. Herbert Keenor eased himself slowly

back like someone who has heard a tale many times but always wants to listen again.

'Hine had lived in the United States for years,' said Irving. 'In peacetime he'd even served in the US Army. Before World War Two he returned to Germany where later he was trained as a spy and saboteur. On a foggy June night he came back to this country with three companions – armed and, so it was said at his trial, prepared to kill.'

The lawyer's voice was slow and compelling. I doubted if he was often interrupted. 'The same month a further four Germans landed undetected on a beach outside Jacksonville, Florida,' he went on. 'They were scheduled to rendezvous with Hine's party in New York, a place where it has always been easy to hide. The object of these men was not only to cripple American war plants, but to organize an espionage network throughout this country, drawing on German-Americans with Nazi sympathies, of which there were not a few.'

Herbert Keenor turned heavily away from the lawyer Irving towards me, as if to gauge my interest.

'It's a tragedy,' Irving went on, 'that might have been written for the Marx Brothers. Hine waited until what he considered to be the opportune moment, then betrayed the others to the Federal Bureau of Investigation, who had spectacularly screwed up the spy-hunt. J. Edgar Hoover, the director of the FBI at the time, wiped the egg from his face, told the nation what a clever boy he was, and got a medal. Six of the spies were summarily tried by military court, were taken to the electric chair and executed. Hine and another man, Konrad, got off the hook. They each served only four years of thirty year sentences and were smuggled back to Germany in 1946, right after the war.'

'Why do you want to find Hine?' I asked.

I thought Herbert Keenor was going to speak but Irving said: 'For years the case has been argued in legal circles; there have been articles in law publications; there have been unending discussions among attorneys. The plain fact of the matter is that these Nazis, even though guilty as hell, were *illegally* tried and *illegally* executed. It was an unconstitutional military tribunal set up by the President, Roosevelt. It was a farce, a trick. And the White House *knew* it was fixed.'

'Who cared?' I interrupted. 'Spies are executed. It goes with the job.'

Keenor spoke. 'Michael, if you are defending a constitution,' he said in his deep, measured way, 'as the United States was at that time – on the battlefield – then you have to defend that constitution in all places – and especially in the courts.'

'Otherwise you simply undermine the very thing for which men are dying,' put in Irving. 'The whole business was a travesty. Three months, less even, elapsed between the spies, saboteurs, call them what you will, landing in America and the electric chair.'

I spread my hands, the glass askew in my right fingers. 'It's all a bit late now, isn't it?' I said.

'Pretty soon,' Irving said. 'Probably within the next few months, there's going to be a move to set the legal record straight. You'll be familiar with the matter of the Japanese-Americans who were sent pre-emptively into the desert in California after Pearl Harbour. That was a gross injustice and it is in the process of being righted, or at least acknowledged. Americans have long memories and long consciences. It's one of our better points.'

He smiled, a thin, courtroom smile.

'And you are instrumental,' I said to Irving, 'in bringing this case up again?'

Keenor said: 'Brant is the major mover.'

'And you want Hine as a witness.'

'We'd sure like him,' said Irving. 'We don't know what happened to Konrad, the other man. He just disappeared. He may well be dead. But Hine has surfaced in Germany and various places.' Leaning over the desk top, Keenor said: 'I own, as you may possibly know, several newspapers and two magazines. When the time is ripe, Michael, I want the full, exclusive, story. Every word from Hine's lips.'

'I'm flattered,' I said. 'But Herbert, if you own newspapers, magazines, surely they have people they could assign to a story like this. Why not send *them*? A team of good reporters. Send them to Germany if you think he's there.'

Keenor was shaking his head before I had finished. He said firmly: 'I need the matter dealt with quietly, *secretly* if you like, by someone outside my news organization.' He glanced at Irving and then studied his own hands on the desk. 'Those people, my own executives, think I'm finished,' he muttered moodily. 'They can't believe I'm in touch with any goddam thing. I'm eighty, a museum piece; even my son, Sam, thinks that although he denies it. He won't hurt my feelings.' He folded his fingers together. 'We publish *News Now* magazine,' he said, 'and I want to go there with the exclusive story and drop it on that editor's desk, at the exact moment when the whole legal thing has come to the boil, and say "publish this".'

Abruptly he half-laughed. 'I'm looking for some belated glory, recognition,' he admitted. 'And you're the man I want to get it for me.'

Quietly I put the glass on the table; looking first at Irving and then to Herbert Keenor, I said in a level voice: 'Thanks, but no. I've finished, retired. I promised that to myself. From now on, I'm only interested in whales.'

Just as quietly, Keenor said: 'I'll pay you a hundred thousand dollars, plus fifty per cent of syndication, and a fifteen percent royalty on any book. You'll also get a thousand dollars a day while you're working on the assignment and, of course, expenses. You'll have an entirely free hand.'

'I'll go back to Thoughtful Creek,' I sighed. 'And lock up the house.'

III

We talked far into the summer night. I went back to the hotel but I could not sleep, and at first light I drove to the beach where all those years before the German spies had come ashore. It was five miles along the coast from Sag Harbour. At that early time of day it was deserted except for a few joggers. The beach was long and easy-shelving, sand and shingle, with substantial dunes topped with rough grass on the inland side.

I was forty-seven years too late to see anything. I have always been, however, a great believer in reconnaissance, even retrospective. After taking a series of photographs of the shore and the dunes, I went back to the hotel for breakfast. It had been my intention to drive back to Massachusetts by the same route as I had taken on the outward journey, the series of ferries across to New London, Connecticut. Now, however, I decided to go to New York.

For three days in the city I spent my time reading everything in the New York Public Library which mentioned the landing of the Long Island spies. There was surprisingly little. There was considerably more, however, in the 1942 files of *The New York Times*, the *Herald Tribune*, and the *Washington Post*.

In the early afternoon of the third day, I began to drive up the coast road towards New Bedford. I did not hurry. In a way I was angry with myself for being diverted from something I had been promising myself for so long. New London, where I had stayed on the outward journey, was lying quietly in the evening sunshine when I reached it. I decided to stay.

The harbour was soundless; boats floated on the reflection of the sky, there were men fishing from the pier. Now that I had allowed myself to be purchased again, I wanted to enjoy a time like this. All my promises to myself were broken, so quickly and so easily. At the sound of money. I felt moody when I again checked in at the Ferryboat Motel. The old lady and the cat were still together behind their counter. The walls of the rooms were flimsy and in mine I could hear a couple next door skirmishing. She said he did not make enough dough.

After I had showered, I walked across the road to the diner. I had a steak and a few drinks, chatted with a couple of locals and joined one of them in a game of pool with two truck drivers who were on their way downstate.

It was eleven o'clock when I got back to the motel. The old lady had gone to bed leaving the keys on their hooks, but the cat was still edging about the corridor. It seemed glad to see me, as if it had been waiting. Somehow I took the key to the wrong room. I walked back for the right key and then went to bed. The couple next door were both snoring, and I lay in the dark listening.

I did not sleep. I am good at sleeping and it worried me. At one time in my life I always knew when something was wrong, an intuition developed from years of practice. But now, turning, watching the lights of sporadic cars drift across the sparsely curtained window and over the ceiling, I began to get impatient with myself. What reason was there to be edgy? Here I was in an unremarkable motel in a small and placid place. There *was* no reason. It was a warm night and the air conditioning

42

was groaning. I got up and went to the bathroom. On the way back to bed I looked through the gap in the curtains. The road was lit and empty. Grumbling at myself I got under the sheet again. Then the door opened.

Christ! I sat bolt upright. Somehow I stifled a shout. The door was swinging like a finger in the dimness. Then something jumped up on the bed. The cat.

I began to laugh at my own idiocy. I got up and closed the door. The catch was deficient. It was a cheap motel. The best I could do was to wedge it with some paper. The cat had settled at the foot of the bed so I left it there.

At last I went to sleep. Then, I believed, the dream had come back . . . the damned wine and blood dream. There was the fire . . . I could smell the fire.

By now I was so familiar with the nightmare that I mentally stood back and waited to see which form it would take, Belfast, Beirut . . . Madrid. But none of the usual characters appeared; no policeman, no militiaman. The burning went on. I jumped awake. The cat was on fire at the bottom of my bed.

And not only the cat. Abruptly the opposite wall exploded into flames. Smoke began to gush from the floor. The cat was going berserk. It rushed towards the door and then swerved back with its tail blazing. I had never heard myself scream before.

I fell out of bed, snatched the cat and put its tail out. Then I pounded on the thin partition wall behind my bed. The smoke began to stifle me. The flames were flaring around the walls.

Then, against the wall, I saw my harpoon. The cat was cringing against the bed, its tail still smoking. Staggering and shaking, I picked up the harpoon and smashed it through the thin wall. The sharp end went straight through. My neighbours began to shout. Repeatedly I hit the wall. The fire and smoke were engulfing the room. Christ, I was frightened. Again and again I struck with the harpoon, I tugged away a piece of the partition. A man's startled face appeared like a picture in a jagged frame. 'What's going on?' he inquired stupidly.

'The place is on fucking fire!' I told him. He could see. He turned away and told the woman who began to scream in earnest. The cat jumped over my shoulder and through the hole.

With my bare foot I kicked through the bottom section of the wall. I fell into the other room. My hair was on fire. I was trying to beat it out. The couple were both in striped pyjamas, standing side by side, immobilized. When she saw the harpoon the woman began screaming again. I went to the wash bowl and turning on the tap extinguished my hair. My feet were raw, skinless. 'Get out!' I bellowed.

We all got out, finding ourselves running across the lawned area in front of the motel to the road. The siren of a fire truck sounded and there were people converging on us, but very slowly, as if they believed we might explode. The motel was blazing like a torch. I shouted to a man to go and find the old lady. Then I sat on the grass and began to rub the dew over my feet. The cat was washing its tail. The woman from the next room sat down near me and began to cry directly into my face: 'I want a divorce!' she howled. 'And soon!' The man was standing transfixed in his pyjamas staring at the flames.

'Don't tell me, madam,' I bellowed at her. 'Tell him!'

*

'Do you have any enemies?'

'Most of us do.'

'In this locality? In New London?'

The hospital was nice. My window overlooked the harbour and I could see the moored boats and the comings and goings of the ferry. On the wall there were two paintings of scenes in the Maritimes. They had bandaged my feet and my head so that I looked like a panda.

'I don't think I have any enemies here,' I told the police lieutenant. 'I don't even *know* anybody.' He sat on the edge of a chair by the bedside, hardly anything written in his open notebook. He looked like he wanted to go home. 'What makes you think it was started deliberately?' I asked him.

He sniffed. He was pale and more studious than you would think a cop would be. Perhaps he normally worked inside. He had rimless glasses. 'There was evidence of an incendiary device,' he shrugged. He stared at the notebook as if to confirm he was allowed to reveal the information. 'In which case it's murder. Mrs Williams died, you know. The old lady.'

'So I heard. It's very sad.'

'She had enemies,' he observed tonelessly. Reflections of things in the room were visible in his glasses, images thrown by sunlight coming in from the window over the sea. I could see he thought I was staring at his eyes. 'People in business have enemies,' he philosophized. 'But nobody who would want to burn down her motel. Not that we know.'

'Did they stick the incendiary underneath?' I asked. 'That building was on legs, stilts.'

His eyes got smaller. 'What makes you say that?'

'I know something about setting fire to places,' I told him. 'I've been a war correspondent.'

'Right,' he said checking his notebook. 'It says here you're a reporter.'

'Was,' I corrected. 'I've retired.'

'What are you interested in now?'

'Whales,' I said.

He looked mildly surprised. 'You're kidding,' he said. 'You like whales?'

'Love 'em,' I said.

'That accounts for the harpoon. We have it at the station.' He became businesslike. 'What were you doing in town anyway?'

'Returning to New Bedford from New York,' I said. 'I'd been over on Long Island visiting Sag Harbour, the Whaling Museum.'

'Sure, I've seen that museum,' he replied briskly as if there were suddenly some bond between us. 'I took my kids there. It's quicker to use the ferry.'

'I had to go to New York City.'

'Oh, sure. What did you do in the evening, after you checked into the motel? Did you go out?'

'I went to eat. That place across the street.'

'Happy Dan's,' he murmured. He looked as though he was going to ask if I could recommend it.

'I had a meal and a couple of drinks there,' I said.

'Talk to anybody?'

'A few locals. And I played a couple of games of pool. With two truck drivers and one of the local men.'

'The truck drivers. What did they look like?'

'One middle-aged, paunchy, not much hair. The other one was younger with a bit of a moustache. Tallish. They both wore jeans and sweatshirts. One smoked a cigar. The older one. The local was called Jake.'

'I'll check. When you went back to the motel did you go straight to fifteen, your room?'

'Yes . . . oh no, wait a minute, I didn't. I went into the room before it, fourteen, I suppose. I mistook the number. It was dim and the number on the key was almost worn out. Fourteen was open, the door was ajar, and I went in there but the bed wasn't made up or anything, so I realized I'd made a mistake.'

'You saw, so you must have switched the light on.'

'Yes, I did.'

'Did you leave the light on for any period?'

He was not so dull as I thought. 'Yes. There was a cat there. It was hanging around my ankles. It ended up in my room. It was burned.'

'Just its tail,' he said. 'And the cat made you forget to turn out the light?'

'Not for long. When I realized I was in the wrong room I went back down the corridor and got the correct key from behind the desk. The old lady, Mrs Williams, had gone. I went back up the corridor, opened the right door and then went back and turned out the light in fourteen.'

The policeman began to sniff again. He needed several sniffs before he was ready to go on. 'The incendiary device,' he said slowly, 'was placed *below* the motel, *under* room fourteen. If anybody had wanted to kill you then maybe they were watching as you went into the motel. They waited until they saw the light switched on, the wrong light as it happened, and pushed the device underneath. It was on a timing clock activated at one a.m.'

There was quite a long silence between us. He looked as wordless and awkward as any other visitor to a hospital bedside. Suddenly he shut his notebook. 'They say you'll be out of here soon,' he said. 'Your lungs are free of smoke. You'll be heading for New Bedford?'

'I've rented a house there. At a place called Thoughtful

Creek. But I'm probably going back to Long Island within a few days.'

'That's a real interesting museum,' he nodded. He took the notebook out again and wrote down the New Bedford address. 'Maybe you could call in at the police station when you go through here again,' he suggested. He regarded me seriously. 'For a guy with no known enemies, you had a lucky escape.'

'Didn't I just,' I said.

After two further days they let me out. My injuries were described as superficial, even if the hospital bill was not. My feet were sore but usable, and the only visible damage was to my hair, now shaved like an Apache's down both sides and at the back.

After claiming and signing for my harpoon at the police station, I drove out of town past the Ferryboat Motel. There has been no shortage of burned buildings in my life but this one gave me a pang. It was as though a bite had been taken from it. Both ends were intact apart from boarded windows, but at the centre was the charred gap where my room and the two adjoining rooms had been.

As I drove by I saw the cat sitting on the doorstep. I stopped the car and got out. After a moment's caution, it gave a token meow, merely moving its mouth without sound. Half-turning it gave its browned tail a lick. 'It's all right for you,' I said. 'Look at my hair.'

There was a gritty saucer on the doorstep so someone had fed it, but not recently. I decided to take it with me up to Thoughtful Creek. It probably needed a change of scene. It allowed me to pick it up.

When I put it in the car it sat without fuss. Perhaps it thought that our destinies were bound together. I started the engine. 'It's just the two of us now,' I said.

We drove to New Bedford, stopping for refreshment. I bought the cat some fish which made the car reek and purloined a dish from a hamburger place so that I could give it some milk. Replenished, it rolled up on the front seat and after a few licks at its sparse tail, went to sleep.

I had no idea what I was going to do with this cat. Had I been continuing to live in the house at Thoughtful Creek there would have been no problem, but now I was likely to be trailing half-way across the world looking for the man Hine. That is no life for a cat.

When we reached the house by the inlet at New Bedford it was again a fine, pale evening, the sky like the water, the water like the sky. There were squadrons of midges down by the jetty but that was the total movement. Then whoever played 'As Time Goes By' on the piano across the creek began to play it again. It became, in my imagination, a slim and beautiful woman wearing a long white gown and feeling lonely.

I sat on the jetty with the cat and watched the day go, my mind crowded with regret that I was giving this up so soon. It crossed my mind to quit now but I knew I would not do it. When it was almost dark the piano playing ceased, the door of the house opened and a fat man came out and got into a car which he drove away. So much for long white dresses.

Casually, the telephone began to ring in the house. It was a strange repeat of that first morning but this time I knew it was for me. Putting the cat down on the wooden boards of the jetty, I hurried over the grass. The ringing stopped as I got to the verandah, but then started again. It was Brant Irving.

'Michael, I've got you at last.'

'Sorry. I've been in hospital. I was caught in a fire.'

'How . . . how the hell did that . . . ?'

'I was in a motel in New London, on the way back here, and somebody set it on fire.'

'My God, it was deliberate?'

'So the police think . . . But I'm okay.'

'Michael . . . I have some bad news . . . Herbert Keenor died last night. It was an accident with a gun . . .'

Before I slept, I went outside. The night was close and cloudy. There was only the sound of the moving creek. In the distance a button of red light stuttered from a radio mast. It was difficult to be comfortable. I walked around the exterior of the house and examined the garden. The building was on stilts, as the motel had been. I got down on my knees with a torch and shone it underneath. There were only some beer crates. I pulled them out and checked them. Big, healthy, rich Herbert Keenor was dead. I went inside, poured myself a drink and began to think about things.

Irving had asked me to drive down to Washington to see him. 'Herbert would have wanted you to go through with the assignment,' he said. 'And I'm going to ask you to do just that.'

Before driving down-state again the following morning, I called at the real estate office and told the surprised man I was moving out.

'You didn't like the place?' he asked anxiously.

'I loved it,' I said truthfully. 'I hope I won't be away too long.'

The contract was for six months and I had paid for three in advance. Now, while he shook his head at the waste, I wrote a further cheque for the second period and handed it over. He asked if I would like him to look out for casual bookings, but I said it was not necessary. I wanted to be able to get back, open the door, and start where I had left off. Did they have any objection to pets? They had no objection.

By afternoon I was back in New London. There had been a rainstorm and the gap in the burned motel was soaked and peeled so that it looked like a set of bad gums. At the police station the reflective cop who had come to see me in hospital was on duty. He looked even more studious behind a desk.

'Did you take a cat from the motel?' he asked.

'Yes. I've still got it. Does somebody want it back?'

'No,' he said. 'It's nobody's cat. We noticed it had gone missing, that's all.'

'You're keeping a close eye on the place,' I said.

He looked as if he could not reveal police secrets. Then he said: 'We checked out poor Mrs Williams. She had a few business troubles and some family disputes, but nothing that would make anyone want to cook her.' He picked up a report sheet from a pile on the side of his desk. 'And there's nothing big on the other people who lodged there that night. Three commercial travellers, who always stay there, were somewhere else at a poker game that went on late.'

'They tend to,' I said.

His lazy eyes came up over the top of his rimless glasses. 'They were twenty miles away,' he said. 'We've checked.' He shifted the report sheet. 'And there's nothing suspicious about the couple in the next room, except they weren't married.'

He saw my surprise. 'She was shouting she wanted a divorce,' I told him.

'Maybe she did. From some other guy,' he said. 'Our information is that they weren't married, just sleeping together.'

'In striped pyjamas?'

He shrugged. 'You never know with people.' He turned the page. 'And that just leaves you, Mr Findlater.' The wan eyes rose, drifted up again. 'We have a forensic report. It *was* an incendiary device.'

'So you told me before.'

'And the two men you played pool with. Nobody knows them in this town. Dan, of Happy Dan's, knows just about every truck driver who passes through and he didn't recognize those two. The third guy who played, Jake Macormick, he didn't know them either. And he's always in there and it's where all the truckers go.'

He put the piece of paper inside a folder and closed it. 'Where are you heading now? Back to Long Island?'

'My plans have changed,' I said carefully. 'I'm going to Washington first.'

'Not too many whales in Washington,' he observed.

'I want to go to the Library of Congress and the Smithsonian,' I lied. 'Research.'

'You taking the cat with you?'

'If nobody else wants it.'

'I think you can assume that.' He rose from the desk. 'Okay, Mr Findlater.' To my surprise his hand came across the desk. I shook it. 'But stay alert,' he said quietly. 'You've got enemies. Somebody is after you.'

IV

Brant Irvine had reserved a room for me in the May-flower Hotel, Washington. I got there in the evening and went to his office on A Street, a few blocks from the Supreme Court, the following morning. I left the cat in the car and went up in the elevator with two nuns. They turned out to be Irish and in a brief elevator conversation we fell to wondering why, after the wide Roman glory of their city, the Washingtonians had been reduced to calling their streets by the bald letters of the alphabet.

'They have a legal advice service in this building,' Brant Irving told me when I mentioned the nuns. He smiled abstractly. 'You'd think the kind of lives they lead, away from this dirty world, there would be no need for lawyers.'

'There'll be lawyers in Heaven,' I said. 'And Hell.' I sat in the chair he offered. 'I'd like to say how sorry I am about Herbert Keenor,' I said.

'Sure,' he said. 'So am I.' He looked tired, ringed under the eyes. He sat narrow in his wide leather chair behind a big desk. Through the window behind him the dome of the Capitol Building rose like a bright hill in the sun. Irving wore a black tie. 'He was my friend for thirty years,' he said heavily. 'From when I first went out to Eastern Long Island. I'm going to miss him.'

'How did it happen?'

'He was alone in the gun room, the Armoury he called

it, the room he showed you the other evening. Lucette, the secretary, heard a shot and found him. He was sitting in a chair and the gun, a handgun from the thirties, was on his lap. It had gone off and killed him. There was a brandy bottle and a glass on the table.'

'It's terrible,' I said. Then inconsequentially: 'He was such a big man.'

'A vital man,' he said. 'The only other person in the house, apart from Lucette and a couple of servants in the staff wing, was your daughter.'

'Susan?' He glanced up at my surprise. 'But I thought they had come here to Washington. That was their plan.'

'Sam was called to New York instead so Madelaine and Susan went up to Middlehampton intending to stay over the weekend.'

'Where was Madelaine . . . when it happened?'

'She was in Easthampton having dinner with friends at the Lobster Pot.'

'But Susan was in the house.'

'She slept through it. Didn't know a thing until next day.'

'Thank God for that,' I said. 'Where is she now?'

'She's gone back to the coast.'

'When is the funeral?'

'It was yesterday.'

'Oh, I'm sorry. Being out of touch . . .'

'In hospital,' he said. He leaned forward, his fingers touching his chin. 'Somebody started that fire *deliberately*?' he asked.

'So the police believe. Somebody put a timed incendiary device underneath what they possibly thought was my room. But it wasn't.'

'Shit,' he said seriously. 'Do they have any idea . . .?'

'At the moment the chief suspects are two truck drivers. I played pool with them that evening and nobody's ever seen them before. On the other hand, they may just have been two new truck drivers. But the police think I have somebody after me . . .'

Irving got up and went to the window. He tapped his knuckles on the glass. 'You could quit now, Michael,' he said. 'Nobody could blame you.'

'Was it an accident?' I asked slowly. 'Herbert's death?'

Still facing the window he said: 'The father of a man like Sam Keenor, a future President maybe, only dies naturally or by accident.' He turned to face me. 'There *is* no other way.'

Irving turned and sat in the chair behind his desk. 'Those nuns,' he said suddenly, 'had quite a case not too long ago. It got in all the newspapers. They complained because in their convent each one was required each day to dig a symbolic spadeful of earth for her own grave. It wasn't healthy.'

After a silence I said: 'Are you trying to tell me something, Brant?'

'In a way,' he said. 'Michael, I have the authority to sign a contract with you on the basis that we discussed that night with Herbert. Nothing has changed. I know he would have wanted to go through with it and the money is available. That's no problem.'

'Herbert won't be there to get his satisfaction,' I pointed out.

The lawyer nodded. 'I'll receive it for him,' he said. 'I guess he'll be lurking somewhere. Guys like Herbert Keenor don't die just because they're killed.'

'You think he was killed?' I asked quickly.

'Accidental death,' he said. 'It's still killing.' With

scarcely a pause, he said: 'Have you left your cat in the car?'

'He's fine,' I said. 'He's quite at home . . .' My voice slowed. 'How did you know I have a cat?'

When he shrugged, his neck became a receptacle for his head which sank into it. 'I called the police at New London,' he said. 'About the fire. I told them I was your literary agent. They told me you'd taken the cat.'

'If anybody claims it they can have it,' I said. 'Its tail is almost healed now.' I watched him. 'You found it necessary to check it out?'

He did not answer. 'That was one hell of a thing,' he said instead. 'Thank God you got out.'

'I've already thanked Him,' I said. 'But I still don't feel very comforted by the thought somebody might have been trying to toast me in my bed. Or the fact that the old lady who owned the motel died.' Still looking at him steadily, I said: 'Have you got any ideas?'

'I have no ideas,' he admitted. 'I can only repeat, Michael, that you are free to quit now. You haven't signed anything.'

I had already made up my mind. 'I'll stay,' I said. 'I'm getting interested.'

His smile was brief and all he said was: 'Thanks. I'm glad.'

He stood and went to a big safe against the wall. 'One further thing,' he said. 'This office was burgled on the same night that Herbert Keenor died. Not ostensibly. But we have ways of knowing. Papers were taken from this safe, presumably photocopied – we have a convenient machine in the outer office – and replaced. This file was disturbed.'

It was a wad of folders, each one a different colour. He lifted the top folder and showed me a label. 'Hine and Company', it said.

'I think our friend Peter Karl Hine undoubtedly has his reasons for not wanting to be found.'

'Very good reasons by the look of it,' I said. 'But Herbert's death was accidental.'

'An accident,' he insisted. 'The police say so. The gun went off in his hand and the bullet travelled through his jaw and lodged in his brain.'

The brown bald dome of a head was lowered like someone trying to make sure of his figures from pad on the desk. 'In the circumstances,' he said, 'I can authorize the payment of a further fifty thousand dollars on the completion of the assignment. That makes a total of one hundred and fifty thousand dollars, plus the percentages, the daily rate of a thousand dollars and, of course, expenses, as agreed.'

Eventually his eyes drifted up. I knew it was my last chance to quit. I was silent. 'And we will have you insured for a half a million dollars, payable in the event of your death. I take it you have a beneficiary?'

I nodded. 'Alice, my wife. She would probably consider it a good exchange. So would I. Perhaps Susan as well.'

'That's fine. We'll name them jointly.'

'How many people know about this?' I asked bluntly.

'Difficult to say. Herbert had staff, of course, and you can't guarantee where their eyes and ears are focused. There are also people working in this office, and those outside who to one degree or another, are aware of our interest, legal people and so on . . . and there's the FBI.'

My eyebrows rose. 'Why should the FBI – I mean, Nazi sympathizers in the FBI?'

'All I said was that there are some employees there who know of our involvement. We've made a lot of use of their files.' He regarded me quizzically. 'They're not faultless. You have traitors in your own top security services, don't you?'

'Not half,' I agreed. 'A mole isn't just a character in *The Wind in the Willows*.'

Irving got up and moved to the door. He walked in a pedantic line like a tightrope man. He opened it and ran his finger down the edge, then closed it again. 'But the most likely source,' he said as he returned still rope-walking to the desk, 'is the intruder who broke into this office. Your dossier, photograph, and so on were in the file. Before Herbert commissioned you he had you checked out.'

This surprised me. I told him so and said: 'Herbert Keenor must have been obsessed with this business, to want it done so badly, to put up the money.'

'Obsessed,' he agreed. 'He was once quite a famous man, remember, and famous men always want one last fling of fame. This was to have been his. He wanted the story talked about, long and loudly.'

'The money is very generous,' I remarked. 'I can spend much longer with the whales.'

He smiled and said: 'Obsessions.'

'It's a deep interest,' I shrugged. 'If it were an obsession, then *nothing*, not even something like this, would get in my way.' I paused. Irving was the sort of man to whom people told things. 'The whales are also a means of sorting out my life,' I confessed.

'Sure, I thought so,' he said. With only a little pause, he said: 'I think we ought to tell Madelaine about this matter.'

I was surprised. 'She doesn't know?'

'No. Herbert kept it secret. That *was* an obsession.'

'So Sam doesn't know either?'

'Especially Sam. He's a busy man right now. Herbert

would not have confided in him for that reason and for another, politicians talk and Sam's a politician. His father wanted real secrecy.'

'But you're going to tell Madelaine?'

'I think so. Somebody in the family must know. She won't tell Sam. She keeps his interests close to her heart.'

I felt embarrassed. 'Yes,' I said. 'I imagine she does.'

He got up and went to a drinks cupboard. He asked and I said I would have a gin and tonic. 'Suppose the fire at the motel and what happened to Herbert Keenor are connected,' I put to him. 'The Nazis, or whoever they are, must have a good organization here.'

'It's possible,' he agreed. 'There's a lot of old, dried shit left lying around in this country – things that happened years ago, and they still smell.'

He drank the gin straight, without tonic, something I'd never seen before. Then he went to the filing cabinet and took out a series of boxes. 'You can look through some of this stuff at some other time,' he said. 'But right now I thought I would just give you a run-down on the whole story, as it happened. The matter has all sorts of legal names, but for our purposes we have always called it "Hinc and Company". In the official records, however, it's been titled "The Pastorius Case". Pastorius was the code name which our friend Peter Karl Hine took on when he landed in from the submarine in June 1942. It's a kind of joke.'

'What kind?'

'Franz Daniel Pastorius started the first German settlement in America,' said Irving. 'Mid-seventeenth century. Germantown, Pennsylvania. In his mind Hine was also establishing, or trying to establish, a colony – of Nazis.'

He shuffled the dossier around his desk as though uncertain how to go on. Then he selected a bunch of photographs and handed them across to me. 'The spies in question,' he said. 'Herbert showed you a picture of Hine. As you see, he's still smiling.'

It was a crooked grin, the expression of a man who believed he was safe. The others did not look so sure. Each one was posed beside a measure recording his height. Each stood, heels abutting, feet splayed, arms vertical, eyes apprehensively straight at the camera. Each man was hung with an identification badge upon which was his name and a number. Hine wore a coat and tie as well as his grin. There was a suspicion of a slouch in his posture, insolence. The others were in shirt sleeves. Every man had his short nineteen-forty-two hair parted sharply and greased back. Under each photograph was the prisoner's name – Ernst Kerchin, Peter Müller, Johannes Vass, Karl Broger, Werner Konrad, Boris Kraft, Wolfgang Schmitt, and Peter Karl Hine.

'When the spies look young it's a sign of geting old,' I observed, putting the pictures on the desk.

'Schmitt was nineteen,' said Irving. 'Hine was the oldest at thirty-eight. Schmitt was an American citizen. As such his least entitlement was to a civil trial.'

'I'll need copies of these pictures,' I told him. 'And photostats of as many of the documents as you can. When I was in New York I checked on the general background. Now I'll have to do some real reading.'

'We have the documentation,' he answered. He picked up a heavy package from the top of the filing cabinet. 'That should keep you occupied.'

I took the package and reminded him: 'You mentioned the other night that it was like the Marx Brothers.'

'I certainly did. Just knowing about America in wartime, I mean generally, would give you some idea of the farce. This was the land of Mickey Mouse in forty-two.

But the *Nazis* were *supposed* to get things right, they were supposed to be smart. Yet they trained these men, these spies, for close on a year, risked two submarines to send them across the Atlantic, landed them – not just landed, *marooned* them – and *hoped* everything would be okay. The four who came ashore on Long Island . . . well, you couldn't write that as fiction and get away with it. The U-boat ran aground in fog and was stuck fast two hundred feet offshore. Two hundred feet! *And nobody in America noticed!* Her engines made one hell of a noise, just trying to get her off the shoal, but nobody thought of telling the coastguard.

'Hine and the three others were put off on a small boat which overturned in the surf, soaking them. They came on the beach wearing *German marine uniforms* but once they got ashore they changed into civilian clothes.'

'They had *that* much thought out then,' I said.

'They had. They figured that if they were captured on landing they would be treated as prisoners-of-war, because they were in uniform. The civilian clothes, all bought from New York stores, were to be worn from that moment on. They had just changed on the beach, in the fog, when a coastguard accidentally turned up. He was walking along the beach, unarmed. He was only a kid, a nineteen-year-old local called George Fleming. Hine told him they were Southampton fishermen from just across the coast, then, for God's sake, they began conversing in *German* between themselves. Finally Hine pressed what he said was three hundred dollars into the boy's hand and told him to go away and forget what he had seen.' Irving laughed wryly. 'It turned out to be two hundred and sixty dollars – the Nazi short-changed him. Fleming was so scared that he accepted the money and ran away.

By the time anybody believed his story and the alarm was raised the four Nazis were aboard the Long Island Railway heading for New York.'

'I read it,' I said. 'They escaped by train.'

'You see what I mean. They walked across the sand-dunes to the Montauk Highway and then to Amagansett Station, bought tickets, waited for almost an hour for the train, boarded it and vanished.'

'And nobody stopped them?'

'Not a soul. Four wet, sandy, furtive men attracted no attention, let alone suspicion. Hine carried something like *one hundred and eighty thousand dollars* – in a bag. That was a fortune in those days. He paid for the railroad tickets out of it. They rode the train as far as Jamaica Station. It was close enough to the city and they didn't want to walk into the hands of the FBI at Pennsylvania. They needn't have worried. The FBI wasn't waiting. It was Sunday and nobody told them until lunchtime. By that time even four blundering Germans were competently hidden.'

I shuffled through the photographs again. 'And four others landed in Florida?' I said.

Irving hunched his shoulders. 'Even easier. They got ashore at Ponte Verde, a beach south of Jacksonville. There nobody even spotted them. They walked up to the highway, waited for the bus and rode into Jacksonville where they washed-up, had a few drinks, and some steaks – they'd been in wartime Germany for more than two years remember – and eventually set out for the rendezvous in New York.'

'It's difficult to believe it,' I said.

'Difficult,' he agreed. 'But it's true. If Hine the traitor hadn't turned *double* traitor, then they could still be somewhere out there now. They hid up for ten days before they were arrested. The youngest guy, Wolfgang Schmitt, even went home to live with his parents in Chicago. *He even registered for the draft for the US Army.* Not many spies have ever done that.'

'Do you believe that Hine always intended to shop them, from the beginning?' I asked.

'That was his story, his defence, and that's what saved him from the chair eventually. He telephoned the FBI and told them he was one of the saboteurs, as they called them. By that time there was a nationwide hunt and nobody had found anybody. But, incredibly, the FBI *didn't believe him* and they just filed the message. To them he was just another nut. It was not until he called again from here in Washington, telephoning the army and God-knows-who-else, that anybody even suspected he was for real.'

'Why do you say the trial was a sham?' I asked carefully.

He answered: 'Listen Michael, I'm Jewish. I'm not devoted to the Nazis. But the fact remains that it was all fixed, cut and dried, and entirely unconstitutional. That's the point Herbert Keenor was making. If you're fighting and dying for freedom, for the Constitution and the Law, then you've got to protect it *everywhere*. It can't just be bent.'

'I bet that wasn't the popular view?'

He shook his head. 'It certainly wasn't in nineteen forty-two, and it probably wouldn't be now. But it's always niggled lawyers.' He passed across another package. 'In there are clippings of the articles and arguments which have appeared in legal journals, the *Military Law Review* and others, over the years. And they're still being written. I've contributed several myself.'

'At this trial,' I said. 'What did the defence do?'

'Everything they humanly could. They were frustrated at every turn. They even found a precedent, God help me – *Ex parte Milligan*. Milligan was a Copperhead Indian at the time of the Civil War, accused of helping the Confederates. Lincoln was supposed to sign his death warrant, but the President went to the theatre, fatally, leaving it unsigned on his desk. A fragment of history.'

I felt the weight of the packages he had given to me. 'There's a lot of reading here,' I reiterated. 'Where was the trial held?'

'A few blocks from here,' he said. 'Right across from what is now the FBI building on Pennsylvania Avenue. There's a plaque on the wall of the courtroom.'

'It's all very convenient,' I remarked.

'You've still got to find Hine.' He looked up. 'He could be in Germany, he could be anywhere. It's a big world. I had a reason for fixing for you to stay at the Mayflower here in Washington.'

'What was it?'

'Hine stayed there. That's where they caught up with him. You're in the same room.'

On the way to the Mayflower Hotel I stopped off and bought a shirt. I did not need a shirt, not urgently, but it came in a big, show-off bag with 'Pierre's' written extravagantly across it, handy for smuggling the cat into the hotel.

According to the proud bellboy who took us up to room 264, the hotel had been restored in detail to its looks of the nineteen forties. Herr Hine certainly knew the best places to surrender, but it was difficult to imagine him, after all this time, still in the room. In those days, with far fewer lofty buildings, his view over Washington must have been spectacular.

I had been in the room only five minutes when there was a diminutive ring at the door and I had to hide the cat in the bathroom.

It was a bellboy with a message. I waited until I was back in the room and then opened it to find myself looking at the now-familiar smirk of Peter Karl Hine. It was a copy of the same photograph, the line-up shot, that I had seen in Irving's office. There was a note attached which said: 'CONFIDENTIAL, Forty Bewley Street, Georgetown, Washington. At 8 pm today. Dial 43987-4. You have an appointment with Mr Shogghelly.' I went into the bathroom. The cat was curled around the base of the lavatory pan.

I ate early at the polished bar on the ground floor and smuggled a piece of New York prime rib upstairs for the cat. Shogghelly sounded Armenian. Initially I considered telephoning Brant Irving about the message, but then decided against it. I've never been one for seeking advice or protection, although I have occasionally sought consolation. This was a one-man job and it might as well begin now.

The dial instruction in the note was not a Washington telephone number. I guessed it was some sort of entryphone combination, and I was right. At eight o'clock I was in the lobby of a dignified apartment block in one of those Georgetown streets where even the shadows look refined. There was an elevator with no call-button. It would have been a real test for a Jehovah's Witness. On the opposite wall was a panel with a series of digits quietly lit. First checking the number on the message I dialled it with care. Inclined to dyslexia with figures, I have a history of interesting but incorrect telephone numbers and wrong faces at wrong doors. I depressed the buttons: 43987-4. Ten seconds went by and then a thick male voice issued through a speaker. 'Please come up. The elevator is waiting.'

So it was. It had sibilantly opened behind me. Inside it was like a mildly-scented padded cell, grey velvet walls, floor and ceiling. There were no buttons. You went where it took you. We ascended in uneasy silence. I began thinking I ought to get a gun.

The door opened with a sigh like an oven in a crematorium. There was only one way to go. I stepped out directly into a seemingly boundless and, some might say, beautiful room, the carpet continuing the quality and shade of that in the elevator, which now closed with soundless finality behind me. There was no one there. I looked around at the furniture; cream sofas and armchairs, puffed up as clouds; side tables and upright chairs in metal and glass, polished and poised, seemingly floating an inch above the floor. Prodigious modern paintings occupied three walls and a barricade of heavy drapes the fourth. With all the modern stuff, and looking sure of itself, was a glowing antique bookcase full of books. There were other books on one of the glass tables. Occupying another was an array of bottles and silver syphons like the towers of some slender city viewed from a distance. The room's air-conditioning may have purred, but you could not detect it above a muted recording of Bach's 'Sheep May Safely Graze', which I recalled used to be played on hot afternoons at Mamma Jo's bar and whorehouse in Saigon.

No one appeared but the place was not threatening. Someone was going to arrive. I stepped deeper into the room. Pretending I was engrossed in the paintings, I was posed with my hands behind my back gazing up with a knowledgeable tilt of the chin, when there came a soft footfall behind me. I turned a touch more swiftly than I had intended. It was Madelaine.

The only uncertain thing about her was her smile. The rest was superbly presented; a dark and flowing velvet dress, a diamond, solitary as the evening star, on a velvet band at her throat, her hair piled up displaying her neck to its very best, her attractive face become beautiful with light and cosmetics. 'You look wonderful,' I said. 'Are you going out?'

'I've just come in,' she answered shortly, not expecting the question and not pleased with it. 'You came to see Mr Shogghelly?'

'If only to find out how he pronounces his name,' I said.

She settled on the arm of one of the cloud chairs. 'Sit down, Michael,' she invited. I did. 'I'm sure you'd like a drink.'

'You know me,' I said. 'Was that Mr Shogghelly who answered me over the entry phone?' She rose and went towards a cabinet against the far wall. 'That's a recording,' she said. As if it had been waiting for her all day the cabinet slid open and a light illuminated its contents. 'Gin?' she asked.

'I've gone off gin.' I was looking over the back of the chair at her. 'I saw a man drinking it neat today.'

'Brant Irving,' she said without turning around. 'He always does. He doesn't like tonic water. What will you have then? We have champagne.'

'Who is "we"? Does that include Mr Shogghelly?' I inquired. She was pleased, I could see, to keep me waiting. 'Yes, champagne please.'

'This was Herbert Keenor's apartment,' she eventually answered. 'He used it when he was in Washington.'

'It was a tragic thing,' I said. She had walked towards me and she was close enough for me to touch her arm. 'I'm very sorry.'

'Thank you. So were we all.' She shook her head. 'I still can't believe it.'

I opened the champagne but she poured it, not very well, for her hand shook. When she handed me the glass her smile was no more certain than her hold.

'Somebody tried to set fire to me last week,' I mentioned.

'God ... I heard from Brant,' she said putting her fingers to her mouth. 'That must have been terrible.'

'An old lady died,' I said.

'Brant told me. He told me about this business ... this assignment that Herbert asked you to undertake.' I could see how anxious she was. 'Do you still want to go through with it?'

'I've said I will,' I shrugged. 'It's a lot of money.'

'What about the whales?'

I raised the glass in a toast. 'Here's to my return to the whales,' I said.

'Safely,' she added oddly.

'You're worried about me?'

'None of it seems right,' she said. 'I was very shocked by Herbert's death.'

'You believe it was an accident?' I asked.

She did not look surprised or upset. 'Of course,' she answered. 'What else?' She reached below the glass table and brought out a polished games board. 'Would you like to play Scrabble?' she inquired.

'English spellings,' I said. I poured two more glasses from the bottle. I was surprised how empty it had become.

'American,' she said, then backed down. 'All right, either.'

On occasions during our marriage we had played drunken Scrabble. Now, without mentioning it, she

68

handed me another bottle of champagne which I opened and she poured. We took the letters from a velvet bag. They were of incised ivory. She played first and spelled 'Harbour'.

'I knew it,' I grumbled. 'Seven letters. English bloody spelling. Bonus points.' We began talking about our daughter. We had some more champagne. At one point my face must have been pushed for emphasis towards her. We were sitting on the floor, the board on the low table, the champagne within distance. She was telling me something about Susan's school and our noses almost collided. In an amazing and gratifying moment we were rolling over, locked in each other, mouths agape, kissing like fury, our faces glistening with saliva and surprise. Christ, she was always so easy to lay! I was overwhelmed by the sensation of her clothed body, her silken face, her perfume, her indecent eagerness. I eased the dress down over her shoulder and kissed her pale breast. 'Who is Mr Shogghelly?' I inquired.

I thought she was going to cry. 'You bastard, Michael,' she muttered. She regarded me as if she were looking through a keyhole. 'You'll never change, will you?' She eased herself up on her elbow and replaced her bosom, forestalling my hand. 'All right, I'll show you.'

On her knees she went complainingly towards the adjacent low table. Picking up one of the old books arranged there, worn as a glove, she opened its frontispiece. 'Remember Mary Shelley and her diary?' she asked. 'And Hogg?'

'Ah yes, Hogg,' I recalled slowly. She crawled back to me. 'Hogg who kept coming.'

She regarded me as if I ought to have the answer by now, as if I were not very bright. 'Yes, Hogg,' she emphasized. 'And Shelley.'

Abruptly I realized. 'Mr Shogghelly!' I laughed. 'And I thought he was an Armenian!' Then I realized why she had done it. 'You . . . you . . . sent that message to get me . . .'

'I suspected I might still fancy you,' she said with sudden English bluntness. 'I don't get many opportunities for this sort of thing.'

Pulling her towards me I kissed her again. 'Any more champagne?' I asked. 'Don't drop off to sleep then,' she warned. 'You've done that before now.' We drank another glass each and lay close again. She lifted her dress and took her white pants off. I recognized her thighs like friends. I took off everything but my new shirt. My hands explored her. 'Darling,' I said. 'You have a pussy like a swamp.'

'Don't be so bloody literary,' she said softly. We were both loving it. The carpet was excellent. Languidly she pushed me gently away and slid out of the velvet gown. Her naked breasts blinked at me as if wondering where I had been all those years. It was better than I could ever remember. I got out of my shirt and she began to softly bite my chest. We had a delirious half an hour. Afterwards, while we were spread like a couple of massacre victims on the floor, she whispered, 'You always were good in bed, Michael. It was out of bed you were such a bastard.'

We sat up and had another drink. I made 'High' out of the Scrabble letters in my rack. It was the best I could do. 'How do you know we're not being watched?' I said to her.

'We're not,' she said. 'just accept that we're not. You don't need to cover your nakedness.'

'How do you know you can trust me?' I said. Sometimes I know I should shut up. 'How do you know I won't tell?'

'You won't tell,' she said. 'But I'm glad you asked. Before you could tell I would have you killed.' She began to cry.

V

Most of the following day, Sunday, I spent in my room at the Mayflower Hotel reading through the files that Brant Irving had given me, and wondering about Madelaine. Peter Karl Hine had been some days in that same room forty-seven years before, trying to get himself arrested. I double-checked it was the right room. It was the same number, 264, but I rang the desk to make sure and they put me on to a public relations man, who was at home enjoying his Sunday, shooting rats so he told me. He said he did on Sundays what he would like to be doing all the week. He called somebody else who knew the history of the place and this person confirmed that the numbers of the rooms now, after the Mayflower's refurbishment, were identical with those in the nineteen forties. I did not give the rat-hunter any reasons, although he sounded as if he would have liked some. Eventually the man's killer instinct overcame his curiosity and he returned to his hobby. Before he hung up, though, his public relations caution had reasserted itself.

'When I said I do on Sundays what I would like to be doing all the week,' he explained, as if I had made an accusation or a note, 'I didn't want to indicate any connection with the hotel.'

'Are there rats in the hotel?' I asked.

'No, no.' This was getting difficult for him. 'I thought you might think I mean human . . . rats. What I meant is I'd like to be out here in Virginia shooting rats all the week. That's what I meant.'

'Sure,' I said. 'I'd like to shoot a few rats myself.'

Taking the file which contained the photographs, I spread them on the bed; individual faces as well as the group. Each spy had that cleaned-up look of men who wanted to look their very best in front of the judge and eventually the executioner. All except Hine. The smile remained smug.

From this very room he had telephoned the police and the army and told them he was a Nazi spy, a hunted saboteur, just eager to be picked up. But the police were busy and the army was out to lunch. It was not until he had seriously pleaded once again with the FBI that somebody at headquarters had put down his sandwich.

Going to the window I was again confronted with the long view over Washington. A hot and empty Sunday look was hung over the city, trees and buildings dumb in the summer heat. Random tourists plodded in a search for somewhere open. There was a line of people emerging like a tail from the coffee shop across the street. My cat jumped softly onto the sill beside me. He was no more a secret cat. The chambermaid had discovered his presence when I had gone out for five minutes to buy the *Washington Post*. The cat, apparently, did not care for the Hoover and the chambermaid knew why. 'In that machine,' she said to me, 'there is dog's hairs. We got dogs in this hotel. Several dogs. And your cat can smell those darned dogs.'

I turned the radio on by the bedside:

You go for me and I'm taboo
And then my baby it's the end of you . . .

There is no telling with women. I once knew a girl in Prague who made a point of wetting the beds of her lovers. It was a perverse thing to do, literally a urinary

73

test, as she said, to ascertain those who were serious about her and did not complain, and those who were not serious and did. Madelaine had left me with a bite on my left shoulder. I had forgotten she was a biter; sometimes both shoulders. In the old days, when we were friendly, my shoulders sometimes took weeks to heal. The telephone rang. It was Brant Irving.

'How are you doing?' he said. His tone was more relaxed. I could tell he was out on Long Island, by the ocean. 'It's great out here today. Herbert would have loved it. How is Washington?'

'The air-conditioning's cool,' I replied. Quietly he laughed. 'Have you given that cat of yours a name yet?'

'Phoenix,' I told him.

'Felix?'

'That's good, Brant, but it's Phoenix.'

'Arisen from the ashes. Sharp, Michael,' he approved. His voice altered. 'I have a contact for you at the FBI. He'll help you. He's a good guy. His name is Fred Robinson, Agent Fred Robinson. He's an archivist and he knows this case. You call the FBI and ask for 3876. He'll answer. They have the complete files there.'

I wrote the information down and let him get back to his sunshine. I informed Phoenix of his new name, and promised that we would go out and get some sunshine of our own later. I stretched out on the bed and took up the documents again.

There was a lot that was surreal, but it was the landing I could scarcely believe. Reading the depositions made at the trial of the spies, it was apparent that neither could anyone else, judges, prosecution, defence, the FBI chief, J. Edgar Hoover, or even the spies themselves. The plot was total farce.

On that June night a fog was lying over the shores of

Eastern Long Island. Creeping through it, the German submarine could hear sounds from the land; music, cars. Then she stuck on the sandbank, not far from the spot which had been planned as a landing place back in L'Orient, in Occupied France, several months before. It had been a formidable feat of navigation by the U-boat commander. It was a shame about the sandbank. The German sailors were only too glad to be rid of their spies. The quartet had drunk too much and talked too loudly for the confines of a submarine. Fortunately they had been able to accomplish the journey across the Atlantic mainly on the surface, and Hine and his three companions had been on deck taking in the calm sea air for most of the way. Apart from a crash dive when the captain believed that Allied aircraft were in the vicinity, they had remained on top of the sea until they were almost in sight of the eastern coast of the United States. The spies, all of whom had lived in America, took turns looking excitedly through the periscope. They had spoken of the USA with a familiarity that sounded odd and suspicious to the German sailors, as if they were returning to their own land, their first country; going home. The U-boat commander had always harboured doubts about the mission, and now these were much increased. He was anxious to get his unwelcome passengers ashore and head back into the vast fastness of the Atlantic.

They went to the beach in a small boat with a line paid out from the submarine. In the night and fog, nothing was visible. They could hear the crunch of breakers on the shingle. The two German sailors manning the boat were eager to be gone and, in their anxiety to get the four invaders disembarked, they capsized the small craft and all six men ended up idiotically splashing about in the foggy shallows.

As soon as they reached the beach the boat was righted, baled out, and pulled back with its relieved two-man crew to the submarine by means of the line. By this time Hine and his companions had changed from their uniforms into civilian clothes, collected together their belongings, including explosives in the shape of fountain pens, and the bag containing 180,000 dollars in notes. Then they looked up to see a coastguard approaching.

The lone unarmed youth, George Fleming, aged nineteen, stopped, looking towards the figures in the fog. He related to the court how he walked towards them, and how Hine said to him: 'Under the stern.' Somewhere concealed in the dark offshore he heard the heavy throbbing of marine engines. Then Hine advanced over the shingle, explaining, as he trudged, that they were fishermen from Southampton, a few miles along the coast. 'Where's your boat?' asked Fleming.

'Somewhere,' said Hine pointing into the murk, 'out there.'

Then Fleming realized that some of the men were breaking into a foreign language, he thought German. He became frightened, and his fear was increased when Hine asked him threateningly if he wanted to see his mother and father again. Fleming, only a boy, answered that he did.

At that moment 260 dollars was pressed into his hand ('Here is three hundred dollars') with the order that he should go away and forget everything he had seen that night. Fleming, staring at the money in his palm, turned and walked away fearing for his life, into the fog.

While the boy had staggered over the rising sand, back towards the coastguard station, the Germans had dug a hole in the beach and buried their uniforms, explosives and other equipment, leaving clear tracks leading to the hiding place. Their clothes were wet, sand adhering to them, but the four men nevertheless tramped over the sand-dunes to the Montauk Highway. Dawn was lightening the fog. Hine guessed right and turned along the road to Amagansett station on the Long Island Railroad. It was an hour early for the first Sunday morning train so they stoically sat until the stationmaster arrived to open up the little wooden booking office. Hine delved into the bag containing the 180,000 dollars, less the 260 dollars he had pressed on the coastguard, and purchased four tickets to Jamaica station, just short of New York City. No one, employees or early morning passengers on the Long Island line, seemed to think there was anything curious about these dishevelled men in city suits, damp and sand-covered, travelling at that early hour of a Sunday.

Fleming had eventually roused his coastguard officers, and a party went down to the beach where, by following the indents in the sand, they easily found and disinterred the Nazi uniforms and the explosives. They returned to their post and called the local army commander. Troops called from their Sunday beds rattled to the seashore.

They searched along the beach and the sand-dunes. It was now a full summer morning, the fog dispersed. By this time people were at church, visiting, at their picnics, or out playing golf. It was not until midday, almost twelve hours after the saboteurs came ashore, that the Federal Bureau of Investigation was informed. By then Hine and his companions were safely in the labyrinth of New York.

My telephone brought me back to the present. It was the public relations man. Would I mind not mentioning in the hotel his joke about human rats? In fact he would be grateful if his shooting rats was not mentioned at all. It was a hobby that might be misunderstood. I promised and he rang off.

I thought I would take Phoenix out to lunch. I never have enjoyed room service. Spooning soup by yourself is the second most lonely occupation known to man.

Phoenix flopped with a single mew into his 'Pierre's' bag. I carried him downstairs and walked a few blocks to the Lafayette Park, where you can sit and watch the White House. There were some hobos and drunks sitting staring in the same direction, towards the house. I let the cat out of the bag, and its attention was at once taken with the squirrels who bounded over the grass and fell clumsily into the trash baskets. Phoenix squatted on the seat and narrowly studied their activities, moving his head as they moved. His tail was almost renewed now. It was twitching. Soon I would have to think of what to do with him.

At that moment a squirrel jumped upon the seat and bared its squared and vicious teeth at my cat, who jumped with a high loop into my arms. I shouted at the squirrel, who spat back before hopping away. The cat was trembling, his fur like a brush. 'They're only rats, really,' I told him.

We returned through the buildings, hot and with only Sunday stragglers around, back to the hotel. A Puerto Rican in a tight dinner jacket tried to charm me into a daytime girlie show. I took Phoenix back to the room and went to the coffee shop. I dropped a lamb chop into my trouser pocket for the cat. A woman at the next table saw me do it; in my confusion I pocketed it without putting it in a napkin. When I got up to go I could see her staring at the grease stain oozing through the front of my trousers.

In the middle of the afternoon I telephoned the FBI, said who I was and where I was calling from, and asked for Agent Fred Robinson. The girl on the switchboard seemed a little offended and told me it was Sunday. 'Doesn't the Bureau work on a Sunday?' I inquired. 'I mean, *nobody*? What if there's a big crime? Or I have some incredible information? What if I'm going to be rubbed out before tomorrow?'

She replied flatly: '*Has* there been a big crime? Do you *have* incredible information? *Are* you going to be rubbed out before tomorrow?' My answers were all negative. 'Call back tomorrow,' she said.

I put the phone down and went to the window. What did you do on a steamy, solitary Sunday in Washington? Madelaine had gone back to Long Island. She was leaving for Los Angeles, to be with her husband, the following day. Christ, but I had really enjoyed her. It was familiar yet all new again. Like visiting somewhere you once knew so well.

From the window I looked out on sun glaring over the white capital. I wondered what the girlie show was like.

Phoenix was curled at the foot of the bed breathing so deeply it was like a snore; I crept out and went to the Smithsonian. It was the sort of thing people did on a Washington Sunday; rowing a boat on the Potomac might qualify as the third loneliest occupation known to man. The cabbie dropped me where he dropped everybody, outside the American History Building, and I went in and joined the human crocodiles wending their way through the halls. There was an exhibit, photographs and videos and tape-recorded witness voices, about the uprooting of the California Japanese after Pearl Harbour. A woman's voice, pure American, issued from the exhibit describing the hardship of being sent into the desert to fend for themselves, but the queue was too long and slow-moving. I moved on.

There was another exhibition called 'The First Roosevelt Years' dealing with the thirties in America, the New Deal years. I wandered through it, almost aimlessly, moving from one showcase to another, until I came to a big photograph of an assembly of men in suits on a Washington lawn in the summer of 1936. Roosevelt was at the centre of the group, his strong head and crooked grin made small by the distance but still discernible. Banked around him, in the wide coats and trousers of the day, were members of his party of the Senate. My interest quickened. Nineteen thirty-six. There was a caption beneath the picture and I ran my finger down the names until it stopped at Senator Herbert Keenor. Even after half a century and more he was readily recognizable. The same tall grin, the thick hair, the air of firmness, self-knowledge, and beaming good nature. He had his arm across another senator's shoulder.

As I was looking at the photograph a short, neat, black man came and stood beside me, studying the picture too. He was so close that I felt I had to converse with him.

'Those were the days,' I said lamely with a nod towards Roosevelt. 'Sure,' he said. 'Sure.'

'Not many black people present, though.'

'Sure,' he said again. 'They didn't go in for them.'

He looked minutely, pushing his head forward as though hoping to spot a black face even on the periphery of the large photograph. After a time he shook his closely barbered head. 'Not even a drinks waiter,' he observed.

I laughed and moved along. He moved along with me. I stopped at a photograph of Roosevelt in a wheelchair. The black man halted beside me. 'You seen the exhibit about the American-Japs who got sent into the desert in the war?' he asked.

'No,' I said. 'The line was too long.'

'There's a lot of interest,' he agreed. 'It's really strange how people get interested in old things, history things.'

After a moment I said: 'I think I'll get a drink.'

He said: 'You don't get alcohol in here, not in the Smithsonian, except you can get wine in the cafeteria. Outside it's soft drinks. How about a root beer? Maybe I'll join you.'

We walked from the building onto a terrace. The daylight was hot after the coolness inside. He told me to sit down at a table while he went and joined a brief queue. He wore a quiet grey sports coat and darker-grey trousers. His shoes shone and I could see he wore red socks. When he returned with the tray and the root beer in polystyrene beakers, I said to him: 'I'm Michael Findlater.'

'I know,' he said, sitting down. He drew some of the beer through his straw.

'How do you know?'

'I'm an FBI agent.'

'Fred Robinson?'

'You got it.'

'I thought you took Sundays off.'

'I had some spare time. I heard you called, and Mr Brant Irving told me you would be around. I went to the Mayflower. They've really made that place swanky.'

'But I'd already left?'

'No, you were still in your room. But I followed some other guy. I thought it was you. He was English. I ended up in a flower market. When I got back I just caught you leaving the hotel. So I tailed you. Anyway, here I am.'

We shook hands over the table. 'Don't let the "agent"

fool you,' he said amiably. 'It just makes me feel good. I work in the archives. That's why I trail the wrong goddam people.'

'Even FBI agents make mistakes,' I pointed out, smiling. 'Look at Hine and Co.'

'They made some then,' he agreed. 'But everybody got medals in the end.' He paused as though uncertain whether to tell me something important. 'We call it "The Pastorius Case", by the way.' He shrugged. 'It's nothing. It's just how it's filed. If you ever need to refer to it at the FBI that's it – The Pastorius Case.'

'It sounds better than Hine and Co.,' I said.

'Hine and Co. could be bootleggers,' he nodded.

'Brant Irving said you were the expert.'

'I've lived with those spies for years, so I guess so. There's always somebody interested in them, lawyers mostly, but always somebody.' He looked at me over his polystyrene beaker. 'You're writing a book?'

'Yes . . . I'm writing about it.'

'Too bad about Senator Keenor.'

'Very sad. He was in that photograph I was looking at inside.'

'Sure. That was his time.'

'What do you think about the spies . . . the saboteurs . . . or whatever?'

'Spies,' he said as one who has a firm category for everything. 'I have them under "spies". They were intended saboteurs but they didn't sabotage anything.'

'From what I understand they didn't do any spying either.'

'True. They just got to the United States and disintegrated. They didn't do very much of anything except disperse. Some people call them invaders, but that's too grand for those guys.'

'People think the trial was fixed.'

'I don't have any opinions about that.' He regarded me as if he had opinions about it. 'I just work on it.'

'What do you think of the Nazis, the spies. Are you allowed to have an opinion on that?'

'Assholes,' he said quietly. 'Whoever picked them didn't know how to pick spies. They weren't just assholes, they were incompetent assholes.'

'It's strange how the case keeps coming up,' I said. 'It seems like it won't stay buried.'

'Right,' he said. 'It won't. And every time it comes up, it stinks more than the last time.'

He had given me concise directions for locating him at the Federal Bureau of Investigation. 'Come in from Pennsylvania Avenue, cross the yard with the fountains. You'll see the entrance. There's a guy screaming abuse outside.' He was right. Outside, standing in the summer dust on the sidewalk, was a threadbare black man howling threats and accusations at the FBI Headquarters. Most of the tirade was unintelligible, but the name of J. Edgar Hoover kept coming up. Either the man thought Hoover was still alive and in charge, or the complaint must have gone back into history. I went in, around some perpetual fountains and the courtyard, and in through deep glass doors. It was like the lobby of a mundane hotel. Piped pop music infiltrated mindlessly. Waiting people sat around with unparticular expressions. There was a security guard in a little pulpit inside the door and three armed receptionists behind a glass-screened desk. One of these was a tall, pretty but businesslike-looking redhead. After her hair and her form, the next thing you noticed was her gun. She was reaching to get a stapler from one of her male colleagues. Both watched her tentatively as she bent towards them as if all-too-ready to catch her if she fell. She had a wonderful hip for a gun.

When I reached Fred Robinson's office, he was spread out on the floor. People were rushing around and telephoning. Two medics arrived with a stretcher. Shocked, I moved back against the corridor wall to let them go by. Robinson was still, his black face frozen, his hands splayed out. The medics lifted him onto their stretcher and carried him out. As he passed me in the corridor, he opened one eye and said: 'Be right with you.'

He was back, whole, and drinking coffee, a few minutes later.

'They require us to do all this stuff,' he sighed when he was restored to his desk. 'Life preservation, they call it. But I'm never the lucky guy who gets the kiss-of-life from that big lady cop downstairs.'

'I saw her,' I agreed. 'The redhead. She'd inflate you.'

'She could certainly try,' he agreed, his eyes coming up appreciatively. His thoughts remained on the prospect until he focused on me again and said: 'Okay – the Pastorius files.'

'I'm looking forward to reading them.'

He spread his small, pale palms. 'Under the US Freedom of Information Act nobody, not even the President of the United States, can stop you,' he said. 'It's all available. And there's a lot of it.' His deep eyes went down to a note on his desk. 'Thirteen thousand, nine hundred and forty pages,' he said.

'Jesus,' I said.

'That's what I say. There's just about everything. The trial, all the depositions, the evidence, the correspondence. The case notes of the G-Men – they used to call them G-Men in those days you know.'

He smiled wistfully. 'They really used to wear those big hats, remember, the ones with the brims. And the suits like you see. I enjoy watching those movies.' He shook his head. 'It's a different world.'

He got up. 'It's no trouble. I can show you the files,' he said. 'And you can just sit down and start at page one.'

'I'm a quick reader,' I said.

We went down two floors. He had obtained a pass for me at the outside desk. It was encased in stiff plastic, and at the entrance to each department it had to be slid into a turnstile and left there, projecting like a shiny tongue, until there was a click and the barrier was released. The room where the files were stored was as long and calm as a vault, lined with metal shelves. Down one side was a long bench with stools. Inside the door a girl in uniform, with a badge bigger than the shoulder it emblazoned, sat in charge. She looked about seventeen. Her name was Sheree and while I was there she called her husband ('To tell you it's okay'), her friend ('It's okay, Marjie') and her dentist to tell him the bridge had stayed in place this time and she felt okay.

Visible on the shelves were the FBI files on Marilyn Monroe and Elvis Presley. Robinson saw my interest. 'The place of the stars,' he smiled. 'We just bring these out when we know somebody is going to need to consult them.' He shrugged: 'Freedom of Information Act,' and added, with what sounded like a private satisfaction: 'But we got lots more files downstairs. And they stay there.'

Fred walked along the shelves. 'The Pastorius Case,' he recited, indicating a long rack of maroon-covered books as solemn as account ledgers. 'There it is. Thirteen thousand, nine hundred and forty pages.' He eased one of the volumes from the metal shelf and ran the type-written sheets through his stubby fingers. 'Some people think it's ancient history.' He glanced up at me.

'With current overtones,' I said. My first random touch of the documents opened at a page headed: 'District Jail, Washington, DC, July 31, 1942.'

Robinson looked over my shoulder. I sensed that Sheree at the desk was watching, but when I glanced that way she turned her head. Fred read aloud like a preacher. ' "The following statement is given of our own free will and may be used in any way our defence counsel thinks it advisable . . .

' "Being charged with serious offences in wartime we have been given a fair trial . . . our defence counsel has represented our case as American officers unbiased, better than we could expect and probably risking the indignation of public opinion. We thank our defence counsel for giving its legal ability, which is recognized as the best in this country – on our behalf . . . General Cox's officers and men we have come into contact with during this time have treated us better than fair." '

I counted the names written below. 'They all signed it,' I said. 'Except Hine.'

'By that time maybe he didn't need to,' said Robinson. 'He knew he was okay.' He half turned to the girl. 'Let me out of this place, Sheree.' He said to me: 'If you don't really like food you could have lunch in this building. I'll come and pick you up.'

As he was going out he said: 'That trial was held right across the street, in the old FBI headquarters. They've got a plaque on the wall there now, outside the room. Maybe you'd like to take that in too.'

I thanked him and he said it was nothing. Sheree unlocked the door and the concise black man went out.

'It's all yours,' she said extending her hand across the files. 'The beginning is at that end.'

To my great relief, the start of the file was a summary of the whole case. By now I had begun to put faces to the men. I began to read. After an hour Sheree asked if I would like some coffee and she telephoned a messenger and unlocked the door for him when he came in with the plastic cups on a plastic tray. While we drank the coffee I asked Sheree how her tooth was now, and she seemed glad but unsurprised that I knew about it. It was the sort of place, activity cocooned in silence, where people picked up drifting words and conversations. 'It's good.' She smiled as if to demonstrate. 'It's really okay now.'

The file which Fred Robinson had selected at random remained on the bench. As I drank the bland coffee I turned a chance page. It contained a memo to J. Edgar Hoover, the Director of the FBI, dated August 7, 1942. It said: 'Arthur Cox called me and advised that word had been given to the Provost Marshal to carry out the executions of the six saboteurs beginning one minute after midnight, August 8, 1942. He advised me that the saboteurs were showing no adverse reaction, but that Schmitt had toothache and that an army dentist had been called and extracted the tooth.'

I glanced up at Sheree. 'Terrible thing toothache,' I said.

'The worst that can happen to you,' she said.

Agent Robinson said that the best time to go across Pennsylvania Avenue to view the room that had been the scene of the trial was during the lunch break when the typists and secretaries who now worked there would be out. As we left the FBI building the man was still outside haranguing the high, unanswering walls.

'He's there all the time,' said Robinson with a certain fondness. 'Every working day. When he didn't show for a couple of days in the spring everybody missed him. People started inquiring about him, where he had got to. When he came back it got around that he'd been sick and people kept asking him if he was better now.'

'What's he saying?' I asked. 'I just can't pick up what he's saying.'

'Nobody can. Maybe he knows, maybe not. He's just a man who thinks he's been done an injustice. Maybe he has.'

We were waiting for the traffic signals. People came out and went into the FBI building, walking by the bawling man without giving him a second look. Nor did he seem to be aware of them. 'He's like a mascot,' I suggested.

'A conscience,' said Robinson.

We crossed the expansive avenue. The darker, older building directly opposite had no security, only a janitor reading a book, a dusty-jowled man with dropped eyes. We went up three floors in the elevator and came out into a corridor. A door framed a solitary woman eating sandwiches at her desk and attempting to knit at the same time. It was difficult. She glanced up, munching, as we got to the door, and then continued clicking the needles furiously as if trying to impress us.

'This is the room,' said Robinson. 'It's just a room. Once they utilized it for interviewing candidates for the Bureau. I came here myself for my first interview. That's when I first saw the plaque, when I first heard of the Pastorius case.'

The plaque was modest. The typist appeared puzzled that we should be studying it at all. It recorded that in that place in July 1942, eight Nazi saboteurs, captured by the FBI, had been put on trial and that six of them had been sentenced to death. There was nothing else to see. 'No vibes,' shrugged Robinson. We went down to the street again. The janitor did not even raise his face.

It was a beautiful Washington lunchtime, full summer, and we walked up towards the Capitol Building, curved and glowing roundly like a great pure egg, before re-crossing the street and going back towards the FBI Headquarters. Robinson sighed as he walked. 'Only I could get assigned to a case forty-seven years old. When lawyers and other parties began to get interested, I was instructed to familiarize myself with it and to take it under my arm. It's been under my arm ever since. I keep Pastorius.'

The man remained shouting up at the J. Edgar Hoover Building, his fervour undiminished. 'In summer he always stays in the same place,' said Robinson as we went under the arch and into the fountained courtyard. 'When it rains there's a dry area where he's been standing.' We pushed our plastic cards into the successive turnstiles and went up to the cafeteria. There were lines of employees taking food from the stainless steel counters. 'It's just salad and soup and stuff,' said Robinson taking a tray and handing one to me. 'They don't encourage fat people here.'

'Will you let me pay?' I said.

'I will, but the Bureau won't,' he answered. He began picking up greenery with tongs. 'I can't pay for you either. It's a Federal Agency.'

'It's difficult to bribe anyone with salad,' I smiled. 'Except rabbits.'

He shrugged, the tongs still in his hand. 'Everything has to be seen to be right.'

To confirm his words, the girl at the pay desk solemnly

weighed my salad before charging me by the ounce. I watched the ritual before following Robinson to a shiny-topped table. We had pear juice to drink. We were surrounded by FBI agents crunching through lunch.

'My father always wanted me to be an FBI man,' Robinson ruminated. 'Always. He even had me baptized Frederick Byron Ivor Robinson – FBI. So that in the fullness of time I could spend my days coughing the dust off files.' He dropped his tone. 'And come up here every day and see them weighing fucking lettuce.'

After four days enclosed in that time-locked vault with Sheree, I decided to go back to Eastern Long Island. The files were getting too much for me and so was Sheree. Thirteen thousand, nine hundred and forty pages turned out to be a box to frighten Pandora, quite apart from being a lot of pages. Facts, figures and farce spilled out all over the bench. I began with a smiling white pad, a pen and a spare pen. But most of my professional life has been out-of-doors, shouting down a commandeered telephone which is cut just before you get through to London, with explosions and deaths occurring off and, not infrequently, on stage. This room, this ticking place, was strange, and it became stranger. Each morning I clocked in at the front desk and collected my plastic tongue from the armed redhead who looked more distant each day. The muzak in the lobby was unchanging. I would put the plastic ticket into the turnstile and poke my tongue out in return. Sheree would say a meaningful good morning, and I would collect an armful of the files and take my place at the bench. Sheree just sat at the door in her little place, occasionally making a phone call, but mostly just sitting. At eleven she was invariably surprised as to how quickly the time had gone and asked would I like some coffee. I too professed amazement at the swift passage of the day, and said I would love some coffee. She would ask about sugar and cream, there would be a phone request, the coffee would be brought in by the same messenger, and we would have five minutes' nebulous conversation while we drank it. She never discussed the files or her marriage. To me she still looked seventeen.

Each page I turned of the Pastorius files uncovered something else to stare me in the face. Two thick pads were full of scribbled notes when I stopped. 'I think this is swallowing me,' I said to Sheree. I did not know whether she was allowed to talk about the files.

'No kidding,' she said. 'Most people come in and know exactly what they're looking for. They just turn to the right page, make their notes and go away.'

'Have you had many people looking at this material?' I asked.

'Now and then,' she said with no suggestion of caution. 'But they come for an hour and they go. Lawyers, guys interested in the war, people like that.' She looked as if she might be about to make a confession. 'I just don't understand it,' she shrugged. 'All this stuff is so *old*. Who cares now?'

During these four days I did not see Fred Robinson. I called his extension a couple of times but a girl said he was at home, a few days' special leave. I got to eating my lunch at a place two blocks back from Pennsylvania, passing by the indomitable protester, his unwavering voice and shaking fist. By now I realized that he was shouting the same scarcely intelligible accusations over and over again, like a loud litany.

'I need a break from this,' I said to Sheree at the end of the fourth afternoon. I stood up and slammed the file. 'I'm going out to Long Island.'

'The ocean's nice,' she said. She had looked a touch offended at my fierceness with the file.

As I was folding the notepad, putting my pens away and arranging the files on the bench like a pile of paving stones, I asked her casually: 'Would it be possible to have a list of the people who have consulted these files over the past year?'

Her voice did not change. 'That's not available, Mr Findlater,' she said. 'The files are subject to the Freedom of Information Act, but the details of who consults them are not.'

'I see. Well thanks for your help. I'll be back some other time. Goodbye.'

'Goodbye, Mr Findlater,' she said.

We had been locked up in a room together for four days and she still called me Mr Findlater.

VI

There must be a name in psychology for a person whose dreams travel with them, changing location as the dreamer moves from place to place. I stopped in New York overnight and I had the blood-and-wine nightmare again, but this time it was happening on Park Avenue. After what happened in the motel at New London I was afraid of this dream, and I made myself wake up to ensure that the flames were only in my imagination. Reassured, I returned to sleep to enter into an adventure where Madelaine was standing on top of the Chrysler Building, on the very edge of the escarpment and *leaning* out and over the top with nothing to save her falling but the wind. She was wearing a blue dress that she held out each side of her like wings, and the wind was filling the wings and holding her there. She was pitched at a terrifying angle, way over the overbalancing point, and down below the traffic was churning.

She had really done that once. Not on top of the Chrysler Building but on the lip of a cliff in Oregon. It was while we were married. We had gone up to that wild place in wintertime, for no special reason as far as I can remember, but because it was the sort of thing we did in our happier days. One morning we went out walking in a gale. It was pounding off the ocean, blind force; even the birds could not fly. Below the cliffs the sea was great and white. We were fooling about as we did at times, and I lay on my stomach and crawled tentatively

93

to the last inch of the cliff, one push at a time, and stared down at the incredible mayhem of the water.

'That's nothing!' she shouted seeing me lying there. She was about thirty feet away, stone cold sober, and standing a few yards back from the edge of the cliff. 'Get this!' I could not believe what she did. Lying there, transfixed, I watched her as she walked into the enormous wind to the lip of the drop, and spreading her arms leaned slowly over. Madelaine leaned over that soaring cliff, into the gale, leaned and leaned, until she was at an angle that was unbelievable. I could hear her laughing crazily – even over the roaring wind. Her hair was stiff as a cowl. She looked as if she were flying. 'Don't!' I managed to call at last. And pathetically: 'Stop it! Madelaine, come back at once!'

I shut my eyes. When I opened them again she was still there, still suspended and laughing like fury. Then, with a final bow to the waves, and as though following some prescribed formula for people who habitually hang over cliffs, she backed away. Each leg retreated in a stilted thrust, a backward stagger, one, two, one, two, one, two, until she was clear.

Once she was safe she fell forward to her knees, still laughing violently, and by the time I had risen from my knees, she was crying. Staggering, the gale hitting me side-on, I ran to her, fighting against the gusts. When I got there her forehead was pressed like a prayer against the earth. As I bent over her the wind hit me so powerfully that it pushed me on top of her. 'I won't do it again, Mike!' she howled. 'I promise. I won't do it!'

Gabbling, I covered her with myself and we grappled, me pinning her to the earth, as if I did not believe her, and then as she weakened, embracing her to me. We hugged each other madly. I kissed her all over her face

94

and crushed her to me. She was wearing a red coat and I still see that coat, blood red, over the cliff in the great, grey storm. Eventually we became silent and still, lying against each other on the hard, cold, dry ground. It was some minutes before we got up and brushed each other down. Then we walked back inland. We were holding hands. 'You silly bloody cow,' I said to her bitterly. It had always been an unusual marriage.

Lucette Harvey, the secretary, was sitting alone by the tennis court as I drove up the final rise to Flagstaff. The sun was on the sea and the garden; the house basked but the outsized Stars and Stripes hung its head, for there was no breeze.

She was wearing a pale green track suit. She made no sign that she saw me coming or heard the car, only remaining seated, unmoving.

'Waiting for someone?' I asked when I had left the car and walked over a stretch of clipped grass to the court. She did not appear unprepared, turning slowly, to see me through the wire mesh.

'Sort of,' she said. Her eyes were glistening.

'Oh yes,' I said, realizing. 'I'm sorry.'

She moved towards the gate. I opened it for her and she thanked me quietly. She peered over the lawns and out towards the ocean. 'Even the sunshine is empty now,' she said.

'I was very sorry,' I said inadequately.

'Thanks,' she replied. 'Brant said you would be coming,' she said. 'I expect you'd like a drink.'

I said I would and we walked together towards the house. She was an athletic woman with a plain face. 'Almost every afternoon we played tennis,' she said miserably. 'Herbert was an excellent player.' Then she said:

'Hardly anybody's been near the place.' We reached the terrace where we had sat only two weeks before. 'They came at first, of course. The family and the police, everybody. But the funeral, you know, was in Washington. I didn't go. I stayed here with the house. And I've been here ever since.'

She poured a beer for me and a lime juice for herself. 'This doesn't taste the same,' she said, making a face at the glass. 'Not when you haven't been playing.'

'What are your plans?' I asked. We sat in the wicker chairs. Herbert Keenor's chair had been pushed to the end of the terrace and was facing the wall.

She shrugged: 'I find it very difficult to care.'

'You were very fond of him.'

'I loved him,' she said flatly. 'He was the most remarkable man. I've been here for twelve years. Herbert was a friend of my father's in the old Washington days.'

Shakily, she lit a cigarette. 'Brant Irving has asked me to stay here for a while, until everything is fixed, sorted out. Sam and Madelaine say they would like to keep the house on, and Herbert would have wanted that . . . but I just don't know. They said they would want me to stay, as a sort of housekeeper, caretaker, secretary, all-in-one. But somehow I don't think I will. It's ended.'

I asked her if Irving had told her I would be arriving and why.

She nodded. 'I know about it. Quite a lot anyway. I typed your contract and working with Herbert . . . well, naturally, I know things that were going on.' I put my glass down. 'He had great faith in you,' she said looking at me frankly. 'He was like that with people. He could sum you up in an instant. And he wanted this done, more than anything. I'm glad you have said you will go on with it.'

'Are there any of Herbert's papers, appertaining to the Pastorius business, that I can see?' I asked.

'There's a file,' she said. 'But most of the documents are duplicates of the material that Brant Irving has. You're familiar with them?'

I said I was and asked if I could see the file. 'Brant said it would be all right,' I told her.

She rose and put down her glass. 'I can show you now.'

We went into the house. A maid was dusting a spotless room. Lucette led the way down the panelled corridor. The house was clean and echoing. 'Suddenly it's just a museum,' she said. 'Just artefacts. Furniture, paintings, books, all lifeless.' Her final step through the door of what I remembered was the room with the guns was deliberate and determined. 'Even these,' she said looking around with a sort of malice at the weapons set out around the walls. I walked in behind her. She stopped and said: 'This he called the Armoury. It happened here.' She pointed, her voice dropping. 'In that chair.'

I touched her arm sympathetically. 'Leave me, if you like,' I said. 'It must be very difficult for you. Just tell me where the file is.'

'Not at all,' she replied. 'I *have* to come in here. I had to come in here then, that night. When he was in that chair. I had to come in a good many times after that and I'll have to come in again. It's only a room, Michael.'

On a leather table was a single gun. 'That's it,' she said. 'The police brought it back yesterday. They took it away for tests but they brought it back. It belongs over there . . . ' She nodded to a space among the weapons on the wall. 'See, it fits in the space. I just haven't been able to bring myself to handle it.' She looked at me.

'Do you want me to put it back?'

'Would you mind?'

'Not at all.' I picked up the clumsy, old, heavy weapon. Its metal was like a cold clenched hand. First checking that it was unloaded, I took it to the wall and clipped it into its fitting.

'Exhibit A,' I heard her say behind me.

'There's no more ammunition around is there?' I said.

'The police took it. They didn't send it back.' She smiled sadly. The shadows in the room made it like a grimace.

I could see that she did not want to remain in the room. She went into the study where Herbert Keenor, Brant Irving and I had sat the night they told me about Pastorius. 'Even this place is just without spirit now,' she said. The blinds had been down. She lifted them with a single touch of a switch. The sun was on the other side of the house so it did not come into the room but outside illuminated the green of the lawns, framed by the window. A gardener went slowly by pushing an empty wheelbarrow.

As though coming into the study had changed her mood, Lucette became businesslike. She unlocked a cabinet and took out a file. 'This is the only material which Brant doesn't have,' she said. 'They did not show you it that night, so he says. He says he wants you to take it with you now.'

Leaning over the desk I took the file from her. 'It's mostly concerned with the night the German submarine came in,' she said. 'Eye-witness accounts of what took place afterwards. It makes quite comic reading.'

Laying the file on the desk, I opened the top. The first document was a list of local names and addresses. 'Zeb Smith,' I read.

She came around the desk and stroked a sunburnt

finger down the list of names. 'Some of these folks are dead now,' she said. 'The list was compiled a few years ago. But Zeb is still around. He still lives at that address.'

I put the file under my arm. 'And that's all?' I said.

'All there is,' she replied. I followed her from the study, through the room with the guns. Here I hesitated and she stopped also.

'May I ask you one more thing?' I asked.

'Sure.'

'There was only one glass and the brandy bottle wasn't there?'

She nodded grimly.

'Did he often drink alone?'

'Quite often. Late at night.'

'Brandy?'

'Herbert was a rye whisky man.'

'But that night it was brandy. Is the bottle still available?'

She moved at once towards a cabinet against the wall. 'The police checked it as well,' she said. 'But they didn't take it away. When they had finished I put it back in here.' She opened the cabinet.

'And the glass?'

She half turned. 'I broke the glass,' she said evenly. 'By accident.'

'I see. Is the bottle there?'

'Yes, it's here.'

She took it from the cabinet. It was four-fifths full. She handed it to me. I turned it so that I could see the label. It said: 'Hine'.

'Hello Brant. I went to the house.'

'Good, Michael. You took the file.'

'Yes. Lucette Harvey gave it to me.'

There was an almost imperceptible hesitation. Then he said: 'How is she doing?'

'Facing it. With difficulty.'

'Yes. She was very close to Herbert. She wiped his blood from the walls and from the floor, you know. She wouldn't let anyone else touch it.'

The list given to me by Lucette was indeed out-of-date. Several of the names had been deleted. One had gone to Iowa to live with his son and another had drowned.

'Two miles offshore, they reckon,' said Zeb Smith with a sniff of finality. 'Went out and didn't come back.'

'Just like that,' I said.

'That's how it happens,' he confirmed. 'Always went out by hisself. Didn't need no crew, sort of bit fishing he was about.'

The old man's house was white-board, single storey, a patch of garden against the creek. It appeared that sections had been added and to no special plan. One of the additions was a deck facing the water. He had a stumpy little jetty down the foot of the garden and nudging it, his dinghy, fidgeting as the morning tide ran away.

He must have been tall once but now he was old; his shirt bulged as if it were concealing a number of packages, his headtop shone, his teeth grew at random, but he moved surely and his eye was bright. 'See this house,' he said. He walked towards one wall and then another, banging them with the flat of his hand. 'Take a guess how much it cost? Long time ago, but take a guess.'

I could see the game would please him. I guessed low. 'Ten thousand dollars,' I said. 'Depends how long ago it was.'

'End of World War One,' he answered. He struck the wall with his palm again. 'My dad bought it.' He smiled with a sort of wicked happiness, unable to contain the answer: 'For *one* dollar.'

We both laughed, me politely, him uproariously. 'But I ain't kidding,' he said wiping his mouth. '*One* US dollar.' He grabbed my arm and sat me down in an old chair. He liked visitors. 'See, they was building these huts, like Quonset huts we called them in World War Two, and when the first war finished, when was it, nineteen eighteen, they had a whole lot of huts and nothing to do with the goddam things, no place to put them. So they sold them to veterans, doughboys back from the war, for *one dollar each.* One dollar!'

'It's worth double now,' I joked.

'Quarter of a million,' he corrected seriously. 'Two hundred and fifty thousand bucks. All for one dollar. Sure, he had to buy the land, but land here wasn't much in those days.'

Reminiscence drifted over his face. 'He was a great guy, you know, my father, a great guy. He used to say that there was two most explosive things in this world – women and dynamite. He was a kind of philosopher.' His eyes came into focus. 'But naturally that was before the nuclear bomb.'

He got up and rolled into the house, returning to the deck with two beers. 'You want to know all about them spy guys,' he said. 'So you said.'

'Yes, I'm writing a book about them.'

'Not many left on the South Fork who was here then,' he ruminated. His eye sockets creased as he tried to think who was.

'What happened to Fleming, the young man, the coastguard?' I asked.

'Took off. Went without trace. Somewhere up in New Jersey.' He shook his head. 'He got a medal.'

'I know.'

'But he wouldn't talk about it. Clamped up. Not a word. It was a crazy thing. Shit, there they was, sitting offshore in their submarine, a goddam *Nazi* submarine, and nobody knew. And this young guy, George Fleming, the coastguard, goes right up to them and they tell him they're fishermen from Southampton. Talking *German*! But he's scared and he high-tails it off.'

'It's difficult to blame him. What do you remember about it?' I said. 'You personally?'

'Just about the same as other folks around here,' he said slowly. He took a sip then a large drink of his beer. 'Didn't know much, not till it was over, or darned near. Everybody was getting down to the beach to see where the Germans had landed. I was working in a boatyard at Westhampton in those days, but of course this being Sunday, I wasn't. Me, I was just going fishing when I heard the news, so I hurry on down to the beach. I guess I was one of the first because there weren't too many folks there then, a few people and the soldiers and the coastguards and the cops. They were just digging up the stuff that the spies had buried in the sand. Everybody was excited. It was like a goddam picnic. There was guys wearing Nazi caps and swaggering around with guns, you know, just local guys, and everybody joined in. The cops tried to stop them but everybody knew everybody in those days, and it was no use. Look . . . wait a minute . . . I'll show you if I can find it . . .'

He rose heavily and returned to the shadows of the house, coming back with a threadbare box file, the lid pushed up with the bulk of the contents. He sat down, slid the elastic band and opened it. 'Look there,' he began to chuckle. He produced a worn photograph. 'That's my old dad. Before he died.'

He handed me a picture of a man who could have been him, face like the winter sun, eyes alive, mouth cracking into a grin. His face was to the camera but his body was side-on. He was wearing a Nazi Swastika on his upper sleeve and pointing to it. 'See, he got the German armband,' said Zeb. 'Folks was strutting around wearing them, showing off, you know, until the cops and the army guys came along and started collecting up the stuff. Even then some of it got left.'

'Like what?'

'Oh, caps and these Nazi arm things. A guy over at Montauk, he had one of them explosive fountain pens. He used to show it off to people. It was like a regular fountain pen but inside was a bomb. I guess the idea was for the spies to leave them about so Americans could blow themselves up. Well, this one worked because this man had the pen for years. His wife wouldn't let him have it in the house because she said it was dangerous, and it sure was. He kept it in his shed in his yard and one day, for no reason, it went off. Bang! Blew the shed to pieces. Nobody in it, which was lucky for them.'

'Is any of this stuff still around?' I asked.

'Could be,' said Zeb. 'After the shed exploding anybody who had anything which could be alive like that, they got rid of it quick. But there's people got pictures like this one. One guy had a pair of shoes. Spies' shoes! When he fell on hard times he used to wear them.'

Some big clouds came from the sea, their shadows moving islands on the water of the creek. 'Do much fishing these days?' I said.

'A bit. Not as much as I used to. Don't go out in the bad weather now. Stay right here in the house.'

'It's a good place to live,' I said.

'Bit lonesome sometimes,' he answered. 'In the winter. We get storms and we get a deal of snow here, you know, out on the South Fork. I used to have a dog but he died and I ain't seen another dog I like. Anyway, I got to thinking I was too old. Dogs don't like to be left when somebody dies.'

'What about cats?'

'Cats? They're different. They can carry on, adapt.'

'Would you like a cat?' I inquired, leaning towards him. 'I happen to have a spare cat.'

'You've got a cat?'

'I have.'

His face brightened; talking about death had shaded it, but now he grinned his lively grin again. 'Maybe I could take a look at it some time,' he said.

'You could now,' I told him. 'It's in the car.'

He appeared delighted. 'No kidding! You got it with you?'

'I'll bring him in,' I said rising from the wicker chair. 'It's a good cat.'

He followed me through the house to his front door. 'Why ain't you going to keep him?' he asked cautiously. 'Maybe he's fierce?'

'I've got to go abroad,' I said. 'I have to have someone who'll take him.'

'Let's see. Let's take a look.'

He remained at the door while I went to the car and lifted the cat from the back seat. He blinked in the sunlight as I lifted him out. I carried him to Zeb Smith at the door.

'He seems okay,' he said looking closely while I still held the animal.

'Oh, he's a complete cat,' I assured him. 'His tail was burned in a fire but it's growing again now.'

The old man did not even ask about the fire. He took the cat from me. 'He got a name?' he asked. The cat was looking him straight in the face.

'Phoenix,' I said.

'Felix,' he said. 'Felix the cat.'

'Phoenix,' I repeated.

'F-E-E-N-I-X,' he spelled out. 'I got you now. Okay, I'll keep him.' He looked at me anxiously. 'Do I owe you anything?'

I laughed and patted his arm. 'Nothing at all,' I said.

'Gee, a free cat,' he murmured in a pleased way. He carried the animal into the house and dropped it gently to the floor. 'Let's see if he gets to be at home.'

'He'll be at home here,' I said hopefully. 'He's been living in hotel rooms.'

'He looks like he'll settle.' Zeb watched the cat pad across the room and out onto the wooden deck. It sat down and began to wash its face. 'That's great,' said the old man. 'I been thinking about a cat but it's difficult to know how to come by one.' Then he repeated, 'Feenix.'

'An Irish name,' I said, giving the cat a farewell touch with my foot. I drained the glass and moved towards the door.

'The man whose shed blew up,' I said to Zeb. 'Where will I find him?'

'You won't,' said the old man. 'Not easy. Harry Filling's dead. He was the one I told you about. Drowned off his fishing boat, back end of last year. Went out by hisself. Never seen again. Boat came back empty.'

Driving towards Washington I realized I was going to miss the cat. Our conversations had been long, if one-sided, during the journeys we had shared, and now when I looked to my right all I saw was an empty seat.

Phoenix had been useful when I needed to explain things to myself.

He would have been convenient now. I was clicking over the names, the characters, who had started this business years before. By now I knew them well: Ernst Kerchin, Peter Müller, Johannes Vass, Karl Broger, Werner Konrad, Boris Kraft, Wolfgang Schmitt, Peter Karl Hine.

Müller, the leader of the party which had come ashore near Jacksonville, Florida, had been a convinced Nazi since the nineteen thirties. He had once blatantly flown the black and red Swastika from his boat off Miami Beach. He had also been an associate of Lincoln Rockwell, the leader of the Bund, the American Nazi party, which had attracted so many Germans who had settled in the United States in the nineteen thirties. He had attended their camps and their conferences, he had helped to set up the skein of sympathizers upon which the spies, had they gone undetected, would have relied for concealment and aid. He had never flinched from his political beliefs, even in the face of the Military court, and had given the Nazi stiff-armed salute at the announcement of the sentence upon him. His final words before going to the electric chair were: 'Heil Hitler'.

But, Hine apart, it was the character of Schmitt, Wolfgang, Wolfie as he was known in Chicago, his hometown, which most intrigued me. Like Fleming, the hapless coastguard who walked into the invaders on the foggy Long Island beach, Schmitt was nineteen, a naïve nineteen. The bemused Fleming got a medal and the bemused Schmitt a death sentence.

It was fading afternoon when I reached Washington and checked in at the Mayflower. Several of the staff inquired after my cat. There was a message to call Brant

Irving, another to call Fred Robinson at the FBI and a third from Mr Shogghelly, with a number.

They had given me the same room. I telephoned Robinson first, but he had gone home. They said it was his softball night. Irving was in his Washington office.

'You saw Zeb Smith,' he said.

'You know.'

'Sure. He's the only one who has any real recall.'

'The others keep dying,' I said.

'People do. All the time.'

'I thought I might take a trip to Chicago,' I told him.

'Schmitt,' he said. 'That may be a good idea.' He paused, then said: 'Just keep in touch, okay. And look after yourself.'

'I'm good at that,' I said.

'How's your cat?'

'Solved,' I said. 'I found him a home. With Zeb Smith.'

'That's good news. He'll like Zeb.'

Sam Keenor on television was something extra. The *New York Times* political columnist had said that he left no stone unthrown, and the throwing of them was spectacular. He was handsomely abrasive, challenging, articulate and increasingly popular. Watching him on ABC News gave you the feeling that he would not be in the general pack unduly long. He was already beginning to act the part, to sound the part. He had a presidential look in his eye.

'Your husband is really very good at it,' I said to Madelaine as we lay watching. We were in the Georgetown apartment.

'He's trained,' she said. She was wearing only a pearl-coloured robe. She was lying face down on the bed with her backside wriggling under the silk. 'He's trained like hell. I mean, he's done it himself. I've seen him practise everything. Over and over.'

Turning her, I kissed her, although her eyes swivelled around towards the screen as I did so. 'Don't you feel this is taking voyeurism a bit far?' I suggested.

'What? Being here with you and watching my hero-husband on television? Maybe ... ' She rolled towards me and reaching out with her naked foot she turned off the television. Sam was finished anyway. 'Listen,' she said putting her face an inch from mine. 'You're never going to be President so don't philosophize about it. We're here and that's all there is to say – we're here.'

'Mr President,' I said mockingly. 'And Mrs President. You won't want to know me then.'

'I certainly will *not*,' she said honestly. 'I'll disown you absolutely. Some things are good for a limited time.'

'Limited Company,' I said thoughtfully. 'I never thought I'd come into the category. Michael Findlater, Limited Company.'

'Well, you do. *We* do. We always did. Take a look at our marriage.'

Our bodies were touching all the way down. I was wearing only my 'Pierre's' shirt, the one I had bought to put the cat in the bag. I was seriously missing that cat. 'Do you want to make love again?' I said to her. The last time was almost an hour away. We had drunk some champagne, eaten some chicken sandwiches and watched Sam since then.

'I want you to screw me,' she said.

'That's more or less what I meant. I phrased it nicely, that's all.'

'"Make love" sounds too involved.'

'All right. I'll screw you. I never was one to bandy

words.' I moved away from her so I could see her. The pearl robe open all the way down her front, showing one pale breast and concealing the other. It fell completely away over her hips, forming silk curtains to her navel and pubis.

'You'll have to get closer,' she murmured, looking at me at my distance.

I smiled at her and she smiled back. Again we made love.

'Just like old times,' I said, my nose close to her sweet and damp neck.

'Better than that,' she answered. She moved so my mouth travelled crossways over her throat. 'You've improved a lot, Michael, and I don't mean just in bed, you were always passable when you felt inclined, but just *generally*. I mean, you were such an asshole when you were young. And when you didn't care at all it was terrible. About sex, I mean.'

I said I was surprised she remembered. 'In the end you used to . . .'

'Lie back and think of England,' she finished. 'Sussex mostly.' We both laughed.

I kissed the inside of her breasts. 'Sorry about Sussex,' I said. 'I should have known. My life has been one long discovery of unsuitable women. And now you're another one.' She squirmed among the silk sheets.

'You made me what I am,' she joked although she did not smile. I told her I doubted it. I looked at the ceiling, and then at the thick folds of the drapes, and said to her: 'This seems like the safest place in Washington.'

'It is. Now I know how to turn the bugging machines off, and the surveillance stuff.'

'I've also been in the loneliest place in this town,' I said.

'Where is that?' I had turned on my front and, as if she subconsciously remembered, she began casually massaging my buttocks, first the left, then the right. There was more residue of our marriage than I had given it credit for.

'The FBI,' I murmured. 'Down in the vaults. There I was in the middle of a city of three million, in the centre of a building where God knows how many thousands work, and I was *lonely*. There was a girl down there, a child-bride.'

'I was one,' said Madelaine. She abandoned my backside and slipped her long and pleasant fingers below me.

'You're bringing Hogg back again,' I mentioned, shifting to make it easier. 'When will you be satisfied?'

'Eventually,' she answered.

I turned to my side and with a continuation of the movement eased her onto her back. I pushed her knees down and opened her thighs like the covers of a book. I slid my head down there and began kissing her. 'Christ,' I heard her say in the distance. 'You could suffocate.'

After a while I began to think she could be right so I ascended again, length to length, skin to skin, and at the end, lip to lip. It was a shame it was not heart to heart.

'I had a dream,' I told her when we were quiet once more, trying to drink champagne lying down. 'You were on top of the Chrysler Building and leaning out, right out, with only the wind keeping you up. You did that once, remember, in Oregon. When you went mad that day.'

'Defying gravity,' she muttered. Only her profile was visible to me. 'I still do it. All the time.'

'There's another file,' said Fred Robinson.

I thought there might be. There is nearly always another file; the one they hold back until they are sure of you. We were sitting at the restored bar in the Mayflower, long and polished.

'It was right here,' Robinson had said. 'Peter Karl Hine sat right here waiting for the FBI – or anybody – to believe him. I guess he thought he'd have to shoot the President before he got any consideration. They let Hine finish his drink before they took him up to his room. It says in the G-Man's report. It wasn't until he opened the bag with all the dough in it, thousands of dollars, that they began to think he was really real. There's nothing so convincing as bucks.'

'Schmitt is an interesting case,' I suggested.

'Sure, the kid. Went home to his mom in Chicago. Have you read that stuff?' A half-a-grin touched his neat, black face.

'Nobody would assist the FBI,' I nodded.

'They would *not*. The place where he lived was full of Germans, little Berlin. Nobody would tell anything. Everybody in the neighbourhood knew Wolfie Schmitt was back, and *some* of them knew where he had been, but nobody would say. They were Germans first and Americans second. The G-men couldn't even find anywhere for a stake-out. Nobody would take them in. Then Wolfie tried to get himself *drafted* – a Nazi spy drafted into the US Army!'

We had another couple of drinks and then he told me about the other file. 'It's not freely available,' he explained. His round, slow eyes came up cautiously. 'But it's not classified, not seriously classified.'

'I'll come down and see it,' I said.

'Sheree's not there any more,' said Robinson. He was peering into his glass as if it contained a message or a fly.

'She quit because it was lonely. Subterranean and lonely she said. They transferred her.'

'She was keeping an eye on me, I imagine,' I said.

'Both. She could keep both eyes on you and you wouldn't know she was looking. But you don't have to go to the Bureau to see the other file. We've had good clearance on you, Michael, although you're not supposed to know that. That information *is* classified.' He waited and examined his drink again. He made the decision and took a sip. 'I'm not a guy to put my neck out, but this seems okay so I made a few notes, extracted from the file.'

He took a small envelope from his pocket. 'Has anybody tried to kill you recently?' he inquired casually.

'Not for three weeks,' I said.

'Oh, sure. The fire in the motel. Well that may or may not have been. We don't have any strong views.'

'If anyone kills me, I'll let you know.'

'We get buzzes. You know, stuff filters. It just gets to us. It's our business.'

'What did the buzzes say?' I asked.

'Listen, I never get *all* the background, the whole story. Only so much as they need to tell me. I've just had instructions to keep you generally alive, you know. It's an additional responsibility as well as the archives. Do you have any personal defence procedure?'

'Yes. It's called running.'

'It's the best,' he nodded. 'And hiding. That's a good one too. But you might just need a gun. I'm going to make it easy for you to get one. Here.'

He looked around and then handed me a gun. 'Neat, like me,' he said, adding a box the size of a ring box but weighty. 'You ain't going to fight any war,' he said. 'There's enough there.'

I opened the box. The ammunition lay like sleeping pigs. 'It looks like I'm going to be earning every dollar,' I said. 'It's getting serious.'

'Every cent,' he corrected. 'Old crimes die hard, Michael. Forty-seven years and it's still with us, like a ghost.'

He picked up his notebook from the bar. 'You want to know what was in the extra file?'

'Yes, of course. I'll make some notes myself.' I glanced towards him.

He nodded and murmured: 'Sure.' We sat at the bar like a couple of salesmen totting up business. 'I've got a gun,' he said as if he had just won it. 'I'm an archivist. I just work among the dust. But I've got a gun.'

I told him I was pleased. He returned to his notebook and me to mine.

'Hine got life, along with the other guy — Konrad — who didn't go to the chair,' said Robinson. 'Konrad helped out after Hine had talked. Both these guys only served just over three years. Hine was in the State Penitentiary at Jackson, Mississippi. Every now and then he would file a complaint against other prisoners. Once there was a riot and he had to be protected by the warders. He sounds a character — an asshole. There's a bunch of his letters back in the records. He wrote the President, and J. Edgar Hoover, and Winston Churchill. Everybody except Hitler, naturally. He got the idea that he shouldn't be in prison at all. As far as he was concerned, Peter Karl Hine was a *hero*, he'd planned all along to betray the others . . . but for him they would never have been caught.'

'He could have been right,' I said.

'Right. Without him they'd have certainly been around a little longer than they were. He was a real rarity, our friend Hine. He was a double traitor, to *both* his countries, his friends and everybody, and he came out of it smelling of roses. His life sentence lasted just over three years. He and the other guy Konrad were shipped secretly back to Germany just after the war. The Germans were short on admiration too, so he tried to become an *American* again. He had the fucking nerve to ask for his citizenship back.'

While he was speaking I began watching two men sitting at a table in one of the alcoves. It is as difficult for two men to sit inconspicuously and silently in a secluded seat as it is for two men to be photographed together. It looks awkward. Robinson had his back to them and he was reading further from his notebook. 'He actually *worked* for the US forces in Germany,' he went on. 'He was a barman in a services club in Frankfurt and at another place in Munich. He used his real name and he made no secret of the spy episode, although, naturally, he always came out of it like Batman.'

He finished his Scotch and put it back on the counter, the notebook still in his hand. 'You watching somebody?' he inquired quietly.

'A little. There are two men sitting in the window over there, in the alcove.'

'I got them,' he replied. He was looking in the bar mirror.

'Maybe they're just holding hands,' I said.

As we spoke one of the pair, the thinner of the two wearing a sports coat and a red tie, rose at the approach of a waiter. They settled the bill and both men went out of the far door. The second man had a blue suit. They may have been animal feed salesmen.

'Peter Karl Hine,' recited Robinson looking carefully back at his notebook, the archivist all at once apparent, 'went to Berlin, where he set himself up as a hero, this time the German variety, the old Nazi. He got mixed in with a cell of political no-hopers and then, if you can believe it, changed colours again and got himself hired as a guide taking tourists around Berlin. We received voluntary information from US tourists who had come in contact with him and he made no secret about his past, he even boasted about it. Then he wrote, get this, he wrote to Renate Schmitt, the sister of Wolfgang Schmitt, in Chicago on the anniversary of her brother's execution, this was in 1982, pouring out sorrow and grief ... you should read that crap.'

I said: 'I was thinking of going to Chicago to see any of Schmitt's family who are still there. Have you got an address on that letter, Hine's address I mean? And the Chicago one would be useful too.'

'Hine,' he read from the notebook, 'was at 112a Bremenstrasse, Berlin 3, when he wrote this. That was eighty-two, remember. Renate Schmitt lived at 2346 Brewster Avenue, Chicago. It's the last address we have for either party.'

We had both finished our drinks. 'Want to go on the town?' he suddenly asked. 'We could go somewhere if you like. I don't have to go home. My home life ain't too friendly right now. I went to play softball last night but I didn't have the heart for it. We could eat right here.'

We did. Two hours later we walked out to get a few drinks somewhere. I liked him and he liked me. I asked him about the two men who had been in the bar earlier. 'They could have been somebody, or maybe they were nobody, I don't know,' he shrugged. 'Maybe they were from the Bureau. We got a lot of agents. I'm just an archivist so I don't know many.'

VII

It was about 10.30 pm, warm in Washington, when we walked along K Street going east. The girlie show which had looked so deathly by daylight was now alive with lights. A man outside, sweating in a tuxedo, accosted us: 'Mimi's on tonight, fellas. Taking 'em *all* off. And Bonnie Belle, the Ding-Dong Girl.'

Robinson nodded towards the glowing entrance: 'Want to take in Mimi?' he suggested. 'Or the Ding-Dong Girl?'

'All right,' I said. We turned towards the door. The doorman looked pleased and tried to shoot his cuffs as he opened it, but the tuxedo was too tight.

There was a girl already on a small, bright stage, a young girl, about eighteen. She looked pink and wholesome, like a cheerleader, a pretty face, a good natured smile. Silhouetted men leaned forward around the dais. Robinson and I waited in the darkness. She never stopped dancing, a strong beat, whirling, swaying, flexing her legs, her torso rolling. When she bared her breasts, white in the lights, it was with a flying gesture, almost a defiance of the men four deep now around the stage; the bra swung like a banner. It was only then I noticed that she wore a garter.

That was all, because she took off the cobweb that was strung between her legs and spread them tauntingly wide. The men seemed struck dumb. Their eyes never left her. A man spilled his drink and cursed. She danced, unhurriedly now, along the fringe of the stage and eagerly the men began pushing forward to thrust dollar, five dollar, ten dollar notes, into the blue garter, each one hanging onto it for as long as she permitted. Artfully she slapped their fingers. One old man who ought to have been safe at home, was holding out a fistful of money, trying to date her. She teased him, pulling her thigh away and wagging a smiling finger at him. 'Is this Mimi?' asked Robinson shifting sideways towards a waiter standing with the glasses slithering slowly sideways on his tray, as fixed as anyone else. The man righted his tray. 'Ain't Mother Theresa,' he muttered.

At the end of her show, Mimi, with almost housewifely deftness, picked up her garments, did a pleasant naked curtsey and went off into the wings, where you could see her counting the money. We went to the bar. The barman said that Bonnie would be performing next but if we wanted to catch Mimi again, from the beginning of her show, then she would be dancing upstairs in four minutes. We drank our drinks and went upstairs.

The word had travelled because the tables around the dimmed stage were already full. We managed to get two chairs in the second row back and then had some luck because the two men directly in front, after checking their watches, got up and left.

We now had a prime place almost at the corner of the low stage. The rock music was already thumping. Robinson asked a waiter for some dollar bills in his change after he had bought two drinks. 'You want to participate?' said the waiter.

'Sure,' said Robinson. He half turned to me: 'I usually finish up listening to the music,' he said. Despite the air-conditioning the place was humid. Some late men came in and stood behind the first row on the other flank of the stage, and then Mimi came on. The girl made her entrance on the move, as though she had danced up the stairs. She was in a sort of tunic, whiter than her legs. She had changed her garter: this one was red and just visible under the silvered hem of the single garment. The man at the next table gave a skittish little wave to her. Mimi began to take off the tunic. She took a long time taking it off. Her fresh skin was pale, her face round and pretty, the smile unaltering.

The tunic was open and discarded, revealing the lace piece between her legs and a bra drilled with two holes through which blinked her pink nipples, like someone peeping through a fence. There was also the garter, circling her thigh. She made her first collection swaying before likely contributors. She came really close so that I could smell her scent. The music was insistent. Her pounding navel was just in front of my eyes. The smile was confident, as if she knew she would never come to harm. For half-a-minute she performed solely for us, her big, pleased eyes moving from Robinson's black face to my red face. We put our contributions in her garter, both taking our hands away guiltily.

This time she removed only half of the bra. It was on a kind of hinge and it was left hanging like a spare ear, one rich breast exposed in the lights. She then plucked away the crotch cobweb and dropped it daintily to the stage. The second half of the bra was peeled. The watchers pressed forward like men sharing a secret. Then Robinson screamed: 'Drop! Get down!' He told me later he meant the girl but his arm pushed me. I fell backwards over the chair, shouting, landing in the fat lap of the man behind. His drink went over and he swore. The first shot sounded, a concise crack, followed by another. It was the second bullet which hit Mimi.

Nothing seemed to happen for a measurable time. Still sprawled on my back I began to apologize to the man behind. I thought it was part of the show. The music went on and some men later said that the girl kept dancing until she let out a sob, which I myself heard, although I could not see her, and fell on her naked back on the garish stage. She was lying there when I managed to struggle to my feet. Everywhere was bedlam, men shouting, trying to get out.

I was aware that Fred Robinson was attempting to get to the door. He had rough-housed his way through the crush before I fully regained my feet. All around the stage the chairs were upturned and some of the audience were still sitting on the floor or crawling on hands and knees away to somewhere they imagined might be safe. Mimi lay on the platform, her blonde hair spread like a fan, her breasts trembling like jelly. Somebody cut the music. It was amazing because nobody went to help her. The men who had been so aching to feel her a few moments ago now hung back, staring at her but keeping their distance as if she had suddenly become untouchable. I have had experience of *making* myself move, and I was first on the low stage. I knelt down by the bare girl. There was a hole the size of a lipstick, bleeding only a little, below her right breast. She was still alive; she looked up at me, her baby blue eyes frightened, unrealizing. Her right hand went down and closed over the dollar bills in her garter. I took off my coat and covered her with it. She died before they found a doctor in a bar next door.

Someone had thought to put the house lights on. They showed the dusty room, the ragged drapes, the patched wooden dais and that poor girl lying under my coat. People behave in strange ways at such moments. The waiters began righting chairs and busily collecting glasses on trays, all the time their gazes going back to that dead heap of young womanhood. People said the police were coming, and they wanted to leave. The doctor was drunk and confused. But there was nothing for him to do anyway, except say Mimi was dead, which anybody could see. I began to move towards the door. Robinson had gone somewhere.

'Nobody leaves,' said a pitted-looking man at the upstairs exit. 'The police are on the way.'

I told him I was going downstairs to find my shocked and aged father, and he seemed to think this was reasonable. He stood aside but repeated: 'Nobody leaves. The police are on the way.' Men were standing around, mostly silent, looking worried. A barman knocked over a tray of drinks.

Robinson I found sitting moodily on a chair at the bottom of the stairs. He was holding his jaw with one hand and dabbing a blood-soaked handkerchief to his nose with the other. He was glowering at the doorman who was trying to look away.

'What happened?' I said.

'They got away,' Robinson sighed still dabbing his nose. The bleeding had stopped but he was making sure. 'This fucking ape let them out.' He looked at me for sympathy. '*Let them out*, I tell you. I'm going to hang something on him and it ain't going to be just a punch.'

The doorman turned sulky. 'They said they was police,' he shrugged.

'So you open the door and let them *out*!' retorted Robinson. 'There's a shooting and two guys come down the stairs and you *let them out*. For Chrissake, the fucking police ought to be running *in*, not out. Cops don't run *away* after murder, you dumb bastard . . . not many, anyway.'

'I ain't the regular security,' said the man. 'He's sick.'

'Then he hit you,' I guessed. His jaw was visibly swelling.

'You got it. I was right after them but he decides to stop anybody leaving. So he hangs one on me. I tell him I'm FBI and he lays another on my nose.' His lined eyes lifted malevolently towards the doorman. 'I could have made my name,' he added in a mutter.

'Fred,' I said. 'They killed that girl.'

'Sure, I know,' he said dismally. He repeated her name 'Mimi' as if he had known her well. 'She got right in the way of it. Poor little girl.'

'Who were they shooting at?' I asked.

He eyed me sombrely: 'Looks like you got away with it again.'

Outside the J. Edgar Hoover Building the black man was still howling abuse at the FBI. He occupied the same spot on the sidewalk, as surely as a statue occupies its plinth. Nor was there any boredom in his voice, no sign of flagging in the face of a total lack of response from the blank walls. The tirade remained incomprehensible to me, but it was delivered with verve, rising at times to passion, over and over again, as if he always meant it and was more convinced of his cause with every repetition. As I approached I felt a touch of familiarity.

He paused to breathe between accusations. His brimming damaged eyes came to face me.

'Good morning,' I said involuntarily.

'Good morning, sir,' he replied with great civility before returning to confront the façade of the building, drawing a deep breath and emitting a renewed blast of protest. This time, as before, I could distinguish the word 'Hoover' and I wondered if the man knew that Hoover had been dead some years. He probably did. Death does not render people guiltless.

They had changed the tape in the lobby and Barry Manilow was singing 'Weekend in New England'. Several people were occupying the waiting seats, clutching files, briefcases or documents and all staring into space as if they were there only on behalf of someone else. The redhead was absent. Fred Robinson came down and saw I was looking for her and asked the replacement, a puffy man with distinct pink spots on his cheeks. He said she was on vacation and that everybody was missing her, including him.

We inserted our plastic passes in the successive turnstiles and when we were through, as though the gates represented more than merely a physical frontier and we could now talk, Robinson said: 'The girl had no enemies. She came from Albany.'

He led the way into his office. Someone had put some flowers on his desk. 'People here are sympathetic this morning,' he shrugged. 'I got questioned by the police.' He sat heavily in the chair and I, looking at him, lowered myself slowly into the chair opposite. 'Me,' he said pleadingly. 'An FBI *agent*, and I get questioned by the police, for chrissake. I showed them my card but they wouldn't believe me. Have I had a hard time.' Soberly he added: 'But shit, then did they get a hard time from me.' He looked momentarily reassured. 'Okay, I'm an archivist – but I'd make a great operative.' His expression fell again and he tapped the desk with a pen. 'Then my section head wanted to know what I was doing at the girlie show, anyway. They get very straight and narrow here you know, the FBI.'

He studied me as if he had an unpleasant surprise.

'Those guys in the bar at the Mayflower, maybe. I don't know. But whoever it was, I think they were shooting for you, Michael,' he said.

'I thought they might be,' I answered.

'They missed you twice now.'

'And two others have died,' I said with sadness and guilt. 'An old woman and a young woman. I feel terrible about it, Fred. I wasn't sure last time.'

'It's an expensive book you're writing,' he said. I dropped my chin into my hands. I saw her again; the pure white girl naked on the naked stage. Her last look had been at me, the final person she ever saw, and I was the reason for her dying. 'I didn't know *anybody* would be getting hurt . . . killed,' I said, 'least of all bystanders.'

'Bystanders do,' he said. 'And dancers. All the time. Now the police are involved. So is the FBI.' He asked me what I was going to do from then on. 'The cops will want a statement from you about the shooting of the girl,' he said. 'But we can do that through the Bureau. There are ways. You only have to say what you saw, nothing more. We'll do it our way. We'll get them.' My doubt must have shown. 'I'd have got the bastards right then and there,' he grumbled. 'If that ape hadn't hit me.'

I said I wanted to go to Chicago. 'Schmitt's family may still be there,' I told him. 'Maybe they'll have some idea where to find Hine. Maybe I'll have to look in Germany.'

His mood changed at once. 'Germany,' he said dreamily as if I had said 'Tahiti'. He closed his eyes. 'I've always wanted to visit those places. Castles and beer and fun and suchlike. And those crazy windmills.'

'Holland,' I told him. 'The windmills are in Holland.'

'You don't say. Maybe they moved them. When are you leaving for Chicago?'

'Tonight,' I said. 'I can't read any more files. I'm going word-blind.'

'What I don't get,' he said thoughtfully, 'is the dumb way they've tried to get you. They don't have any . . . well, finesse.'

'They're incompetent,' I agreed.

'It didn't stop them killing other folks,' he pointed out. He leaned back in his chair. 'Germany,' he breathed. 'It sounds good.'

'You can go instead of me,' I said. 'I'm getting less enthusiastic.'

Fred shook his head. 'No way,' he said. 'They might start learning to shoot straight.' He unlocked a drawer in the desk and took out a file. 'I just got together all the most recent stuff available on this case,' he said. 'And it ain't much and it's not very recent. But there's a handbill here that might give you a lead on Schmitt's family. It just had to be *Schmitt*, didn't it. There's still a big German community in Chicago and they get together now and then, a kind of social club, to talk over old times, you know, drink some beer and play at windmills, I guess.'

He handed the file across. 'You can take it away,' he shrugged. 'It's declassified. But I need ten cents for each page that's been photocopied.' He looked a little shame-faced. 'You have to pay eighty cents to the cashier,' he said. He shrugged. 'I can't pay it for you because of the rules. It's like they won't let me buy you a lunch, and you can't buy me lunch and why they weigh the lettuce. Rules.'

We went out into the corridor and down two flights of stairs. In the cashier's department I paid over a dollar, received twenty cents change and was handed a solemn receipt. Robinson took me to the main lobby where I handed in my security card. We shook hands. He said: 'Have fun and don't get killed.'

Back at the hotel I called Brant Irving and told him I was going to Chicago. I said nothing about Mimi. Then, cautiously, I tried to call Madelaine but I could not get my Spanish-American accent right and when the man in California began asking me to repeat who I was, I panicked and hung up.

On the plane to Chicago, I sat next to a man who quietly opened his business case and took out a gun. He had said nothing, just walked through and slumped down like any other grey traveller. But when he took out the gun he turned to me with a creased grin and said: 'You worried about this?'

'A little,' I said.

'It's a toy,' he said. 'They know me. It's gotten to be a joke. Every time I come through they say: "Hey, here comes Mr Corax with another concealed weapon." We all laugh.' He took the gun out, shielding it with his case from the passenger across the aisle. 'It's a great toy.'

'Great,' I said.

'We sell other things, too,' he said as if in justification. He put the weapon away and brought out a mechanical bird. It was black, shaped like a crow. He pulled a lever and the bird flapped its wings and opened its yellow beak.

'I used to like jig-saw puzzles,' I mentioned.

'Jig-saw, pig-saw,' he grunted, putting the bird in with the gun and shutting the case. 'Kids don't have that sort of patience now. It's computers and stuff. We stick to soft toys and guns.'

He said his company was in Chicago. He gave me his card and seemed surprised when I did not return the compliment. I explained I was a writer. He nodded. 'Having "writer" on a card looks lonely,' he said.

'It's solitary,' I said. We had a drink and he said he had been at a toy convention in Atlanta, confirming orders for the following Christmas. 'In this trade we never stop,' he said rolling his head tiredly. 'Soon as Christmas is over we start over. Kids have birthdays. Thank God. All the time. Parents split so the kids get double presents.' I asked him if he knew whether the German community in Chicago lived in a well-defined district. He shook his head. 'They did once, years ago,' he said. 'But they got spread out. After the war they got spread out, with guys coming out of the army and wanting to move away. But there's still plenty there, plenty of German people.'

We reached O'Hare at eleven-thirty and I went straight to the Regent. I had one Scotch in the bar before going to my room. As I was drifting to sleep the bedside telephone rang. It was only a purr but it made me jump like hell. I picked it up. 'Hello.'

The man's voice sounded almost dreamy. He began to recite a nursery rhyme which I now know word for word, even though it is in German:

> 'Hoppe, hoppe Reiter,
> Wenn er fällt dann schreit er,
> Fällt er in den Graben,
> Fressen ihn die Raben,
> Fällt er in den Sumpf,
> Geht der Reiter . . . plump!'

As the rhyme was spoken I sat gradually upright in the bed. My throat had gone ashen. I turned on the bedside light as if that would help me see him. But I still let him finish. Then I said: 'Where are you? Come on, you bastard, where are you?'

'In the Toy Shop,' he said before putting the telephone down.

Turning on more lights, I went, for some reason, to the window and peered down on Clark Street, as if he might be seen loitering on the opposite side. I realized I was sweating. Late cars cruised by and there were some early morning people walking but nobody standing about. My coat was on the back of a chair. From the pocket I took the man's business card. A home number was listed and after a full minute, the call was answered. It was a woman who had never heard of Mr Corax and was mad as hell at being woken at that hour, just when her husband had settled down. I almost asked her what she meant by that but she abruptly terminated our conversation. Then I dialled the business number but it was unobtainable. Crossing the room I took the telephone directory from its drawer and turned up both Nathaniel Corax and the Corax Toy Company Inc. Neither was listed. I rang Information and they had no information.

Next I called the hotel reception desk and asked if there had been anyone inquiring about me, and they said no one had. I was feeling unsafe. I made sure the door was double-locked and I took the chain off and re-engaged it. Then I lay awake until daylight.

'Mike, the airline say that nobody called Corax was on that flight last night. Also the check-in staff are not familiar with any guy who regularly comes through with imitation firearms or toys. Their security people say they wouldn't knowingly allow anybody aboard a plane with that kind of thing anyway. They thought I was crazy just for asking.'

'He took risks then,' I said.

'He wanted to scare you.'

'He certainly succeeded. I never thought I'd shit at the sound of a nursery rhyme, Fred.'

I heard him laugh. 'And there's no Corax Toy Company Inc. in Chicago or even in the state of Illinois. Nor any Nathaniel Corax. We checked the numbers. The business number is phoney. It's got one too many digits. The other one is a widow called Toomey.'

'She said she had a husband,' I told him. 'He'd just settled down.'

'She was a widow this morning,' said Robinson. I could almost hear him shrug. 'Maybe Mr Toomey died in the night. Maybe that's what she meant by "settled down". Anyway, she's no threat.'

'I'm relieved. Thanks, Fred.'

'What are you doing next?'

'Going around in circles I expect,' I said. 'As usual. I'll have to start bothering all the Schmitts. Ask them if one of the family went to the electric chair.'

'There's nothing smarter I can think of,' he admitted. 'By the way, they're holding the inquest on Mimi tomorrow. I have to appear because I was the boo-boo who chased them. We've managed to get together a story, a reason for me being in the show in the first place, which does not involve you or what you're doing.'

'Thanks, Fred.'

'It's okay. I'm getting interested in this. I hate old bones, if you get what I mean. I'm getting interested. There was no reason anybody had to kill that girl. She just came from Albany. A nice kid with good tits who showed them for a living. Ain't nothing wrong with that.'

'Jesus, I feel dreadful about it. Guilty as hell.'

'You didn't shoot her.'

'I feel as though I did. Perhaps I ought to write to her parents.'

'Don't!' It was a sort of reduced shout. 'It won't help anybody. It won't do any good ... and don't send flowers. They're easily traced.'

'It's on my conscience, Fred.'

'Let it stay there. Maybe we can find these fuckers.'

'You really are interested. Don't get fired for me though.'

'There's no way I'll get fired. I've got a pension.'

VIII

Chicago, flat as a prairie, spreads back into streets and industry, held like a parcel by the Loop, the elevated railway. In 1942 Wolfgang Schmitt's local station was at Webster Avenue and Sheffield Street. The family had lived at Brewster Street.

Schmitt had been born in Germany but most of his life had been lived in Chicago. As soon as he could after landing from the Nazi submarine he had, like any good American boy, gone directly home to his mother. The next day he had made a down-payment on a Plymouth saloon. He also purchased a Bulova watch, a hat and a penknife.

I sat on the bed in the hotel and read again through the report on Wolfgang Franz Godlove Schmitt, born August 10th, 1922, in Essen, Germany, who was executed in the electric chair at the State Penitentiary at Washington DC two days before his twentieth birthday.

The first item in the file was a request from Schmitt that his parents be allowed to visit him before he died. They would, he wrote, be able to pay their own fares from Chicago and that of any escorting officers. To the request was appended a handwritten and initialled note: 'Directed that this not be done'.

Schmitt's parents had left Germany as soon as they could after the First World War, during which his father had fought with the Kaiser's army. Wolfgang was a year old when they landed in New York and made their way towards the hopeful lights of Chicago, as so many of their forebears had done. Wolfgang had grown up in the city and gone to an American school. He had assumed American citizenship through his parents, although he had never taken any oath. Among the material so badly buried on the beach at Eastern Long Island was a German Marine fatigue jacket, and in the pocket the coast-guards found a handkerchief. When subjected to a routine test by the FBI hidden writing appeared: 'Wolfie' and his uncle's name and phone number in Maywood, Chicago.

So many people of German origin and sympathies lived in that vicinity that the Federal Bureau of Investigation had much difficulty in establishing stake-out positions to monitor Schmitt's movements. There was no window from which they could safely watch. 'It was necessary to change surveillancing agents frequently because of the difficulty of concealment,' related the report. 'A hamburger bar at one corner afforded the only consistent view.'

Unknown to these federal agents, a number of their colleagues had already called at Schmitt's house to inquire why Wolfgang had not responded to a draft card. The German spy was required by the US Army.

The times of Schmitt's movements over his last few free days in Chicago in June 1942, were, however, somehow recorded. His visit with his father to the Delight-to-Drive Automobile saleroom for the purchase of his 1938 Plymouth saloon ($480 down-payment) was noted, also his brief stay at the house of a one-time girlfriend, a young widow called Lili Fechner, and his afternoon spent at the Belmont Theatre, a cinema, where he watched the film '49th Parallel', a British drama about Nazis landing from a submarine in Canada.

*

Brewster Street, where the Schmitt family had been living when Wolfgang arrived, smiling smugly, late one night, was no more. It had been demolished and smart apartments had replaced the old German houses. There were more than a hundred Schmitts listed in the Chicago telephone directory.

Under 'German' I found a list of exile organizations, the German-American Friendship Club, the Bavarian Beer Club, the American-German Returned Veterans, the Deutsch Glee Club, Chicago German Brass Band, and others.

Many of these organizations had addresses in the north-west of the city. I locked my door and took the key with me. The taxi dropped me at Webster and Lincoln.

Here there were still German shops, restaurants and several beer cellars. One of these had plastic vines around its cavernous opening. München Beer was advertised and music and singing on Thursday evenings. This was a Tuesday morning. The steps were illuminated by a single flyblown lantern, entwined and supported by more dusty vines. Coming from the street sunshine I had difficulty in finding the edges of the steps. Blinking, I stumbled down into the cellar. At one end, behind the bar, the only lit place, was a man with a Meerschaum moustache.

'No music?' I asked. 'No singing?'

'Singing Thursdays,' he said. His accent was the only American thing in the place. 'Unless you want to sing now. That's okay.'

In the old days I could walk into a bar and sit drinking for two hours – and then start asking questions. But I cannot do it now. After one Steiner I casually asked the barman if he knew whether any of Wolfgang Schmitt's family were still around.

He said immediately: 'Wolfgang Schmitt, the spy?'
Astonished I nodded.

'I don't know now. Not now,' he said. 'They used to be pretty well known in this area, having a spy in the family. Not everybody has a kid who goes to the electric chair. It was talked about for years, passed down, you know. My father knew them. My father, he fought for Uncle Sam but his brother, in Germany, he was rooting for Hitler. We had a foot in both camps. We covered our bets. My dad's brother got killed. Maybe he got killed by my dad.' His uncle had won the Iron Cross and his father the Purple Heart.

He tried to remember who might know where the family of Schmitt lived these days but people moved. All the time they moved. Florida, everywhere. If I went back that night maybe there would be somebody there with some information.

For two more hours I trudged around the district, Irving Park, Belmont, Fullerton, all German-settled areas once. In 1930 Chicago had 377,975 Germans, of whom Wolfgang Schmitt was one. They represented 11.2 per cent of the population. I went into an old-looking shop festooned with German newspapers. There was a man behind the counter, elderly and bald with a beaky nose and wearing an old check shirt and a grey woollen cardigan that hung about him like wings. He looked as if he might have memories. 'You looking for somebody?' he asked, forestalling my initial question. 'I see you outside, looking.' The accent was old German with a coating of American. It was not hostile. 'Years ago,' I said looking straight into his eye-sockets, 'during the war, I believe the Schmitt family lived around here.'

'Schmitt the spy,' he confirmed, like the barman. 'Sure, sure, lived on Brewster. Like it was then. They fried him, you know. So he was a spy. He was a boy. It upset his momma and poppa, I tell you, frying him like that.'

'It would,' I nodded.

He shook his elderly, eager head and began to re-arrange the newspapers on the counter. 'There's nothing worse,' he said.

'Did you know them?' I asked carefully. 'The family?'

'The Schmitts I knew very good,' he said. 'Why you wanting to know?'

'I'm a writer,' I said. I could not think of any other excuse. 'I'm interested in the story.'

His shrug showed he was unsurprised. 'The story is old,' he said. 'I thought everybody forgot it. It should be forgot. It's not nice.'

'Maybe some new light could be thrown on it,' I suggested unconvincingly.

'What new light?' he demanded. 'You can't unfry Wolfie Schmitt.'

'Do you know if any of the Schmitt family are in Chicago now?' I asked firmly. I sensed he wanted to terminate the conversation.

'Somewhere,' he shrugged. A woman, shuffling in bed-room slippers, and wearing a straw sun-hat came into the shop. He went away to attend to her. She bought the *Berliner Morgenpost* and *Women's Wear*. The shopman asked her something in German. She glanced at me heavily. The big sunhat darkened her face; her eyes examined me from below the brim. When she replied it was sharply and in German. He asked her an additional question as she was about to go out. Her reply was brief and unhappy. After she had gone I saw her studying me through the window. I gave her a tentative smile and she scowled under her straw hat and shuffled away.

'She knows,' said the old man. 'But she don't want to tell. That poor boy, he's still got a sister around somewhere, but she won't tell where.'

'In Chicago?'

'In Chicago. But it's a big city, like you see.' He looked at me and his expression changed, as if he had made up his mind to help. 'You know where the canal is? The old shit waterway like they call it. There's a man lives on a boat there, I don't know the place exact, but he's there. He was a friend of Wolfgang Schmitt. If he wants to tell you something, let him. His name is Beckerman. Alfred Beckerman.'

The Chicago Sanitary and Ship Canal seeps through the southern city, making its way inland to Forest View where it is joined by the Illinois and Michigan Canal, and the two progress side by side through Lamont, Lockport and Fairmont to Joliet. From Lake Michigan to Joliet is just over thirty miles.

From the hotel I telephoned City Hall, and they referred me to the Illinois Waterways Authority. There were, confirmed the man at the Waterways Authority, certain places on the canal, small docks, no longer in commercial use, where people lived on boats. He gave me a list of half a dozen. I asked if the people paid rent and the man said that they had to pay dock dues. He did not have time to look up the names of the people right then because they had some problems at the Sanitary and Ship end of the canal, but that if I called him back in two hours, he could have checked by then.

When I made the return call he said: 'We have a Mr A. A. Beckerman listed as paying dues for a dock mooring just by the old Chicago Contagious Diseases Hospital, that's on the Sanitary and Ship Canal.'

'Economical,' I suggested.

'It's okay,' he said. He was helpful but without humour. 'It's convenient for downtown. Mr Beckerman is listed as Mooring A 22.'

I went down to the street and got a taxi. 'I want the Sanitary and Ship Canal,' I told the driver. 'Near the old Chicago Contagious Diseases Hospital.'

'You sickening for something?' the man said.

'It's just an address.'

'That's a great address.'

We went below the Adlai Stevenson Expressway and crossed the canal. It looked like its name except there were no ships. Even the fierce four o'clock sun failed to burnish the water that sagged between the banks. The driver was interested. He seemed to enjoy asking directions once we were in the thick streets beyond the expressway. These led to a narrow fungus-hung passage of old, damp bricks leading directly to the canal bank. The taxi stopped at the edge. The driver said: 'This is as far as we go without getting wet.'

I got out, thanked and paid him. He said he would have waited. His mother was getting either married or buried.

He left me in a humid enclosure, in the gut of a big city, a place steaming like a jungle with weeds and brambles entangled along a ragged towpath that led to an arch in a powdery wall. Beyond that, like some scene from Venice, was a small inlet clogged with decrepit boats that would never sail again, nudging each other knowingly like old people.

The arch itself looked as if it might be due to tumble. Carefully I ducked below it. The dopey smell was not unpleasant. Some of the people who lived on the boats had put rows of flowers in pots. One hulk had a tree growing through a hole in its stern.

'Just growed like that,' said a man sitting on the rotten deck. His coat looked damp. 'Crept through the wood. Can't take it away now or she'll sink.'

I asked him if he knew Mr Beckerman, and he pointed to a barge at the end of the dock. 'Adolf lives right there,' he indicated. 'Could be he'll be out of bed by now. It's after four.'

'Adolf?' I said. Always keep a talker talking. 'I thought his name was Alfred.'

'That too,' he nodded. 'Alfred he was called when he first got here, a few years ago now, but after a while he said his name was Adolf as well. Now everybody calls him that. Adolf. I guess he thinks it's got something about it.'

Beckerman was indeed stirring. He emerged from the interior of the barge like a man ascending from a grave. The vessel was strong and neat, painted green and red, with flowers in buckets and pots on the deck. It was at once apparent that the man who rose through the hatchway was not the person who kept the vessel in such trim. Rubbing his eyes, he grumbled at the sun. His shirt was clean but the man was grim and whiskered.

'Mr Beckerman?' I said.

Although I had been visibly standing on the dock as he came out of the hatch, he blinked as if I had appeared from a puff of smoke. 'Who wants him?' he asked. 'There was no German in the voice. 'You from the rent people? I told them next month. I wrote them.'

'I'm not,' I said. 'But I may be able to help.' He looked the sort of person who is interested in help. 'Can I come aboard?'

He regarded me with watery suspicion. 'You can help with the dues?' he said. 'You got money for that?'

'I have,' I assured him. As I was about to walk up the

short gangplank to the deck he stopped me. 'Don't trust that,' he warned. 'It's a kind of trap. It will drop you into this stinking water. I keep it like that for people I don't need.' He verged on a grimy smile, possibly at some memory. 'Climb over the side,' he suggested. 'It's safer.'

I clambered over the hull of the boat. 'It's nice,' I said looking around the deck. 'You keep it well.'

'My wife does,' he corrected lethargically. 'She comes down here and paints and cleans up. She figures that as long as the boat is in good shape, they won't stop me living here. If they do she knows I'll have to go back with her and the idea don't appeal.' My hand had been extended for some time since I gained the deck, and now he shook it with unexpected briskness. 'You from Canada?' he asked. 'Your voice is strange.'

'No. I'm British,' I told him.

He regarded me watchfully. 'That's a hell of a way to come to pay a man's dues,' he said.

'I'm willing to pay money,' I said firmly. 'But I need information.' His eyes contracted to pins of light. 'What information?'

'About Wolfgang Schmitt.'

He whistled through poisonous teeth. 'Wolfie,' he said. 'What information? Wolfie died years ago. In the penitentiary.'

'But I believe you knew him.' Forestalling the question I said: 'I'm writing a book.'

He looked amazed. 'A book on Wolfie?'

'And others.'

Realizing, he nodded. 'I got you now. How much rent is Wolfie worth? Can tell you a few things.'

'A hundred dollars,' I guessed.

'Not bad, not bad,' he approved. 'Keep me here for a

space. Maybe if it's good information you could pay me a bit more. Keep me here longer.'

'It could be.'

He began to climb towards the hatch again. He was thin and, despite his decrepitude, agile. 'You better come down. It ain't any cooler down there but it's more private.' He looked distrustingly around the fetid dock. No human moved. From somewhere unseen a snore drifted. A dog on the next boat walked two feet and lay down. 'You never can tell,' said Beckerman.

Within the shell of the barge the air was hot and aromatic. Adolf's industrious wife obviously did not go down there because it was filthy. In a greasy galley dishes and pans were piled up. As we walked through, my head bent below the bulkhead, a fat-caked saucepan slithered and its owner gave it a kick back into the galley again. 'Ain't washed up since Christmas,' he boasted.

There were two bunks, one a mess of yellowing sheets and a ragged pillow, and the other with canvas spread upon it. He motioned me to this and pulled across some exhausted curtains. 'Keep the sun out,' he said. 'And people.' He sat up on the bed and regarded me anxiously. 'You going to pay me now?'

From my back pocket I took a bill fold and extracted fifty dollars. His sharp eyes were so intent on the roll of money that he almost forgot to extend his hand. 'Writing sure pays, hey?' he said enviously. 'That's a lot of dough you got there.'

'I'll give you another fifty when we've talked,' I said. 'And if you don't hold anything back, I'll make it another fifty.' I did not need to be subtle.

Folding the bills slowly he pushed them deep into a pocket. 'I won't hold out on you,' he promised. 'Wolfie don't care now, anyhow.'

'How long did you know him?' I asked producing my pocket tape recorder. He eyed it apprehensively and said: 'Is my name going on that?'

'Maybe,' I said. 'How would you feel about that?'

He surprised me by saying: 'Fine. But call me Alfred. Okay ... ? Alfred. They call me Adolf but it ain't my choice.'

'Is your name, or one of them, Adolf?'

'Sure, that's right. My father wanted it. Reminded him of the old country.'

'Were you born in Germany?'

'Sure thing. Düsseldorf, some place near Düsseldorf. But I've never been there. Wolfie went back, but not me.'

'When did you first know Schmitt, Wolfie?'

'At school. Half the kids in school was German. We used to fight the war in the schoolyard. I mean, the war that was coming. We used to march around in the yard and beat up the Polaks and the Czechs. I was proud my name was Adolf then. Wolfie made a great little storm-trooper.'

'He liked the idea of Hitler?'

'Oh, sure. Everybody did. In Chicago the German kids really went for Hitler. We all wanted to join that US Nazi Party, what was it called ...?'

'The American Bund,' I said.

'You know it. But in high school, for chrissake, we had to join the Cadets, like we was good little Americans. Drilling and doing things with guns ready to fight the *Germans*, our own flesh and blood. Wolfie didn't care for that. Nor me to be honest. Not then, though I got used to it later. We used to pretend that it was really training to help Hitler and Germany. And marching about we used to break into the goosestep until the instructor saw us and went crazy. We said we was just joking.'

He took a cigarette from a rusty tin and offered me one. I felt genuinely glad I did not smoke. 'I keep giving up,' he said, giving an exploratory cough. 'For my health. Like they say. But then I start again.' He looked around at the dirt-hung cabin. 'Maybe it helps to fumigate this place.'

He lit the cigarette and, oddly, turned his head and blew the smoke hard towards the shaft of heavy sunlight coming down the hatch. 'When it came to the war,' he said, 'the real one, the USA versus Germany, then we was in two minds. We'd always lived here but we came from Germany. There was no arguing with that. But the US said we had to fight for Uncle Sam.'

'You didn't like that?'

'How would you? If there was a war between Uncle Sam and England, would you like to fight against England?'

'What did you do?'

'Scrammed. We went, me, Wolfie and another guy called Rosenberg. Willi Rosenberg. He was a Jew, like he sounds. German Jew. He didn't want to get caught neither. By *nobody*. He didn't want the *draft* to get him, and he didn't want the *Nazis* to get him. Wolfie and me could go back to Germany, and Wolfie did, but not Willi because he was a Jew and he wouldn't have been welcome.'

'Did you consider yourselves to be Nazis?'

'Jesus Christ, no! Not like they turned out. We didn't *know* then, you get me, and the Nazis to us was no worse than Republicans or Democrats. My folks had always voted Republican, like most of the neighbours. It was just another name. People joined because they thought it was okay, right here in Chicago, I mean. There was the Bund, the American Bund, and it was the US Nazi Party, but we were kids. What did we know?'

'When you went, when you scrammed, where did you go?'

He did not hurry to answer. His riven face softened, his eyes became less brittle, he pulled deeply on the cigarette but not forgetting to project the smoke towards the hatch. The action was slower this time. I told him not to bother to blow it away. The next time he ejected a foul blue mouthful, and it filled the cabin. 'It was good, great,' he muttered. 'I remember it. Getting away from the city and your family, especially your mother and your father, looking for girls, keeping out of the way of the US Armed Forces. For a while anyway. It was great.'

'Wolfie Schmitt had another reason, though, didn't he?'

For a moment he seemed mystified, frowning, but then his expression relaxed. 'Oh, yeah, I've got you now. The girl, Lili her name was. You heard. It was tough, but Wolfie was seventeen and he didn't know whether he was the father or some other guy. There was no baby right then, but one was coming fast, and Wolfie didn't like the set-up, so he came along. We just got in a car, Willi Rosenberg's car, that was one reason we took him – he had a good car.'

'Where did you go?'

'We headed anywhere. Just to clear the city and Illinois state. Going south. We just kept going. We had some dough. I had been working in the stockyards and Wolfie was training to be an optician. The company was making bomb-aiming devices for the air force, which was kind of funny. Wolfie helping to drop the bombs on his own head, if you get me. Willi was in his father's office in the city and he made good money, better than us.'

'Willi was quite useful,' I said.

'He was useful. We went south staying in small places, trailer parks and little motels. They had just begun calling them motels then. They was cheap enough. We just kept going for a couple of weeks until we reached Mexico. Well, it was at the border, before Tijuana, and we had to make up our minds what to do next, whether to do the jump into Mexico and cut ourselves off, make a real escape, or think again and go back. In the end we did three different things.' Abruptly, he looked up. It was as though he had been talking to himself and suddenly realized that I was listening. 'I hope all this is worth another fifty bucks, a hundred maybe,' he said anxiously. I nodded and he went on: 'It's all the truth. I don't care much for that tape recorder but nobody knows it's me, and what the hell anyway, it's all goddam history.'

'It's all goddam history,' I agreed.

'Where was I?' he asked.

'You did three different things,' I recalled.

'That's what I said,' he agreed. 'Willi Rosenberg and Wolfie were not hitting it off. There was a disagreement over a girl in a dance place in some town in California. Willi was a hit at the jitterbug and Wolfie had took a fancy to the girl, but she liked Willi best because of his jitterbugging. Anyway Willi decided to head east again, and I never saw him after that. I don't know what happened to the guy. As the war went on his folks moved from Chicago on account of the German families around them. They got to being afraid on account of their Jewishness. But anyway Willi blew. There was no bad feelings, we all shook hands at the Mexican border and he took off. But, of course, he took off *in his car*, which made it hard for us. He might have been a Jew but his car was useful. Also our money was getting low.

We hitched lifts towards Mexico City. We got to the time when we had to make up our minds what we were going to do. I was beginning to get worried, you know, conscience, because by now I'd got round to reckoning I was an American citizen first and a German second. I had thought it out and we talked about it, Wolfie and me, and it got pretty heated at times. Then we had a real bust-up and he said Germany would win the war, and I said America would win it. We'd had a few too many beers, and that didn't help, I guess. It ended up with us fighting, fists and everything, rolling all over the floor in this lousy Mexican house. We broke a wall down, imagine that, we broke down a whole goddam wall! It was just mud and straw, and rolling like we was we went straight through the wall. The room was upstairs in the house and we fell into the street. Gee, I can laugh at it now . . .'

He had lit another cigarette and, in a strangely sophisticated moment, blew a cool column of smoke upwards as he shook his head and smiled at the memory. 'Just think, we fell out of the room into the street. All the Mexes went bananas. Imagine just seeing two fighting gringos come straight through a wall! There was a deal of trouble and it was difficult getting out of there in the end. We had to give them just about all the money we had left. That was when we split up. I'd had all the travelling I needed, and I wanted to get back to the US. Wolfie was going to get to Germany some way. We shook hands in the end and he got a hitch to Mexico City and I got one going the other way. I got to San Diego and went to the Draft Office and said I wanted to join the US Army and they took me. I ended up on Guadalcanal fighting the Japs. At least it was the Japs, but it was shit, I can tell you. There was plenty of times when I wished I had gone with Wolfie.' He became pensive. The cigarette burned idly in his stained fingers. 'But then maybe they would have sent me back like a spy also. Maybe I would have took that walk to the chair. They grilled Wolfie then they fried him.' He half-laughed at his joke but then stopped and appeared ashamed. His damp eyes turned directly to me and then dropped down to the revolving spools of the tape recorder. 'That's all I know,' he said. 'Is that a hundred dollars' worth?'

'I think it is,' I nodded. 'Do you know anything about Wolfie Schmitt when he got back to Chicago after coming from Germany?'

'Only what I heard. I was away, fighting the Japs for Uncle Sam then. I heard all about it from various directions. But his sister knows all about that.'

'Yes, he had a sister,' I said. 'She's still around?'

'Sure. Unless she died. What's her name? She's a fat woman. She lives somewhere round Fullerton Beach. I saw her at a German wedding about a year back. I don't know whether she knows me, recognizes me, but she don't want to know me anyhow, and that's fine by me.'

I got up and gave him another hundred. The very action seemed to drop him into thought. 'You want to talk to this woman?' he asked. We were by the hatch now and he flicked the dying cigarette out of the barge and onto the dockside where it joined many others lying about like spent fireworks. I nodded.

'I think maybe my wife knows where to find her. Women keep track better. Where do you stay in Chicago?'

'The Regent.'

He whistled and looked down at the two extra fifty dollar notes as if he now wished he had upped the price.

'I'll call you tonight,' he promised. 'I'll leave a message if you ain't there. My wife will know. I'll ask her. She comes over Tuesdays to scrub the deck.'

IX

She appeared from the dog parlour at six looking distraught; a big woman in every direction, tall and broad with a mass of trembling chest and heavy legs, and wearing a dress of multi-coloured horizontal hoops.

'Are you Renate Schmitt?' I asked her when she reached the uptown bus stop on Lincoln.

She appeared unworried by the approach. A woman that size can look after herself. She nodded, some wrinkles folding across her brow, her chins overlapping like waves. 'And who wants to know?' she asked.

'My name is Michael Findlater,' I said. 'I'm from England.'

'You're not from Grand Rapids,' she answered eyeing me. Her eyes were big and mauve. 'And I know what you want.'

'You do?' Beckerman's wife must have telephoned her. I said: 'Can we talk?'

The bus was pulling towards us through the traffic, edging towards the sidewalk. 'We can talk on the bus,' she said. 'I need to get this bus, sir. I have to get home.'

It was crowded but she was powerful enough to push her way into the standing people and clear room for both of us. She appeared to have had practice. As we got on I wriggled for the fares.

'Forget it,' she said. An arm like a cudgel was thrust out. Her hand engulfed the small change. 'It's going to cost you more than a bus fare.' The driver looked at us oddly.

'I expect it is,' I said. She shuffled further into the interior and there were protests from passengers standing at the distant end.

'God, it's so hot,' she said to me puffing her cheeks. 'It's like it gets hotter at the end of the day. It's like it piles up and just waits for me when I get out the door.' She regarded me anxiously. I had never seen mauve eyes before. 'Can you smell those dogs on me?' she inquired. Her voice was resounding. People began to shift uneasily and look towards us.

'No, I can't,' I said as privately as I could. 'Not really.'

'Sniff,' she demanded. 'Sniff, you can smell them.'

Minutely I extended my nostrils in her direction. 'Not much,' I assured her. 'Not much at all.'

'Goddam dogs,' she complained. 'Especially this weather. All day they brings dogs in. Washing, cleaning, grooming, talking to them, for God's sake. And they bite. I can tell you they *bite*.' Clumsily she changed hands on the hanger and showed me teethmarks imprinted like a grin on the back of her hand. Several people around had become interested and looked. 'See *that*. They bite,' she repeated. 'And you can only get back at them when nobody's looking.' Again she blew out her cheeks. 'But I get back at them.'

'It can't be an easy job,' I suggested.

'When you hate dogs like I hate dogs,' she agreed. 'And it don't finish when you leave the employment. The smell goes with you. I have other dogs following me down the street.'

At Bay Street, Fullerton Beach, the bus halted and she rolled her mauve eyes at me. We alighted and I turned to see our former fellow passengers crowding at the windows. 'We make a nice couple,' said Renate as she waddled hugely along the fences and dusty trees. 'Fat woman, almost sixty, and a nice young man from England.' There were some children hanging about the street and two black boys began to bark as soon as we had walked by.

'See what I mean,' she grumbled. 'Like about the dogs. I used to chase after those kids, but I never caught them once. Believe me, there could have been blood in this street.' She reached the meshed wire fence of a three-storey block of neat apartments. There was a bay tree in the front garden and a security lock on the gate. She revolved massively.

'You want to know about Wolfgang, I know,' she said. 'Maria Beckerman said.'

'That's correct. I'm a writer. Will you help me?'

'You can't come in now,' she said, her voice dropping for the first time. 'Everybody in this neighbourhood talks. But I'm a straightforward woman. For five hundred dollars I'll tell you.' She looked ashamed. 'I need the money,' she said opening her palms. 'Wolfgang wouldn't care and for sure he won't now. Maybe he'd even like to have a book written.'

'Five hundred is fine,' I said quietly.

'I never ask for money from anybody,' she said. 'But right now I need it.' She smiled, a wide, truly beatific, smile. Together with her mauve eyes it seemed to belong to another body.

'Don't worry, I understand,' I said. 'When can we talk?'

'You can take me out,' she told me firmly. 'Somewhere swank. Somewhere real nice and expensive. I'll dress up. You won't be embarrassed.'

I shook my head unconvincingly. 'If that's what you'd like . . .' I began.

'That's what I'd like,' she confirmed. 'I'd just like to go somewhere swank and I've got nobody to take me. I even thought of hiring a guy, you know, one of these escort guys who take money for taking ugly women to nice places. But I figured that with me it would just cost too much.' She smiled again. Her great hand folded around mine, and we made a pact to meet in the bar at the Regent the following evening at eight.

'We'll have a great time,' she assured me as she opened the security gate. Her legs pounded steadily down the short path to the door, her hooped dress like a top slowly spinning. 'And don't forget to bring the dough,' she called uncompromisingly over her shoulder.

Renate was late. Women have been late before, more often than not. In my youthful years I held the world record for waiting under the Waterloo Station clock in London.

For half an hour I loitered around the hotel lobby. When she did arrive there was no mistaking it. Through the hotel's main door she came like a carnival. People stopped and stared but then smiled, because she looked wonderful. Imagine a two hundred pound woman in a silver dress. She had a blonde wig fixed on one end of her and what must have been specially constructed fashion shoes on the other. The dress was like crushed silver paper, wrapped around and swirled about her great body, with an extra swirl of it over one shoulder flying like a pennant as she flung it extravagantly sideways. Over her thick forearm was a white fur hung like a victim. Her nails were bloody scimitars, and she held them out before her, emptying a path between the people. Her legs clumped across the lobby's marble floor, her smile was like a white beach, and her eyes blazed gloriously. Renate had presence.

'So sorry,' she boomed. Watchers standing near backed off. 'I lost one of my goddamned lenses. And I still didn't find the sonofabitch.' It was no time for handshakes. I attempted to embrace her but she beat me to it. It was engulfing as a quilt. 'Notice anything?' she challenged.

'Several things,' I ventured.

'The eyes,' she urged in a huge whisper. 'Get the eyes.'

It was difficult to miss them, even amid the rest of her. There was only one mauve eye now, the other a drab brown. 'I know how much you liked my eyes,' she said as I propelled her towards the bar. Her elbow was like squeezing an old-fashioned motor horn. 'I could tell you liked them the way you kept looking. They're tinted. But you'll have to take in the right one tonight because I couldn't find the other little devil.' I sat her majestically in a seat in an alcove towards which she had set her own course. She occupied it like a queen. 'The rest of me,' she announced, 'is all here.'

We had Martinis and she drank several. It worried me because I had planned to leave my questions about Wolfie until we were sitting at dinner. Now I thought I ought to start soon. 'This is elegant,' she decided, looking imperially around her. 'Just my style. I feel like one of those poodles I have to sweeten.'

'The money,' I said low-voiced and aware how crass it sounded. 'Would you like it now?'

'God no!' she laughed powerfully. 'You don't have to pay me *now*. I can wait for five hundred dollars.'

Two men left a neighbouring table, almost pulled from their seats by their own raised eyebrows. 'Shit. Five hundred bucks!' one said as they made for the door.

Renate was oblivious to it. 'Where are we going for dinner?' she asked. 'Is it special? I don't want that German junk. If anything was going to turn me against the old country, it was not Hitler, it was the sausages.'

'Is there anywhere special you'd particularly like?' I asked.

'Cave d'Or,' she said in a moment. 'Three blocks from here.'

'You know it?'

'Sure I know it.'

'It's good?'

'It's got to be good what they charge. Not that I've ever been there, but they *charge*. I read the newspaper columns, and the guide books, you know, about the fancy places. Expensive, very expensive, costly . . . and so on. I know every swank eatery in this city, but I've never been to any of them. I just sit and read about them at home eating my cold potatoes.'

'Cave d'Or it is then. I hope they have a table.'

'They do. I already booked it.' She looked at a delicate watch cutting into her broad wrist. She had a small ring on her engagement finger but no wedding ring. 'Nine-thirty I reserved it,' she said. 'We have time for another aperitif.' Before I could raise my hand she had waved down a waiter and he came back with two Martinis on a silver tray which reflected his own grin.

She tried hers, then put the glass down and, glancing about her, the first unostentatious thing she had done that evening, she said: 'Listen Michael, you don't have to worry. I'm sixty years old so I'm not going to eat you.'

'That might be cheaper than the restaurant,' I grinned.

She laughed. I really liked her. 'You won't need to lift me from under the table either,' she promised. 'I can drink this stuff like water. When you drink alone you get to acquire capacity.'

We finished our drinks and went out, slowing, then stopping the bar conversation as we did. Just for the hell of it I turned swiftly around and so did Renate, almost at the same moment, as if we had rehearsed it. We caught them all staring, the customers, the waiters, the men behind the bar. Then we turned back again. She put her arm in mine and we went jauntily out of the place. In the lobby we both began to laugh. I was enjoying myself more than I had for some time. It was less than three blocks, but we got a cab and arrived with some style outside the restaurant. During the short journey Renate had told the driver that I was her son who had returned from Joliet Penitentiary only that day, after an absence of several years, and he seemed to believe her. 'And I thought Chicago was all finished,' he said.

I have rarely seen anyone's expression undergo a change like that of the black doorman's at the 'Cave d'Or'. He could not decide whether to hold the door of the taxi or haul Renate out onto the sidewalk. They eventually managed it between them, with me hovering uselessly. Within the restaurant the man at the door was scarcely less unguarded. His mouth opened several times before he could say: 'Good evening'. Renate grandly handed in her fur to the girl behind the cloakroom desk, and the girl seemed to approve. She stroked it. 'What is it, madame?' she asked.

'Yak,' said Renate. 'It's yak.'

Everybody laughed. We were led to a table, once more stunning idle chatter. She swept her eyes over the luxurious room as if checking that everything was properly in place. She had reserved an alcove table. We sat down and suddenly her mood changed, she dropped the imperious air, her puffy face softened. 'But this is *elegant*, Michael,' she enthused quietly. 'Like I always imagine it.' She arranged the outrageous silver dress sedately. 'I hope I haven't embarrassed you,' she murmured. 'I'm really enjoying it.'

'And so am I,' I said genuinely. 'I don't go to good places enough.'

She ordered pâté de foie gras, followed by almond trout, followed by Boeuf Wellington. We drank two bottles of French Macon, one white, one red. 'I know the menu,' she confessed during the main course. 'I send for them. Every good place in this town, I know the menu. I read them at home.' She ate heartily. Then she said: 'You'll be wanting to know about Wolfie.'

'In your own time,' I said.

'Our father called him Godlove, you know that? Godlove.'

'Yes, I knew that was one of his names.'

'They called me Renate, which means re-birth. I should be re-born, believe me. But Godlove was something else to live up to.'

'You were ten years younger, weren't you,' I ventured. 'So you would be about ten when it all happened.'

'That was it. I remember the FBI coming to the house. Jesus, those FBI men were so dumb, so clumsy. They came around and gave everybody a fright, except me because I didn't know much about what was going on, and then they said they'd come because Wolfgang hadn't *registered for the draft*. Imagine, there's a Nazi spy and right in front of their eyes – and they're grumbling because he hasn't been to sign for the draft!'

'That's what I heard.'

She looked at me a little concerned. 'How much do you know already?' she inquired.

'Bits and pieces. There's a lot to be filled in.'

Her anxiety lingered. She had a curved crust from the Boeuf Wellington poised on the way to her mouth, and she let it drop back onto the plate. 'And this is for a book, you say?'

'A book, maybe,' I said. I couldn't lie to her. 'And some newspaper articles.'

'Me, I'll have to disappear,' she said without emphasis. 'There'll be reporters around the door. It'll be worse than the Feds. Not that I care. I've had Chicago anyway, and especially I've had Chicago's dogs. One day I'm just going to strangle one and quit.' Her mouth flowed into a big smile. 'I even know which dog,' she said. She bit into the pastry.

'Where will you go?'

'Head for Florida, I guess. That's where we all go, don't we? Sit on Miami Beach and wait for God. I've got some savings and the apartment is mine.' She waited. 'I need this money to get my teeth fixed.'

The crust at last was consumed. 'The beef is great,' she said. 'So is the Wellington.'

The wine waiter poured more of the Mâcon Rouge. 'That's a fine seventy-six,' Renate assured him expansively. He himself did not seem sure. As he went away, she said: 'You know the background. How my brother went to Mexico. Beckerman told you that. He's a shit, that guy. Makes his wife scrub the decks of that lousy tub he lives on. She told me.'

I said: 'Beckerman told me up to the time they went to Mexico, but not beyond that.' In my pocket I had the tape recorder. I had intended to leave it there. It would spoil the evening. But she said: 'You going to get this on tape? Like you did with Beckerman. That way you get it right.'

As I lifted the small machine from my pocket, she took it from me and placed it among the flowers at the centre of the table. 'Now nobody cares a damn,' she muttered. 'See that,' she held up the ring on her engagement finger. 'That was my mother's.'

'It's nice,' I said.

'A present from her son. From her Wolfgang,' she said simply. 'With some of the money the Nazis gave him. He only bought himself a penknife, a watch and a hat. And the down-payment on a car. My father had to take the car back as soon as the Government said they didn't need it any more for evidence. The day after Wolfie went to the chair, my old man took the car back to the salesman, and what do you think, two Feds drive up as he's leaving and take back the four hundred and fifty dollars he had in his hand. Uncle Sam wanted everything accounted for. Not that he got it.'

I saved asking her then what she meant by that. Instead I said: 'What happened after Mexico?'

'Well, when he and Beckerman split up, and there was another guy who had parted company with them some time before ... when he and Beckerman split, Wolfie went to Mexico City. Even then, so he said, he had no idea what he was going to do, no real plans. He was no Nazi, Michael, you've got to believe that. When he was a kid he walked into doors and he went on like that. And he walked as far as the electric chair.' She paused in unhappy thought, propelling her fat fingers like legs along the table.

'In Mexico he was running out of money,' she went on. 'So he went to the German Consulate like anybody would. And it was that guy, that consulate, who put him up to going back to Germany. This was before there was war between Germany and Japan and the United States, you understand, only England had a war. Uncle Sam was neutral. But everybody who wasn't crazy knew what was coming and this consul asked Wolfgang if he would like to go back to the Fatherland, and Wolfgang said okay. He was given some money and not too much later he was aboard a ship, out of Mexico and heading for Japan from where they went to Germany. It was full of Germans going back like he was. They went the long way around to avoid the British blockade.'

The tape recorder was revolving silently among the flowers in the now crowded restaurant with its finery; the noise from the tables, the waiters moving and me in this alcove with this large, sad woman. 'The ship,' she went on, 'took a long time, Wolfie didn't care for it because it was full of one hundred per cent Nazis. Every day they had to listen to lectures to show them how great Hitler was, what the Nazi Party had done, indoctrination stuff, etcetera. When my father told me about this, a long time after, when he found out something, and my mother gave me the ring when she was dying . . . when he finally told me the details . . . it was this ship that Wolfgang hated worse than anything. Worse than the trial and the prison and everything else. The only worse thing was when the US Government wouldn't let his mom and pa visit him in the condemned cell. They offered to pay their own fares, and even pay the fares for any guy, if one had to travel on the train with them, but no, it was against the rules. J. Edgar Hoover said it was against the rules, and he was the boss of the Feds. What he said, the President did, so they say. He was the chief.'

Her voice had dropped and to my surprise, she began to cry, only slightly, dabbing at her eyes with a dainty lace handkerchief. She told me what she wanted to order for dessert, crème brûlée, and then excused herself and bounced like a silver orb between the tables, stopping eaters in mid-mouthful as she went towards the cloak-room. The waiter appeared and I ordered the desserts. 'Your mother seems to be enjoying herself,' he ventured.

'It's my wife,' I told him.

He blushed the colour of his maroon jacket. 'She's . . . she's wonderful,' he said. 'Really wonderful.'

When Renate returned it was as though the whole room had been awaiting her. She appeared at the door like a rising silver moon and a hush set in; people at every table looked up. Most of them were smiling, es-pecially the women, not sneering but in admiration for someone who could carry herself off like that. She rolled into the restaurant, and for a moment I thought some-body was going to break the spell by actually applauding. Fortunately it did not happen. As she had passed each table, so the conversation resumed, most of it, I imagined, about her. The head waiter lowered his head diligently as she progressed past him and, standing in the back-ground, the waiter who had mistaken her for my mother performed a still embarrassed bow.

'There were two ladies in the cloakroom who wanted to know where I bought my dress,' Renate said in a pleased way as she edged her way behind our table. 'They thought it was neat.' She rolled her eyes, the mauve one and the brown one. 'I made it myself. There's no way you can buy dresses like this. They don't have the scope.'

She surveyed the crème brûlée in its small round dish as an elephant might regard a mousehole. 'They don't overfeed you with this stuff, do they?' she whispered loudly. The spoon was poised tinily in her hand. She picked at the dessert delicately. 'Where did we leave my brother?' she inquired. 'On the ship, wasn't it?'

'At sea,' I confirmed. 'With the Nazis.'

'And he hated it,' she said. 'They were the real thing, not toy Nazis like before. He was glad when they reached Japan.'

'How did he get along with the Japanese?'

'Not at all. He was no racist, Wolfgang. God, the guy he travelled to Mexico with – not Beckerman, the other guy – was a Jew, but Wolfie still went with him. It could have been because this guy was a car-owner. But my brother just hated those Japs. When he got home to Chicago at last we sat down and locked the doors and pulled the drapes tight, and he told us all the things that had happened. He said it was the Japs he hated most. And they were on *our* side . . . well, *his* side, not ours because we were really Americans.' She lapsed into caution for once. 'In general we supported the USA.'

'He told you everything when he came back then?'

'Spilled the beans, as they used to say. I don't remember it very well because, as you know, I was only a young kid then, but I remember sitting in this room with the doors locked and him telling us about his adventures. It was like a sailor coming home after sailing. I know spies are not supposed to tell *anything*, but there was no way Wolfie could keep this to himself, not from his ma and poppa.

'We were a very close family and so were all our relatives. He told plenty of people but he knew they wouldn't go blabbing to the FBI. They were all *German* people, after all, and they knew him, they'd known him from a kid. They wouldn't have wanted him to get into trouble.'

She was soberly serious. The dessert had disappeared and she tapped the spoon on the table as she spoke. 'In any case,' she said. 'How else could he explain coming back after two years with thousands of dollars? If he had said he'd stolen it, robbed a bank or something, my father would have been shocked. He might have even handed him over to the police. He certainly would have told him to send the dough back. He was that sort of man. We'd never had any criminal trouble in our family.'

'He had thousands of dollars?' I said.

'Thousands,' she said. 'I'll let you know about that.' She paused reflectively: 'I believe, and I've always believed, Michael . . . ' She leaned closer, the stiff silver of her dress touching my elbow. '. . . Always . . . I believe Wolfgang had some plan. He had an idea to *expose* the whole plot, to tell the authorities where the real spies were, the other guys, the baddies, because he was no Nazi. When he was a young kid maybe he *thought* he was, but he changed when he saw what the real thing was like. He was just waiting for his opportunity to snitch on them when a terrible man, the one who got clean away with it . . .'

'Hine,' I prompted. 'Peter Karl Hine.'

She looked at me surprised. 'That's the sonofabitch,' she said, her voice low. 'Hine. He even wrote. He got there first and blew the whistle on everybody, our poor Wolfgang included.'

'Wolfgang met up with Hine in Germany,' I said.

'Right. I don't know how Wolfie got to Germany but it must have been some journey from Japan. But he made it and he spent some time travelling around and seeing all our various relatives still living there. Then, in some way, he got caught up by the Nazis and they sent him to this place somewhere so that he could be trained.'

I almost said: 'As a spy.'

'It sounded like summer camp,' Renate went on. 'This

much I remember because being a young kid I guess I was more interested. It was in some woods, by a lake, all that stuff. He had fun. They even had sing-songs. They sang "Yankee Doodle Dandy". American songs. "Ain't Misbehaving". I remember him saying. The only thing he didn't like was the football. It wasn't American football, it was German football and he didn't go for that.'

'When he came back, back to Chicago,' I said. 'Everybody must have been amazed. He'd been away a couple of years.'

She looked troubled. 'I don't remember too much of that, of him actually arriving, I only know he was back. But it's a funny thing . . .'

'What is?' I was afraid she might not go on: I was anxious about the tape recorder and tried listening for it. It was silent-running but I moved slightly so I could see the eye of red light which showed it was operating. 'It's still going,' she said, leaning over also. 'Just so long as it doesn't fall in the flower-water.'

Before I could move she reached out and wedged the miniature machine more securely between the stems of the roses. She went on without prompting. 'It's a funny thing,' she repeated. 'But my father and mother always swore that they thought he was in Mexico, all the time since he left home . . . that he had gone because of the trouble with the girl who said he had got her pregnant, which I don't think was even true. Even in our own family they always talked about Wolfgang as being down in Mexico, but they must have known he had left there because he sent a postcard from Japan while he was there, and said he was going on to the Fatherland, as he called it. I've still got the postcard.'

That startled me. 'You've still got some of his belongings?'

For the first time she seemed less than open. Then she decided. 'I have some of his things,' she said. 'A few. I guess you'd like to see them. I've never shown them to a soul.'

X

When we were in the taxi I said: 'When do you think your father and mother actually knew what Wolfgang was up to? Was it when they realized *why* he had come back?'

'That,' she said with emphasis, 'must have been some situation.' She glanced towards the driver. His head was nodding to music. 'I guess they must have known pretty fast,' she said. Her tone descended. 'They weren't dumb. He could never keep anything like that to himself.'

'They must have had a tug-of-war with their loyalties.'

'Tug-of-war is right,' she agreed quickly. 'But they always loved him more than they loved Uncle Sam. They came to America because of necessity, and they took the oath and everything. But Godlove was Godlove. Their kid. There was no way they would have turned him in. Nor would anybody else. Not in this town. Not German people.'

'I heard,' I said, 'that the FBI had trouble finding somewhere to hide, to watch your house.'

'You know so much about this,' she observed again. 'Still, if it's a book you're writing, then I suppose you must know it. Where they hid out I don't know, but they watched him from somewhere. He went to the Belmont picture theatre, as they used to call it, in the afternoon when it was nearly empty and he said that two guys sat right behind him. He didn't suspect them. He really wasn't cut out to be a spy.'

We were on Lincoln Avenue, going north, and she gave the driver instructions. She dropped back heavily into the seat. 'Jesus but I've had a good time tonight,' she said.

'So have I,' I replied honestly. I patted her wrist. 'I must give you the five hundred.'

'I won't forget,' she promised emphatically. 'I didn't have *that* good a time.'

We both laughed. Her big frame vibrated. She flapped her hands. When we left the cab outside her apartment, she was still laughing slightly. Then she emitted a small sniffle and dabbed at her eyes with the back of her hand. 'A good time,' she repeated.

'Keep having a good time,' called the taxi driver as he went away. 'Do you think we look strange?' she asked abruptly as she unlocked the security gate. 'Here am I, my size and my age.'

'You're lovely,' I told her. 'And *I* don't feel strange.'

She undid the front door locks and we went up a short flight of carpeted stairs to a door on a landing. 'Keys, keys, keys,' she recited as she opened this door. 'It's like being your own prisoner.' We went into a surprisingly large room furnished without luxury but with some taste. 'I need a big living area,' she said. 'I keep falling over things. I've been here for twenty years, since my father died.'

'I must give you this cheque,' I said. I had already written it. It was in an envelope. She put it on a full bookcase without opening it. She said she would make some coffee and told me to pour myself a drink. There was a bottle of schnapps on the side and I poured a small measure. I called to her, but she said she would not drink any more. I went to the window and looked down on the midnight street. It was empty except for a man sweeping the gutters. He had a small cart. He swept a few yards and pulled the cart up, then swept a few more yards. He was smoking as he worked, and he politely knocked the ash into his cart.

Renate came from the kitchen with a tray. She put the coffee down and sat in an upright chair opposite me. 'I think I've told you just about everything,' she said. 'Unless you've got any ideas.'

'I'd certainly like to see the things you have that belonged to your brother,' I told her. 'If that's all right.'

'Sure. Nobody else has ever seen some of the things. Not even the FBI. They went through this place, took it apart, after they arrested Wolfie. They picked him up at the gas station when he was standing admiring his new car, and they got back here like somebody's army. There were Feds on every corner of the street. They came into the house scaring everybody, although I guess the grown-ups realized what it was about. I was so scared I took myself upstairs and hid under the bed in my pa and mom's room. That's when I first saw the money.'

'The money?' I said slowly.

'Under the bed in a bag. I opened the bag and saw it.'

'Wolfgang's,' I said. There had been nothing in the files about Schmitt having a large amount of money.

'Sure. For expenses, I guess. There was thirty thousand dollars. He'd only bought the watch, the hat and the penknife, and this ring for his ma, and put the down-payment on the car.'

'They didn't look under the bed?'

'Not then. They were so dumb. They didn't look there till later.'

'One thing I missed,' I said. 'Who told Wolfgang to go to the FBI about his draft? It took some nerve to walk in there when you've just been landed from a German submarine.'

She shrugged. 'Maybe my father. But he carried it off like a Hollywood star, strolled in and told the guy that he had been away in Mexico. They wrote everything down and it seems they had no idea that other FBI agents were looking for him at the same time. It was a different department, I guess, and the right hand didn't know what the left was doing.'

'It would have been something if he'd ended up in the US Army,' I smiled.

She shook her large head: 'He wouldn't have done that,' she said. 'He had his principles, so my father told me. He was on the side of Germany even if he wasn't on the side of Hitler, the Nazi. He took precautions. He went to a doctor and took some special pills which slowed up his heart and the doctor, who was a German doctor of course, gave him a certificate to say he wasn't fit for service. Then he went to his boss, or the man who was his boss before he went to Mexico, and he got a letter from him to say that they needed him to work in the optical factory, where they were making bombing-sights for the US Air Force.' For once she seemed to realize the ridiculousness of it. 'It all was very complicated,' she said spreading her hands.

My empty coffee cup was on the low table. She put hers beside it. 'You'd like to see the relics,' she said.

'I would.'

'I've kept them,' she said, rising from the upright chair. 'It's been my secret. It's time somebody else was let in on it.'

I followed her from the room. There was a corridor between a bedroom and a bathroom, and in the wall was a wallpapered cupboard. She produced another small key and opened it. 'One time I used to seriously hide them,' she said over her shoulder. 'But nobody ever tried to find them so I eased off on the security.' She laughed awkwardly. 'Who cares anyway? Mind your head.' She climbed heavily into the aperture. 'I have to be careful with mine. I don't often bother to come in here now.'

Inside the door she switched on a light. It was a bare bulb jutting from the wall. There was just about enough room for us both to stand. 'There's that,' she said flatly.

Squatting at the shadowed end of the cupboard was a human skull. Through the eyeholes were projecting two flags; from the right the Stars and Stripes, from the left the Nazi Swastika. I was wordless.

'The head's not real,' said Renate casually. 'It's just plaster or something. I couldn't keep a real head.'

'No . . .' I mumbled. 'You couldn't really.'

'Wolfgang made it when he was a kid. Still at High School. He was more of a little Nazi then than he was when he came back. It's symbolic . . . of . . . well, like you see . . .'

'Yes, I understand.'

'I didn't even know it was around until my father died. Then it turned out that he'd kept a few things belonging to Wolfgang. Memories, I guess you could say.'

'What else do you have?' I asked slowly, still taking in the skull and its flags.

'Not much.' There was a wooden box standing on an upright chair pushed against the narrow wall. It was not locked. She lifted the lid and took out some small objects. 'His penknife,' she said solemnly. She held it in the fleshy palm of her hand and I took it from her. 'I told you he bought a penknife,' she said.

I nodded and said: 'There was a watch, wasn't there?'

She took the watch from the box, closing the lid again as she had done the first time. 'It still goes,' she said. 'You only have to wind it.' She turned the winder to and fro and then held the ticking watch towards my ear.

'How did these come back to you?' I asked. 'The FBI must have had them.'

'My father claimed them. He kept claiming them, saying they were his son's property and he was entitled to them. Even the families of murderers get belongings sent back, he said. Nothing happened for a long time, and then they sent them back. It was after the war. They must have been having a clear-out.'

From the bottom of the box she first took a grey cap and then a uniform tunic. 'German Marines,' she said. 'See the badges.'

'He was wearing this when he came ashore on Long Island,' I said. I could hardly believe I was touching it. 'They returned this to your father also?'

'No. This was hidden. And the skull. Some relative must have had them.'

I glanced at her in the uncertain light. The evening's ebullience had drained. She looked lined and weary in the confined shadows.

Her big hand went once more into the box. 'Here,' she said, 'is the postcard Wolfie sent. Like I told you. From Japan. The FBI had that too. It was evidence.'

I took it from her, brown with age and inferior card-board. It was a picture, in fading colours, of Mount Fuji. I turned it over, holding it near the light. The writing was round and regular. It was in German and was signed 'Godlove'.

Renate took the card from me and placed it back in the box. 'That's all there is,' she said closing the lid.

'You told me Hine had once written to you or your parents,' I said trying not to press her too much. 'Do you have that letter?'

'It's somewhere,' she said. 'I would not put it with these things. That traitor.' She asked me to turn out the light and I followed her from the enclosed space. 'At some time,' I said, 'could I come and take some photographs of the things in here?'

'For your book? Well, why not. I'll be moved out by that time, anyway. By the time it comes out. Down to South Miami Beach.'

'I'd like to come tomorrow,' I said. 'I'd planned to leave tomorrow. I could come here before I go. But you'll be at work, won't you?'

She shrugged. 'I could take the day off,' she offered. 'They owe me time. I won't be de-lousing dogs too much longer in any case.' We walked now into her sitting room and she said: 'I don't know where that letter is. Maybe I threw it in the trash.'

She offered me another cup of coffee or a drink but I declined. I felt a real friendship and a sadness for her. 'What will you do in Florida?' I asked.

She smiled a little and said: 'There's a whole lot of me to get sunned.' She stood up and so did I. I kissed her on the cheek and thanked her.

'Thank you,' she returned. 'It was a night to remember. And thanks for the five hundred.' As she walked towards the door she said: 'Maybe I'll open a poodle parlour on Ocean Drive when I get to Miami. Those old people have all got dogs down there. They don't eat too well themselves, but the dogs live okay. They spend money on them. And I won't mind it too much if it's my place. They won't smell so bad.'

I was glad she laughed because she had become sombre after showing me the objects in the cupboard. When I was at the door I asked her if she knew a German nursery rhyme beginning: 'Hop, hop, writer . . .'

She appeared only slightly surprised at the question and she nodded. 'All the children from the old country know it,' she said.

'Could you tell me how it goes?'

We were almost at her door now. She said. 'How is it? Yes . . .'

'Hoppe, hoppe Reiter,
Wenn er fällt, dann schreit er,
Fällt er in den Graben,
Fressen ihn die Raben,
Fällt er in den Sumpf,
Geht der Reiter . . . plump!'

'What happens to this hopping writer?'

'It's not,' she said. 'It's a *rider*, a guy on horseback. He hops and hops, and then falls off the horse and cries out. Then . . . let me see . . . when you don't use a language every day . . . yes, now he falls into a sumpf . . . a swamp. And the ravens come along and eat him . . .'

'Ravens?'

'Ravens. Birds. Black birds.'

'I understand.'

'You don't look so good, Michael.'

I smiled tightly at her. 'I'm fine,' I said. 'It's just part of the puzzle, that's all . . . Could you write it down for me?'

She did not ask what I meant. 'There's some more,' she said. 'When the ravens get the rider he sinks in the swamp . . . plomp . . . just like that.' It took her a few minutes to write the words. She handed it to me. 'It's just a rhyme,' she said. 'A kid's rhyme.'

*

The night was humid so I took my time. The street-sweeper had gone. Lone cats and lonely cars used the streets. From the junction with Lincoln Avenue I looked back. The light in her window was still on. I began to recite: 'Hoppe, hoppe Reiter . . .' From my pocket I took the folded piece of paper and, by the light of the street lamps, I read the rest aloud.

> 'Wenn er fällt dann schreit er,
> Fällt er in den Graben,
> Fressen ihn die Raben . . .'

A cruising cab approached. I waved the nursery rhyme and he pulled over. Sitting in the back I read the verse aloud again. The driver cocked his head. 'It's a long time since I heard that,' he said conversationally. 'Hoppe, hoppe, Reiter.'

'Your family came from Germany?'

'A while back. But we used to say it at school and at home. Then it got a bad name.'

'Oh? Why was that?'

'The Bund, you know, the United States Nazi Party. Pre-nineteen forty-one. Especially here in Chicago and Milwaukee . . . Beer country. A lot of German settlers. It was a sort of symbolic rhyme. They had training camps, the Bund, up in the hills and places, and they used to sing it there. Imagine, singing nursery rhymes.'

'Did you . . . have any experience of that?' I thought he was in his early sixties.

'Me? No, I had no dealings with that. When my folks came to the US they took the oath and that was good enough for them. They considered they were Americans from that minute. Nothing less. My old man used to say Hitler could go and shit himself.'

'But there were others?'

'Sure. Plenty in this city. Some torn one way and another. That was difficult. People here had relatives being bombed by the US Air Force in Germany. You get me?'

'Yes, I understand. Do you remember the case of Wolfgang Schmitt?'

He nodded but was silent. 'He went to the electric chair,' I prompted.

'Sure he did. For spying they said. Everybody knew about him. He was just a dumb kid. He went to the chair to make J. Edgar Hoover feel good. Hoover made sure Hoover got all the kudos. The President, Roosevelt, even gave him a medal, for God's sake.'

'Did you know the family?' I asked.

'Not close. I was a kid then. There were a whole lot of Germans here. Thousands of families. I knew where the Schmitts lived, on Brewster, one of those streets, and I knew people who knew them. You know how it is.'

We drove through the hollow city. 'But people felt bad,' he went on, still thinking about it. 'The German families here. But after a while they swallowed it and went back to being good Americans again.'

He dropped me outside the hotel. The lobby was deserted except for a night clerk totting up accounts. I had my key with me. Going up in the elevator I found myself reciting again: 'Hoppe, hoppe Reiter . . .'

As I put the key in the door I sensed something strange. A smell. I turned it and carefully eased the door. I knew that there was something, someone, in the room. My neck began to sweat. The gun was in the room, in my luggage. Pushing the door open I swiftly stepped back. Nothing happened. I was getting jumpy. There was no movement from the dark inside. I muttered an insult to myself and walked into the room. I reached up and turned on the light.

For a second nothing occurred. Then I saw it and heard it. At the same time. A huge black bird with a frightening wingspan and a mad, mad cry came battering down on me from the other side of the room. Christ, I was never so scared in my life! Its wings engulfed me. I let out a howl that was worse than the bird's and flailed about with my hands. It was in front of my face, its beak like a lance, its wings beating, its terrible high croaking shout sounding again and again. My hands beat back against its feathers, and it screeched again and veered off, back to the far side of the room. My hands were bleeding, still protecting my face. Sobbing like a child, I staggered back into the corridor and slammed the door. Shaking, my mouth agape, I collapsed against the opposite wall. People were opening doors all along the corridor. Tentative heads appeared, some in curlers, one in a nightcap.

'What's going on?' complained a man three doors away. 'I've been disturbed.'

'Not half as much as I've been,' I answered him without looking. I was still shaking. There was a house phone a few paces away. I got to it and picked it up. The operator answered: 'Can I help you?' he asked.

'I'll say you can. Get someone up here, will you – with a bird cage.'

'A bird cage?' He sounded only slightly surprised. It was the time of night for drunks. 'You want a bird cage at this time of night?'

'I do. There's a fucking great raven in my room.'

'The largest,' announced the man from the Chicago Zoo at six in the morning. 'The largest of the passerine birds.'

He was vaguely benign and wearing pyjamas under his baggy suit. The ends of the pyjama legs projected from his trousers, and he had spread the collar like a wide-striped sports shirt over his coat. There had been instant amity between him and the raven, and now he looked fondly down as it squatted beneath the dome of a copious cage, and I swear the bird looked fondly back. It was only when the creature revolved its bright black head towards me that its eyes took on a malevolent glaze.

'It's as well you had the odd bird cage,' I mentioned to the night manager.

'We are programmed to handle most emergency situations,' he responded primly. He did not care for me or the raven. 'Are you checking out today, sir?'

'I was anyway.'

'I see. We'll get your account ready.'

'Listen,' I said tapping him on the shoulder. 'I didn't take this monster into the room. It was *put* there. Since you're programmed so well somebody on your staff must have noticed, out of the corner of his eye even, a bloody raven being carted upstairs. It's not easy to hide.'

The zoo man had eyes only for the bird. It had returned its attention to him. 'A fine specimen,' he murmured bending from the waist. Whoever he slept with must have despised those pyjamas. 'Really fine.'

'Maybe you should adopt it,' I suggested. 'I have my considerable doubts about anybody claiming it.'

'Fine feathers, excellent wingspan,' he crooned, ignoring me. The bird, I swear, seemed to appreciate the comments because it half-opened its glistening wings. The man added: 'They can be taught to talk, you know.'

'I wish this one would,' I said fervently.

'So does the hotel,' said the night manager. He still

did not believe me. As if to test its weight, the zoo man lifted the cage. He needed two hands. The raven gave a soft croak, as if it were ready to go anywhere with him. 'He likes you,' said the hotel manager hopefully.

'We could certainly give him a home, even if it's only temporary. Until he's claimed,' said the zoo man. He looked up. There was stubble on his chin and sleep in his eyes, but he was plainly happy. 'They can survive to a good age, you know,' he said. 'One lived to sixty-nine.'

'It put a few years on me,' I said.

'I'll take it back with me,' he decided. 'If anyone claims it, you'll know where it is.'

'Right,' said the manager overwhelmingly relieved. 'Maybe you could drop the cage back some time. We never know when we may need it again.'

'I'd like another room for a few hours,' I told him. 'This thing crapped everywhere.'

'They do,' nodded the zoo man.

The manager looked as if he would have liked to have refused, but he thought the better of it and went to the reception desk where the night clerk, who had been watching in silence and fascination, handed him a key. I shook hands with the zoo man and thanked him.

'It's okay,' he said. 'Any time.'

He looked down at the bird again. '*Corvus corax*,' he said.

'Would you repeat that?' I said.

'*Corvus corax*,' he obliged. 'The common raven.'

XI

'*Corvus corax*, hey? Well, you're certainly teaching me things I never knew. First windmills, now *Corvus corax*, the common raven. What do you know about them?'

'They shit,' I said. 'Everywhere.'

'It was the name of the guy from the toy company,' said Robinson on the telephone. 'The guy on the plane.'

'It was.'

'You've got the gun?'

'The way I feel, jittery, I might shoot somebody,' I answered. 'I think they just want me to be scared, Fred, that's why *other* people keep getting killed. They could pick me off in the street. Why put a bloody bird in my room? They could just as easily . . . easier in fact . . .'

'. . . put a bomb in your bed. Sure.'

'I found Schmitt's sister.'

'Jesus! You did! That's good. You should work here. We have guys who can't find their way to the bathroom.'

'It wasn't too difficult.'

'Did she tell you anything?'

'Just about everything she knows. Well, nearly. She's going to tell me some more today. Do they sweep the streets at night in Chicago?'

'I'll find out.'

'I'll find out myself. I can ring somebody at City Hall. I've seen Wolfgang's marine cap and some other souvenirs.'

He whistled down the phone. 'You *have* been operating.'

'What happened at the girl's inquest?' I asked.

'It was adjourned. The police say they're still investigating. What are you going to do now?'

'I'm hoping to get a lead on Hine in Berlin. That's where he is, I think.'

'Oh, right. I'd have liked to come with you. But now I can't. My wife's come home.'

'I'm glad.'

'I should be, but I don't know. She wants me to improve, she says. I don't know that I can improve. When will you go?'

'In a few days. I've decided to go down to New Bedford. I'm still renting a house there.'

'I remember that. Going to see if the whales are still okay?'

'I just want to go for a couple of days. I'm going to try and unscramble my brain. I'm going to try and fit everything into some sort of logic, everything I now know, and see how it sits. The place is called Thoughtful Creek.'

'I heard. We know all about you here, Mike. We're good, *great* even, on getting facts and feeding them into computers. Facts, we can handle. What we're not good at is fantasy. When are you leaving?'

'Noon flight to Boston. I'm going to see Renate again, that's Schmitt's sister, before I go.'

'Okay Michael. Call me before you go to Berlin. Jesus, but do you have some life. Berlin, Thoughtful Creek. The only place I'm going is lunch.'

'Give my love to the girl who weighs the lettuce. Can you check if someone in Chicago has reported a missing raven?'

'We can only try,' he said.

'Did you have to wait long last night for a taxi?' she asked.

'Not long. I walked up to Lincoln.' Then I lied: 'I had a conversation with the street-cleaner.'

'Those guys,' she said caustically. 'They need somebody to talk to. In the middle of the darned night you hear them hollering to each other, waking the neighbourhood. In the middle of the night. I think they do it because they don't like everybody sleeping when they're working. It's called revenge.'

'Perhaps they do it because they're afraid of the dark,' I suggested. She laughed. She went in for horizontal rings and this morning she was again twirled with bright colours, circling the commodious legs and the formidable tunic of a trouser suit. She had done her hair, piled it up like a harvest loaf, but her face was weary, her make-up accentuating its heaviness.

'I had a real good time last night,' she said touching my hand.

'So did I,' I said truthfully. 'I can't remember when I had such a pleasant evening.'

'Now you're kidding.' She turned away. 'I showed you Wolfgang's postcard from Japan. And I found the letter that asshole Hine sent, and a photo he sent. I must have kept it. Maybe I thought it would be useful if somebody was ever looking for him. He's the sort that someone might want to find.'

'I do,' I said. 'Can I see it?'

She pointed towards the window. The sun was directly over the apartment and its dusty rays fell almost straight down onto a table. The street was busy now. I walked to the table and picked up Hine's letter. At last I was getting closer to him. It was the first time I had felt like this. The letter was still in its envelope. The postmark was 'Berlin, August 8, 1982'. Carefully I opened the flap. Inside was a coloured photograph of old Prussian war helmets and swords. I turned it over: it was written in German. 'I'll read it for you,' said Renate, although with a little hesitation. She took the card with distaste, holding it between finger and thumb. 'Dear Fräulein Schmitt,' she said. 'This is to remind you of some of the glory that was Germany. Wolfgang, your brother, died for it. Today is the anniversary. It is forty years. His sacrifice is not forgotten.'

Her voice began to shake and I took the card from her as if the action would dispose of the emotion. It did. Her face became hard. 'And *he* betrayed him,' she murmured. She handed it to me. 'Do you want to keep it?'

I thanked her and put the card, in its envelope, in my pocket. She was again hesitating about something. 'Have you got something else?' I asked looking at her quickly but without emphasis in my voice.

'You guessed,' she sighed. 'There is. I was thinking about showing you. I might just as well show you now. I've never told anyone else about it, let alone let them see. Maybe I was waiting for you. Sit down a moment, Michael.'

I dropped to the edge of a quilted chair and watched her hurry heavily from the room. She returned, carrying a creased and old brown-paper shopping bag. 'See that,' she said, tapping its side. 'Belmont fruit market. Years ago they closed it down. This is what I wanted to show you.'

She upturned the bag and onto the carpet slid thousands of dollars. She shook it and more fell out, and she looked up with a half-smile into my astonished face.

'Twenty-nine thousand, four hundred and eighteen bucks,' she said. 'I've counted it.'

I felt my mouth agape.

'Blood money,' she answered. 'I guess you could call it that, blood money.' She put her fat hand down and let the notes slide through them. 'It's all there,' she said as though I were about to check it. 'I've never touched a dime.'

'The FBI never got it,' I said.

'Those guys were deadheads,' she said. 'I was only a kid, remember, but when I realized, I snitched it right from under their noses. I took it and walked with it into Mr Huber, who lived next door. He smuggled it somewhere else. My father got it back, but he wouldn't spend it. He was too honest.'

'It's incredible,' I said.

'I know. We had a dog, Wilhelm, just a sort of small general dog. The money I put under the rug in his basket and carried it out like that, the dog as well. I told them, the Feds, that they were scaring my dog. One guy asked the dog's name, and I remember I was going to tell him "Wilhelm" and my father said: "*Bill*, it's *Bill*, the dog".' She smiled softly. 'He was really scared.'

I picked up some of the notes. They were in five, ten and hundred dollar bills. 'This is probably all right now,' I told her. 'Legal tender still. You could spend it.'

'There's no way. I've needed it, believe me, sometimes, but I wouldn't.' She began putting the notes back into the faded shopping bag. 'In fact,' she said. 'You can be my way out. You take it. Do what you like with it, Michael. Spend it, give it to the FBI and say you found it in a trashcan, or throw it into Lake Michigan. I don't care. Just take it away.'

'I'll give you a receipt,' I said putting the dollars back into the bag.

'Please, I don't want any receipt. I never saw that money in my life.'

'I understand. Can I take some photographs? I'd like to get a picture of the German marine cap and tunic.'

'Sure. But, I've been thinking about it ... not the skull, Michael, if you don't mind. Wolfgang's skull with the flags. It puts him in a bad light. And he was only a kid.'

I took the noon flight to Boston, rented a car at the airport and drove on down towards New Bedford. It was high summer and I was glad when I saw the sea. Somewhere out there were the whales. I began again regretting that I had allowed myself to be diverted from a peaceful pursuit to one which had become unsavoury and dangerous ... especially for other people. Then it struck me. Renate! Jesus, what about Renate?

Pulling the car off the road at the first gas station, I telephoned her number, which I had at least taken the precaution of noting, but there was no answer. Then I called Information.

'It's called Woofer Wonderland,' I said. 'On Lincoln Avenue, Chicago, Illinois.'

'Bow-wow,' she said.

'Somebody's life is in danger,' I told her and that stopped her fun, and she gave me the number. I rang it. An irate woman there said that Miss Schmitt had not been in to work that day, and if I contacted her to tell her Mrs Heller was very annoyed. I rang off and called Fred Robinson at the FBI.

'Did you check on the street-sweeper?' he asked.

'No, because Renate told me that they *did* sweep the streets at night. The men kept everybody awake, shouting and singing to each other.'

'This street-sweeper was silent, okay?'

'Yes . . . He was alone.'

'Call me back, Michael. Give me ten minutes.'

Grimly, slowly, I put the telephone down. I sat with a cup of coffee watching the minutes go.

When the last one had gone I called him again. The FBI switchboard said the extension was busy. I hung up and gave it another five minutes. The girl serving could see I was agitated, and asked if I would like another cup of coffee. Thanks, I said, I would. Again I called the number. This time I got him.

'Which street?' he said. 'Where she lived. What was the street and the district?'

'Bay Street, Fullerton Beach.'

'Shit,' I heard him say. 'Hold it. I've got another line open.'

He went away. Now I was very worried. I heard him repeat the information and then he came back. 'Which day?'

'Thursday. Early hours of Thursday.'

Once more I could hear him on the other telephone. He came back. 'They sweep that street Mondays, Wednesdays, Fridays,' he said, his voice dull.

'Fuck it,' I said. I felt sick. What a bloody fool.

'Sure, fuck it,' he said. 'I'll get the apartment checked right away. You got the number?'

'No, I haven't. It was on a corner. Three blocks from Lincoln.'

'Don't worry. We can get it.'

'Woofer Wonderland,' I blurted out.

'What?'

'Woofer Wonderland. I'm serious, Fred. It's where she worked. A dog parlour. They'll know the number in the street. I've got the phone number.'

'Let's have it.

'It's 876 43 234. Got it?'

'Repeat. 876 43 234. Okay.'

'I'll call you in half an hour.'

'Please.'

There was nothing for it but to drive on down the coastal road towards New Bedford. All the way I cursed myself. I felt guilty and stupid. Jesus Christ, two innocent people had died just about under my feet. And it had not occurred to me.

'She's nowhere around,' said Fred when I telephoned next. 'Nobody saw her leave but she's taken off somewhere.'

'Fred,' I breathed. 'I don't want another murder down to my account.'

'Did you see any other person in Chicago?' he asked ominously.

'Only one. A man called Beckerman, Adolf Beckerman.'

'Also known as Alfred?'

My mouth went dry again. 'Yes . . . why?'

'I've had them checking anything strange with the German community. There's a man called Beckerman died. He lived on a boat.'

'Jesus Christ . . . '

'Boat blew up. Gas cylinder they think. Sank and he never got out.'

'I've got the touch of death,' I said.

It rained as evening came over the coast, dark rain on dark roads. I leaned towards the windscreen, muttering to myself, cursing. Had the evening I spent with Renate been her last? Beckerman's death was down to me. I was in no doubt about that. And I kept seeing the dancing girl lying white on that stage, staring at me with her final question. I had been frightened before but I had always had companions then. Now I was frightened and alone. And angry. I drove on towards New Bedford. Few people were about in the wet streets. As I took the shore road to Thoughtful Creek the rain eased and eventually ceased, but the night remained dark. I stopped the car outside the front gate of the crouching house, the place where so recently I had planned to be content. Now it had the look of a threat; low and black against the thick sky. I turned down the car window, watched and listened. The only sound was the rainwater dripping off the roof and running in the gutters.

Reaching into my case I took out the gun. The only occasions I had held it were when I was sitting alone and unthreatened, rolling it over in my hands, trying to warm its cold feel. Now I was glad I had it. As I was about to leave the car, headlights began to grow, yellow in the distance behind me, on the road up which I had come.

At once I closed the door and curled myself low in the seat. The light beams intensified and melted into one. There was the frying sound of tyres on the wet road. It went by swiftly without hesitation, its rear lights vanishing around the bend in the road as it followed the creek. I waited another two minutes before I left the car, and with care opened the flimsy wooden gate which creaked. I looked both ways before going up the narrow path. My nearest neighbours were several hundred yards away on each side, and both houses were without lights. Thoughtful Creek was a place for weekends.

I moved around the outside of the house keeping tight to the walls, narrowing my eyes against the windows but looking only into interior darkness. A ghostly bird screeched out on the creek, freezing me until I realized what it was.

From the back I could see sparse lights across the dim water, but the house where the fat man had played 'As Time Goes By' was a lost shape in the bulky trees. Towards New Bedford the sky was touched by the illuminations of the town, but not much. The creek sucked around the jetty at the foot of the garden.

Returning to the front of the house, I struck my foot against an old watering can and sent it bouncing and banging along the concrete path. I stiffened against the walls, but nothing else happened, no sound from within.

Again, I waited before opening the door, letting it swing back and waiting for half a further minute before putting my shoe inside. The gun was still in my hand. It had become sticky. Within, the house felt close and damp. I switched the lights on to the main room, empty, desolate, cold in the bleak glare. Swiftly I went into all the rooms, turning on the lights, each room hollow and unused. In the kitchen some cups I had left on the draining board were mouldy. My harpoon stood in a corner.

'For Christ's sake,' I muttered. 'Come on. Come on.' I turned on the glow of the electric fire in the main room, and then moved about the place, trying to get some life, some feeling, into it. I flicked on the television. Someone was about to be knifed so I switched channels. It was a talk-show. I was grateful for the voices. After pouring myself a Scotch, I went outside again to get my bag from the car. As I did so a set of headlights turned the corner on the creekside. They swooped past without pause. Again, I dropped out of sight. It must have been the same car. That road goes nowhere.

Back in the house I locked the door behind me and

telephoned Fred Robinson at home. A passive-voiced woman answered and called him to the phone.

'Not a thing,' he said when he knew it was me. 'So far not a thing.'

'Fred,' I said. 'I'm at New Bedford, at the house. I'm just shit-scared they may have done something to Renate.'

'No reports,' he repeated. He sounded as if he wanted to get off the phone. I felt irritated. 'Okay,' I said. 'I'll call you tomorrow morning at the FBI.'

'Call me here,' he said flatly. 'I'm taking a couple of days off. To cement my marriage.'

'Oh, I see. Sorry I called.'

'It's no trouble. The cement ain't dry yet.'

I put the phone down. It was difficult to consider other people's lives. I got myself another Scotch which I drank quickly. There were some cans of food in the cupboard and beer in the refrigerator. I warmed through some beef and mixed vegetables, and afterwards I sat half-watching the television and drank the beer. Before I went to bed I called Renate's number in Chicago again. It rang emptily.

The day had been wearying. I took my only pair of pyjamas from the case. I was not going naked to bed. The sheets felt unhealthy, dank. My eyes were drooping. Then I remembered I had left the car in the street. Cursing, I got out of bed, pushing my bare feet into my shoes and, making sure the door latch was fixed, I went out into the dripping night. There was a broken piece of moon. Curtains of mist were rising like muslin from lawns and paths. The air was thick and warm.

I eased up the garage doors. Apart from a few garden implements, it was empty. I must have looked ghostly wearing pyjamas in the mist. I clattered down the path and went to the car, turning it up the drive and into the garage. When I was pulling down the door I realized how ludicrous the situation was. If someone from Beirut, from Saigon could have seen me. The scared man of Thoughtful Creek. The notion made me smile. I went back into the house, less tentative, got into bed and switched out the light. I fell quickly asleep. Half an hour later I woke *knowing* there was someone standing outside the house.

It was a shuffle, a scrape. I lay listening, frantically trying to find the gun below the pillow. My fingers located it. I eased myself into a sitting position at the side of the bed. My skin was on edge.

Then I saw the shadow. It shifted across the latticed window. My hand clutching the gun was trembling. I felt my blood dry. Still sitting on the edge of the bed I eased myself around. The shadow was moving along the side of the house.

As though of its own mind the gun was half-way raised when I heard a sound from the front door. The handle was being turned, tried. Forcing myself steady, I rose from the bed and moved out into the living room and then into the small hall. The shadow was on the opaque glass of the door. There came a polite knock.

'Who's there?' I croaked. 'Who is it?'

'It's not trick-or-treat.' The voice was soft and amused. Madelaine's voice. Relief and embarrassment flooded me. Half-hiding the gun I reached out, turned on the lobby light and opened the door, and began laughing idiotically. She was standing on the threshold. She looked beautiful, her shape tall and the light issuing out onto her face.

'Pyjamas,' she smirked. 'You do look neat.'

'You would have looked neat with a hole in you,' I

said unsteadily. I opened the door fully and she stepped in. She was wearing slacks tucked into boots and a light jacket. Her eyes took in the gun. 'A gun as well,' she murmured. 'A gun *and* pyjamas. Are you feeling threatened, Michael?'

'Vulnerable,' I said. 'You scared the shit out of me.'

Turning, I went into the living room and turned on the lamps. She looked around. 'Thoughtful Creek,' she said. 'So this is it.'

I sat on the arm of the chair. 'Jeeze, I could have shot you, Madelaine.'

'You can kiss me if you like,' she said. 'If you put the gun down.' I did both. My relief was so overwhelming that I began to laugh again, at myself this time. She had come to sleep with me.

'I'll get us a drink,' I said taking my hands from her. 'Scotch?'

'Anything to restore your equilibrium,' she said sitting down in the armchair. She crossed her booted legs. 'What's been frightening you? I've never seen you scared, Michael. You always went off to wars with such aplomb.'

'*They* were wars,' I told her bringing the drinks back and setting the bottle with the glasses on a low table. 'Other people were there. I had company.'

She took a drink and examined me, creasing her nose, her eyes still half-amused. 'But what . . . what's with the gun? Where did you get it?'

'It's on loan from the FBI,' I told her, sitting again on the arm of the chair. I lowered my face towards her and we kissed again. 'I'm glad you're here,' I said. 'But why are you?'

'I'm here because you're here,' she replied spreading her hands. 'It's simple.' Her face was deep but soft with shadows in the cottage lights. 'I had to be at a dinner in Washington with Sam. We're spending more time there than out on the coast.'

'Susan's in California,' I said.

'Sure. She's back at school. But I have to be with Sam.'

The familiar niggle of annoyance, of envy, caught me. 'You're not with him now,' I pointed out. She reached out with her left hand and slid it into into as I faced her. I could feel the sharpness of her rings and nails and the richness of her skin. 'I'm certainly not,' she said.

'Sorry,' I said.

'That's okay. I kind of like you being a touch jealous.' We both smiled. 'Sam had to go down to Charleston for some duty function. So that let me out. I said I would go to New York and do some shopping, take in a show. We're meeting there on Thursday to fly back to Los Angeles.'

'Busy, busy,' I said keeping the words friendly. 'But New York is New York, this is Thoughtful Creek. I'm flattered. Who told you I was here, Brant Irving?'

'He did. I called him and asked how you were getting on with the business. He said you were coming here for a few days but he didn't say you had a gun or why . . . '

'He didn't know. I can't call him every time something happens.' As I said it, I leaned towards her and pressed my face to her neck. 'It's wonderful that you're here,' I said.

'I think you'd have preferred a cop,' she answered still puzzled. 'What *has* happened to you?'

Seriously I regarded her. 'There's no reason why you shouldn't know,' I said. 'But this Pastorius . . . Hine business is getting nasty. People have died.'

The drink was halfway to her lips. It stopped there and her eyes came up to my face. 'Died?' she said.

'Murdered,' I answered. 'I'm bloody edgy, I can tell you, Madelaine. The bastards put a raven in my room.'

Then she burst out laughing. 'Michael . . . are you going mad? A raven? What's a raven got . . . '

'I believe Herbert Keenor was murdered,' I told her flatly.

Her face went solid. 'Don't *ever* say that. Never say it, Mike. It was an accident.'

'I *know*, I *know*. All right, Madelaine. But, as well, there was a girl shot dead in Washington. In front of my fucking eyes. A go-go dancer. And it was meant for me. Then a man called Beckerman died when his boat blew up. The old girl in the motel was burned to death and a woman called Renate Schmitt, sister of one of those spies, has gone missing . . . '

She half got to her feet then sat down again. Her eyes were alarmed. 'Mike, do you mean this? Do you know what you're saying?'

'Perfectly. We've unlocked a nasty can of worms here, take it from me. The whole business is absolutely crazy. That's why I was scared. God, I nearly shot you.'

Hurriedly she began to kiss me again. 'Mike . . . oh . . . if it's true . . . '

'It's true,' I told her. 'Even I don't make up stories like this.'

It was strange sleeping with her all night again, cleaning our teeth, turning on the late-night radio, seeing her taking her clothes off and brushing her hair. At two-thirty I got up and went to the lavatory. She stirred and I knew she was awake.

'You still go to the bathroom at exactly the same time,' she observed sleepily. She rolled over to see the bedside clock.

'Old habits,' I said climbing in beside her.

She touched me and I could sense her smile. Outside the curtained window the night had now settled, the rain gone, the moon unencumbered. Her fingers folded around me.

Gently she tugged, guiding my stem between her sleepy breasts. Lazily I climbed on her like a tired horseman. I could feel her tongue on my skin. She engulfed me but with difficulty I eased myself from her.

'I do so fucking well enjoy you,' she whispered.

She took me again and slid me between her legs. I felt myself go softly, fittingly, into her. A pendant of sweat trickled between her breasts. I nudged it with my chin. The clock had reached two fifty-five and the moon had set before we lay away from each other.

'It gets better,' I said.

'Think of all the times we've missed,' she observed quietly. 'Thousands.'

'You regret it? Our parting?'

'No. Just the times we missed,' she said. 'We could never have stayed together, Mike.'

While we lay we talked of Susan, our daughter, and some of the old times and the people we had known and what had happened to them. She had been laughing at some memory. Then she stopped and turned nearer, and after we had breathed close against each other for some time she said: 'You were shit-scared when I got here tonight.'

'Fairly shit-scared,' I admitted. 'Some unpleasant things have happened.'

'The raven,' she said wonderingly. 'I can't believe somebody put a raven in your hotel room.'

'It's to do with a rhyme,' I told her. 'An old German nursery rhyme. The American Nazis used it as a kind of allegory. It begins: "Reiter, reiter ..." and goes on about a raven attacking a man.'

'Writer, writer,' she misunderstood. 'That's very strange.'

'It sounds made for me,' I agreed. 'But it means a man on a horse. Rider, rider.'

'I get it.' She shifted against me. 'And it's all because of this Pastorius business. Like some kind of time warp.'

'Old and rotten,' I agreed, thinking what Robinson had said. 'And nasty smells are coming from it. They care enough about it to kill. I don't know why they haven't killed me yet. I'm sure that poor kid in Washington, the dancer, got in the way of my bullet. The others are people who've been ... well, eliminated along the way.'

I had not told her in detail about the go-go girl nor Beckerman nor Renate. Now, as we lay beside each other, I did so.

When I came to describing my encounter with Renate, Madelaine raised herself on her elbow, her dark breasts lolling towards me, and said: 'You saw the guy's Nazi uniform?'

'You haven't heard anything yet,' I said. 'Or seen anything.' Rolling from the bed I went to my case. I took out the old shopping bag full of dollars given to me by Renate. I switched on the bedside light at her back. She sat up and I opened the bag in front of her.

'Twenty-nine thousand, four hundred and eighteen dollars, circa nineteen forty-two,' I said. 'Courtesy of Adolf Hitler.'

'Jesus Christ,' she whispered in a stunned way. 'You have been busy.'

She said she had to leave by ten the next morning. Everywhere was still and sunlit, and I was sorry that she was going. I was falling in love with her, probably for the first time.

'I rented this car at Providence,' she said as I went out into the street with her. Nobody was about. An osprey flew in from the sea, low over the ordinary housetops. 'I left mine there,' she added. 'It might be conspicuous.'

We kissed. 'Take it easy,' I said. 'If you have an accident it's going to need some explaining.'

'I've got all day to drive,' she said. She was thoughtful. 'Bye, Mike . . . and Michael . . . take care.'

'It's other people need to take care,' I said. Then, suddenly realizing, I feared for her also. 'You too,' I said.

'Don't worry. Nobody knows.' She smiled, still thoughtfully. 'But Michael . . .'

'Yes.'

'Don't go falling in love.'

'With you?'

'Don't do it. There's no future in it, darling.'

She started the car and drove off down the bright street with its sharp sunlight and sharp shadows. I went through the house and out into the patch of garden at the back. The creek was green and flush. Trees stood unmoving as the pale houses they screened. From the jetty you could see the white causeway bridge that took the road over the inlet towards the town. I saw her car going that way. My mind was filled with uncertainty and my heart with regret. My desire to stay there for a few days was gone. Turning away from the peaceful water, I went into the house, repacked my bag and left. I drove to Boston, put Hitler's money in a safe deposit at the Bank of America, and caught the evening British Airways flight to London. Perhaps I was hurrying towards something. Perhaps I was running away.

XII

At seven in the morning grey-green fields appeared. Rivers uncoiled below the wing, glinting fitfully; towns like spiders' webs; a motorway like a machine belt; the squares, crescents and parks of London, the dull Thames, and the drop into Heathrow. I was home.

Home, but I had nowhere to go. Standing in a small drizzle outside the terminal, I was unsure where to direct the taxi. My flat now had a new tenant and I could scarcely expect an estranged wife to welcome me at that early hour or, for that matter, at all. In the end I told the driver to take me to the Montgomery, which I had sometimes used as a professional rendezvous. It was strange going to rent a room in your own city.

The taxi driver asked if I had been away long and told me that the weather had changed only that morning. We discussed the cricket season, his wife's back pains and his holiday in Yugoslavia.

At the Montgomery the hall porter, Basset, recognized me and said: 'Good morning, Mr Findlater, sir,' as if I had been there only the previous day. He had been of service to me in the past. He was once a soldier and his stance was straight; he had a measuring eye and a tight moustache.

They had a duplex suite with lofty Regency windows and a spiral staircase climbing from the sitting room to the bedroom. I had dozed on the plane. Now I took a bath and then dropped off to sleep on the bed. It was twelve-thirty when I woke.

There was a pub I used to frequent off Wigmore Street, and I went there and had two pints of bitter and steak and kidney pie. In this place nothing ever altered. Returning from some overseas war, I had always made a point of making for this bar, a reassurance that some things were safe and unchanging.

In Regent Street I bought a suit, a casual jacket and two pairs of trousers, some shirts and underwear. I had a haircut. The barber told me about his two greyhounds. Then I went out into the jammed but unhooting traffic, the pondering red buses, the tourists and the everyday Londoners. The summer sun came out. I bought an *Evening Standard* from a man shouting 'Drama tonight! Drama!' A company in the City had been accused of impropriety and England were taking quick wickets at Nottingham.

From the hotel I telephoned my wife. She was as cool as I imagined she would be. She said she was well, and she hoped I was also. Had I returned to London for good? Had I finished with the whales? I said I was only on a brief visit and she sounded pleased. She probably had somebody else by now, although she had said that after me she was not interested. We arranged to have a drink the following evening at the American Bar in The Savoy. 'We ought to fix a divorce date,' she said.

There had been the annual game of all-change-places at the paper. People had been moved up, down, sideways and out. Andrew Simmons, who had been head of features in my last days, was now occupying the news editor's desk.

'Roll on redundancy,' he sighed on the telephone.

'How I envy you, Mike, getting out like that. How is the whale book coming?'

'Slowly,' I replied truthfully.

'I'd love to do something slowly,' he said sincerely. 'I'm never going to write another word, pick up another telephone nor read another bleeding newspaper once I get out of here.'

I asked if he could arrange for me to spend an hour or two in the cuttings library. 'Whaling treaties,' I lied.

'Sure, any time.' He picked out the weakness in the story. 'You didn't come across the Atlantic to check up on whaling treaties, did you?'

'No. I have to talk to Alice about our divorce.'

'Oh yes. I remember now. Sorry about that.'

'Whales and women don't mix,' I said.

'Sometimes I think men and women don't mix,' he added.

After I had put the phone down I took out my old contacts book. It had been mine, added to, amended, encoded, decoded, for twenty years. Many of the numbers were history now; I would never need them again. Scribbled between 'Society of Asian Missions' and 'Suzanne', whoever she might have been, I found Dennis Sheldon. He had moved but they gave me his new number. He was old now; he had not been everybody's cup of tea when he was young. But we had travelled, caroused together, shared confidences and contacts, although our newspapers were in direct rivalry, and he always swore that I had saved his life during the Six Day War, although I don't remember the incident because we were both drunk. He was unique in that he was a journalist who had been in the intelligence service. Dennis Sheldon knew a lot of things and he had a long memory. At one time, when he was home, he lunched often at a corner table at the Sonning Hotel in Victoria. 'Mike,' he said on the telephone. 'It will be like old times. I could do with some of the old times.'

One of those grand but subdued hotels, the Sonning is unostentatious among old London streets. I was early. The barman said he had not seen Sheldon for many months.

'Still come here almost every day,' breathed Sheldon as we settled at the corner table. 'Just about worn this bloody table out. And how is the placid life suiting you, old boy?'

He looked a little threadbare but better than the last time I saw him because then he was in hospital in Addis Ababa with dysentery. 'Going through the motions,' he laughed when I mentioned it. His shirt collar was frayed; the neck that poked from it was tortoise thin. He had grey hair and grey eyes.

I said: 'I've been sidetracked, Dennis.'

'Aren't we always,' he nodded, arranging his smoked salmon in a pattern. He had another glass of Chablis. 'They're different these days, journalists, you know. Fretting about their fucking mortgages. You and I would have got out of our own coffins to report the funeral.'

I had never appreciated before how much older he was than me. In Beirut I remember how he ran with the best. And he had always had young wives or fiancées. 'What was the sidetrack?' he asked.

My reasons would have to be lies. 'To tell the truth,' I said, 'it's a bit lost in the mists, but ABC television came to me with the idea, so I thought I'd give it a go.'

'For money,' he grunted. 'You always were one for money, Michael. I never knew anybody – anybody – concoct his expenses like you.' He began to laugh. 'I remember when you charged for dinner with a dead man.'

'Ever hear of somebody called Peter Karl Hine?' I said. 'A spy.'

'Not off-hand. Mind, I sometimes suspect there are more spies in the world than non-spies. Well . . . *were*. All this lovey-dovey mush with the Russians has ruined the trade, old boy. Christ, there's no bugger left to *spy on*. No traps, no treachery, not even a decent exchange of captured agents. All the fucking fun's gone.'

'Hine was a German spy.'

'Oh, *German*. Way back.'

'June, nineteen forty-two,' I said. 'He was one of eight Nazis landed in America.'

He recognized it. 'The Pastorius business,' he nodded. 'I was there, in Washington, at the time. Hoover fouled it up and still came out smelling of tulips. Hine . . . yes, I do remember.'

'They want me to write a documentary about it,' I lied. 'And I'm trying to trace Hine. He was still alive a couple of years ago, according to the FBI.'

'They wouldn't know,' he growled, his grey eyes almost submerged in his wrinkles. 'Hine got off, didn't he? And another man. Hine shopped the rest . . . and they went to the chair. Nasty bit of work. I remember waiting outside the Washington DC Penitentiary on the day they were executed, and the army trucks drove out of the gate. We guessed they contained the bodies and we tried to go after them, but the cops stopped us. There was some yarn about the spies being buried inside the prison but I never swallowed that. Why did they need all the trucks?' His head had dropped lower over his brandy as he remembered. Abruptly he realized how close to the table he had sunk, and he quickly jerked his face up.

'How you going to find him?' he inquired. He took another drink.

'I'm going to Berlin,' I told him. 'That was where he was last reported. I don't want to make too much dust because it's all confidential. I'd go and poke around in the Springer group files, but they'd suss me. They'd have it in print in no time.'

'They wouldn't miss a trick like that,' he agreed. 'They've got their new newspaper office built almost on the Berlin Wall, all windows shining like truth.' He paused and looked deeply into the brandy. 'You think I can help,' he said.

'You still have contacts?' I asked.

'In Intelligence? Bloody old contacts,' he answered. 'They might come up with something. They tend to remember the ancient stories. They all live in the past, thirty, forty, fifty years ago even. Some of them even write dreary books.'

We walked out into the mild London streets and he promised he would see what he could dig up. We shook hands. I had enjoyed the lunch. He boarded a taxi and I waited for another. After a minute his taxi returned and Sheldon leaned, grey and anxious, from the window. 'Ah, you're still here. Good. What was the bloke's name again? Forgotten it already.'

'Hine,' I told him. 'Peter Karl.'

'I'd better write it down,' he said.

'Think of brandy,' I said.

'I often do,' he laughed.

I stood in the American Bar at The Savoy feeling uneasy about meeting my wife again. It was hard to forget her readiness, her stand-back-and-watch attitude when I left, walked out of the door and closed it on our marriage. I had been unprepared for such acquiescence.

She walked into the bar. I was shocked at th change in her in a few weeks. Everything about her was thin, her body, her arms poking from the unflattering green dress, her hair, her face and the look in her eyes. I thought she also had a cold.

Alice ordered vodka. Women frequently alter their drinks with their marriages. She had always liked Campari. She was fine, she said. Last week she had quit her job and was just waiting to go with some friends to Juan les Pins.

After I had told her the covering story about my activities in America, there seemed little to add. We idled awkwardly. We estimated how long it would be before we could have a divorce, and then began looking around at other people in the bar.

Abruptly, she asked me where we were going to dinner. I had not said anything about going to dinner. 'Where would you like to go?' I asked. She said she had come to like a restaurant in Covent Garden. She had been there with friends. Her eyes came up as if challenging me to ask about these friends, but I did not ask. As we were approaching the revolving door of the Savoy I touched her elbow. It felt like the elbow of an old woman.

In the restaurant after some wine she all at once began to tell me what was wrong with her. 'After you went, Michael, I didn't know what to do,' she said. 'I wasn't aghast, or anything, I wasn't even all that sorry, but I was lost. God knows, you were away enough during what passed for our marriage and you were not the only one who was unfaithful either, but it was only to pass the time. I always knew being without you was *temporary*, that you were somewhere on earth and you'd be back sometime. I wasn't moping, I was lost. It was just the lack of arrangements.' Her thin face looked fully into mine. 'Although I'm not saying it didn't hurt that you'd pissed off to a lot of whales,' she said with a comic sadness. 'Another woman might have been understandable.'

Her veined hand was on the tablecloth and I patted it, but she withdrew it as if she preferred me not to touch her. 'I started going out with the boss. Well not so much *out* – he was afraid we'd be seen – it was more like going *in*. We used to go back to the office at night and go to the flat on the top floor. McAllister's his name. Everyone called him B.A.L. Even me, his lover.'

'I remember the name.'

She shrugged. 'That's about all I remember now,' she said. 'It's just like it was years ago. And all he ever really cared about was work. He was such a bloody fanatic that after we'd been to bed he'd get me down to the office and start on some project or other. And I was exhausted. You know how I am after sex.'

I smiled at her hurt. 'You have to sleep.'

'You remember that?' she said.

'I remember it,' I said.

A silent sadness came over us. Two people who had never loved each other and now regretted it. We had picked a quiet night, although the place looked as if it had its moments. The ceiling was low and customers had drawn cartoons and comments on it. 'When I was a little girl,' Alice said suddenly, pushing her dessert around the plate as a child might, 'I never minded being sent to bed for misbehaving because I could be *private* there. I *liked* being private. You were the first person that ever made me want to share anything. You were the first one who ever got me *out* of bed.'

I felt myself beginning to grin. 'That sounds like a

back-handed compliment,' I said. 'You never told me that.'

'I imagined you might discover it for yourself. Anyway it's too late now. Didn't somebody, some poet, say that the worst two words in the language are "too late"?' She took a figured metal box, like an old-fashioned vinaigrette, from her handbag and poured a portion of cocaine, like a miniature pile of lime, on the edge of her hand, behind the thumb, and without a glance anywhere, at me or anyone else in the place, snorted it up her nostril.

'Your new hobby?' I suggested. Now I knew why she looked as if she had a cold.

'Fairly new,' she answered. 'It's the company I keep.' She put her hands to her face. Her fingers touched her forehead lightly. 'Everything's gone. You and everything. There's no arrangements,' she repeated.

'We never had many arrangements,' I told her, touching her hand again. This time she did not withdraw it. 'For some reason I thought it didn't matter. We were so casual, no kids. I thought that nobody would be hurt.'

'It *didn't* matter then,' she said bluntly. 'Or it didn't seem to. It's only now that it does. You were a bastard just going off like that for a load of shitty whales.'

She was so bitter I could not smile. Then she said: 'Anyway, now I'm broke. Stoney. I can't get a job. The advertising world is small, God knows and certainly I do. But since the B.A.L. McAllister business it's been bloody minuscule. I simply don't know what to do next. Except now I want to go home. Will you take me? You know where it is. Camden Town.'

It was very strange going back there. In the summer dark we walked down the unchanged street. The same man who exercised three dogs of varied sizes every even ing came down our pavement and wished us 'Good-night' before encouraging the dogs towards a mound of builder's sand. There was always a mound of builder's sand somewhere in the street. Sand and skips.

I said to Alice: 'It doesn't change much.'

'No,' she replied as she took out the door key. 'Not out-wardly.'

Inside the narrow Georgian house it smelled dry but musty, as if it had trapped the warmth of the July day. Tentatively I reached for the switch and turned on the lights. Everything was as I remembered it except for a new plant standing in the hall and a new tape deck in one corner of the living room. Without thinking about it I sat in my usual chair. Briefly she stared at me sitting there, but all she said was: 'I'll get you a drink.'

'Thanks. Scotch if you've got it.'

'Water and one cube of ice,' she recited as she went to the cabinet. Her head bent and I realized she was crying. Rising, I went across the room and tried to put my arms around her, but she struggled them away. 'I don't want your arms, Michael,' she snivelled. 'It's all gone, like I said. There's no getting it back. I'm not at all sure I ever loved you – but I certainly don't now. I'm crying for myself.'

Backing off I said I thought I ought to go but she was at once conciliatory. 'No, stay for a drink,' she said wiping her eyes with the back of her thin hand. 'Please.' Her legs looked like sticks. 'There are letters for you anyway. They've been piling up. I meant to send them on.' She handed the Scotch to me and poured one for herself. Then she walked out of the room. Sadly, I looked around. In the old days I had always been glad to come back there. It was all I had. There had been a picture of our wedding at Caxton Hall with all the Fleet Street people posed around us. It was no longer there.

She returned with a bundle of letters and packages which she put in a supermarket bag.

'Cocaine,' said Alice, 'sometimes make me laugh. Either I laugh or I cry. Usually though it just makes me sneeze.' She sneezed. 'And afterwards it makes me tired.'

'You're tired now, I can see,' I said. The Scotch I emptied with a single tip of the glass. 'I'll be on my way.'

She had sat in her chair, the thin knees poking out like stems. There was a closed look on her face; blank, as if I had already gone. Then she said: 'There's another package. It just arrived.'

With some effort, it seemed, she stood. The sooner I went the better. She left and returned with a brown envelope. 'Since when have you worked for Reuter?' she asked casually, looking at the address.

'Never,' I answered.

'It says Michael Findlater and in brackets "Reuter",' she mentioned. She held out the package and I took it from her. My breath seemed to choke within me.

'It's Reiter,' I muttered. 'It means "rider" in German.'

She laughed bleakly. 'I don't care,' she said. She poured herself a whole tumbler of Scotch as she said it, and drank most of it at once. I did not answer. I just said: 'I'll be going. Thanks.'

'For everything,' Alice finished. She did an unsteady curtsey. Carrying the packet I went out into the lobby. 'You forgot the others,' she said, going back and picking up the shopping bag.

I turned and kissed her, first on the skinny cheek and then on the lips, a forlorn kiss. She was going to cry again. I took one step away and we both said 'Goodnight' as she closed the door, as softly as she had done on the day I had left our house for good.

Walking only as far as the nearest street lamp I opened the packet, tearing it apart. From it slid four photographs: one of a bright, laughing blonde, Mimi the go-go girl, then a picture cut from a newspaper: 'Owner dies in Motel Fire'. My hands were shaking. I knew what the other pictures were, a grubby old snapshot, Adolf Beckerman, squatting on the deck of his boat. Then the fat face of Renate Schmitt staring into the camera. God, I felt sick. My hands shook so much I dropped the pictures onto the pavement and it was only when I was picking them up that I saw that each had on its reverse the drawing of a black bird, the raven.

I looked back towards Alice's house just as the light went on in the upper window. Christ! Alice! It was only a few yards but I ran. I took three paces to get up the front path. I rang the bell.

The first floor curtains were pulled apart and I could see her outlined against the light, like a target. She pushed up the sash. Her head, the dank blonde hair hanging out, was projected and a hand with a full glass.

'What is it?' she inquired, her voice slurring. 'You're not sleeping with me, Mike Findlater, get that straight. I've finished sleeping with you.'

Softly I called to her: 'Alice, please open the door. It's important. Very important.'

I could see she believed me. 'Oh, all right,' she called down. 'But keep out of our . . . my . . . bed, that's all.'

She went from the window and through the opaque glass of the door, her shape grew as she stumbled down the stairs. She had trouble opening the locks. Anxiously I looked up and down the street.

At first she opened the door halfway. 'Why are you

looking so worried?' she demanded. She still carried the glass and now she drank its contents at a swallow, wiping her mouth with the back of her hand. 'People around here sleep like pigs, you know that. You're not waking anybody.'

'It's not the neighbours I'm worried about.' I stepped forward as she opened the door to let me in. 'What's going on?' she inquired drunkenly. 'You're not sleeping . . . you're simply not.'

Pushing her gently into the living room I sat her in a chair. I took the glass from her and put it on a side table but she picked it up again at once and took another defiant gulp. I leaned forward and held both her hands. 'Listen Alice . . . are you listening?'

'I'm listening,' she assured me, attempting to focus her eyes.

'Listen. Tomorrow . . . well, today now . . . first thing in the morning, I want you to go off to your friends at Juan les Pins.'

'Love to,' she agreed simply. 'But I haven't got the money. Not a bean, darling.'

'I'll see to that,' I told her firmly. 'I'll get your air ticket and I'll make sure you're all right for cash.'

A new expression lit her. 'Darling!' she exclaimed. She leaned her drunken face forward and I kissed her extended lips. Her eyelids lifted untrustingly. 'You'd do that for me?'

'I will. First flight tomorrow. I want you to go – and don't tell anybody where you're going.'

'I won't,' she promised. Then like an only child: 'I haven't got anybody to tell.'

'Good,' I said. 'Believe me, Alice, it's essential that you go. And I want to stay here tonight.'

She raised an admonishing finger. 'I told you, Michael

. . . no. You are my past existence. The past is . . . well, whatever it is. But no.'

'I'll sit down here in the chair,' I told her. 'I'll watch the television.'

Alice regarded me quizzically. 'Don't tell me *you* haven't got anybody to sleep with either,' she said. Her eyes drooped. 'Why don't you go and sleep with what's-her-name, your former Madelaine?'

She was sagging forward in the chair. I stood up and lifted her out of it. She was no weight. I could feel her ribs. 'The South of France will be good for me,' she suddenly mumbled. 'I won't die there.'

'You're not going to die anywhere,' I told her firmly. Her arms went around my neck but she seemed to be deeply asleep again. I manoeuvred her from the room. There was not sufficient space to pick her up and carry her upstairs so we stumbled up the short flight like a pair performing a slow, ascending waltz. In the bedroom she opened her eyes and wearily wagged her warning finger at me once more, but then completely collapsed. It was easy to carry her to our bed. Before I left her I took her shoes off.

Downstairs I sat uneasily in the chair for several minutes. Then I got up and looked out of the window, just as I had done at Renate's apartment in Chicago. Now it was no longer casual, but nobody was sweeping the street. The houses, the faintly luminous parked cars and the dusky trees were motionless in the summer night. I sat down by the telephone, dialled the Mont-gomery Hotel and asked to be put through to the night porter.

'Is that you, Mr Basset?'

'Mr Basset it is, sir.'

'Oh, good. This is Michael Findlater.'

'Mr Findlater, you're about early. Or is it late?'

'Both I think. I'm glad it's you on duty.'

'Week on nights, week on days. Turn and turn about, sir. What can I do for you?'

'Have you got anybody spare who could bring something to me in Camden Town?' I asked.

'Could myself, Mr Findlater. Just about on my lunch break, I am.'

I looked at my watch; it was one-thirty. I said. 'If you go to my room – one-o-one – and open the right-hand top drawer of the dressing table . . . '

'Yes sir.'

'Under some clothes you'll find a gun.'

'Yes sir.'

'There's also a box of ammunition.'

'Yes sir.'

'The gun is not loaded.'

'No sir.'

'Bring the gun and the ammunition. I'm at number ten, Bankes Road, Camden Town. Just ring the bell.'

'Yes sir. I'll be right there.'

In twenty-five minutes he was. I heard the taxi pause in the street and I was halfway down the stairs before his shadow occupied the door pane. As I opened it he handed me a table napkin which was wrapped around the gun and the box of ammunition.

'Brilliant, Mr Basset,' I said. 'Can I settle with you tomorrow?'

'Any time, sir. Ex-Royal Army Ordnance Corps, sir.'

'Thanks a million.'

He gave an abbreviated salute and returned to the taxi. I watched it go and returned upstairs. After loading the gun I sat in front of the television set, turned it on, and went to sleep.

When I woke at seven-thirty the London day was streaming through the windows. The gun was in my lap. Upstairs I heard Alice moving about. I put the gun in my pocket.

She came downstairs like a white witch. 'So you did stay,' she said suspiciously. 'I couldn't remember.

'It's all right,' I said. 'I didn't take advantage.'

'Thanks. Did I dream it or did you promise to pay for me to go to the South of France?'

'It wasn't a dream.'

She smiled and lit a cigarette. She was bare-footed, her feet like claws. 'Today?' she said.

'Now,' I confirmed. 'As soon as you can get packed.'

'I'll make some coffee,' she smiled standing up. 'I can't believe this.'

'Frankly, Alice,' I lied, 'you look as if you could do with a vacation. I'm aware that I've never given you a fiver since I went. Quite honestly I believed you when you said you could look after yourself.'

She had walked into the kitchen. 'I thought I could,' she called out. 'But look what happened.' She returned and regarded me suspiciously. 'The ticket *and* some cash?' she queried once more.

I took out my cheque book and wrote a cheque for two thousand pounds. 'I don't have the cash on me.'

She took it and almost swallowed the cigarette. 'Shit,' she said. 'Have you struck gold?'

'Not yet. But I really want you to get away. I'm going to see you get on the plane this morning.'

'I'll get it,' she said. 'Nothing's going to stop me.' The kettle was whistling in the kitchen, a nostalgic sound. It had always whistled like a boy with a tooth missing. Before she went back in there she turned and, almost wistfully, said: 'No strings?'

'No strings,' I answered.

When I returned to the hotel from the airport there was a message to ring Dennis Sheldon. He was breezy. 'We're in luck, old boy. Managed to get hold of the very chap yesterday.'

'Splendid,' I said. 'When can we meet?'

'Lunchtime,' he said as I knew he would. 'Golf Club, Fleet Street.' He was already at the bar when I got there.

'Look at these poor blighters,' he said casting his arm around the room. 'It's no trade now, Michael, all this bonking and blackmail.'

We raised our glasses to the decent old days.

His grey, red-bordered eyes, flicked about. I could see how much he missed it.

'The more things change, the more they change,' he observed moodily. 'In the old days, the paper paid for the lot. They looked after me. Fair's fair, but I've had to move from that nice little pad I had in St James. It's Battersea now. And I get out less. People move on, some get moved on. I've had a full life, been everywhere, *you* know that, Michael. Now I watch the box, EastEnders. My excitements come out of a container, like eating out of a tin.'

He scanned down the menu as if it were a news story. 'These days,' he said sorrowfully, 'lunch seems about the only damn thing there is to look forward to. Lunch and death.' The florid face had become shiny and his silver hair stuck across his forehead. He had already drained his glass. He looked down into it in a hurt fashion. We drank two more before the food arrived. 'I've got some bits and pieces,' he said, his tone dropping professionally. 'Very confidential, old boy.'

'Of course,' I agreed.

'It's an old story, this Hine business, Pastorius as they called it, there's no denying that, but the source is still operational, if you understand my meaning. So it has to be classified – between you, me and that empty wine bottle.'

I ordered another. He had devoured most of his steak and kidney pie before he returned to the subject. 'It's an interesting study, Nazis in America,' he said. He scraped around his plate. 'There were a lot of the buggers there at the start, of course, because of the German immigrants. The Bund, they called it. But the insertion of agents, spies, saboteurs, or what-have-you, was not very clever, not like the Krauts at all. Some of it was botched, most was little short of comical, including these johnnies, Hine and company.'

'Elements of farce,' I nodded.

'I'll say. How they could risk a perfectly good U-boat, in fact *two* perfectly good U-boats, counting the Florida landing, to play out this pantomime defeats me. Nor was it the first time. Two Germans were landed from a submarine up on the New England coast, Maine, in *winter*, in *winter* mark you, and *without overcoats*. Very nearly froze their balls off. A kid spotted them. Just a boy. Even he could see there was something suspicious about them. Nobody goes without a topcoat up there in January. They were picked up right away. No trouble.'

'What about Hine?' I asked. 'You mentioned you had something.'

'Well, you know all the history I take it,' said Sheldon.

'Over and over,' I said. 'It's his present whereabouts I want.'

'Could be South America, Paraguay. There's plenty of

the bastards in Paraguay, or he may well be helping Hitler stoke the fires of Hell,' said Sheldon. 'He hasn't surfaced in two years. Not that anyone has noticed. Had the bloody nerve to get a job in a US Servicemen's club, as a barman, before that. Then he was a tourist guide.'

'Hine's resourceful,' I said.

'You have to be resourceful to escape the electric chair, old boy,' Sheldon dug pensively into the Golf Club apple pie. 'But the last sighting . . . ' He took out a small, stained notebook and, opening it only minutely, peered into it. 'September 1987. Berlin. He was dabbling in antiques.' He looked up with a pleased expression. 'Is that any use to you?' He counted two fingers. 'Antiques. Berlin.'

His crumpled hand was on the table and I patted it. 'Could well be,' I said. 'Anything else?'

'Nothing,' he said. 'Puff of smoke job. There might have been some other minor details, but it was difficult, you understand, and I couldn't outstay my welcome. Security contacts can be very touchy. But it narrows it down, doesn't it.'

'It certainly does,' I said.

That afternoon I sent him a case of brandy. Hine.

There are places where you cannot go back, and a newspaper office is one of them. Yesterday is long ago and you are part of it. They are always too occupied with today.

Andrew Simmons was busy so I took the lift to the fourth floor. The library was somewhere I had always liked, a measured room of books and files, a quiet place in a noisy business in the days before journalists spent half their lives with their heads thrust into screens. The staff of the library stayed for years as if part of the books and files of cuttings, moving almost ghostly between the shelves. They knew nearly everything. The Librarian was Harry Burnett, known for his generations of maroon pullovers. He was wearing one now as he sat roundly behind his desk. I knocked on his glass partition and walked around to the open door. He lowered a cup of tea uncovering a smile of welcome.

'Whales and Whaling, Treaties, Negotiations, Abuses of, Naval Actions, United Nations Reports, wasn't it, Mr Findlater?' he recited. 'They told me you'd be up.'

In a subdued tone I said: 'Actually not, Harry. Not whales this time. I wonder if you could let me loose in your files for an hour. There's something difficult I want to check.'

'Secret is it, sir?' he said genially. 'Well, I've had Whales and Whaling and the other items taken out for you, and they're on the table by the window. But if you have to go off at a tangent, so to speak, then who knows? As long as it's not about the Proprietor.'

'Thanks Harry. It's not. I'll replace the files.'

I went to the table, overhung by a green reading lamp, at the far window. For the sake of appearances I sat rummaging through the files they had prepared for me. A girl brought me a cup of tea. She looked over my shoulder and said in a small, cockney voice, 'Whales are great.'

'Great,' I agreed. I drank the tea, then replacing the newspaper cuttings in their files, I left the table and moved sideways along the metal shelves. The section marked 'Espionage' stretched for yards. There was a comprehensive index, however, and under 'Spies: German, WWII' was an entry 'Pastorius Case. US. 1942'.

Lifting the file out, I returned to the table by the

window. Most of the cuttings were brittle and brown, flaking in the fingers. Carefully, singly, I put them on the table under the reading lamp. There was scarcely anything that I did not already know; the landings, the hunt, Hine's betrayal of his comrades, the trial, the executions. There was also an article from a British law journal discussing the legal implications of the case, a long and complicated setting out of the doubts and arguments similar to those detailed to me by Brant Irving.

At the end of the fourth tightly-printed page, after a section dealing with Hine's release in 1945, after having served only three years of a thirty-year sentence, there came a concluding paragraph which read: 'Peter Karl Hine was subsequently noted in Germany. There were several "sightings" over a number of years. He had worked as a barman in a US service club. He had been employed as a guide in West Berlin. He made no secret of his past when dealing with tourists, or previously with American service personnel. Within the last year he was reported to be dealing in antiques.'

The final line was underlined in pencil. I returned the file to its niche and thanked Harry. I rang Andrew Simmons from the library. 'He's in conference with the editor,' his secretary said. 'It's very busy today.'

'Tell him "thanks",' I said.

Harry and I shook hands. He tapped his nose with his pencil. 'Funny seeing you today, sir. We had an old friend of yours in yesterday. Wanted to check something. Dennis Sheldon.'

'I know,' I smiled

At the hotel was a telephone message which said: 'I got here. Don't know why you did it, but thanks. Alice.'

I called Fred Robinson. 'Anything on Renate?' I asked.

'Not a thing. The Chicago police department think she just took off,' he said. 'This is a whole lot of country.' I told him what had happened in London. 'We ought to have the antique dealer information in the Pastorius file,' he mumbled. 'But maybe not. Things slip through the floorboards here like they do any other place. And it's an old case. I figure the Bureau thinks it's got plenty on its hands with new cases. You're going to Berlin now, right?'

'I'm going tonight,' I said. Then: 'Fred, I was scared about what might happen to my wife, Alice that is. Somebody sent me some photographs. Mimi, Mrs Williams, Beckerman and Renate.'

'Shit. They did? There in London?'

'Here in London,' I confirmed. 'They're watching. But Alice is out of harm's way. She's gone abroad.'

He tapped a pen on the receiver. 'So far,' he said thoughtfully, 'we've had three deaths and Renate Schmitt's disappearance. The only death we've had that's directly connected to Pastorius, somebody who knew Hine, is Beckerman. Mrs Williams and Mimi, they were just bystanders. They just got in the way. They had no connection with this case.'

'It's still three dead people. Maybe four.'

'Do you want to quit?'

'Not now. I'm mad as hell, Fred. Now I want to find *them*.'

'When you're in Berlin,' he said, 'be in touch. If there's anybody there that you think might be exposed to danger I'll try to fix it for the West Berlin police to have them looked after. Who knows, maybe that way we can get our hands on one of these people and find out from which fan this shit is flying.'

'Use it as a trap,' I said.

'Something like that.'

'All right Fred,' I agreed. 'I was really shaken when I got those photographs.'

'I'll make arrangements in Berlin,' he promised. 'You've got the gun?'

'Yes. I got it through airport security at Boston. Now I have to do the same at Heathrow.'

'We can arrange clearance,' he said. 'We've done it so far.'

'Oh, I see. At Boston?'

'At Boston. What time is your Berlin flight?'

'British Airways at five this afternoon. I'll call you when I'm there . . . How's the cement at home, Fred?'

I heard him sigh. 'Still tacky,' he said.

XIII

Before I left for Berlin I telephoned Brant Irving. He knew about Beckerman and the disappearance of Renate. 'I've kept in touch with Robinson at the FBI,' he said. 'It certainly looks as if we're stirring up a nest of serpents. How do you feel about it, Michael?'

I knew what he meant. 'I've signed a contract,' I said. 'They've been trying to frighten me with that bloody raven and one thing and another – and believe me, Brant, they've succeeded. But I'm *angry* now, Brant. I'm damned-well livid. I'm going on and I'm going to turn over this pile of shit. I won't let go now, don't worry. I'm going to stuff Mister Hine and whoever he's got working for him.'

'When are you going to Berlin?'

'Almost immediately. There's a flight at five this afternoon. Robinson says that he thinks the FBI can make arrangements with the West Berlin police to have anyone protectively watched.'

'Sure,' he said. 'Good.' I thought the conversation was finishing, but then he asked: 'Have you heard from Madelaine?'

'She called me,' I replied cautiously.

'She and Sam are busy, busy. As you might guess. Sam's Mister Everywhere and she's with him. By his side. But I keep her informed of what's happening. In general. I think she should know, even if Sam shouldn't.'

'I'm sure that's right,' I said. 'She really telephoned

me about Susan. The school doesn't encourage phone calls from parents, particularly ex-parents, and anyway I feel that after not seeing Susan for so long it would be wrong to go over the top with it now.'

'That's reasonable,' he said.

'It doesn't mean that I don't want to hear about her. I feel ashamed of not bothering with her in the past. I've sent her a couple of postcards and I've written. I'd like to hear from her if I could stop still in one place for a while.'

'Mike, I'll fix something. So you can speak on the phone.'

'Thanks. I'd be grateful.'

I left London on time on British Airways and two hours later I was in a taxi driving out of Tegel Airport, West Berlin. Outside the airport was a large advertising sign. It said: 'Eternité'.

Some cities shine, some glisten, Berlin glints. It was hot and gritty that day, with the towers metallic in the sun. Across the Wall the great bulk on the top of the East Berlin Television Tower caught the rays and displayed them, curiously, as a shining evangelical cross.

It was ten in the morning. I had only been in the hotel for an hour the previous evening, when the telephone rang and it was Susan from California.

'What are you doing *there*?' she asked.

'Working,' I said, taken off-guard.

'Writing? I thought you were writing about whales.'

'I was. I'm doing this one thing, then I'm going back to Thoughtful Creek to carry on with the whales.'

'Do you think I could ever come up to Thoughtful Creek? I'd really like that.'

'Why not? In your vacation. If it's all right with your mother – and Sam.'

'Sure. I understand. We don't get a vacation until Thanksgiving, and that's not long. After that it's Christmas.'

'I'll be working up there for two years. At least.'

'It would be dreamy. I'd like to be up there with you.'

'I'd like it too,' I said sadly.

She seemed to detect my feelings because she asked brightly: 'What are you writing in Berlin?'

'It's more research than writing,' I said attempting vagueness.

'Is it something to do with what Grandfather Keenor wanted you to do?'

'How do you know about that?'

'I know, Daddy, I listen. People don't think so, but I listen. *I'd* make a good spy.'

'You mustn't mention it, Susan,' I said. 'Not to anyone. Understand? You must keep it secret.'

'I will,' she said. 'That's what a good spy does.'

Fifty-eight antique dealers are listed in the yellow pages of the West Berlin telephone directory. There are also five markets dealing in antiques, remnants and relics.

There is a flea market off the Ku'damm, some stalls piled with undisguised junk, debris, but others which deal in real antiques. There was one specializing in military mementoes, hats, buckles, badges, swords and medals. The stallholder, wearing a Luftwaffe flying jacket despite the warm day, was examining some medals held out hopefully by an old, halting man, his face engraved with war, his hands shaking.

'Soldiers,' shrugged the dealer after sending the man away. He unbuttoned the leather jacket and scratched. 'Who needs medals?'

'It's all they've got,' I said. He grunted and said: 'You want to buy?'

'Have you ever known a man in this business called Peter Karl Hine?' I said.

He shook his head at once. 'No one,' he said. His attention had already gone from me to a man poised above a tray of buckles.

'Is there anyone else here dealing in military things?' I asked.

Impatiently he nodded his head. 'Over there, next line.'

Moving through the market and the shuffling customers, I reached the next row and spotted the military stall, its wares jumbled as though left on a recent battlefield. The stallholder had never heard of Hine but she was more disposed to talk, and tried to think of someone who might have known him. I produced the photograph which Hine had sent to Renate Schmitt, the picture of German military headgear. The woman had a prolonged nose and she was already wearing spectacles. Without taking them off she put on an additional pair to examine the photograph, nodding approvingly at the items displayed. She pointed to each hat and recited its name. A man came to the stall and she showed him the photograph, putting her second set of spectacles on his nose. He nodded at the headgear and named the hats as she had done.

'Do you know *where* this is?' I asked. 'What place? What market?'

The man understood. He looked once more at the photograph and a beam of achievement crossed the stubble on his face. 'Ja,' he said triumphantly. 'Ja, ja.' He made a movement with his hands, flattening them against his face and then pushing them together outwards. He repeated the movement 'Reflektieren,' he said. 'Spiegel,' pointing at the picture.

I saw what he meant. The hats were displayed behind a small window and there was a reflection of the glass. 'Nollendorfplatz,' he said triumphantly.

His wife agreed. 'Ja, Nollendorfplatz. U-bahn.' She pointed into the distance of Berlin.

The man indicated the picture again. Just visible on the outside of the frame was a curve at each corner of the window. 'U-bahn,' he repeated and tooted like a railway train. They were enjoying the game. When I took out my map, they pointed out Nollendorfplatz, off the Kleiststrasse.

I bought from them a framed photograph of a long-ago Prussian officer heavily uniformed and girded, his expression comically threatening. We parted with handshakes.

At Nollendorfplatz there were students sitting outside a café in front of an old theatre. There was a ramp going up to what was outwardly just another U-bahn station, but at the top there was a sign 'Flohmarkt' indicating what had once been a station hall but was now lined with former railway carriages, polished and decorated, each one an antique stall.

In two minutes I was standing in the place where the picture which Hine had sent to Renate had been taken. The bevel-framed windows of the railway wagon were full of military hats and helmets. Inside was a fluffy blonde woman conversing with two tourists. They were taking a long time so I strolled around the market watching for the tourists to leave. I saw them making for the exit, carrying a wrapped sword, and returned to find the blonde was locking the door of the stall and putting up a closed notice. I made entreaties to her through the glass but she shook her head vigorously. Then I waved the framed picture I had bought at the other fleamarket. She opened the door and I said quickly and firmly: 'I am looking for a man.'

I was still holding the faded, framed photograph and she took hold of it roughly with one hand and turned it towards her. 'This man I do not know,' she said heavily.

'Not *this* man,' I corrected. 'A man called Herr Hine. Peter Karl Hine.'

'Where do you stay?' she demanded.

My heart jumped. She knew something. 'Hotel Ambassador,' I said hurriedly. 'My name is Michael Findlater.'

'I will telephone.'

With that she shut the window of the railway carriage with the finality of someone embarking on a journey. I stood staring in at her. She was sitting opening a parcel. She looked up and saw me still framed hopefully in the window. Annoyance creased her blonde face, and she stood up and waved me away, mouthing some words through the glass before briskly pulling the blind down. It said: 'Erste Klasse'. First Class.

Going back to the hotel I stayed in my room. I had lunch there and dinner. I dozed in front of the television and dreamed the blood-and-wine dream, Belfast version, but in which the roar of lions intervened. Startled, I awoke. The roars came from across the Budapester Strasse, from the Berlin Zoo.

She telephoned at ten o'clock.

'Hine I have not seen for a long time,' she said. 'But there is someone.'

'Who is that?'

'Are you to buy this information?'

'Perhaps,' I told her. 'It depends how good it is.'

'I will meet you. Tomorrow at the Strandbad Wannsee.'

'Wait a moment,' I said. I got her to spell it and I wrote it down. 'The taxi will know,' she said. 'I am there by ten-thirty. Perhaps it will be some trouble for you to know me. Recognize me. And me to know you.'

'I will wear a rose,' I said. I had seen a flower seller outside the zoo across the street. 'A red one in my lapel.'

She laughed harshly. 'This I will like to see,' she said.

Although West Berlin is distant from the sea, it has the almost unique advantage of having bathing beaches within its environs. The River Spree is enjoyed by Berliners both East and West, and the Wannsee moves inland in a broad swathe providing sand beaches and lidos for the land-bound population.

Self-consciously I walked into Strandbad Wannsee with the red rose in my hand. The area is designated for nude bathing. It was a comfortably warm morning and the naked bodies of West Berliners were stretched out on the grass and the sand.

I tried to look as if I always walked about in the nude. But as I advanced into the bathing area with my rose I was aware that my body stood out like a pale target among the browned limbs and oiled torsos all around.

'Ah so, I think I would have known you even without the rose,' she said. She looked better without clothes. In the flea market she had been hung with a shawl. Now she appeared as a sturdy woman with bronzed tureen-like breasts, a formidable but firm stomach and athletic legs. Her face was commonplace but even in daylight she had outstanding eyes.

We shook hands. I repeated my name. 'I am Gerda,' she announced. She was squatting on a collapsible canvas chair. In the changing room they had handed me a miniature towel, and I spread this on the ground.

'This is a good place to talk,' she said. She turned her powerful eyes towards me, having first cast them around the suburban beach. 'No person can hear here,' she added. 'There are many conversations in the antique business which must not be heard, you understand. Always I come here.' She cupped her large breasts in her equally large hands and rubbed them unselfconsciously. 'So, you want to know about Peter Karl Hine.'

'Do you know where he is?'

'How many Deutschmarks is this to you?'

'One thousand,' I said looking straight at her.

'Good, that is okay,' she said to my surprise. I had expected to have to bargain. Her eyes gazed down at the grass between her open thighs as if she was making a mental calculation. 'I need to buy two Russian sabres,' she said looking up. She cupped her breasts again, pushing the brown nipples disconcertingly inwards. 'I will meet you seven o'clock at the Café Einstein. In the garden. I have something for you and you will have the money – in Deutschmarks, no cheque. My bank is not co-operative.'

'Can't you tell me anything?' I said. I did not want to lose her now. 'When did you last see Hine?'

'We have company,' she said.

'Who?' I whispered. 'Where?' I tried to look secretly around.

'I will stand,' she said doing so. 'And now move to this side. Do not let them see you.'

She turned, spread her big legs and stretched her arms as though exercising. I was able to peer through the arch of her opened thighs like someone looking from the aperture of a tent. 'Two men,' she continued calmly, 'have come to this place while we have talked. They are white-skinned also. I have not seen them here before and I think I recognize most of the men who always are here.'

'I don't see them,' I whispered.

'They stand by the trash bin, you see. They stand too long. People here do not stand for a long time. And not by the trash.'

Now I could see the men. One was thin and pale, with shaggy hair. As I watched he squatted down next to the rubbish bin. The other man was squarer, putty-coloured, with hairs all over his stomach.

'Don't move, Gerda,' I said. They could not be armed, not naked, unless the gun was in the bin. I got up and as casually as I could moved back towards the changing rooms near the gate. Two muscle men in leopard-skin trunks were outside, performing press-ups, counted by a weedy attendant who sat on a chair by a pile of towels.

There were two doors to the changing room. Looking directly ahead, I went in and waited on the yellow tiled floor to see which way they would come. I did not hear them outside because of their bare feet. They came in separate doors, one each side of me. The one with the hairy stomach said: 'Herr Findlater?'

He took a step nearer and as he did I hit both men at once, a difficult technique I learned from a Cambodian postman. I caught both of them, one on the chin and the other on the nose. Both staggered and bellowed. A flower of crimson opened at the end of one man's nose. He had fallen backwards, naked, to the floor and was sitting upright pointing at me and spitting blood. He was also blocking my exit. The thin man had gone sideways against one of the cubicles but he was still on his feet. I attempted to hit him again but the thick man got up and we all tumbled in a rude, nude heap, legs, arms, torsos and testicles flying.

Crying: '*Die Schwulen! Die Schwulen!*' the tawdry attendant came in. It turned out he was disabled, and he began laying about all three of us with his crutch. '*Die Schwulen!*' he squeaked. '*Schwulen!*' The rubber stopper at the foot end of the crutch caught me, and I felt my lip split. The two muscle men, who had been pressing-up outside, now arrived and joined in. They dragged and rolled me into a lavatory cubicle, slamming the door.

'These men have got guns. *Kanons*,' I tried to shout although my split lip was spouting. '*Achtung! Kanons!*' From what I could hear from outside my two adversaries had been closeted like me and the police were on their way, so I sat on the seat and tried to stop the blood by holding the pieces of my lip together and damming the flow with lavatory paper.

The police were no help They caught hold of the three of us, each one by the hair, and bundled us, still naked, out into the sunshine and into an armoured van. Nude onlookers had gathered. One man shouted: '*Schwulen!*' I could not see Gerda. With a brief touch of humanity the attendant threw three towels in after us and these were followed by mixed deliveries of clothes. We were all permitted to put our trousers on. We were divided by several policeman, who watched us do it. Vainly I tried to collect the words to warn the police that the other two men were dangerous. My lip kept bleeding. My adversaries, bruised and bloodmarked also, scowled in silence. I began to wonder if something had gone wrong.

'You did *what?*'
   'I told you . . . '
   'I can't hear you, Mike.'

'My lip is split. It hurts to shout. This is not easy, Fred ... These two bastards came at me in the dressing room, stark naked because it's a nude bathing beach ... '

'Shit. This gets better.'

'Not for me, it doesn't. I thought I was going to be jumped. There was a fight and the attendant mistook it for a poofters' punch up ...'

'Shit.'

'Don't keep saying "Shit", Fred. This is serious. I'm at the police station. I was in handcuffs, for Chrissake.'

I could hear him laughing all the way from Washington. 'Mike, we'll sort it out. Don't worry, we'll fix it.'

'How the hell was I supposed to know who they were?'

'The FBI wouldn't sanction official protection,' he said all at once sounding official himself. 'Not in a foreign country, and I have to tread carefully with this one. But I wanted you looked after, Mike, so I got Brant Irving to make arrangements. Those guys were there to protect you.'

'I can't believe this.'

'They come from the best private detective agency in West Berlin.'

'*Now* you tell me.'

'Listen, Mike, just sit tight until somebody gets you out, okay?'

'I've got no choice, Fred.'

'We're working on it now. Brant is too ... By the way, Chicago police found a body in Lake Michigan.'

I felt myself go cold and shiver.

'Renate?' I said.

'Looks like it,' he said.

It was fortunate that Gerda lacked a sense of humour.

Sitting opposite her in the garden of the Café Einstein that evening might have been difficult with someone who had, because I had two stitches holding together the sundered parts of my lower lip, and another two below my eye. Eating and drinking were difficult. The aproned waiter studied my injuries but remained professionally set-faced. He suggested an egg and milk mixture, as a dish not a medicant, and some watered wine.

Gerda ate enthusiastically. 'It was very strange seeing you taken by the police,' she observed soberly. 'It is not good to be hurt for a mistake.'

I grunted. I was now anxious about her. But antiques is not a trusting business, and she had come prepared for trouble. Against the bar in the house two slab-faced men watched while we were sitting under the garden tree. 'They have come to look after me,' she explained. 'They will guard my body.' She paused and glanced towards the pair. 'They will see I am paid, also,' she added.

Since it was going to be businesslike, I said: 'Tell me what you know about Peter Karl Hine.'

'It is not possible to tell you where to find this man,' she warned as though anxious to see fair play. 'But maybe I can lead you towards him.'

'Try,' I told her. Long sentences I found were difficult.

'My father will tell you,' she said. 'He is here in West Berlin, but you must speak to him soon because tomorrow he must go away. He knows Hine from the time of the training camp for spies. My father was there also. And when Hine came back to Germany from the USA he met my father again and asked him for money, for help. They know themselves – each other – for years after that.'

She had already written down the address and now she handed it to me across the table. I sensed her companions, inside the large, lit room, peering out into the garden to see what was going on.

'But you must go tomorrow,' Gerda warned again. 'In the early morning. Before eleven o'clock. After, he must go away. He goes to jail.'

Helmut Fechner was all packed for prison when I arrived at his grim flat in Kreuzberg overlooking the rusting railway bridges of the *S-bahn*. The line begins in East Berlin but has been long abandoned. 'When I was a little boy,' he said looking out of his dirty windows, 'I liked to play at railways. Now I have a train set below my house – but it does not run, nothing moves, mate.'

Below his window the railway lines were tangled with weeds, and a line of decayed wagons stood under the unused bridges. 'Did my daughter, my little girl, tell you why I was going to prison?'

He spoke a strange hybrid language, German in tone and English with Cockney colloquialisms. He had, he said, worked for the British Army in Hanover.

'She just mentioned you were going,' I told him. 'How long will you be gone?'

'Two years,' he sighed. 'Which seems like a bloody long time to me. I done a deal with them, chum. I got bail and I showed them where the ikons were 'id and the arrangements was that I would only get two years. The bugger what shopped me, a Turkish bugger, got off with six months and deportation.'

'It's a long time,' I sympathized.

'*Ja, ja*' he groaned. 'I'm not looking forward to it, not one little bit.' He pointed around the dire flat. 'Mind, I won't be sorry to leave this 'ole.'

He was a meagre man, his body hung forward. His

eyes were rimmed red, his nose damp, and his mouth creased.

'Gerda talked about money,' he said. His eyes became a little hopeful. 'I'll need some for comfort when I'm inside, just believe me.'

'I gave your daughter a thousand marks,' I told him steadily. 'I'm willing to make yours a bit more. Providing what you have to tell me is good. I am writing a book.'

'About Hine.' The purse-string of his mouth pulled tighter. 'The old arse 'ole.'

He went to a cupboard high on the wall and brought out a plastic bottle and two pink, dirty plastic cups. 'Schnapps,' he said pouring a portion into each. 'There's no bloody point to keep it for Christmas now.' He lifted his. 'Cheers, mate,' he said with a dry crack of a smile. His fingers were like twigs. I told him I could not drink because of my lip. Then I took out the tape recorder and set it on the table before sitting back on a shaky chair. 'I'm used to these gadgets,' he assured me. 'The police get it all on tape. Can't write, some of them.'

Gloom settled upon him. He went lower in his seat. His lips curled as if jockeying for position on his face. 'Everything goes wrong,' he complained. 'I don't care what. Gerda, I wanted her to be a ballet dancer. Look at the size of 'er!'

'Do you know where Peter Karl Hine can be found?' I asked uncompromisingly.

'Hine? Now? These days?' He sniffed in thought. 'I got no idea, mate.' He saw my disappointment and at once thought of the money. 'But I bet in South America. There's still plenty of Nazis in Paraguay and Argentina, and he wanted to use them to get hold of some antiques they nicked from Europe. All sorts of stuff they took. One of them pinched a whole church. Everything; altar, candlesticks, the lot. Hine went down that way. Always said he would.'

'How long since you saw him?'

'Not so long. Only a year. He was here in Berlin. He was a tourist guide once, you know, and he played about.'

'Women?'

'Antiques. And women.'

'You met in the training camp near Brandenburg, didn't you?'

'That's it. We got there on the same day. With about twenty others. We'd all lived in America. I lived two years in New Jersey, before I got back to Germany. I thought this training camp would be better than the army, especially Russia. We had a good time. Hine even screwed the woman at the inn. Husband on the Russian Front, poor bastard.'

'Why didn't you go on the final mission, to America?'

'Pox,' he answered simply. 'They gave us leave before we were going off on the U-boat and we went to Paris. We were at L'Orient in France then, in Brittany, and we went to Paris and I got it. Some of the whores in Paris were giving it to our boys like hot cakes. Anyhow, I got it. You ought to 'ave seen it. Like a turnip. And they took me off the operation, court martial, the lot. Luckiest dose of clap I ever got.'

'What about Hine?'

'What was he like, you mean? Well, he was always conceited. Know-it-all. Not that he did. Once he nearly drowned us in the lake. Turned the boat right over. That place! I tell you it was funny. *Speak* American, they told us, it was orders; read *The New York Times*, the comics, *think* American again, see. We sang Yank songs marching along the roads. In Germany! They taught us about explosives. When we got to the US we were supposed to sabotage aluminium plants and that sort of place, but nobody thought we would do it. It was somebody's crazy idea. It was just a good chance for a holiday.'

He got up from the chair and went to the window to gaze out at the rusting railway yards. 'There is a lot of scrap metal there,' he sighed. 'Under my nose. I should have thought of that before now. Not ikons. I've been too artistic.'

Turning, he poured the last of the Schnapps into his grim plastic cup and said a cheerless 'cheers'. 'Here I am,' he said. 'My last time before prison and I'm talking about things that went on so long ago that don't matter.'

'It matters,' I told him.

'For your book?' he shrugged. He became businesslike. 'The money is agreed?' he said.

'It's agreed,' I assured him. I took the notes from my wallet and handed them to him. His eyes glinted with brief pleasure and his ribbed mouth relaxed. But then he said: 'In prison they'll ask where I nicked it.'

'I will tell them,' I promised. 'By the time you come out there ought to be some accrued interest.'

He brightened. 'It will give me a start,' he said. He leaned forward. 'Where was we? At L'Orient ... ach so ... but I had this pox and they took me out of the squad. Not that I was sorry about that, old man. I should cocoa! The U-boat crews, even the commanders, reckoned it was madness. To go to the coast of the US and put off these spies. Madness, rubbish. Some fool in intelligence, the *Abwehr*, dreamed it up when he was pissed.'

'Did Hine always mean to betray the others?' I asked.

'Maybe. Maybe not,' he shrugged. He upturned the

plastic bottle, but nothing came out. 'Hine would always go the way of the wind, you understand. When he came back after the war he always *said* he did, meant to shop them. It was natural. He said the US President should have given him a medal. A medal! If Hitler had won he would have wanted the Iron Cross. He was . . . what you call it? . . . a turn-coat. That's when I met him again. He was working as a barman in a US club in München when I met him again.'

He shook his head at the memory. 'Hine told everyone. Yarns, all of it, yarns. He even told them about my pox. They would all be there, American GIs, all drinking and laughing and asking him questions about how it was being a spy and so-and-so-on. It was strange, I can tell you. He stayed there a long time, but I went to work for the British Army in Hanover and I didn't see him again until I came here to Berlin five years ago.'

'What was he doing then?'

'Nothing. Like me, skint, no money. We used to stand outside the zoo by the Tiergarten and get paid to push old women around in their wheelchairs. It was a regular thing. You pushed and they saw the flowers and the trees or the fucking polar bears. One of these old women sold us some little Japanese figures, *netsuke* they call them. Nearly a hundred. For a few marks. But they were the real thing, and they made a lot of money for us and started us in the antique business, a very good business if you know about it. Hine specialized in military things, swords and guns and big hats. But then he tried to cheat somebody and lost all. Then, like I told you, he was a tourist guide. He used to tell the Americans he had been a spy in their country, but they would not believe him. Mostly not. Then he said he could do this deal in South America somewhere and get some ancient stuff. Now I think of it, he said he had a good contact in Paraguay, some bloke from the spy-training days, some *Abwehr* officer, who remembered him from then. This bloke was going to help him. That was all I heard of him.'

From the front door downstairs came a single, brisk ring of the bell. The old man grimaced and said: 'Will you answer?'

I went down the stairs and I heard him following. To my surprise his daughter Gerda was at the door with the two policemen. She ignored me but spoke sharply to the old man. With a sulky shrug, he handed over to her the money I had given him. She put it in her purse and shut it with a fierce finality. The policeman looked embarrassed and asked the old man if his name was Helmut Fechner, and when he confirmed it was, told him to go with them.

Carrying his small worn case, he obeyed. He suddenly seemed to remember I was there and turned and shook my hand, jerkily as a blind man might. 'Toodle-loo, mate,' he said.

XIV

The immediate country south-west of Berlin, in the German Democratic Republic, is spread with small lakes and rivers, many of them joined together by the Plauer Kanal. On the horizon there is a smudge of smoke from Potsdam. The old city of Brandenburg is south of the region, and Quenz Lake is a few miles beyond the city. Turning the car off the main road I drove through prim villages alongside the waterways, and then down close lanes to the lake's fringe.

The farmhouse was standing reflectively among the trees by the sunny water; it looked like Thoughtful Creek. I knew it was the same farmhouse. In the FBI files there were plans and several photographs of the house and one of a spies' football team, with the house in the background. The roof was different, replaced after the war I thought, but the layout and location were recognizable. This was the place.

A man wearing new, vivid blue overalls stood near the gate. I asked if this was Quenz farm and he appeared to have to think before he nodded. '*Ja, ja,*' he said. 'It's famous,' I ventured looking about. 'The place where they used to train the *Abwehr* agents.' I had put my German carefully together, rehearsing it in the hotel room. I wondered if he would understand.

He wiped the back of his hand across his nose and saying, '*Abwehr,*' turned and went into the yard, entering a studded door in a back wall which crashed heavily as it closed behind him. He emerged with a square woman, wearing a bright red dress and gumboots. She stood vividly beside the man in his blue overalls. 'This is the place,' she confirmed, after examining me and the car. 'But long ago. Everything was brought down in the war, you understand. There is nothing here left. People have before come to see it.'

The man was more interested in the car, a rented Moroodoo. He began to circle it, prodding the windows, tugging at the door handles and kicking the tyres in an inquiring way.

'What sort of people?' I said to the woman.

'Only tourists. Sometimes they say they had been here in the war, but I do not know.'

'You don't have a visitor's book?'

'*Nein.* This is not a hotel. Here we farm.' She was becoming impatient.

'Where is the inn?' I tried finally.

'This is in the village,' she pointed. The man had returned from his check of the car and now stood beside her.

'American,' he said nodding towards me. 'American.'

They stood together and, slightly to my surprise, firmly shook hands with me before I drove on. When I looked back through the mirror they were still at the gate, a small blot of red and a blob of blue, their faces watching me go.

Appropriately the inn was called 'Der Bär' — 'The Bear', but its sign depicted an ancient king. It was old and dry, a long tiled roof and trees like fans about it.

'He was Albert of Brandenburg,' said the woman in the bar. It was noon. There was no one else there. 'He was called Albert The Bear. He built the city, so they tell us at school.' Her English was spoken with a Birmingham accent.

'You have lived here all your life?' I asked.

'All of it,' she sighed. 'Except for time, one year, in England. I was working.'

'How long have your family been here?'

'My mother and my father, it was their house,' she said. 'Now it is mine, with my husband, but he is in hospital. The *Zehennagel* . . . what is it? . . . toenail went the wrong way.'

Locals came in who drank quickly and mostly in silence and went out. I walked in the garden. There was a bordering wall, leaning and crumbling. A tree grew through it. It had made room for itself by pushing the wall aside. In the shade of the wall and the tree were three long oak tables and benches. I took my beer and a plate of cheese and sausage, and sat at one of these. It was incised all over with initials and dates, deep and worn, some dated in the nineteen-forties. I ran my finger along the furrows and then moved to the other tables. From the open door of the inn I saw faces watching. One of them belonged to the man from the farm who wore the blue overalls. There were a lot of initials, roman numerals, probably signifying a military unit, and the dates. I took my time.

On the last table, carved in one corner, I found a group of initials with a border cut around them and the incised letters 'UDS'. It was dated 1942. At the head of the group were the initials 'PKH'. Peter Karl Hine.

'I heard that this place was the only building for miles left standing after the war,' I suggested.

'Nothing else,' she said. Her name was Ursula. I had a room for the night, we were the only people in the bar and she seemed glad of the company. 'The Russians were very complete.' She corrected herself. 'Thorough.' She was polishing glasses, the unending chore of anyone who stands the other side of a bar. In Beirut once, I saw a barman weep because the pyramid of glasses he had shined were shattered with a sweep of automatic fire from a man who strolled in. Three drinkers were killed, blood was everywhere, but the barman was crying for the lost glasses.

'Not even the stones by the church,' she continued referring to the Russians. 'The tombstones.' She pronounced it: 'tom stones'. She put a glass to her eye like a telescope. 'Nothing was left. But they did not hurt this place. They liked to drink. The officers lived here. My mother served them.'

'Your father went to fight in the war?'

'He did not return for one year. To mother he was dead. Then he walked in and sat down here, where you sit. He asked for beer and my mother, his own wife, had served it to him before she knew who he was.'

I said: 'Who carved these initials and the dates on the tables outside?'

'Also from the war,' she nodded.

'They're well preserved.'

'Ah . . . preserved? Ah, yes, I understand. They have been in a barn a long time, for years. Hans, my husband who has the toe, he brought them into the garden. Many people have been looking at them.'

'They come especially?'

'Sometimes a man will come back and it is interesting for him to find his letters made there so long ago. And his comrades.'

'There was a camp down by the lake, wasn't there? Where the farm is.'

'Ah, yes. I know that is true. My mother knew some men there in that place, training, and they came here to drink. One came back, old now, last year only. He was one of them. My mother knew him. He sent her letters.'

Carefully I asked: 'Was his name Hine? Peter Karl Hine?'

'You know him?'

'It was?'

'Yes. It was this man. Hine.'

'How long ago. Do you still have the letters?'

She looked only a little surprised. 'My mother, perhaps she will still have them. She keeps things. I can ask her.'

'She is . . . still here . . . ?'

'Ach so. She is in bed over this room.' She pointed at the beamed ceiling. 'She is always in bed now. She cannot get out.'

'Is there . . . ? Would it be possible to speak with her?'

Now she looked surprised. 'With my mother? But she is in the room, in the bed. Nobody she sees, but the television.'

Getting up and going to the bar, I leaned over confidingly: 'I am a writer, about the war. I want to find Peter Karl Hine. He has a story to tell.'

She nodded but still doubtfully. 'I knew there was something with this man. He helped the Americans, did he not? He was a brave man in America, a hero.'

'Oh, he was,' I agreed. 'That is why I would like to speak to your mother.'

'She has no English,' she said. 'And she is in the bed.'

'You could translate.'

A smile of small enthusiasm touched her plain face. 'I will tell her,' she said decisively. 'Nobody will come here now tonight. It is *kaputt*. There is a football match. All the men look at the television. It is time to shut.'

She bustled around the bar and threw the bolts on the door. Then she went to the back door and did the same. Then she said: 'One moment.' She put a fat finger to her lips and went towards the dark disappearing stairs, pausing at the foot to repeat the warning. Standing by the bar I watched her tramp heavily around the bend in the staircase. A light dimly moved as she opened a door on the unseen landing. I heard her voice through the ceiling. An extended discussion went on but eventually Ursula's substantial legs reappeared on the curve of the stairs and she plodded down.

'*Jawohl*' she said. 'It is fixed. She will talk to you. Come.'

I followed her up the stairs. She raised the latch of a dim door, it creaked open and we walked in on an old woman in a yellow bonnet, sitting up in bed, watching television.

'My mother has put on her hat for you. She likes the football,' said Ursula apologetically. 'Mutti,' she addressed the old lady.

'Hist!' hushed her mother waving a thin and deprecatory hand at us, and not taking her eyes from the screen. She had given me only the shortest of glances when I had come into the room. Now her attention had wholly returned to the soccer match.

'*Gut, gut,*' she enthused. '*Ach . . . Dummkopf!*'

Ursula motioned me nearer the bedside and we stood respectfully watching the brightly coloured action. 'What's the score?' I inquired lamely. The daughter asked and the old women responded 'Hamburg' and held up two bone-like fingers. 'Und Bayern München,' and held up one.

Her bonneted head was thrust forward towards the

screen. The goalkeeper was about to take a kick and she glanced swiftly at me during the time the ball was being placed. 'Good match?' I inquired.

'*Gut, gut,*' she agreed, returning to the picture.

We sat for another five minutes during which Bayern Munich scored. The old lady bounced in the bed and threw her nightgowned arms wide. 'Goal!' she cried. 'Goal!' Her toothless mouth opened longways, oddly like a goal itself. I nodded with restrained enthusiasm. Ursula said: 'She will not speak until it is ended.'

It was fortunately only a few more minutes before the game was over and the old woman, apparently satisfied with a draw, leaned back against her pillows and opened her arms with a yawn. Ursula was searching for something among the bedclothes and retrieved a set of false teeth which she placed in her mother's mouth. 'In case of accident she takes away her teeth,' she explained. Her mother manoeuvred the dentures around in her face and when they were settled, turned towards me in the lamplight and said: '*Ja was ist's?*'

'I must tell her,' cautioned Ursula. She turned off the sound of the television although the picture remained. Then she leaned over and spoke to the old lady.

To my relief the woman looked interested. She made a motion towards a wooden chair in the corner of the room, and I took hold of it and put it by the bedside. I sat on it looking solicitous.

Ursula said to me: 'I have explained that you want to meet Herr Hine because of a book. My mother, she says she will talk to you.'

First things first. 'Has she still got his letter?'

She asked the old lady who nodded strongly, spoke and pointed to the floor. Her daughter said: 'Later I will show you.'

'When did he come back?' I asked. 'How long ago?'

The old lady tried to calculate. She was not sure. Perhaps a year. 'But after the war he came here for three months,' Ursula said with a certain dryness. 'He stayed in this room.'

Her mother had taken on an uncertain expression. '*Ja*,' she remembered, this was the room. He came to the inn when he came back from America. He told them he was a hero.

'Does she recall when she first saw him, during the war, when he was at the training camp?'

Ursula put the question and her mother looked jovial. She clicked her bonnet from side to side as if enjoying the memory. Then she spoke at length, at one time making curious up and down cow-milking movements with her hands. The younger woman appeared embarrassed. Her reply was hesitant. 'These men from the camp, they would make jokes, not good jokes, about my mother.'

The old lady abruptly broke in with a long and agitated monologue. It was as if she had been saving it. Abruptly she began to sing, a snatch of la-la-la, and cupped her veined hand to her ear as though listening. Then she continued her story, words tumbling, often laughing, but at the end her face falling to sadness. Then she threw her hands sideways and looked first at her daughter and then at me. It was concluded.

'That was a performance,' I said to Ursula.

'She wanted to be an actress,' shrugged Ursula. 'She says she was beautiful once.'

'What did she tell us?'

Ursula seemed abruptly chastened, reluctant to translate. Her hands toyed with the edge of the bedclothes. 'It was about the wartime,' she said eventually. 'How these

243

men, this man Peter Karl Hine and the others, came to the training place. She says they were special soldiers, learning to be saboteurs. They used to march to this inn along the roads singing and she would be listening and say: "Ah, here come the spies".' The younger woman shrugged her shoulders. 'Spies who sing,' she muttered. 'How foolish.'

Her mother, her face retreated further into the bonnet until she looked as if she were peering from a hole, had leaned back against her pillows and, in between impatient glances at her daughter and myself, now concentrated on the pictures on the silent television. Something occurred there to engage her interest and she began saying '*Auf . . . auf . . .*' making small knob movements with her hands. Sulkily, Ursula turned up the sound. 'It is finished,' she said. 'We must go.'

We went from the room with the old woman now absorbed in the programme. She made no sign she saw us go although I wished her goodnight.

Downstairs Ursula went behind the bar and drew two glasses of beer from the pump. She handed one to me and then replaced her hand on the decorated china pump handle. 'This is what she was meaning,' she said quietly. 'This is where they made the jokes with her.' Without emphasis and not looking at me, she moved her thick fingers up and down the handle. 'Such jokes,' she shrugged.

'Is it possible I could see Herr Hine's letters?' I asked, keeping my tone casual.

'They are in German. They are somewhere,' she said. She moved from behind the bar and went into a panelled side room. I stood where I was but I could hear her opening a heavy drawer. Then another not so heavy. She returned holding two letters.

'This letter,' she said, 'he wrote to my mother two years ago. There were others, but I do not know where. It is written from Berlin.'

Tentatively I held out my hand for it but she did not give it to me. 'The other,' she continued, separating them, 'came here two months ago only.'

It was all I could do not to snatch it from her. 'Where is it from?' I said as quietly as I could. 'Which country?'

'Mexico,' she said. 'Some place. I have not shown this letter to my mother because he is asking for money. When he wrote before he asked for money also, and my mother sent it. She was not all the time in bed then. Now I opened this letter. I do not want him to have money.'

'May I?' I asked. Afraid that she would not show me, I held out my hand firmly. She handed the sheet to me. All I wanted, just once, was to see the address. It was disappointing: PO Box 376, Mexico City, Mexico. The signature was the same as Renate had shown me: Peter Karl Hine. The date was the previous June 23rd.

'You would like me to read it?' she asked.

'Please, would you.'

'"I love you still," it says.' I could see that it was hurting her. I thought that she might have been glad I was there, that she needed someone to tell. 'And it goes on with such things,' she said. 'I do not want to read these. Then it asks for money. As much as she can send. He wishes it for antiques. He can buy antiques, he says, and do big business. 'She gave a short snort.' And then he will send the money back to here plus twenty per cent.'

Ursula folded the letters away. 'I do not like this man,' she said. 'I believe he is my father.'

I looked at her. Her face was creased. 'Things happen,' I said inadequately.

'He came back to Germany in nineteen forty-six, when he came from America. It was then.'

Her eyes had dropped. When she looked at me again it was with a shrug. 'My mother was always a foolish woman,' she said. 'The actress. And always ... of the senses ... sensual, you say. For sex and those things. My God, but she still is. That is why she watches the footballers. She enjoys their legs.'

Before I left the following morning, I went into the garden and photographed the column of weathered initials under the letters 'UDS' on the beer table. The weather had been hot but on that morning, the sky was ponderous and the green trees stationary, waiting for the rain.

It began as I was setting out from the inn. Ursula came to the door and waved, but quite suddenly went in. The downpour was intense for the first few miles. I was thinking about 'UDS', what it might mean, and trying to allay a sneaking fear about Ursula and her mother. I was certain that no one had followed me to the inn beside the lake at Quenz. I was in East Germany where traffic is always light, and it had been a journey made on clear highways giving way to smaller roads and eventually, to tight lanes. If anyone had followed me, I would have known. But I remembered Renate. The rain stopped suddenly and I was driving north-east on shining roads. Turning through East Berlin I reached Checkpoint Charlie. The Iron Curtain here was guarded by middle-aged bespectacled ladies with pursed lips and grey, curled hair. One of them brought out an appliance like a manual carpet sweeper and pushed it below the car. It had a mirror on its top surface. I had forgotten they did that.

'Find anything?' I asked, but she did not reply.

When I reached the hotel I had lunch and then called Brant Irving in the middle of the afternoon. He was at breakfast.

'Mexico,' he said. 'When are you going, Michael?'

'I'll fly back to New York tomorrow,' I said. 'I'll go on from there.'

'You seem to be piecing it together,' he said. 'I knew you would. So did Herbert.'

'I get the feeling I'm not too far away,' I said.

'Come and see me, won't you. I'll be out on Long Island. I'm taking a break.'

I said I was going back briefly to Long Island. 'There's a few things I want to clear up in my mind.'

'They're selling the house,' he said. 'Flagstaff.'

'Selling it?' I said.

'They are. You're not surprised?'

'Not really.'

Next I called Fred Robinson. He was taking part in air raid drill so I telephoned an hour later.

'Did the bomb drop?' I asked.

'They said it did,' he sighed. 'But I didn't hear a thing. It's crazy. How can you *pretend* you've been nuked?'

'It must be hard,' I agreed. 'Hine's in Mexico.'

'You found him!'

'I hope so. He was there two months ago.'

'Do you want an operative to check down there?'

'No thank you,' I was emphatic. 'I can do it.'

'We'll keep an eye on you. I promise. Mexico's no problem.'

'Thanks. Listen, Fred, can you keep an eye on a couple for me? Mother and daughter.'

'Maybe so. If it's priority. A1 risk.'

'No private detectives, please.'

I heard him laugh. 'Jesus, no. Where are they?'

'In East Germany.'

'Beautiful. That's really beautiful.'

'I thought you'd say that.'

'Listen Mike, any hassle that's happened, happened here in the United States. Nobody over there has gotten hurt.'

'I like the word "hassle".'

'It's a general term. I know how you feel, Mike, but I don't think we can stretch things that far. How many people have you talked to in Europe, people who you think might be threatened?'

'One, my wife, I've sent into hiding.'

'Does she know anything about this case?'

'No, but I spent some time with her. It worried me, that's all.'

'So you've made arrangements. Okay. Who else?'

'A man and his daughter in Berlin. I was talking to her when those clowns turned up from the agency. She just put me on to her father, so I don't think she's in any danger. She's not close enough to it.'

'And the father?'

'He's safe. He's gone to prison.'

I heard him whistle. 'You certainly find them.'

'Then there are the two women in East Germany.'

'Where are they located?'

'At The Bear Inn at Quenz Lake.'

'You got there. You're some operator.'

'Thanks. Is there anything you can do?'

'I doubt it, Mike. East is East, man. Did anyone follow you there?'

'I don't think so.'

'Okay, well, I'll see if there's anything I can do. But I doubt it. Maybe we ought to call the KGB.'

248

'Fred, do the initials UDS mean anything to you?'

'Not a thing.'

'I thought you might have come across them in the Pastorius files.'

'Only UDS I know is the United Diaper Service. Maybe I'll be needing them soon.'

'You're having a baby?'

'I ain't. The wife is. She's been away, remember.'

As soon as I had replaced the telephone, the red message light began to blink. I picked it up again.

'Herr Findlater,' said the operator. 'There was a message for you but you were busy.'

'Yes. What's the message?'

'Will you please ring Shogghelly . . . that's SHOG . . .'

'I know, I know.'

'Right. Shogghelly at 294.231.803.'

'Sam had to come to a conference in Brussels,' she said on the telephone. 'Somebody fell ill and he had to take their place. So I figured Brussels wasn't too far from Berlin. I got the first Lufthansa flight and here I am. I said I was going shopping in Paris.'

'Christ, I wouldn't like to be married to you.'

'Well, you're not, so don't worry about it. Brant told me where you were.'

'Do you think he knows?'

'Maybe. But he won't say anything. He's not a rocker of boats. He's set to become Sam's attorney.'

'Everything fits together, doesn't it.'

She heard the cynicism but it did not worry her. 'Almost everything,' she said.

She was twenty minutes late at the Café Oberon that afternoon. 'It's going to be a brief visit,' she said.

'Even I can't spend too much time shopping in Paris.'

Around us were Berliners taking their afternoon chocolate and pastries, eating stolidly, gazing from the round tables out onto the Ku'damm traffic running below the trees. By now I was in the habit of looking around me and over both shoulders.

'Expecting somebody?' she asked. She contrived to poise her glass below the tip of her nose so that it cleared the froth on the chocolate by a centimetre.

'After what's happened in the past couple of months, I generally am.'

'In Berlin?'

'Anywhere.' I looked at her seriously. 'Renate Schmitt, the woman in Chicago, the sister of Wolfgang Schmitt, was found drowned in the lake.'

'God, that's terrible. She was the one you said you were worried about.'

'That's her. Poor woman. I've already had to smuggle Alice away . . .'

'Alice! But what is it to do with Alice?' She realized how loudly she had spoken and looked around guiltily. A heavy German couple were regarding her without expression, their loaded pastry forks hovering.

'Nothing. Nothing directly,' I said levelling my voice. 'But I'm worried about anyone . . .' I stared at her. 'You . . . even.'

Madelaine laughed nervously. 'Don't be crazy, Michael. You're becoming paranoid.'

'Maybe,' I said. 'I had a ridiculous punch-up with two men who turned out to be protecting *me* . . .'

She laughed more easily. 'I wondered what had happened to your face.'

'It's almost healed now.'

'Tell me.'

I told her and she stifled the laughter as far as she could, but more chocolate-consuming faces were turned towards us. We got up, paid the bill and left. I took her down to the zoo, and we walked around the wide, flowered paths, between pelicans, bears and chimpanzees. Two men walked by pushing two old women in wheeled chairs. The women wore identical red straw hats with wide brims.

'That's quite a trade here,' I said. We sat on a seat in the shade. Another young man approached with another old woman. 'Hine once did it.'

'Hine? You've traced him?'

'Not quite. But I know where he is, I think.'

'Where?'

'Mexico. He was there two months ago anyway.'

She regarded me with frank admiration. 'My God, Michael, you are good,' she breathed. 'How did you manage that?'

'Brilliance,' I smiled. The sun had moved sufficiently to make a veil of tree shadows on her face.

'No. How?'

'A friend of his told me. The poor chap was on his way to prison at the time.'

'It's . . . it's like . . .'

'A novel. I know. Perhaps one day I'll write it.'

'Who else have you found?'

'Two women, mother and daughter. They own an inn at Quenz Lake near Brandenburg. Ursula thinks she may be Hine's daughter.'

She put her slender hand on my chest. 'I knew you'd be terrific,' she said softly. 'I told poor Herbert. I'm glad I was right.'

I grinned at her frankly. 'What are you doing for the rest of the afternoon?' I said.

'I have to get the plane at eight. How far is your hotel?'

'Right across the street,' I pointed. 'From my bed you can hear the lions.'

At six I went in the taxi with her to Tegel Airport. I kissed her before she got out. 'Stay with the cab,' she said. 'From here on I'm alone.'

As she went into the terminal, the slim, smart back, the fine legs, going through the opening doors, I directed the driver back to the hotel.

The room key was in my pocket and I went immediately into the lift to the fifth floor. The door of my room was ajar, a chambermaid's trolley outside. As I walked along the corridor towards it, the woman suddenly emerged screaming. Her face was full of terror. She was trying to say something and cry at the same time. Her shaking finger pointed towards the room. Now I carried the gun all the time. I took it out, keeping it close to my chest, pushed the door with my foot, and went in.

Lying on the bed, wings grotesquely spread out, was a dead raven.

Its throat had been severed and its blood was smeared all over the sheets.

XV

The road out to Eastern Long Island was easy once the
dormitory settlements, Hicksville, Plainview, Islip, were
behind. Signposts, real estate offices, car lots, Hamburger
Heavens, Tire Traders, Bed Sales and ice cream parlours
drifted by. The air cleared. Pilots descending into Kennedy say the smog belt visibly begins at the Nassau
County border. Once I was driving in Suffolk County,
fields and orchards and smart houses occurred, advertising signs diminished. Sunshine warmed the reddening
trees, Old Glory rippled from enormous patriotic poles
on village greens. People looked richer. I lowered the
window of the car and felt the sun, and got a scent of the
ocean.

When I reached The Hamptons I drove directly to
Flagstaff, away from the main highway and through the
tended lanes redolent of wealthy quiet. There was a
glimpse of the autumn sea, pale and rolling up an
unpeopled beach. Seabirds sniffed the air.

As I drove towards the house, up the final gradient, I
saw that the big flag was not flying. The pole stood bare
against the sky. The house itself appeared changed,
unused and sad. There were crates on the terrace and a
pile of trash outside what had been Herbert Keenor's
study. Sitting solitary inside the cage of the tennis court,
as she had been when I last was there, was Lucette
Harvey. She was wearing white tennis clothes.

'You probably think I've gone mad,' she called when

I left the car and stood at the gate to the tennis court. She had scarcely glanced up at my approach. Now she looked around. Her face was bleak. There were rings below her eyes.

'The flag isn't flying,' I said. 'I thought it had to fly. It's in the deeds.'

'One of Herbert's stories,' she smiled. I opened the gate and walked into the court. 'He had a lot. I don't know whether it's altogether true.' Her voice was sad but firm.

'I telephoned,' I explained. 'But there was no answer.'

'Sometimes there isn't,' she said. 'In fact, more often than not.'

She picked up the tennis racquet and we began to walk together towards the house. 'You must think I'm crazy,' she repeated swinging the racquet. 'All dressed up and nowhere to play.' She looked back at the court. 'But the sun is on that bench at this time of the day.' She walked more firmly towards the house. 'The racquet is just an accessory,' she said.

I felt awkward being with her. We walked up to the dumb house. There were dead leaves on the terrace. She asked me to sit there while she brought some drinks. I sat in one of the big wicker chairs, the soft sun filtering through the pillars. Half turning, I looked through the long end window into what had been Herbert Keenor's study. There were spaces in the bookshelves like the gaps of removed teeth. Lucette returned with the drinks on a tray.

'I can't bear it,' she said. 'Seeing it all go. You would have thought this house and all it contained, the people, and everything they had, were here for ever.'

Her spoken memory seemed to embarrass her. 'Sorry,' she said. I reached and patted the back of her hand. She wore no rings at all. We sat down in the crossing shadows and she poured a scotch and water for me. She drank lime juice. Her knees were round and brown. 'We always drank lime after playing,' she said. She looked at me suddenly and earnestly. 'Did you mention that you played?' she asked.

'Tennis? Well, I used to play.' She had caught me unawares. 'I played quite regularly in Vietnam.'

'Vietnam? And I thought it was all war.' She gave a swift snort of amusement.

'War and tennis,' I told her. 'On the last day before the Viet Cong moved into Saigon, there was a club tennis tournament. Some people think that nothing will ever change.'

She was regarding me steadily. 'I know what you mean,' she said. She did not shift her eyes. 'We could play now,' she said.

It caught me unawares. 'Now? . . . play . . . well, yes, I suppose so . . . But I haven't any . . . '

'Herbert's tennis clothes will fit you,' she said eagerly. 'Truly. Shirt, shorts, even shoes. What size shoes?'

'Nine. British size,' I said helplessly.

'They should fit.' Her face became a plea. 'Please. Would you?'

I was cornered. 'Why not?' I answered. I choked over the whisky and refused another.

'Come,' she said like a girl. 'Let's go.' She rose from the wicker chair. The canework had left bars on the back of her thighs. 'I'll show you where everything is. Herbert had just bought a new racquet.'

She led me through the french window into the study and then into the room they called the Armoury. At once I glanced towards the place where the gun which had killed Herbert Keenor had been displayed. The space was vacant. She saw my look.

'What's going to happen to the guns?' I asked her.

'They'll be auctioned with the rest of the contents,' she said. Then firmly: 'Except one. I'm not letting that gun go. It's not going to be shown off as a curio.' She continued through the room. 'But nobody knows that – yet.'

In the corridor she turned right. There were no loitering servants now. Through the windows I saw that the lawn was littered with leaves. A fallen bough lay like a bone.

'In here,' she invited, opening a panelled door. She walked in and opened two drawers. 'Shirts, shorts,' she indicated. 'Shoes in the locker over there. And here . . . ' she reached up almost lovingly and took down a racquet in a leather case, '. . . it is.' Handing it to me she said: 'He had scarcely used it.'

I made a show of swinging the racquet. It was difficult to feel that this was really occurring. She left me and I slowly undressed and put on the dead man's tennis clothes. As if it were planned, everything fitted, the shorts, the monogrammed shirt, even the shoes. Hesitantly I retraced my steps out into the sunshine. Lucette was waiting by the court. When she saw me coming she quickly turned away and then pretended to adjust the net.

We played the strangest match. She was a strong player. I was rusty and she took the first four games, but then I began to improve. It was hot in the September afternoon sun. Sweat broke on my face and ran down inside Herbert's shirt. She won the first set six-three, and I won the second six-four. She ran for everything, heavy chest bouncing, legs gleaming. I realized she needed to win. She jumped and sprinted and back-pedalled. Her smash was fierce, she covered the baseline madly, she grunted like a hog as she served, she shouted when she won a point after a sweating rally. The third set went to a tie-break. My eyes were salty, my legs were stringy, my lungs heaving. She won the final point and the match with a forehand to the last corner inch of the court.

'Brilliant,' I croaked across the net, 'just . . . amazing!' I exaggerated the stagger towards her and she laughed.

'Wonderful! Thank you. Thank you.'

At the net she leaned forward and I held her hand and kissed her on her glistening cheek. She was still laughing but, in the middle of it, she collapsed in great sobbing tears. Her arms came across the tense wire to me and I involuntarily put mine around her. Grotesquely we hung onto each other out there on the court in the deserted sunshine.

'He was . . . he was *killed*!' she cried. 'He didn't do it, Mike. He didn't.'

She pushed her hands across her face like a sobbing child. Her stark eyes stared through the wet, dirty trails. 'There was a car, I saw it.' The words tumbled out. 'That night. It came up the drive without lights. I saw it, I tell you. I was in my room. It stopped and somebody got out. I heard the door open . . . After . . . the shot, I ran down . . . I found him sitting there . . . like I told you . . . but the car wasn't there. It's the truth.'

Her expression had become almost mad. 'Somebody killed Herbert Keenor,' she sobbed. 'My Herbert.'

At Zeb Smith's one-dollar house, Feenix, my former cat, was lying on the evening step. Cats easily change lives and loyalties, and he had forgotten me. His tail was fully restored. He rolled sideways and yawned.

There was a newly painted sign saying: 'Buck House' and someone had polished the brass bell hanging in the porch. I tinkled it moderately. When the door opened it revealed an old lady who was so much like Zeb, the long chin, the creased forehead, the damp grey hair, and the silvery eyes, that for one odd moment I thought I had chanced upon the old man at an inopportune moment. Even the voice, although higher pitched, had Zeb's intonation. I told her who I was.

'Zeb's in bed,' she said. 'He's due to die.'

'Oh,' I said inadequately. 'I am sorry.'

'So is he,' she shrugged. 'And me too. I left my house to come and look to him. Better come in.'

As we walked through the now-tidy room and into Zeb's bedroom she said she was his sister. Zeb was groaning in bed but he seemed to rally when he saw me. 'Come for your cat?' he asked.

'No, Zeb,' I smiled, shaking his hand as he lay. The hand was without strength and it was cold. 'I gave him to you. For keeps.'

'For keeps,' he ruminated. 'However long "keeps" is.' He looked challengingly at his sister. 'Did you tell him I'm dying?' he demanded.

'I mentioned it,' said the sister. She began to waddle towards the door saying she would get me a beer.

'That's Chloe,' sniffed Zeb. He shifted into a more upright position in the voluminous bed. 'When I got took, some busy-body called her and here she is.' He glanced slyly towards the door. 'Don't even care for her,' he whispered. 'Twins we are, but you wouldn't know it. She's gotten so old and ugly.'

Chloe returned with two beers. She handed one to me and dipped her finger in the other before handing it to Zeb. 'Don't do for him to drink too cold,' she said. Zeb grimaced and took the beer.

'She's very concerned for you,' I told Zeb when she had gone again.

He emitted a soft snarl. 'I managed all these years,' he said. 'Now, when I'm dying, she gets herself into my house.'

'What's making you die?' I asked.

'Her, mostly,' he replied. A roguish smile rolled over his worn face. 'But she don't know. I might be here longer than her. It happens, that sort of thing.' He looked at me for reassurance.

'But what's wrong?' I insisted. 'What does the doctor say?'

'Not a thing,' he complained. 'Chloe wouldn't tell. All she'd say was "You're dying".'

'We're all dying,' I pointed out.

That cheered him. 'She didn't give me no date,' he said. 'How have you been?'

'Fine,' I said. 'Travelling, playing tennis and such-like.'

'Tennis? Now that's a game I should have tried. You still interested in the spies?'

He had been holding something back. The way he looked I knew it. 'Very,' I said as unhurriedly as I could.

'It's so long ago,' he ruminated. 'Forties. World War Two.'

'Do you want to tell me anything else, Zeb?' I asked him.

He looked curiously abashed, like a little old child. 'Got something to show you,' he decided. 'Didn't mention it before because it's against the law, always was, and I didn't know you that well. But after you gave me the cat, I figured I could show you.' He attempted to fumble below the bed. 'I got it right here,' he said. 'Some . . . where.'

He located what he was seeking, a tobacco box worn to the metal, which he brought up to his lap. It had once

259

been painted yellow. 'Don't tell nobody,' he warned. 'Not till you hear I'm dead.'

He appeared as if he were about to lift the lid of the box but then he passed it solemnly to me. 'Take a look,' he said. 'Help yourself.'

The lid was firm but I lifted it. Lying inside, bedded on a pad of sere newspaper, was an aluminium bracelet, half chain, half Maltese cross. There were some words, small, across the face of the cross. They said: 'Unter den Sternen'. Under the Stars. Now I knew what UDS meant.

It rained the following morning, drifting coastal rain, loitering over roofs and among the masts of harboured boats, diminishing the colours of the town. The roads shone like an empty smile, the sky lay against the ocean.

Brant Irving was at his house. He always took a week's vacation at that time of the year, he said, when the crowds had gone. He was working on the hulls of a catamaran hauled up on his jetty. By the time I got there the rain had ceased. The trees dripped and there were remnants of mist.

'Summer,' he said, 'finishes with Labor Day. We fix that in the United States. It can't go on a day longer.' He had been scraping paint and he put down the tool to shake my hand.

'It was beautiful when I drove down yesterday,' I said.

'It's a trap.' He was wearing a blue sweatshirt and long grubby jeans. I asked after Mrs Irving.

'Mrs Irving?' he paused as if trying to recall her. 'Oh, well, she's okay, so I believe.' He looked at me with dark humour. 'We don't keep track of each other.'

'I know how it is,' I said.

'But you and Madelaine, you get on terrifically, I can see it.'

'It's a wonderful thing, divorce,' I said cautiously.

He put his hands in the pockets of his jeans. 'As a lawyer I don't believe in divorce,' he said.

We both laughed and he patted the slim hull of the catamaran. 'Cat is an old sea name, you know. Cat-boats.'

'So I believe,' I said. 'Is Dick Whittington a familiar story in America?'

'Sure, I've heard it. He was Lord Mayor of London, right?'

'Right. And he had a cat. But it wasn't a *cat* cat, with tail and fur. He was a ship-owner and his cat was a coal-boat.'

'Things get mangled with time,' he said. We moved down the jetty to where his white cruiser was moored. The rain had made it glisten. 'You think Hine's in Mexico,' he said.

'That's the latest.'

'Great. Herbert was right about you, Michael. He had an instinct for people. Want to take a trip?' He glanced around. 'We can talk some more out there.'

We climbed aboard the cruiser. The engines started with a well-fed growl. I cast off the stern mooring and we moved out into the creek, flat, faintly luminous, interspersed with grey moody mist. A heron croaked and flew off in slow and solitary motion.

Irving stood at the wheel tugging an oilskin over his shoulders. At his invitation I had picked up a thick jersey from the entrance to the cabin. 'Tell me all about it,' he said. 'Pour a couple first. This damp gets into the bones.'

The bottle was in the cabin and I brought two glasses

onto the deck. We were heading towards the open sea but still within the wide arms of the land. The boat's engine sounded deeply and the bow cut a ribbon in the glassy water. Behind us the wash spread sluggishly. On that downcast day there were no other craft in the creek. A buoy clanged like a funeral bell. He stood against the small wheel, whisky glass in one hand, looking out casually. I related with as much detail as possible the events in Chicago and in Berlin. He asked few questions, and these only to check times and places. Occasionally he shook his head and sent a low whistle into the grey air. He laughed out loud as I told him of the naked fight in the changing room in Berlin.

By the end of the narrative we had reached the out-spread entrance to the creek, so far out that the fingers of land were engulfed by mist and the sea became longer and heavier as we touched the verge of the Atlantic. 'I guess it's time to go back,' he said turning the wheel steadily. 'It doesn't look good out there.' The cruiser tilted as he changed course. One wave rolled her roughly and his whisky glass slid sideways on the shelf in front of him. He arrested it deftly and handed it to me. 'Why not have one for the way home,' he said.

He had turned the craft entirely by the time I emerged from the cabin. Before us the creek and its enclosing land were indistinct. As we journeyed back a strange thing occurred. I had not mentioned my visit to Flagstaff the day before. Now I did. It was quite casual.

'It was beautiful driving from New York yesterday,' I repeated, adding: 'I went up to the house.'

'Flagstaff?' he said at once. His tone had an edge.

'I thought I ought to take another look, since it's going to be sold.' He recovered himself as though closing a door into a rarely opened room. The boat, I could see by the wake, had heeled quite abruptly to port. He brought it strongly back on course.

'Sure. Why not?' he said. His eyes were ahead. 'There may not be too many further opportunities. Sad, eh?'

'It was. Flagstaff without the flag.'

'Most of the staff have gone,' he said.

'Lucette was up there,' I said.

The cruiser gave a sharp heave to the side, so swift I stumbled to the rail of the cockpit. 'Lucette!' he half shouted. 'Lucette Harvey! Fuck her!' He pulled the boat savagely the other way, so that I stumbled towards him. We were rolling like a snake across the indolent creek. I pulled myself upright.

'She has no right to hang around there!' His face had gone hard and pale. 'She was paid off and she left.' As if to emphasize the accusation he turned the wheel the opposite way.

'I'm sorry, Brant,' I said. 'I didn't know what the situation was. I drove up there . . . ' I held onto the rail as he brought the cruiser back, '. . . and I thought that was okay. You gave me a free hand with this. I don't want to come to you for clearance every time.'

'No, no.' He waved his hand in a conciliatory way 'No, it's not you. I apologize, Michael. That woman is out to make trouble. I'll have to make sure she doesn't go to the house again. What was she doing when you got there?'

'Sitting alone by the tennis court,' I said. He had calmed himself but the cruiser was still turning in wide swathes across the gunmetal water.

'They played tennis a lot,' he mumbled staring over the bow.

'She was all ready to play, dressed in tennis gear,' I told him.

'Lucette's crazy,' he said firmly.

'She plays tennis all right,' I said. 'I played with her.'

He started to give the wheel another tug but thought again. I could see he was holding himself with difficulty. 'She looked pretty woeful,' I went on. 'There didn't seem any harm in it.'

Irving sent the boat on another meditative zig-zag. He had cut a trail like a great whip across the creek. Filtering sunlight broke through beyond our stern somewhere and lit the furrows of the wash.

'Michael,' he said with sighing patience, 'as you know I was Herbert Keenor's attorney . . . '

I almost said: 'And you are about to become his son's attorney.'

'It's important, essential, that nothing untoward happens to Herbert's reputation. The greatest wish, ambition, object, in his life was that Sam should brilliantly succeed in politics, even get to the White House. Nothing could be – nor will be – allowed to get in the way of his progress.'

He tightened his hands on the wheel. 'This goddam woman, Lucette Harvey, could make a lot of trouble. Whether she was Herbert's mistress or not is not of importance. He had been a widower for years. But you know as I know that one lonely, depressive woman like that can do a hell of a lot of damage. She was generously paid off, over-generously in my view, and told to go away and start somewhere else. She is trespassing at that house. She had no right to . . . play tennis there. She entertains fantasies.'

'I'll say she does,' I agreed carefully. I thought I would try it. 'She told me a car went there that night. She saw it. No headlights.'

His head began to come slowly around to me. 'She said that?' he muttered.

'She did. She says Herbert Keenor was murdered.'

Brant Irving lost control of himself and the boat then. He threw the wheel sideways and cursed and shouted, bawled, incoherently, banging his fist on the woodwork. The cruiser curved madly over the deadened water.

XVI

It was still the rainy season, and it does not drizzle in Mexico City. Water rolled in rivers from the roof of the arrival terminal at Benito Juarez International Airport. Vehicles passed behind it like shadows across a window.

People were crammed under the roof of the exterior concourse, shoving and shouldering each other in an attempt both to make progress and keep dry. I pushed my way to a bar where at least the crowd was constant. A weary waiter appeared, his moustache hanging like a support to his black apron. He balanced his tray on one hand, as though about to perform some feat of magic. I ordered a beer and he rolled his tired black eyes. The humidity had defeated the air-conditioning. I had left New York in a light grey suit which was sticking to me.

A young woman appeared with a suitcase and a brown paper package which slipped and almost fell as she passed me. I attempted to catch it and knocked the arm of a man behind me, spilling his beer. He made no comment and did not even look in my direction, but brushed away the drops of beer as if they were dust.

'I'm so sorry,' she said. The parcel was caught between her legs. She retrieved it. She had pale, almost sallow skin, a bare neck, black hair tied back. I found myself looking directly into promising eyes. From her ears hung golden rings, each like a trapeze.

'How do I get out of here?' I asked her, looking around at the crowd.

She smiled and shrugged. She was quite small. 'It's not easy,' she said. 'Once you leave the plane – then the journey begins.' Her voice was American with a touch of Spanish, a curl at the end of the sentence. 'A car is coming to pick me up but I'm not going to look for it, and the driver won't come and look for me, so I guess I'm here forever too.' She laughed and nodded towards the throng. 'Mexico City has eighteen million people, you know,' she said. The waiter arrived with my beer. I asked if she would like a drink but she shook her head.

A sorry-looking man in a wet white shirt appeared through the crowd. 'Jesus Christ,' murmured the girl. 'He's found me.'

'Señorita Brown,' said the man with a bow. Water was wriggling down his forehead. 'The car is outside.'

'Like magic,' I said. She saw my look. 'Where are you heading?' she asked.

'Anywhere,' I answered. 'Away from this. I'm going to the Hotel Carlos Underwood but anywhere will do. I'd be very grateful.'

'Hotel Carlos Underwood is no problem,' she said. 'It's central.'

'Rio Misisipi,' confirmed the man. He picked up her luggage and mine.

'Thanks,' I said as we began to move through the crowd. 'I had no idea how I was going to get out of this.'

She said: 'Mexico City gets a lot of rain. But the season is almost over now.'

The driver had not been able to get a space at the kerb. He staggered out into the downpour, to a

Mercedes, with the luggage, putting it quite studiously in the boot. He then opened the rear door. 'Let's run,' she said and we made a dash, wriggling through the nearer cars, the rain bouncing from them and out into the road. We were both soaked within seconds. She laughed as we unravelled ourselves in the back seat and the dripping driver started the engine.

Her blouse was soaked and sticking to her. She tugged it away from her body. 'I should have known,' she said. 'I know this city so I should have known.'

'I'm very grateful,' I repeated. The car was nosing speculatively into the traffic. Then I said: 'I am Michael Findlater.'

'From England,' she said. She held out a slim, damp hand and I took it in mine. 'And I'm Cara Brown, of Mexico City. What are you doing here?'

'I'm a journalist,' I said. The car made an impressive bow-wave as it turned from the airport and onto the main highway. Traffic moved by in the rain.

'Boulevard Capitan Juan Sarabio,' the driver called over his shoulder.

'Boulevard Capitan Juan Sarabio,' repeated the girl with a private smile at me. 'He likes to keep us informed. Are you going to do some reports here?'

'I hope so. There's a fair amount of smuggling of antiques, ancient artefacts and so on, out of Mexico.'

'It's true,' she said. 'If you can get some of those old things out, there's big bucks in it. But if they catch you, then don't plan to get home for a few years.'

The windscreen wipers could scarcely keep pace with the rain. Traffic around us was reduced to coloured balloons. The driver leaned and peered through the glass.

'You live here now?' I asked her, thinking of her American voice. 'For a while,' she said. 'My mother is here. She and my father split up. She is Mexican, he's American. Not a good mix, I can tell you. They met at a showing of *Gone With the Wind*. They had me christened Tara but I was having none of that, so I changed it to Cara.' She tried to look through the opaque window. 'We'll be going right past the Hotel Carlos Underwood and I can drop you. How are you going to find your smugglers?'

'I've no idea,' I said. 'Do what I always do. Ask around.'

'They operate mostly out in the country,' she said. 'Near to the ancient places, Yucatan, Oaxaca, and so on. The people there have always lived with these things, these relics. Then the gringo comes along and shows them a handful of dollars and that's it. It's getting the stuff out, of course, that is the problem. Anybody can buy it. Getting it out is something else.'

'Do you know anybody who might be able to help?'

She shrugged. 'Not really *help*,' she said. 'My mother knows some people in the antique business but they're here in the city. They don't touch anything that's suspect. They cannot. The Government may not build houses or put enough drains in, but they protect the history like mad. I'll ask her.'

'Can I call your mother?' I asked carefully.

'If you like,' she laughed. 'You'd like her, Mr Findlater. But maybe I had better get the names for you.'

'Paseo de la Reforma,' chanted the driver. The rain was still solid. 'Your hotel is a few blocks,' said the girl. 'I will telephone you.'

'Thank you. That would be a great help,' I said. 'Would you like to go somewhere to dinner? It would be some way of repayment.'

'Can I bring my mother?'

'Of course,' I said. 'What does she like to eat?'

'Expensive,' she smiled.

'Rio Misisipi,' said the driver over his shoulder as we turned a further corner. 'Hotel Carlos Underwood.' I could hear the water gushing around the car. The girl tried to peer from the window. 'It is just like the Mississippi,' she said.

We attempted to shake hands in the car. It pulled up and the driver ran out to open the boot for my case. 'I'll call you,' she said again.

'I'm looking forward to it,' I said. 'And to meeting your mother.'

'If we're going to dinner,' she said, 'it will have to be tomorrow. She is afraid of the rain.'

Even the doubtful hope I held that after several months the Mexico City Post Office would retain the address of Peter Karl Hine, otherwise PO Box 376, vanished upon my first attempt.

'Ees not,' answered the clerk, a huge man, his great white shirt filling the picture-frame aperture of the counter like a sail. He lowered his body to see me. I apologized for my lack of Spanish and asked to speak to someone who might better understand my request. He took on a thoughtful look and went away, returning with another white-shirted man, so small that he might have been his little son. I repeated my request. He looked back at the first clerk who was filling the space behind him and spoke in rapid Spanish. Returning to me he also said simply: 'Ees not.'

'Ees not, what?' I asked.

'Ees not possible,' he shrugged. 'We not tell of people's names or address who have box numbers. Never or ever.'

I smiled at him and he became co-operative. 'Also,' he said, 'ees finished. No more this person. Some more person take the number.' He decided to become even more helpful. He opened a ledger and checked down the entries. 'Señor Mendoza,' he read aloud. He now appeared concerned on my behalf. The large eyes in the small face looked up. 'But ees not, not Señor Mendoza?'

'No. This person was Peter Karl Hine. Señor Hine.'

'Not this person,' he muttered, shaking his head as though blaming the ledger. 'Not same.'

'Not same,' I agreed, leaning forward speculatively, as a man might who has money to spend on bribes or gratuities. 'Do you keep the records?' I inquired. 'Maybe you still have Señor Hine's address in the records?' I decided on lying. 'He is my father . . . I have lost him.'

He looked sad but unbelieving. 'Not this place,' he said shaking his small head. He turned again to the great man still filling in the background, and inquired again in Spanish. The white shirt crinkled as he shrugged. The small man's face reappeared in the foreground. 'No records,' he said. He smiled as if he had thought of something special. 'Thrown to pigs,' he said. 'Garbage.'

When I described it, Cara said: 'There is a point, a moment, when you know, by your instinct, that money is in order – that a bribe is okay. But when it comes you *know* it, and this does not sound like it.'

The rain had finished for the day. We were in a courtyard restaurant under the trees. Through the iron gate I could see the street floating with steam as though from a geyser; water still dripped from the wall which enclosed us. The tablecloth was unspotted, however. 'They dry the trees overhead,' she explained. 'They have a machine and they dry them.'

'I am sorry your mother could not come,' I told her gravely.

'It is a pity,' she replied simply. 'You would like her.'

Cara was a musician, a violinist. 'But after five years' study my heart knew that what I had was just not good enough,' she sighed. 'I was at the Boston Conservatoire and then I went to Los Angeles. But I knew very soon that I would never be a soloist, a big name. Nobody needed to tell me. But I continued with the studies, hoping something would happen to change me. After five years I was certain that it was never going to. That's why I've come back to cry on momma's cheek . . . Now I've got to decide what to do.' Her intense eyes moved around the courtyard, and then she smiled slightly. 'Maybe I could play the gipsy fiddle in a place like this,' she said. She turned the food over on her plate. 'Are you very good at what you do, Michael?'

'Was,' I corrected. 'Too good for my own good. That's why I got out. I freelance now. It's much easier. When I was employed by a newspaper I came to realize that nobody cared a damn – the editor, the people in the office, nor the readers. I was getting too old and too wise for the business.'

When afterwards we were walking along the Paseo de la Reforma, cars and people passing, the lights gaudy and flashing, the damp pavement reflecting the colours, she said, as if the idea had abruptly occurred to her: 'Michael, would you like to hear me play the violin?'

I said: 'Yes, I would.'

'I do not play to anybody,' she said as if emphasizing that the offer had not been made easily. 'Only to my teachers and only to myself. But I am at a time when I would like some other ear to hear it, if you understand. Soon I may be working for a computer company.'

It was walking distance. Unself-consciously she took my arm and I felt the pleasure of the familiarity. She guided me off the main road at a big circus with Christopher Columbus looking out over the traffic. 'Perhaps, I think,' she smiled, 'Columbus is still wondering what he has discovered.'

The street where we walked was enclosed; the traffic noise all at once diminished. 'This,' she said, her voice hardly above a whisper, but not secretively. 'Here.' She opened a studded door leading into a small courtyard. A single tree dripped onto a metal table as regularly as a metronome. 'Here I do not dry the trees,' she said.

She began to unlock another studded door in a lofty white wall. 'My mother is in a different part of the house,' she said, as if I had asked the question. 'She sleeps well. If she hears me playing she will only smile and go back to her dreams.'

We entered into a hallway where the air was tepid. She touched a switch and a gentle light filled it. On one wall was a fine gilt mirror. Cara turned towards it and touched her hair. The lamplight made her face look almost elfin, her eyes even larger than before. 'Can you think of them giving me the name of Tara,' she giggled, regarding herself once more. 'Tara was not even a person, nor the house of *Gone With the Wind*. It was the fields, the land . . . the estate.'

'You do *not* look like an estate,' I told her, smiling.

'Crazy, my father especially,' she said. She walked up a brief flight of stairs and into a wide room where a single lamp was illuminating a corner, its light fanning out against two walls. '*Gone With the* goddam *Wind* was all they had in common in the end,' she shrugged, switching on two more lamps. 'If they were going to fight, I used to stop them by talking about it.' The floor was patterned with fine Mexican tiles, cool looking and warm to the touch; the furniture was modern, the cushions and drapes dramatic colours. There were two landscapes of mountain country on one wall, and a painting of a child with a violin on the other. I sat down near the window overlooking the silent street. She said she would get me a drink. 'When they had their big house north of San Diego,' she said, as she was arranging the glasses, 'they actually called the butler Rhett.' She giggled engagingly again. 'Don't you think that is amazing. His name was not Rhett, of course, but he had to take that name with the job. Rhett Butler!'

'Is this you?' I asked getting up and going to the picture of the child with the violin. The head of the girl was serious, her hair black.

'How I wish,' she sighed. She came over with two glasses containing white wine. The light shimmered through them. 'See her hands,' she said. 'They are beautiful.'

I took one glass and said: 'Your hands are also.'

'Ah, but not to the violin,' she said, adding: 'Very soon I will play for you. First I will go and see that my mother is in bed. She asks me to kiss her.'

She opened one door and I heard her opening a further door in the room beyond. It must have been a big house. I sat down with smug male anticipation, enjoying the sensation of unexpectedly being in someone else's house, an intruder, suddenly in from the outside, my eyes going around a place where a stranger lived and looking at the stranger's possessions. I looked at her books: travel, biography, *The Foundations of Music, The Bach Family, Chopin's Musical Style*, and the tapes on a deck fashioned into the bookshelves: Dire Straits, Mendelssohn, Genesis, Saint-Saëns. There was a tape already slotted into the deck. I touched the button and a violin began to play, heady as a lark, with the orchestra flowing into the theme just as she walked into the room again.

'Beethoven,' she said. She had put on a pale robe, almost colourless. She carried a violin that caught the subdued light of the room on its deep wood. She smiled and her eyes came up to me. 'The most beautiful of all.'

'Like you,' I said. I took two paces towards her. She reached up and kissed me politely and switched off the tape. 'You must hear me play,' she said. The pale hand that was not holding the violin and its bow came towards me in invitation. I put my fingers around hers. 'Follow me,' she said. 'It is here.'

If, even an hour before, I had been given a vision of the next few minutes, I would not have believed it. At her request I stretched out on her soft bed, arms behind my head, while she sat almost at the foot, her legs curled below her, and played a piece she told me was composed by Fritz Kreisler and played by him at the Manchester Town Hall in 1933.

The light gown fell away from her as her arm studiously worked the bow. Her slight face was set with peace and concentration, her body moved under the silk, her bare bent knee reflected the lamplight.

The piece had only a single movement, no more than a study. When it was finished she remained poised as a faun, listening to the last drifting note. Then she lowered the violin and turned her face entirely towards me, and with a serious smile she said: 'I am not good enough.'

'It sounded beautiful,' I said. She moved over the silken bed towards me, and kissed my shirt, my chin and my face. My hands held the breasts lolling in the shadows below the gown. She climbed on top of me. 'I am glad you like my playing,' she said. Toe to toe, her hair was under my chin. 'I loved it,' I muttered. 'I love Kreisler. Love him.'

She laughed mischievously. 'I lied to you,' she said. 'It was your own Elgar.'

'Love Elgar,' I amended. 'More than Kreisler.' She eased herself a fraction away from me so that she could look into my face with her deep eyes. 'I have taken advantage of you,' she said.

My arms went around the silken robe. 'It's perfectly all right,' I said.

Intently she undressed me, easily too, even the potentially farcical moment of pulling my trousers off. No coins fell from my pockets. I kept stroking her and kissing her. When I was naked she surveyed me, turned out the bedside light and, sliding off the gown in the dark, eased herself above me again. Then she began to talk.

Throughout the whole time of our love-making, she conversed about so many subjects, the weather, Mexican food, her parents, *Gone With the Wind*, a dog she had once had, a man who had run away with her violin. I kept muttering: 'Yes,' and 'Yes, of course,' but I realized that she was really talking to herself. Her eyes were closed and her lips moved with the discourse, but her body was taking and giving.

Several times I thought we were almost there but then she would postpone it by pausing, poised, and then embarking on another topic of conversation. She mumbled as she moved. I began to feel like an eavesdropper.

Then she opened her eyes and looked slightly surprised to see me. She stared for a moment and then smiled recognition. 'Do not wait, darling,' she said. 'I am ready now. I have stopped talking.'

'When you make love why do you have to talk?' I felt I knew her well enough to ask.

'Sometimes, at first, it is necessary for me,' she said. 'I am nervous. I get away the tension. And also so that I do not . . . not finish . . . too soon.'

'The copra prospects in Guernero state are fascinating.' I laughed at her and pulled her nose. It was afternoon and we were on her bed again.

'Anything I read in the newspapers is good enough,' she said. 'It is just a conversation with myself.' She continued to regard me with engrossing seriousness. 'It is not necessary for you to listen,' she said.

'Hearing the commodities market from you,' I said, 'is always worthwhile.'

'I can hum,' she suggested. 'Now that we know each other I can hum instead. I hum well. Next time I will show you.' She continued to regard me gravely, almost examining me. 'You are a good man,' she said.

'Thanks. No one can say anything better.'

'There is some news you may like to hear.'

'What is that?'

'There is an exhibition. At the Museo de la Ciudad de Mexico. It is not far from here. Recent finds of Aztec Art and Antiquities.'

'Somebody may know where Hine is,' I said.

'All the experts will be there,' she nodded. She eased herself from the bed and put on a robe. It was too big. 'My mother's,' she smiled.

'She is still here?' I asked. 'In this house?'

'This morning she went to her sister's house in Tepotzotlan. She gets up from bed early.' She looked a little embarrassed. 'I did not tell her about you. She did not know you were here. She would think you were too old for me.'

'I am,' I said, reaching out and holding her hands.

'Perhaps,' she responded with a shrug. 'I do things on the impulse. Come we will bath together.'

The bathroom was sumptuous, the bath an ivory shell in the centre of the black tiled floor. There was a green parrot in a palatial cage. The parrot and I had already become acquainted. It regarded me now with silent-eyed suspicion whereas previously it had squawked a spasm of Spanish at me. Cara paid genuine attention to the temperature of the water, trailing her fingers in it, varying the flow of the ornate taps. When she considered it was right, I helped her into the bath, and climbed in after her. We washed each other while the parrot quietly cawed and fretted on its perch.

'What is he actually saying?' I asked her. There was a silver container at the side with a bottle of glimmering wine in a cooler and two glasses.

Her eyes looked very fine in her wet face. Her shy breasts were just below the soap level and as she laughed, their snouts surfaced like the noses of twin otters. 'He is telling you the commodities,' she said.

We had several glasses of wine in the bath. I tried to appear as though I drank it like that all the time. She looked as though she did. When, after twenty minutes of sheer indulgence, we climbed out, she took a huge towel and dried me with almost motherly detachment, but would not allow me to do the same for her. The parrot cackled in a muted way, rolled its eyes and strode sideways on its perch.

We dressed and then left the house walking through the afternoon streets, below trees fragmenting the sun. There was no rain today. She said that the season was far gone and that there would be some days when the rain forgot to arrive at all. The Museo de la Ciudad de Mexico was only ten minutes' walk, a Baroque building with a fanged serpent, a relic of an Aztec temple, as its cornerstone.

Inside was a notice pointing the way to the exhibition, and she touched my hand as we walked towards it. It was housed in a cool, large room and two smaller galleries. Light from high windows flowed across the curved ceiling. It was the customary studious scene: murmurings and footsteps and people moving with solemn attention. The exhibition had been opened only the previous evening and there was a scattered stream of visitors walking around the cases and cabinets. The exhibits were mainly pottery, some complete, bulbous red and ochre jars and bowls, some jig-saw pieces. There was a section devoted to ancient weapons and masks. We progressed slowly around the perimeter. At one case a tall man with a goatee beard was explaining something to an attentive group of three. I touched Cara's hand and we moved towards them. He had just finished his discourse as we neared him and the trio thanked him and moved off.

'I wonder,' I asked him, 'if we might also benefit from your knowledge.'

He smiled kindly and said: 'If there is anything that I know, you will know it also, señor.' He bowed towards Cara: 'Señorita.'

Waving his long arm towards the showcases, he announced: 'I am Professor Mañuel Lopez. These are my discoveries of last year from Chichén Itza, a district of the Yucatan Peninsular.'

'I am Michael Findlater,' I said. 'And this is Señorita Cara Brown.'

Again he bowed. 'What would you like to know?'

I did not rush it. First I asked him about his finds, about the region of their discovery, the tribes and how long ago they had been living there. Then I said: 'Have you ever met a man called Hine, Peter Karl Hine? He is a collector, I believe. Of sorts.'

His face drew in. He looked at me, fingering his beard. 'I know of this man,' he said. 'But not very much. He is a friend of yours?'

'Not a friend,' I told him prudently, 'but I am anxious to know where he might be found.'

'This I do not know. But there is someone who will know, I think. Señor Paco Gonzales. He is the one. I will take you to him.'

He glanced at his relics as if he feared they might run away back to Chichén Itza while he was absent, but then decided they were safe. His smile reappeared, a studious, straight smile, like a lid to his beard, and he repeated his tall bow, indicating that we were to follow him. As we did so, through the current people and the remnants of people long past, he waved his long arms and said: 'This man I have heard about.' He looked cautiously sideways at me. 'He is not a good person, you know.'

'He never has been,' I agreed. 'That is partly why I want to find him.'

'Are you police?' he asked with a deeper interest.

'No, I'm not police. I am a private investigator.'

He ushered us into a side gallery where the walls were arrayed with spears. 'Señor Gonzales,' said the Professor, 'is right here.' A crowd of masks grimaced down.

Gonzales was a bulky man in a creased fawn suit. He had spilled something down the front. He nodded unhappily when the Professor had spoken to him in Spanish. 'This Hine,' he said to me. 'We have come to know. Nothing can be proved against him, but we know he has tried to smuggle valuable artefacts from Mexico. This is against the law. We require our history to remain here.'

'I thought he might be up to something like that,' I

said. 'That is why I would like to know his where-abouts.'

'The last time I knew of him,' muttered Gonzales, 'he was living the other side of the Rio Atoyac.' I sensed Cara nodding beside me.

'This is in Oaxaca State,' she said.

'That is the place. The village is called San Miguel del Rio. There are some famous ruins there.'

'It is about two hundred and fifty miles,' she said turning to me.

'That is very useful, señor,' I said. 'Thank you. Do you know anything else about him?'

'He is a German,' shrugged Gonzales. 'But there are many Germans in Mexico. Here in Mexico City there are many thousands. He has kept out of trouble with the police . . . but he is doing something. This I know. Maybe, after you have found him, you can tell me.'

'I will,' I promised. 'I have a lot of questions I want to ask him.' I repeated the name of the town: 'San Miguel del Rio.'

'That is the place,' said the Mexican. 'He lives there in a castle.'

She lay in my arms and hummed that night. Humming with intermittent la-la-ing until we both slept, her tender thigh between my legs, her hair flung over my chest. The humming included, so she told me, a Bach toccata and fugue, part of the second movement of the Mendelssohn Violin Concerto and 'Land of Hope and Glory' (Elgar) which I recognized for myself. She only hummed a snatch of each. Her melodic voice would drift away and then return later as though it had been on some journey within her.

During a break in her tunes, she informed me in a

whisper: 'Oaxaca is the most beautiful state in Mexico.' I felt her eyelashes brush my skin as she opened her eyes. 'There it is always spring. The mountains are green. Will you take me with you, Michael?'

I eased myself up in the bed. She moved her head away, lay on her back and looked up. The room was dim. 'I have to tell you a little more about this,' I said.

She sat up like a child being promised a story. I could just make out her nose, her shoulder and her small, bare breasts. Reaching out, I touched her. She turned fully to me. 'What must you tell me?' she inquired.

'The man Hine is not only a shady character in the antiquities business,' I told her. 'He has spent his life being a shady character. He has arranged to have people killed.'

I felt her react. 'Killed? How?' she whispered. 'Why?'

'It's a complicated story,' I said. 'Even I haven't worked it out yet, and I know as much about it as anybody, I think. He was a Nazi spy during the war.'

She pulled away from me again and I thought she was trying not to laugh. 'War?' she whispered. 'But Michael, that is history. It was long ago.'

'Not that long,' I said defensively. 'In any case, the people who have died have been murdered. All within the last few months.'

'This Hine, he arranged this? He is hiding something?'

'They were all people connected with his past,' I said. 'Either that or innocent parties who happened to get in the way.'

'In that case,' she said firmly, 'I must be with you.'

She studied my reaction in the dusky light. 'I would be a good guide,' she promised. 'I know Oaxaca very well. We will find this village, San Miguel del Rio together.'

I was still going to say that she could not come with me, when she slipped and wriggled over my body and, in the middle of our discussion, we once more made love. It was a long time since I had known anyone so young and passionate as Cara. We lay softly sweating, listening to the muted night sounds of the street. Her breathing became slight, and I thought she was sleeping. But she shifted and said: 'Your name is very good for this, Michael.'

'How is that?'

'Your name, Findlater. Someone who is searching.'

It had never occurred to me. I stroked her hair.

'You always believed you would find it later,' she said. 'Can I come with you?'

Smiling, I kissed her. God, when I think of it now, I can scarcely believe it all happened. 'All right, you can come,' I told her. 'You can show me the way.'

'Always I will,' she said gravely. Still sitting on the bed, she reached for her robe, her naked shape outlined in the near-dark. 'First,' she said, 'I will serve some drinks for us. Then I will tell you about Oaxaca and its mountains.'

'They're green,' I smiled.

'All through the year,' she agreed. 'It is never too hot but not too cold. There is much to see there.'

'Including Herr Hine, I hope,' I said.

'Yes, including this man. I hope so too.'

She eased herself from the bed and went from the room. At once I fell asleep. She told me in the morning that she had held a glass of whisky right under my snoring nose, but it had not caused me even to stir. When I awoke the tumbler was by the bedside and she was sleeping on the far side of the bed. I could hear the parrot muttering: 'Cor . . . cor' in the bathroom. I went in there, crossing the white beams of the Mexican day coming in between the shutters of the house. Outside cars were honking.

Cara appeared unclothed and half asleep at the bathroom door, and without a word began to run the water. 'How long will it take?' I asked her, 'to San Miguel?'

Shrugging indolently she said: 'All day, perhaps. I do not think I will come with you.'

I felt a keen disappointment, almost a hurt, but I said: 'You must do whatever you think is right.' I climbed into the bath and she stayed on the side and slowly, absent-mindedly it appeared, washed my back, my chest and under my arms. 'You will see the village women washing their clothes in the rivers,' she said. 'Like I do now.'

'I'll look forward to that,' I muttered. 'Are you sure you want to stay?'

'I think so, Michael.' She ran her small fingers down my wet face. 'One day perhaps I will come to visit you in New England at Thinking . . . '

'Thoughtful Creek,' I said.

'Yes. There. And you can show me the whales.'

It sounded like goodbye. I climbed from the sunken bath and picked up a towel and a robe. The parrot, which had pretended to sleep, opened one eye and recited: 'Cor . . . cor.' I left Cara in the bathroom. 'I will make the coffee,' she called after me in a sad voice. 'I will come soon.'

In the Mexico City yellow pages I looked up Hertz and called them. They said they would bring the car to me. I told them ten o'clock. I wanted to be on my way.

She emerged from the bathroom with a towelling robe

around her. I wondered then if I would ever again see her naked. She looked sulky and sad. I did not ask her why. Moodily we sat down in our robes and drank the thick coffee she had prepared.

'The bird is from today called Michael,' she said ending our silence.

'Thank you. What about its real name? Won't it get confused?'

'It has a Mexican name – Tlacochahuaya.'

'Michael should make life simpler for it,' I agreed. I thought she might smile or cry, but she did neither. I got dressed and waited for the car. She stayed in her robe, moving around without speaking. Going into the bedroom again, she played for a few minutes on her violin. I stood at the door, leaning against the jamb, and watched her but she never glanced towards me. I went back in to the main room and she ceased playing and came into me. The bell in the courtyard rang.

With a strange formality we kissed at the centre of the room. Our hands touched each other's bodies after the kiss. There is only one way to get out of these situations, and that is to go. I went towards the door and, my hand holding her fingers, she walked just behind me, as if I were leading her.

She unbolted the door and we blinked at the vivid sun on the courtyard. The car driver, outside the door in the white wall, pulled the bell again. We moved out under the courtyard tree. Then we saw it.

It was on the iron table below the tree. It had been there some time because there were two fallen leaves on its lid; a child's coffin, white and small and frightening. Cara caught her breath. 'Go back in,' I said. I made it harsher. 'Go inside, Cara,' I ordered. 'This is part of it.'

Her response was almost a whimper. 'No. I stay,' she said. 'I cannot.'

Leaving her by the door, I slowly walked across the courtyard. Maddeningly the man from Hertz rang again and I snarled back towards the door. I reached the coffin and put my hand on the lid. It was warm. The Hertz man called over the wall: 'Señor! Señor!'

'Fuck off,' I shouted back. My eyes were on the coffin. I reached out and eased open the lid.

'What is it?' I heard Cara say behind me. 'Michael, what is it?'

'It's a raven,' I said without turning around. 'A dead raven.'

The man at the gate shouted. 'Señor. Your Hertz car.'

I turned and looked at Cara. Her face was like powder. 'Now,' I said firmly, 'you definitely *are* coming with me. I'm not letting you out of my sight.'

By evening we had reached the mountains. They were olive in the late light; the villages, necklaced by their own refuse and trash, dim pink and white. At two places along the highway they had been burning the refuse, and the smoke still ringed the habitations. Dogs and black pigs wandered about in the company of slow children. Coconut husks were piled outside the villages; rural people hung onto trucks they used like buses. Dust-covered men stood at the side of the road waiting to go home, their straw-hatted heads bowed with the weariness of heat and labour. But then we passed a young man riding a lively horse bareback along the fringe of the same road, leading another, its pale mane flowing. We came to a river where women were washing clothes on the stones and hanging them to dry below a bridge.

I had told her why they sent the dead raven. I told

her of the other times they had sent it, and how they had killed Renate among others.

'I do not understand,' she had said, 'how these things matter *now*. It is so long ago. Why do they care so much?'

'Enough to kill,' I said. 'They have something to hide.'

'I do not understand,' she repeated.

By now I had driven the car into the foothills of the Sierra Madre del Sur, and then up to the plateau that accommodates the city of Oaxaca de Juarez, the capital of the region, called The Jade City because of its green walls. By the final light of the day, we descended into the valleys again, where oil lamps hung in the hamlet houses, across the river of Atoyac and on to San Miguel.

'This place is very old,' she said. 'The Mixtecs, the earliest people, were here until the Aztecs conquered them. You can see the signs of how they lived. The people here have always been among the remains of the past.'

San Miguel was a small town, hardly more than a village, with a hill at its centre and a ghostly white church at the apex of the hill. There was a single hotel built around a tiled and tree-shaded courtyard, and we got a room there. The window was the shape of a rising half-moon and it let in the cool evening air to us. The furniture was local, carved and heavy. There was a glowering mirror in an ornate surround. But across the bed was a bright quilt of woven colours. We lay on this and rested after our journey.

A melancholy had come over her. We lay, clothed, and she pushed herself into me, into my side, under my arm, like an uncertain animal seeking solace. 'I wish we had not come to this place,' she whispered. 'I wish that we were going tonight to New England to the whales.'

I laughed and told her: 'This is the last stop, Cara. It has been a long business but now, once I have seen this man Hine, it will be the end.'

She said: 'Perhaps he will not speak to you. If he knows you are writing about him. If there is something to hide. If there have been killings, he will be a dangerous person.'

I nodded against her face. 'I know,' I admitted. 'I've thought it all out. Indeed, if he knows I am here he may decamp. I think I must go and see him now. Tonight.'

She sat up and stared at me. 'Now? This moment?'

'He may not be around tomorrow,' I said.

Easing myself off the bed I went to the lavatory. I thought I heard her crying, and when I returned she was still lying on the bed but with her face to the wall. Gently I reached out and turned her light body towards me. Her eyes were wet.

'Tomorrow,' I promised, 'we will begin our journey to the whales.'

Her smile was unconvincing. 'Tonight I must come,' she said softly. 'You must not go alone.'

'I think it would be better if you stayed here,' I said. But I was not sure.

'No. I will come.'

I held out my hand to her and easing her from the bed, I said: 'Let's go and see the Nazi in his castle.'

We went out into the town; two or three little lit cantinas were open in the square with a few men drinking, a peasant rode a donkey, each as tired as the other; there were children fighting over a hosepipe gushing water, women with baskets on their heads standing in a gossip circle. The first man I asked, the waiter arranging the tables on the terrace outside our hotel, pointed up beyond the church. 'Torre,' he said.

'There will be guards with guns?' suggested Cara as we went up the incline of the street.

'God knows,' I admitted. 'I don't know what to expect. The tower may be more like a fortress.'

'You have a gun?' she said anxiously.

'You know I have.'

'Yes, I have seen it. I did not like to say.'

It was less than a mile but the road was broken and muddy. Gradually the houses diminished, their lights and people were left behind us. A night breeze blew quite strongly over the side of the hill. But the air was full and warm, and there was a big, early moonrise.

The castle grew before us at every stride, its walls humped and irregular. 'It's quite a *small* fortress,' I joked to reassure her.

It was not a fortress at all. It was mostly a ruin. The outer walls had slid and fallen in places, the remaining parts standing up thin and jagged like burnt candles against the night sky. There were stone steps leading up to what had once been a door but was now a hole in the masonry. From somewhere within came the diffused light of a lantern and the sound of a man singing wildly:

> 'In olden days a glimpse of stocking
> Was looked on as something shocking,
> Now Heaven knows . . . anything goes!'

Stunned, we halted. I felt my mouth open and shut. I turned and she did also, staring with astonishment at me. Then a heavy shape appeared, not the singer, but a Mexican carrying a lantern.

'Señor Hine, *por favor*?' I asked tentatively.

'He is here,' said the man. 'You can hear him.'

'That's him singing?'

'He is drunk, señor. When he is drunk, he sings.'

'Can we come in?'

'Come in, okay,' he said standing aside. 'But he is drunk.'

We walked into an area surrounded by the broken castle walls. The moonlight revealed that it was full of old cars and tractors, wrecked agricultural machinery, coils of cable, wooden crates, and piles of coconut husks. The singing had quivered and stopped. It had emanated from one corner where some semblance of the original building still stood. It was illuminated by lantern light which filtered outside. All around were the shapes and shadows of ancient urns and ruined pots. We moved closer. The front of the room, if it were a room, was entirely open, shored up with stones and props of random wood. The props formed a frame and within the frame hung a hammock, bulging with someone, and gently swaying. At the side of the hammock was a table upon which was a bottle and a glass rolling on its side. As we watched, an ashen hand emerged from the hammock. It went like a crab across the table and after searching briefly for the glass, caught the bottle around the throat and lifted it back into the confines of the hammock. We saw it being tilted. The Mexican who had silently accompanied us repeated: 'Señor Hine is drunk.'

The man in the hammock reacted to the voice and looked over the edge. At last I was face to face with him. It was one of the big surprises of my life. Hine was white and ravaged and riven, ancient as a ghost. He waved the bottle convivially, although its weight seemed too much for him. 'I'm drunk!' he shouted. 'Drunk!'

He began to sing grotesquely once more:

'In olden days a glimpse of stocking
Was looked on as something shocking . . . '

The Mexican touched my arm. 'You see him,' he shrugged. 'But he cannot see you.'

I misunderstood. 'He's blind?' I said.

'Blind drunk,' he repeated. He was ushering us towards the hole in the wall. 'Tomorrow,' he said. 'I will tell him. I will keep him sober. You want to do some deal with him?'

'Yes, in a way,' I said.

'I will fix it. I will bring him into the town tomorrow. You can talk to him about the deal. He will keep sober for that.'

Cara and I walked down the hill in the starlight. I was silent. 'This,' she asked eventually, 'is the man who organizes murders?'

XVII

As we descended the hill we could hear the evening noises of the village, music and the honking of a car horn; voices echoed, a donkey brayed. The path, before it became a road, dipped below drooping trees, and the lights of the small place shone up and below the leaves and branches as if they were gleaming from a cavern.

We were unspeaking. Her hand had slipped itself into mine. When we reached the habitations we saw that there were a few people at the tables in the cantina next to the hotel. Without speaking I guided her in there and we sat a little away from the rest. A sinewy-looking short man in a greasy white shirt and stained dungarees came immediately to the table and placed three glasses of wine there. Suspiciously I glanced at him. His eyes and his moustache were pendulous. He sat without invitation and moved two of the glasses in front of us, each movement deliberate, like a chess player. 'You been up to see the old Hun,' he said.

'That's right,' I answered. 'He was drunk.'

'Come evening, he generally is.' His accent was midwest American. 'He was singing, right?'

' "Anything Goes",' I confirmed.

'He likes the old ones. My name's Bill Sherling.'

'I'm Michael Findlater and this is Cara Brown.'

We shook hands awkwardly across the table. 'Thanks for the drink,' I said. He raised his glass and we followed suit. 'It's only wine,' he apologized. 'But I figured you'd need it. If you'd like something else . . .'

'Wine is fine,' I said. 'What are you doing here?'

'This and that. I'm a pilot. Got my own plane. I shuttle things to and fro.'

'Shuttle?'

'Some shuttle, some smuggle. Across the border into Texas . . . New Mexico.'

'Drugs?'

'Parrots mostly.'

'Parrots!' I laughed and Cara giggled into her hands.

'Sure, parrots,' he confirmed gravely. 'There's bucks for parrots. Big contraband. You can get five thousand dollars for a good parrot. I fly in fifty at a time. The old Hun wants me to fly out some of his ancient pots and pans.'

'I understand he's been shopping around for somebody to do that.'

'It's his dream. He's a fanatical old bastard. But I'm not too sure about running relics. Here they don't mind the parrots. It's the US of A don't like the parrots. They say they've got fleas and disease. But the Mex police don't like you shipping their antiques. That's big trouble.'

Cara said: 'I thought the drugs was the big business.'

'For some,' he shrugged. 'But it's overcrowded. Too many people in it. And they keep killing each other. Or they double-cross each other so that they're picked up across the border. And they've got blimps over there now.'

'Blimps?' I said. 'Airships?'

'Unmanned balloons,' he nodded. 'But with radar. To pick up planes sneaking over. It's like you see in the war movies.'

He looked over his shoulder and a waiter in a huge apron wrapped twice around his body brought a bottle to the table and poured another round. 'What do you know about Hine?' I asked.

Sherling grimaced. 'A character, I guess,' he said. 'But old.'

'He was a spy once,' I said.

'Sure, sure. He told me. He's told everybody. How he won the war for Uncle Sam and then got no thanks. In fact Uncle Sam threw him into jail. But he's crazy. You don't know what to believe.'

'Does he have any money?'

Sherling's drowsy eyes rose from beneath his heavy lids. He wiped the wine from his moustache. 'Anybody who wants him for his money had better forget it,' he said. 'There isn't any. That's why he wants to export his pots and pans.'

'He could not finance any network, any illegal network, in the United States then?'

The lines cracked all over his face as he laughed. 'He can't finance his eating,' he said. 'No way could he do anything like that. Not out of the country. He made a trip a few months ago. Some cowboy got him across the border some way. He has no visa. He was back here in a couple of weeks.'

'When was that?' I asked him.

He scratched his sparse hair. 'Oh, I don't know. Let's see. About July sometime. But don't get me wrong. I didn't take him. He had no dough. He said he was going to get some dough – but I guess he didn't get it because nothing's changed with him.'

'You don't believe he could have *any* organization behind him, let's say ex-Nazis for example, that he just puts on a front here?'

Sherling laughed dryly again and shook his head. 'The only organization Hine's got is what you see up there where he lives. There's ex-Nazis in Mexico like there are in Paraguay and Argentina and Chile. They came to South America in truckloads after the war. But they're old, like he's old. They're just hanging on to die.'

'I came to write something about Hine,' I said.

'So I hear.' He looked at me apologetically. 'You hear most things pretty quickly around here,' he said 'Well, he'd like that. Particularly if you pay him. But he'd do it for nothing, if necessary. He's a vain old bastard.'

At five thirty in the morning with a dawn breeze seeping through the half-moon window and touching us as we lay on our bed, Cara murmured to me and eased herself into my naked arms. I had been sleeping and now I awoke to the cool luxury of her skin. She rolled above me and we lay unmoving while the light grew in the window and the cockerels sounded in the village.

'I am very sad,' she whispered.

'Why is that?'

'Because I feel that we are coming to the end of our time.'

'The end of this part of our time,' I told her. 'But there will be others. Remember the whales.'

'Your whales,' she breathed.

'Not mine. They belong to themselves. But we can look.'

'As long as we do not touch,' she said. She began to touch me down the points of my body. She followed her hands with her lips. I lay back, enjoying the luxury of what she was doing, but looking out of the window at the daylight now filling it. We had known a remarkable time together and I would always remember it, as indeed

I do, but even then I knew it would be finished. These things always are. They are good for so long only. They go away and you cannot retrieve them, which is perhaps just as well.

We made our last love while the morning activities of the Mexican place sounded outside. There were clatterings, the barking of dogs, the reluctant starting of a motorcycle, and the calm ringing of the single bell from the church.

Someone in the street, a woman, began shouting: *'Peor es nada! Peor es nada!'*

We were lying still, thinking and listening. 'What is she saying?' I asked.

'Peor es nada,' she said. 'It is better than nothing.'

We waited all the hot day for Hine to come down to the village. It did not rain. At six o'clock, after the sun had gone from the dusty square and the single street, a man passing by on a mule leaned towards me sitting under the shade of the hotel verandah and called: 'He is coming.'

The mule plodded on, the man lolling from side to side on its back. Hine did not appear. Half an hour later two children, boys, came down the street dragging a three-foot iguana between them, the back of its head trailing in the dirt. They stopped and surveyed me. The iguana was still alive because it wriggled. The boys looked back up the street towards the hill-path that led to the ruined castle. The older one said something in Spanish.

Cara, sitting at the opposite side of the table, said: 'They say he is coming.'

'What's the iguana for?' I asked.

'Their supper,' she said.

Then I saw him descending through the town. The

big Mexican came first, the man who had been at the tower the previous night. Then Hine appeared, trudging. It was obvious that he was an object of curiosity, even reverence, because people came from their houses to view him as he walked by.

He was wearing a threadbare long-sleeved bush jacket and faded khaki trousers tucked into long, scarred, brown boots. Even at a distance you could see he was decrepit and strained. He hobbled to one side and his arms hung straight down. He looked like the ghost of some long-dead Afrika Corps captain.

'This is it,' I said to Cara as I stood up. 'Now we're face to face.'

'It is a poor face,' she said.

It was too. He arrived outside the hotel and it seemed he would have walked past if the big Mexican had not stopped and pointed me out. Hine turned and looked straight at me. I knew for certain then I had been chasing a shadow.

'Ah,' he croaked. 'So you're the guy who wants to see me.'

The voice was half-American, half-European. He walked towards me with his skinny hand outstretched, poking nine inches beyond his tattered khaki sleeve. There was nothing for it but to shake the hand, as poor as a chicken's claw. 'I am Michael Findlater,' I said. 'And this is Cara Brown.'

'Nice,' he said looking Cara up and down insolently. 'Real nice.'

'Sit down,' I invited pulling out a chair. I wanted him to sit directly opposite me. He took the chair next to the one I had offered him. The waiter with the wrap-around apron appeared and I asked Hine what he would like to drink. He said he drank mezcal. Cara nodded and the waiter brought a bottle and poured out three glasses.

The Mexicans who had been observing Hine as he walked down the street had followed him, in an oddly biblical way, and now they stood in the street, twenty or more of them, and watched us. Some others came to the tables and sat looking. The waiter began to be busy. I saw Bill Sherling arrive and sit on the wall in the background, a glass hanging sideways in his hand. He lifted it when he saw that I had seen him.

The two boys who had carried the iguana now returned and stood in the street singing tunelessly, one knocking two bones together, apparently hoping for money. A third child came and sat down beside them with a pained and hopeless expression. Sherling told them to go away and they eventually did so, muttering.

'So,' said Hine. 'What's all this about? Do I get paid?'

I had planned it carefully. The fatal move would be to rush things. It would be necessary for me to lead him along the way. I could not believe that this wreck of a man could have organized the killings and the dead ravens and all the other things, but he might know who did. Also, I needed his story.

'I'm interested,' I began, 'in the antiquities in this region.' I decided to lie boldly. 'I am writing a series of articles for *Time* magazine. I need some characters too, and you appear to be a character, Señor Hine.'

The flattery pleased him as I guessed it would. He rubbed his thin hands and a smile wormed across his rheumy face. His eyes were sharp and bright. 'How much do I get?' he asked. 'I've got to live. Like everybody I've got to live.'

Leaning forward across the table, I said quietly: 'Five thousand dollars.'

298

'Make it six,' he said.

'All right. Six.'

'When?'

'Tomorrow.'

'Let's have some more mezcal,' he said. The big Mexican who had accompanied him was sitting at another table ten feet away, arguing spasmodically with two locals. It was he who nodded to the waiter and he came to our table once more with the bottle.

'How did you come to be here in the first place?' I said to Hine. He lifted his glass towards me and then towards Cara, his lips leering.

'I've travelled,' he said. 'Everywhere I've been. This just happens to be where I am now. I'll move on.' He regarded me doubtfully. 'You came up to my place last night?'

'Yes.'

'Sure. I was tired. But you saw the urns and the decorated pots. And I've got weapons and beads and everything. Aztec and Zapotec. It's all there. Come up tomorrow and I'll explain it all to you. After you've paid the money.'

'Right,' I said calmly. 'I'll do that.'

He regarded me across the table as though wondering whether to confide in me. He threw the drink in his glass down his throat and leaned over the cloth. 'I got other relics,' he ventured throatily. 'Real good stuff.'

'Like what?'

'Nazi relics,' he said with hushed triumph. 'From the war.' He fumbled in his pocket. 'Priceless.' He brought out two small boxes. 'Take a look at these.'

He opened the first box, lifting the hinged lid. 'See that,' he whispered. He looked about us as if ensuring that nobody nearby would understand. I thought he was going to pass the box to me but he withdrew it at the extreme of his reach, holding it so I could see. It contained a curl of hair under a perspex cover.

'What is it?' I asked.

'Hitler's forelock,' he answered. He glared at me as though daring me to laugh. 'His famous cow-lick,' he added. 'Taken from his dead body in the Reichstag bunker. For a price it is yours.'

Attempting to look astonished and impressed, 'And what's in the other one?' I asked inadequately.

'See.' He withdrew the first box and extended the second in the same manner. He flicked open the lid and displayed another scrap of hair. Triumph filled his measly face. 'The Führer's moustache,' he announced.

It was difficult keeping a set expression. 'Cut off the body in the bunker,' I suggested.

'Sure. What a relic! Just think what it's worth! Half a million dollars maybe. With another quarter of a million for his cow-lick. I have certificates of authenticity.'

'From who?'

'The barber who cut them off Hitler,' he said. 'He has signed a certificate. I have also signed it. You want to buy them?'

'It's a lot of money,' I stalled. 'How did you come by them?'

'Me? I was close to the Führer at one time,' he said. It was a muted boast. 'I didn't like the guy. In fact, I played a big part in his defeat, you know. But that's another story.' He had shut the lids of the two boxes and now he proferred them across the table again, but now both held in one hand. 'Twenty thousand dollars,' he offered.

I said: 'That's more in my range.' I thought the time had come. 'Not too long ago,' I lied, 'I was in Paraguay.

I met a good friend of yours. He told me how he trained you as a spy.'

His creased face softened remarkably. He put the two boxes away. 'Dieter Gottinger,' he said. 'Of Villarica.'

'That's him. Dieter Gottinger. I met him in Villarica.'

He held out his glass and it was at once replenished from the bottle. 'Did you know I was a famous spy?' he asked. He threw the drink down his throat, again in one movement. His eyes were like red coals. 'I was the guy who won the war. Peter Karl Hine, the spy, won the war. Gottinger must have told you.'

Giving it a moment, time enough for him to lie back and look satisfied, I leaned forward and said firmly: 'Unter den Sternen.'

He looked amazed. 'Unter den Sternen,' he repeated hoarsely. 'It was our password. You know it ... you know about the landing, then, and the man who was supposed to . . .'

At that moment the most incredible thing happened. During his speaking Cara had been searching in her handbag. I thought she was reaching for a handkerchief. Instead she brought out a gun. A small, dull, gun. I felt my mouth sag. I could not move. Calmly, she brought it up above the table and fired it once. The bullet went straight between Hine's eyes. The explosion sent birds screeching from the trees, but no one in the cantina moved. Then she turned to me, as if about to explain what she had done, and the gun came up with her eyes. *She was going to kill me.*

I could not even make a sound. She was four feet away. She levelled the gun, straight at me. She was crying. There was a flash of light across my eyes and two quick reports. I thought I was dead. A burning furrow went across my cheek and I fell backwards over the chair. Now there was panic. A third shot was fired, smashing the light above the table. Everyone started to scream and run at once. I felt myself being lifted by the armpits and heard Bill Sherling's voice saying firmly: 'You're not dead. Let's get out of here.'

He pulled me to my feet. The air was full of acrid burning. Cara was lying across the tablecloth, blood oozing out from her like a tide. Hine was hung back against a wall, his arms petrified in their final spread above his head. I began to babble but Sherling put his hand across my mouth. 'This is where we blow,' he said in my ear. 'Move your ass.'

He pulled me into the street. People were running away, including, as even I noticed at that confused and agitated moment, the two village policemen. Blood was soaking my collar and was sticky around my neck. 'Come on, come on,' Sherling urged. He pushed me like a child. My legs were trembling. 'Christ,' I kept saying. 'Oh, Christ.' Before we went into the street I had looked at her a last time, hung across the table as if she were weeping. That was Cara. She was dead.

We reached Sherling's car. Two of the tyres had been let down. The boys who had been playing and singing so tunelessly had not run away with the others. They now crouched in a doorway and were laughing. 'Bastards!' bellowed Sherling shaking his fist. 'Bastards!' they called back.

Looking over his shoulder towards the cantina he pushed, manhandled, me further into the street. A dust-coated car was rumbling down the rutted road. Sherling put up his hand to stop it. The driver, a squat old man, did not change his expression when confronted with Sherling's gun.

'Señor?' he queried.

'Out!' ordered Sherling. 'Get out!'

The man left the driving seat in a dignified way. Sherling told him to hurry. He looked quite closely at the gun, then opened the door so that we could get in. '*Muchas gracias*,' said Sherling getting behind the wheel.

'Gringo shit,' said the Mexican amiably.

Still no one had emerged from the cantina. I fell in beside Sherling and he charged the rattling car down the street towards the main highway. The owner had left a dirty white scarf behind and Sherling handed it to me, and I pressed it to my bloodied neck. 'You okay?' he said.

'I'm okay,' I said. 'Did you *have* to kill her?'

He stared at me and angrily shouted: 'Of course I fucking well had to kill her!' He gunned the car along the road. Pieces of mud fell from the roof. He bellowed at me again: 'Do you think I go around shooting girls for a hobby? It was her or you, buster. A tenth of a second more and that cut on your cheek would have been an extra hole in your nose.'

'I know, I know,' I moaned. 'I'm sorry. I just can't believe it. Fred Robinson had you watch me, did he?'

'The FBI did,' he answered grimly. 'I'm not on first name terms with anybody there.'

We were silent for several miles. He knew where he was going. We turned away from the main route, the road climbed into the dark hills and the wind began to blow against the car. We stopped at a village and filled up with gasoline. 'Thank God it's kept in one piece,' he said tapping the car roof.

'Where are we going?'

'I'm not telling you,' he replied bluntly. 'I'm not telling any bastard. It's somewhere where you can hole up for a while before we try to get you out of here. There's more of them, you know. She wasn't working alone. She had back-up, there was a getaway car which drove off. They'll still be after you. And me.'

'Shit,' I said. 'I just can't believe it.'

'Don't keep saying you can't believe it, because you'd *better* believe it. You may be a great reporter, friend, but you don't know the first fucking thing about this game.'

'What an actress she was,' I said after a few more minutes. 'She was a beautiful actress.'

'Brilliant,' he said sourly. 'When I shot her she was crying. They don't come any more convincing than that.'

'She was sent to kill Hine, when I had led her to him, and then kill me.'

'You got it at last. End of story. A couple of village shootings in this country don't make a lot of waves.'

'Well, thanks anyway.'

'That's okay. It's my job, as they say in the movies.'

'I thought you smuggled parrots.'

'I do. The FBI is casual work.'

We drove on through the mountains. I fell miserably asleep, hunched in the seat beside him. When I awoke we were still snaking around bends and descending into valleys, only to climb again. It was pitch dark. I put my head in my hands and then felt my cheek. There was a cake of blood there.

'It's stopped bleeding,' I said.

'It's a graze,' he grunted.

'I've been trying to work out the whole thing,' I said. 'Why did they send Cara . . . her to kill me?'

'My guess is that it was because you'd come to the end of your usefulness, fulfilled your role. You'd found Hine. Somebody did not want you to talk about it. I don't know the whole story, because they didn't tell me it. They just told me to keep close to you.'

'Thank God you did. What a bloody trail it's been. Halfway across the world and back again . . .'

'Tell me some other time,' he muttered. 'I think we're here.'

He stopped the car. There were some low buildings outlined against the dim sky. 'This,' he said, 'is as out-of-the-way as anywhere I know. It's a fishing camp. Owned by a friend of mine. You hole up here for a few days until I can sort a few things out. Okay?'

'Okay, of course.'

He got out of the car and again patted its roof as if it were a horse. I got out also. My legs held me up now. There was the sound of swiftly running water.

Sherling walked a few yards down a path and knocked on a window. A light showed in the room and a curtain was pulled aside. Then it dropped again, and a light went on behind an outer door which then opened. There were exclamations and explanations. I walked towards the door.

'This is my friend,' Sherling said to the man in the door. He was a big, sleepy Mexican wearing only a shirt. 'This is my friend,' he said to me.

We shook hands with odd formality. The man went to get his trousers and shoes. We heard him talking to a complaining woman. He reappeared and led the way with a torch to a cabin at the bottom of the short row. The river ran noisily but out of sight behind the building. 'Not many customers right now,' said the Mexican. 'Good peace and quiet.'

'That's what I need,' I said. He unlocked the door and led us into a frugal wood-walled cabin, a bedroom, bathroom, galley kitchen and a small sitting area with two chairs, a table and a huge, old-fashioned television set. 'Home sweet home,' said Sherling. It smelled damp.

'How long will I be here?' I asked him.

'A few days. Maybe a week. Depends. You'll be out of Mexico as soon as I can fix it.'

'The quicker the better,' I said.

The man, who was called Arturo, went away and brought a pot of coffee. We told him there was nothing else and he left. Every inch of me ached. I could not keep my eyes open. I lay on one of the twin beds and Sherling lay on the other. Before I slept I heard him snoring. He had saved my life.

Every second of the horrifying minute, and that is all it could have been, went through my mind. The way she had so casually and expertly shot Hine. Her stark look when she turned the gun towards my face. The flash and the double explosion. Her body bent across the table. Why then? Why that moment? What had Hine been saying?

I remembered. He had said 'Unter den Sternen . . . it was our password . . .'

Then I began to realize.

Sherling rose early. I was already awake, lying watching him and wondering. 'I'm going,' he said. 'Stay here and don't move, okay? You've got a gun.'

'Yes,' I said. 'And I've got nowhere to go in particular. When will you be back?'

'Tonight or tomorrow,' he said. 'I hope. I've got to make some arrangements to get you out, still vertical. I'm supposed to look after you.'

'Well, you've done that so far,' I said dismally.

He reacted to my tone. 'Maybe you'd have preferred

me dead and her being holed up here with you,' he said. He was already in the bathroom. 'It would be more fun.'

'Sorry, Bill. I still can't believe it all. I'm bloody numb from it.'

'Well, be numb for a couple more days. Don't go out and don't answer the door unless it's Arturo. I'll tell him to call so you can hear it's him. He'll bring you food. Just stay, okay? Watch the TV, read.' There was a Mexican comic paper on a side table. He had finished in the bathroom. He came out and threw it towards me. 'Meditate.'

I caught the comic. On the front a donkey was saying: 'Caramba!' Sherling was pulling on his shirt. 'Shit,' he said. 'I've got to drive that bundle of guts back. I hope it makes it.'

'So do I,' I told him. 'Thanks for saving my life. I meant to mention it yesterday.'

'You did. Anyhow, it was orders,' he said. He grinned for the first time since I had met him. 'You wait till the Bureau get the bill for this. The parrots I can buy!'

He left then, shutting the cabin door firmly behind him and shouting a reminder to lock it. I did not need to be told. There was a lock and a bolt on the door and I engaged both. Then I went to the back window. The curtains were drawn and I left them like that. I peered through over a scrubby bank falling away down to where the river was, although the drop was so steep I could not see it. It was a grey morning. What I took to be clouds in the distance turned out to be mountains. It was an isolated and lonely place.

A knock on the door startled me. I had put my gun under the pillow and I scrambled across to get it. But the oddly high voice of the big-bodied Arturo called out his name. Still cautiously, I went and opened the door. He was standing there gravely with a tray upon which was a breakfast of coffee and eggs and tacos. Taking it from him, I thanked him. He said: 'Next time I call it is more food.'

Putting the tray on the rough table, I sat on the bed and ate the eggs and drank all the coffee. I looked at my watch as I was going to do every half an hour thereafter. There was no telephone in the room.

After eating I lay back on the bed and slept again for three hours. It must have been a deep sleep because I awoke staring uncomprehendingly at the wooden-beamed ceiling for a full minute before I recalled where I was. I heard myself groan. Arturo's approach aroused me; something extra must have been ticking like an alert in my brain. He once more called in his peculiar voice outside the door: 'Señor! Señor! Arturo with the food.'

He brought in some steamed fish and tough taco chips, a can of beer and some fruit. He also brought a razor and some soap. I thanked him and we exchanged trays through the door. I did not feel like eating the fish, but I did because I knew it would smell if I left it. After drinking the beer, I turned on the television. There might be some news. I imagined pictures of the wrecked cantina at San Miguel, the chairs thrown over, the two bodies, Hine leaning back as if crucified, and Cara's hair spread over the bloodied tablecloth. But there was no report. The news came on and I listened to the Spanish carefully to pick up any identifying words. The television set was old and jumpy. After the news I watched a film about a potter living in the mountains of New Zealand.

The tray which Arturo had brought was lined with a paper napkin. It was only slightly marked. I took it and folded it, longways into four columns. Resting it on the Mexican comic paper on the table, I took a pen from the inside of my suit jacket. My passport was in there. The pen, the passport and the gun were my only possessions now.

Very carefully I wrote down, in sequence, every significant thing I could remember about the whole Pastorius business. Every move, every remark that seemed to be pointing somewhere, the characters of the people. I even remembered the names of the senators standing next to Keenor in the old photograph at the museum in Washington. In the end the list occupied both sides of the stiff paper napkin. There was still a lot more. I searched the room. The toilet paper was porous, but in the top of the cupboard that served as a wardrobe was some paper lining the single shelf. It was almost brown but it would do. I took it out and folded it in a dozen columns. Then I continued with the chronology.

Everything I could remember went down. Single lines, single words even. It was a long story. When I got, at last, to the moment when Cara had insinuated herself at Mexico City Airport, I smiled grimly and realized, not for the first time, how easy it had been, what a beginner I was.

When I had finished I lay down again and slept for another two hours. Arturo's voice outside awoke me. He was standing with a bashful smile holding a tray upon which was an ice bucket, and in the ice bucket a champagne-shaped bottle, leaning jauntily to one side. 'To make you cheer, señor,' he said kindly.

Touched by the gesture I let him into the room. It was Mexican champagne, and he put it down on the table with a comic flourish. The ice was packed up both sides. With a sleepy bow he withdrew. It was almost dark outside now. 'Food after,' he promised. 'I come back.' He went out and I locked and bolted the door again.

Within ten minutes the call came from outside. 'Señor. Señor. The food.' I had not opened the champagne. I put it out of sight so that it was hidden by the table lamp near the bathroom door, in case he should be offended at my lack of response to his gift. Then I opened the door.

Arturo was not there. A man pointing a gun at me was. Behind him was another man. Their faces were in the shadow. 'Wrong door,' I said attempting to close it. The first man pushed it in and the second man followed. The second man was not holding a gun. They were not Mexicans. They had white, nervous faces; their eyes moved and flickered. The one in the front had a moustache and an expensive wristwatch. Perhaps you notice details like that when you are about to die. I wondered if hangmen wore wristwatches.

They moved in the room, the second man closing the door behind him. They were very jumpy, looking about. Moving back I almost fell over the bed. It was pressing behind my knees. Somebody had to say something. 'You've got the wrong place,' I said lamely. 'I'm just here for the fishing.'

Neither said a word. They just looked at me. Their faces were full of alarm. Then the man in front cocked the gun.

'I'm only interested in fish,' I whispered. How odd if these should have been my last words.

The Mexican champagne was standing in the ice bucket behind the table lamp near the bathroom door. It was behind the two intruders and slightly to their left. It was warm in the room and the ice was melting. As it did so it shifted quite loudly and the bottle made a noise as it settled further down in the bucket.

Both men spun around in the direction of the sound.

The one with the gun fired a shot, then another towards the bathroom door. The second shot wrecked the champagne bottle. By the time he had fired, I had leapt backwards over the bed and grasped the gun from beneath the pillow. I found it first time, thank God. I shot the man with the gun as he turned back towards me. I, who had never before knowingly killed anybody, shot him full in the chest and he went down with an amazed expression on his face. The second man panicked and turned towards the door. I fired again and hit him in the back of the neck. He howled once and pitched forward. It was all too easy. Two shots, two men. I stared at the gun as if it had produced magic. 'Fucking hell,' I whispered to myself.

I was afraid to come out from behind the bed. I was like a soldier in a trench. I watched the bodies for movement. The man nearest the door shuddered and I almost shot him again, but he was only twitching in death. For a good five minutes I hid there, waiting for something to occur, not knowing what to do.

A knock came on the door.

'Who is it?' I heard myself croak.

'Arturo, señor,' came the familiar reply. 'I come with the food.'

Sitting there with a pair of dead men I ate fiercely. I also drank half a bottle of wine straight-off, like water, and began to laugh hysterically. Arturo had not heard the shots because he had been some distance away. He viewed the bodies and said he did not know what to do. That made two of us.

Half an hour later, however, Bill Sherling arrived. The bodies were still where they had fallen. 'Shit,' he observed quietly. 'You have been busy.'

'What are we going to do?' I demanded. I was still fighting hysteria, trying to straighten my voice. Arturo went out and came back with some whisky and I began to laugh unreasonably again. 'Quit,' said Sherling. 'For chrissake, quit will you.'

Sitting down on the bed I looked mournfully at the two corpses. 'I never realized it was so easy,' I said. 'Bang, bang. And there you are.'

'Don't start discovering your conscience,' muttered Sherling. Arturo, curiously, said there was a programme he wanted to watch on television and, stepping heavily over the dead men near the door, went out into the night. Sherling bent over the first man and searched his pockets, then the second. 'Not a thing,' he grunted. 'Maybe they knew they were no good at it.'

'Is that what you think?' I said.

'Well, they didn't do a great job, that's for sure,' he said. 'A medium professional would have got you the moment you opened the door.'

'Thanks. That makes me feel a lot better.'

'I'm glad. Now, the question is, getting rid of them. We don't want the police here. Arturo's got his living to consider. I think they had better be fish-food.'

'In the river,' I said.

'That's where the fish are.' He studied the man who had entered with the gun. 'Where does your suit come from?' he asked thoughtfully.

'My suit . . . well, London. What . . .?'

He walked over to the chair where my grey jacket was suspended. He looked at the label inside. 'Aquascutum,' he read. 'Is that right?'

'Right.'

'Regent Street, London, w1,' he read again. He looked at the corpse. 'Should fit him.'

'Christ . . . you're going . . .'

'*We're* going,' he corrected. 'Got your passport? Ah . . . yes . . . here . . .' He tapped the inside pocket and took out the passport. He looked at the coat-of-arms on the cover. 'Pretty,' he said. He opened it and looked at my photograph. 'Not so pretty,' he added.

'He's going to be me?' I said. 'Into the river . . .?'

'That's the general plan. We'll have to dispose of his buddy some other way. Can't have too many stiffs floating downstream. The fish will think it's Thanksgiving. We just drop him in wearing your suit, passport in pocket. A couple of days in that river and his mother wouldn't know him.'

He leaned down and lifted the man, turning his shoulders so he could view the dead face. 'Hell,' he said. 'He's got a moustache.' He dropped the body heavily. 'That will have to go.' He glanced at me. 'Got some shaving gear?'

'Yes. Arturo brought some.'

'Good. Let's get to work.'

It was a gruesome fifteen minutes. The moustache took some removing. Sherling held the head while I shaved. The blood from the bullet hole had spread like a fan all over the man's shirt and the front of his jacket, and his eyes stared, hurt and helpless, as we went about the task.

At last it was done. 'I'm glad that's finished,' I breathed as Sherling dropped him again.

'Thank God he didn't have a beard,' said the American wiping his hands on his trousers. He glanced at me. 'Maybe you'd better have one! Okay, let's get him rigged up.'

I have never undressed a man before and certainly not a dead one. We pulled his trousers down revealing

Mickey Mouse boxer shorts, and eased him out of the bloodied coat. Then we put him in my suit and I put on his trousers. 'Made to measure,' approved Sherling. He looked at me. I swear he was enjoying it. 'The river is as fast as hell below here,' he said. 'There's not much risk of him being washed up too soon, not intact. Downstream there's a logging camp and various dams and docks, also plenty of big logs jumping about. That's where he should be found. Maybe it will be a few days or a few weeks.'

He sounded like someone discussing a friend's holiday schedule. 'As for buddy-boy,' he said, 'I guess we'll have to take him along.'

'With us?'

'That's what I said. We can't leave him here. Arturo's a good guy but he's not that good.'

'We could bury him,' I said. I almost felt I was entering into the spirit of the thing. 'Deep.'

'He'd come back with the rains,' sniffed Sherling. 'And that would not be nice. We'll have to take him.'

'Where are we going?'

'Eventually to the United States of America,' he announced. 'I just hope you like parrots.'

XVIII

When we took the first of the dead men out, there was a
curl of moon just above the mountains, and Arturo
appeared with a lantern. Sherling and I were carrying
the corpse between us. 'Our friend is going to the river,'
Sherling called to Arturo when he was still some distance
away. 'He likes to swim.'

The Mexican's big head was nodding wisely in the
uncertain lamplight as he neared. 'So,' he said: 'It is
good to swim. The fishes enjoy.'

Without another word he led the way. We skirted the
cabins and clambered heavily down some broken steps
which, in turn, gave way to a muddy downward path.
We slithered and stumbled towards the river. It was
swift, running heavily in its chasm, almost below our
feet. Arturo's lantern bounced as it descended ahead.
The angle was steep and the way became even more
difficult, with bends and boulders in the path. The river
seemed so directly below that I feared that one slip
would send all of us to join the body we were carrying.

'*Si, si,*' the Mexican ahead eventually whispered. He
had made no attempt at secrecy at the upper level, when
he had first appeared, but the presence of the rushing
water and the darkness of the deep place, caused him to
whisper now. I understood how he felt.

He had arrived at a flat stone platform, a fishing stage
I imagined, and he again said: '*Si, si.*' We paused,
breathing hard. People are always much heavier when

they are dead. We laid the burden down with odd gentleness on the stage and looked down towards the black awesome run of the river. Arturo lifted his lamp and the light caught the fringes of white water. It was still a long way down.

'It is a fine coat he is wearing for swimming,' suggested Arturo looking down at the man in my London clothes.

'He needs it,' returned Sherling. 'The water is cold.'

He glanced up at me in the uncertain light. 'Okay?' he said.

'Okay.' We lifted the corpse. Then Sherling, who was at the head and shoulders, nodded to me to lower it again. He felt on the inside pocket to make sure that the passport was secure. The pocket could be closed with a button and he checked this also.

'Now, really okay,' he said.

We lifted the body and, like two boys playing a swinging game with another boy, we swung him back and forwards three times. '*Uno, dos, tres,*' recited Arturo, his face devilish in the upward lantern rays. It was the most animated I had seen him. At '*tres*' we both let go and the man in my light grey suit flew off into the darkness, hitting the river heavily, sending out visible rings of spray.

Solemnly Sherling said to me: 'Now you're dead.'

I felt an intake of relief that we had done it. Arturo went past us on the stage and began the ascent. We trudged behind him. I was wearing the trousers of the man now presumably shooting rapidly through rough river waters downstream.

'Another señor to go swimming?' inquired the Mexican. As we reached the top, next to the cabins, his voice rose in confidence again.

'No,' said Sherling. 'Another señor going for a ride.'

He went with him to the top cabin which was the Mexican's house and his office, presumably to settle what must have been an unusual and considerable bill. I waited in the room. The second man had become almost part of the furniture. I stepped over him to reach the bathroom. Apart from my gun, my pen and my shaving kit, I had no possessions to take. I could go at once.

Sherling had obtained a new car, a sturdy station wagon, and into the back of this we lifted our second body. We also had a plastic bag containing the first man's bloodied shirt and coat. Arturo brought out some sacking and we laid it over the man. He then produced armfuls of great onions, still with their thick stems, and threw them across the sacks. 'They make a good smell,' he said.

'It's a long drive,' warned Sherling as he started the engine and switched on the headlights.

'How long?'

'Ten, twelve hours,' he said. 'North. Get some sleep if you can.'

'Thanks,' I said. 'I'll do some of the driving if you like.'

'Later. When we get on the main highway. Three or four hours from now. Get across to the back seat and sleep. Our friend doesn't snore.'

The body was rolled just inside the tailgate of the car, concealed by the sacking and the piled onions. I glanced over the back.

'What are we going to do with him?' I asked.

'There's a place,' said Sherling dependably.

I stretched on the back seat and as he drove down the mountain I fell into an exhausted sleep. The elbow turns and the steep braking scarcely disturbed me. When I woke the car had stopped and Sherling had climbed out and was walking easily towards a group of men with guns. I observed the scene cautiously. We were at a military checkpoint. There was a single floodlight and a boxlike cabin. The soldiers, three of them, were small and held onto their automatic rifles tightly, as though afraid they might be snatched from their hands. Sherling was speaking to them in rapid Spanish. Two of them advanced almost timidly. I sat up in the back seat and startled them both. They were boys, no more than eighteen, in greasy camouflaged fatigues, round-faced with black aslant and uncertain eyes. They did not look safe with the rifles.

Sherling continued talking to them as they approached. I saw him offer them a packet of cigarettes which, after the briefest hesitation, one of them grabbed and stuffed in his ammunition pouch. '*Buenas noches*,' I said to them.

They returned the greeting politely but nervously. One of them circled the car and actually looked through the back window at the onion-covered body. They then moved aside and the soldier who had been left behind lifted the barrier which had blocked the road. '*Buenas noches*,' they all cried, suddenly childlike and cheerful. Sherling slowed and threw them another packet of cigarettes which they scrambled for. Then another. 'One each,' he called as we drove on.

'Conscripts,' he called over his shoulder to me. 'Backwoods boys.'

'Why the road block?'

'Marijuana,' he returned. 'That's the excuse anyway. They grow it up in the hills and bring it down to the towns, and these guys are supposed to stop it getting through. That bunch looked as if they came from where the stuff is grown.'

'That might have been difficult, though,' I suggested.

'Certainly could,' he agreed. 'The sergeant was sleeping, which was lucky because he might have taken a closer look. And those boys, I bet they've hardly ever seen a gringo. They were too scared to do much.'

'Two gringos in a car with a load of onions,' I mused.

'Sure, but they don't know.'

'Will there be any more?'

'Road blocks? I doubt it. There's usually one on each highway. I'd overlooked it. Anyway we're soon going to part company with our passenger.'

Five minutes later he turned the car off the highway and once more we began to drive into the hills. The road was as canted and as indifferent as before. We went through a village with not a single light showing anywhere. Dogs barked but nobody got up from their bed.

After an hour we were driving along a plateau, way up near the moon it seemed. Huge, low clouds rolled almost in touching distance. The earth seemed far below as if we were flying. Sherling pulled up the car. It was getting light.

'This is it,' he said. 'This is where he gets out.'

I had trusted him this far. I had every reason to do so. He had saved my life. But suddenly an unreasonable alarm bell started ringing inside me. Here was I, alone and exposed again. I felt for my gun.

He detected the hesitation at once. 'What's the trouble?' he asked. 'Worried about me?' He snorted. 'So you should be. Don't trust anybody in this game, as you ought to be the first to know.'

'Sorry. But you know . . .'

'Sure I know. You're learning. That's how to stay living.'

He took a gun from his pocket and threw it on the driving seat. 'Now,' he said spreading his hands, '*I've* got to trust *you*.'

I laughed but still nervously. 'Okay. Sorry, Bill, but I've become jittery.'

'A good sign,' he said. 'I must be getting old not taking into account the road block. But somebody's got to lift our friend out.'

'Where's he going?' I asked. Dawn began to spread quickly. I could see him clearly now.

'Down El Gordo,' he answered. He walked around to the back of the vehicle and lifted the tailgate. 'The fat hole.'

I put the gun away and helped him lift the body. It had stiffened. It was like carrying a large piece of wooden furniture. 'Where's the hole?' I asked.

'You're almost on it,' he warned. 'Just step carefully. Over here, left.'

The dawn was helped by the car headlights that illuminated our feet and the rising ground before us. 'Hold it,' said Sherling abruptly. 'Just drop him for a minute.'

We put the body down. Sherling moved forward, up the slope, through the pale light. I saw him stop. 'It's still here,' he called back. 'The biggest hole in Mexico.'

I walked up as carefully as he had done, to where he was standing, at the top of the rise. He was two yards from the lip of a great misted chasm, a gap in the earth that stretched around us and disappeared into vapour and infinity far below our feet. 'Nobody has ever been to the bottom,' he said. 'Not to tell.'

He turned and I followed him. We picked up the hard body and carried it towards the precipice, stumbling over the rough ground. We laid it down at the place where we had stood before.

'One, two, three again, I suggest,' he said. 'We don't want any accidents.' He grinned. 'It would be sad if we went over the edge and left him here.'

We picked up the man for the last time. 'Okay,' said Sherling. 'Let's count together. Then we'll keep in time. Now.'

We swung our load and counted. '*Uno, dos, tres.*' We flung him out as far as we could from the edge. We saw him fall like a piece of paper. Fall and fall and fall, until he vanished into the fog far below. Strangely, his arms and legs were stretched out, as if he were trying to fly. He whirled and whirled. But silently, when it almost seemed that he should have screamed.

By the time Sherling drove the car down the mountain road again the Mexican day had grown around us; the sun, large and low, beamed across the land, thick trees split with its light, bulbous red boulders glowing like coals.

'There's nothing so advantageous as being dead,' observed Sherling. 'Not in this business. Dead like you are, I mean. So everybody thinks you're dead, but you know you're not. Then you can move about, make enquiries, watch people, take actions, without anybody knowing it's you. It's a great freedom.'

'Thanks,' I returned. 'I don't feel so great now. All these bodies are beginning to get me down.'

'They will,' he nodded sagely. 'But after a while one body is much like another. Especially if they're your enemies.'

'It's difficult when it is an enemy and you *do* care for them,' I said moodily.

'The girl?' He managed to combine a shrug with a vast spin of the wheel which sent the vehicle swerving in a dust cloud around one of the final corners of the downward road. 'Well, it was tough. I understand very well. But she was out to kill you. There's no arguing that. Even if *she* felt anything for *you*, she certainly wasn't going to let it get in *her* way. No sir.'

We reached the main highway. 'Do you want me to drive?' I said. 'You need some rest.'

'I do,' he acknowledged. He pulled the station wagon into a rutted lay-by where a man had a stall selling coffee and tacos. 'Breakfast,' he added.

'I'll get it,' I said. I glanced at him. 'But I don't have any money, remember.'

'We left it in your pants,' he nodded. 'That's okay. The Bureau instructed me to arrange financial support, within limits. I guess a dollar fifty won't break any rules.'

He handed me two dollars. Leaving the car I went to the taco stand and bought two cartons of thick Mexican coffee and tacos with bacon.

'Throwing people down holes makes you hungry,' observed Sherling. I still could not work him out; I still could not bring myself to trust him, despite everything. We ate the food and drank the coffee. 'Tacos,' he said, 'get in my teeth. If there's one thing I'd like to quit this country for, it's the fucking tacos. And guacamole. Only the Mexes could turn out a dish that looks like pale green shit and call it a delicacy.'

'Would you like to work . . . go . . . somewhere else?'

'Any place. Almost,' he said. 'I hate the goddam country. But this is *the* place for smuggling parrots. Try getting them in from Alaska or Honolulu.'

'Where do you get them?'

'All over. Dealers, guys who catch them. From all over Central and South America. It's an expensive business. First you have to get them here, alive, because a dead parrot's no use to any bastard. You have to assemble them, co-ordinate the whole thing. Get the plane fixed up. Some place quiet where you don't have to file a flight plan or if you do, you don't need to keep to it. Then you have to wait for the right moment, and that's difficult right now, as I told you. They've got these new goddam blimps all along the border, Stateside. They're supposed to spot the drug runners, but parrots are not too different as far as the US Customs is concerned. It gets difficult. We need some bad weather. When they don't fly the blimps.'

'Do the parrots make a row?'

'Fucking hideous.' He climbed over into the long rear scat and settled himself to sleep. 'You'll find out.'

I started the engine. 'Do we turn off anywhere?' I asked over my shoulder. I was uncomfortable that he was behind me.

'Keep going,' he said tiredly. 'It's five hours, depending how you drive. Maybe six. Just stay on the Inter-American Highway. The turn-off is to Santa Maria del Nieves. They say the clouds look like snow, so they called it that. But I'll be awake before you get to it.'

The highway, at this point, was only a two-track road, but it widened as we reached a long plain. The traffic was spasmodic; trucks labouring north, and truck-buses, with people crammed into and hanging onto them. It became hot and bright outside. I was glad of the air-conditioning. The road went spilling out before me. As I drove I began to think the whole thing out from the beginning again. I believed I almost had the answer.

Sherling woke after two hours and remained in the

back seat, sitting saying nothing, until we came to a small town. 'Want a beer?' he asked, adding, 'I do.'

Without waiting for an answer he said: 'This place ahead. Pull in there. We could get some hamburgers or something.'

I drove the car off the road into the red dirt. A man on a donkey was coming sedately towards me. Both passed by without a change of expression. Children stood shyly around watching the vehicle and saying: 'Money, money', but not insistently, almost as a suggestion. There were the usual black and grey pigs rummaging in the trash piled at the side of the road. A goat had put its horns through the skin of a pink plastic bag and was pulling out the rotten contents with its teeth. Sherling got out of the car and went to the food stand. My mouth was dry and I was grateful for the beer he brought back. He gave some coins to the children.

'Just to show you I'm not a bad guy,' he said as he handed me a hamburger through the window, 'unless I find it necessary.' He knew what I had been thinking. There had probably been a lot of people who did not trust him.

'How long will it be, do you think, before we can fly over the border?' I asked.

He shrugged, his mouth crammed with hamburger. 'Couple of weeks or a couple of months,' he said.

'Christ, that long?'

'I told you, I've got to co-ordinate the parrots, fix the plane and make sure the time, the weather, is right. That doesn't happen on the dot.' He looked through his cracked eyes at me in the driving seat. 'And, you've not been found dead yet.'

'No. I see.'

'No use you going back in secret, to catch them

unawares, if your death hasn't been announced,' he said. 'They won't *know* you're dead, will they? The effect is diminished.'

'What if they don't find me in the river?' I asked. 'Maybe that corpse is trapped in some logs or wedged in a side-channel or something like that.'

He thought about it then said: 'In that case we'll have to kill you again. And keep on killing you until somebody notices.' He opened the door. 'I'll drive now,' he said.

He climbed behind the wheel as I moved over. 'At Santa Maria you'll have to hide up again,' he said. 'Maybe for a long time. You'd better get yourself a good book. Or maybe write one.'

The car turned onto the main road. A truck-bus overtook us while we were still gaining momentum, and all the passengers waved in simple triumph. 'That's the idea,' I said. 'To write a book. But somehow I don't think I'm going to be paid for it. Not now.'

'It should sell plenty,' he said.

'Who is going to believe it?' I asked. 'What proof do I have? Nobody will think there's a shred of bloody truth in it.'

'That's how it often is,' he agreed calmly. 'There's no justice in this business.'

'Nobody would believe it, anyway,' I repeated. 'And, frankly, I don't feel inclined to spend the rest of my life as a prospective assassination victim.'

'It's not the best life,' he agreed but added: 'But people do. One day you must tell me the whole story.'

He did not sound convincing. 'You really want to hear it?' I asked.

He shook his head and glanced in the driving mirror at the traffic behind. There was a junction sign ahead. 'No,' he sighed. 'I don't really. It's interesting, but I find

I'm happier, and safer, if I don't know too much. A little of this and a little of that. It's all I need. Strangely enough, parrots don't tell tales.'

At the turn off the sign said: 'Santa Maria del Nieves' and we followed it. 'It's no fishing camp,' said Sherling. 'Let me warn you.'

'I've had enough of fishing camps,' I told him. 'What is it?'

'It's an apartment.' He seemed doubtful. 'I guess you could call it that. Yes, an apartment. Top floor of a crummy hotel in the middle of a crummy town. Hot and crummy.'

'But it's safe?'

'I guess so. As safe as anywhere is. It's noisy. There's a lot of people around. But it's safe . . . sure . . .'

He still did not sound convinced. 'I'll be gone a few days,' he said. 'Maybe a week. Keep your head down. Your food will come to your room. They may still be after you. Or maybe we threw them off, I don't know.'

The road went up so steeply in places that even the powerful car groaned. 'How do they get up here normally?' I asked. 'The locals.'

'They don't in general,' he said. 'They live up there and that's where they stay. They've got everything they need. It's like a separate country. Nobody comes out unless they have to, certainly not in this direction. I keep my plane up here for that reason. Anybody approaching is seen and people talk about them.'

'That goes for us too then.'

He sniffed as though testing the air. He had turned down the window and there was already a change in the temperature. Ferns and flowers grew at the flanks of the road. 'They've got used to me,' he said. 'Because they know I've got the plane. Sometimes I've brought other people up here. They won't think it's too strange.' There was a sense of relief about him that we had reached this place. 'It's a good place to fly a plane from,' he continued. 'You're at three thousand feet before you start. Great saving on gas. And nobody sees you come and nobody sees you go.'

The greenery hugging the road had become luxuriant, sometimes encroaching across the broken tarmac. The going was rougher as we climbed. The firm surface became cracked and convoluted at the steep bends. In some places a great bite of the road had disappeared over the side of a precipice. Bright geraniums in pots warned the driver of the danger. 'They come down from the villages or the town,' said Sherling. 'And take a look at the road, or where there was a road, and put the flowers out. They're prettier than a barrier or red lights. And cheaper. They show up plenty at night. Not that there's much traffic.'

I said that if the road was so rarely used it was a wonder it was repaired at all. 'They're not stupid, these people,' he said. 'They know that if it gets too bad then the government's going to take an interest and send up gangs to repair it; send up gangs and probably officials and then soldiers to guard the officials, and so it will go on. The people up here don't want that. So they repair the road themselves and nobody comes bothering them.'

'They sound as if they've got a lot to hide,' I said.

'Sure. There's a big marijuana industry, other drugs too, and sometimes fugitives.' He glanced at me. 'People who need to hide. There's a monastery up here where half the fucking monks have been in jail, and some still ought to be. They specialize in privacy.'

As he spoke he curved the car around a broad bend, part of which had disappeared forever over its own edge, and we drove abruptly into a ragged but substantial town. The main street climbed between adobe houses, each with its porch, its open drain and its hammock in the shade. In the street were some shops beneath threadbare awnings, and a little café where people sat and stood around a counter occupied by a woman pouring coloured drinks. There were half a dozen vehicles, mud-caked and leaning, some horses tethered to a tree, its bark rubbed away from years of such use. There was the customary mixture of children, pigs and goats. In the centre of the place was a faucet from which spouted a stream of water, thick as an arm. Two women bent with pots to collect the water and a small girl in a filthy red dress walked away precisely, balancing a rusty jerry-can upon her small head.

'We got here,' sighed Sherling pulling the car up outside a fly-blown awning. As we arrived the awning was pulled aside and a man with no legs came out pushing himself on a wheeled trolley. He greeted Sherling joyfully and insisted on showing the American his trolley with the enthusiasm of the owner of a new car. 'He used to have roller skates,' explained Sherling.

I followed him below the dirty canvas and into a dim, wooden room, with a bar running along one side and a rough array of tables and chairs occupying the rest of the place. There was a picture of Jesus behind the bar but that was the only decoration. A man came forward and rubbed his hands on a foul apron. 'This is Jesus,' said Sherling. He glanced at the picture. 'No relation. Jesus Morales. He runs this shit-hole. He's your host until we can get out. God knows when that will be. What would you like to drink?'

The Hotel Grande and Excelsior at Santa Maria del

Nieves was a dire place to stay for two months. Sherling had not exaggerated. The moment Jesus Morales took me to the room I knew that. He turned on a heavy brass switch at the door, and with the groan of a rudely aroused drunk, the rusty fan on the ceiling began to revolve. Jesus introduced it proudly, pointing his finger up in the manner of paintings of his namesake. 'Señor, ees air-condition,' he said.

The fan was loose and it wobbled as it revolved turgidly. If you attempted to speed it, pieces of plaster fell which Jesus picked up sulkily when he came in to the room. As the fan wobbled it clanked like an elderly engine. Even so, its poor efforts at distributing the gritty air were necessary. Nights and mornings were blessedly cool, but as the beat of the day increased and the dust rose from the street below, to be without it would have been unbearable. I sat near the torn and yellowing gauze curtain at the window and looked out over the town. Jesus brought me food and beer three times a day, and also thoughtfully offered me the comfort of his widowed sister, which I declined. Instead he produced the only book in English he could find in the town, a guide to Nova Scotia. I became an armchair expert on Nova Scotia. If ever I go there I will be treading familiar ground.

Twice during his first absence Sherling telephoned to see that I was safe. I was gratified. My ambition was to get out of this place in one piece; my plan was forming. I had not shaved for a week. Before he left I had asked Sherling if he had reported my safe-being to the FBI. He had shaken his head. 'I wanted to make sure you're *really* safe before I did that,' he said. 'I'm not a regular operative, just when I'm required. I don't have to tell them everything I do.'

'Good,' I had told him. 'I think it would be better if when my death is announced *everybody* should believe it.'

'Right,' he said. 'You should get a good press. It's a matter of timing.' We had been drinking in the room just before his departure to co-ordinate his consignment of parrots. He said he was having trouble with the plane. There would be delays. 'You ever see those guys at Acapulco diving from the rocks into the sea?' he inquired.

'No, I've never been to Acapulco.'

'One hundred, thirty-five feet they dive. It's terrific. Into the ocean. But it depends on the right wave and the right wind and the right guy who is diving. Everything has got to be right. Timing.'

Every morning in the room I would be awakened by the shouts and sounds in the street below. Children being scolded to school, men trudging to work, donkeys snorting. Sometimes a woman sang. Weeks went by like this. Unending and unchanging. I never went out. Sherling came and went. He needed new parts for the plane. Some of the parrots had died.

After eight of the longest weeks I can ever remember, during which I not only had time to sift the present phase of my life, but all I could remember that had gone before: marriages, affairs, work, frustrations and anger, and my late shot at happiness with the whales; after those eight weeks, the news arrived of my death.

I had paid Jesus to bring a television into my room and I watched American films dubbed in Spanish. There was an English film with Big Ben and red buses. Alec Guinness sounded strange. The news was broadcast from Mexico City twice a day, in the early and late evening. When I had all but given up hope of the body in the river being found its discovery was mentioned on the late newscast. Because I was dozing I almost missed it. I heard my name and sat abruptly upright on the bed. I jumped up and got closer, turning the volume up. The body had been found at a log jam in the river. It was only identified by the London label of the suit and a soaked British passport. That news would already be in Washington and in London. I wondered how many glasses would be raised in my memory.

Now all I could do was to wait for Sherling. He arrived four days later. He had seen the news in a Mexican paper. He brought the cutting and showed it to me. 'They also got your picture,' he said. 'Wire service picture.' He handed a second newspaper to me. It featured a photograph taken at a wedding. I looked drunk. The wedding might have been one of mine.

'I've fixed the plane,' he said. 'And I've got the parrots. It's taken a long time.'

'When do we go?' I asked.

'When the weather is okay,' he repeated. He had brought back a bottle of brandy and we were drinking it in the room, sitting on each side of the dirty window. 'I've organized everything else. Now it's just the weather.'

It took two further days. I stayed in the room as before but he was absent throughout the days, returning at nightfall grimy and tired. 'You earn your dough parrot smuggling,' he said.

At four o'clock on the third morning he woke me, banging on my door in the dark. 'Mike, get up,' he called. 'We're going.' Outside I could hear the wind shifting. It only took me ten minutes to get downstairs, but he was already waiting. 'We don't want too much crap,' he said going to the door and examining the wind in the darkness. 'But just crap enough.'

He had changed the car again. Now it was a jeep. We climbed into it, and Jesus came sleepily to the door to see us off. He asked if he could have his Nova Scotia book back, and I told him it was in the room.

Sherling kept looking out at the sky and smelling at that wind. I began to get apprehensive. 'What do you think?' I asked.

'It's not good enough for safety but it's too lousy for the blimps. They don't fly them in this weather. But they're a hundred miles away, remember. It may be peaceful as fucking paradise there. But you can generally tell. If it's crap here, it's probably crap over there. Let's hope so.'

We drove down the mountain and then up on another slim track. It was still dark and the headlights revealed the rocks and chasms we were skirting. I kept silent. Eventually the track flattened and as the first dawn was scraping the eastern horizon, we arrived on a plateau lined with thick, blowing grass. There was a single silhouetted shed, and next to it the outline of a small twin-engined aeroplane fidgeting in the wind.

Sherling clambered out of the jeep. As he did so I heard a concerted scream. Sharply I looked around, staring into the grey light. 'Parrots,' he shouted over his shoulder. 'They sound like that when they're sore.'

These parrots were sore. As we opened the door of the aircraft, they screamed their fury. They were in cages occupying the entire back compartment of the plane. In the dimness I could hardly see them, only their angry eyes, the disturbance of their flapping feathers, and the clatter of their beaks on wire. I got into the co-pilot's seat. A man, a shape, appeared from within the solitary hut. He began to laugh coarsely. Then he went away and Sherling climbed into the pilot's position beside me.

332

'This ain't going to be any trip by Concorde,' he warned. He grimaced out of the window. 'But this time we need to go. That guy says some soldiers are due up here tomorrow.'

There was only a curtain, which was open, between us and the rest of the plane. The parrots' cages were only two feet behind my neck. They stank too. They cackled and screeched. A great green creature was in the cage immediately behind me. Sherling pulled the curtain across, but I could feel its eyes on my neck. 'How many?' I asked Sherling.

'Fifty-three alive,' he said. 'Now, can you quit the questions for a while? I've got to get this fucking menace out of here.' He turned on the power. The lights on the control panel lit up like a silent pinball machine. He made a conscientious check, and then switched on the port engine. The parrots screeched. The bird behind me, beyond the curtain, was flapping its wings and shouting in my ear.

Outside the early day was dim. The wind was still up and, as Sherling turned on the starboard engine, gobs of rain began to pattern the glass in front of us. The American swore vividly. The racket of the engines was doing something to drown the racket of the parrots. 'Right,' said Sherling. 'Let's see if she still flies.'

He edged the machine away from the shed. I caught a moment of the fat stationary Mexican watching us go. He did not wave but flapped his hand downwards in a dismissive motion. 'He thinks we're mad,' grunted the American.

Rain splattered against the windscreen. The wiper on my side did not work. Sherling turned the bouncing plane in a half circle, and then we sat for five minutes while he warmed the engines. They covered the protests of the parrots. The pilot had ample doubts. The rain thickened but he said: 'We can't wait. We've got to go. If you feel like quitting, now's the time to do it, brother. In ten minutes it's going to be too late, because I'm not coming back in this shit.'

'I'm here now,' I said unconvincingly. 'Is this going to ease?'

'It had better,' he grunted. 'I'll give it as long as I can.'

The minutes went by on the clock almost in front of my nose, the only dial that did not seem to be trembling with indecision. Then the downpour briefly eased. 'The wind is swinging around,' said Sherling. 'This is where we go.'

He gave the engines another boost. The parrots sounded like distraught and distant old ladies. The plane was tugging to go. He released the brakes and we began to make speed along the heavy grass of the strip, bouncing and banging until at last we pulled clear and the only noise was that of the engines and the parrots. The aircraft bucked in the turbulence. 'We've got to go right through the middle of this crap,' muttered Sherling. 'There's no way around it or above it. Just hold on tight and try not to vomit in my lap.'

The following half an hour was terrifying. We were thrown about the clouds like a piece of board. Every time we sailed into a blue patch my relief was terminated by another onslaught, and we were back in the storm again. He was a wonderful pilot, but I was not sure about the machine. The parrots had gone thoughtfully silent.

At no time did we get above four thousand feet, and somehow he had to pick his way between the sharp edges of mountains that loitered among the clouds. They seemed very close. But he knew what he was doing. He made no radio contact with the ground at any stage, but flew by skill and instinct. 'I have never seen anything like that,' I said to him eventually. 'Your flying, I mean.'

'Nor me,' he agreed laconically.

We had emerged from the worst of the weather and were bumping along in a mushy grey sky, but flat, and we had left the wind astern. The parrots, possibly as relieved as me, had reduced their sounds to a general cawing. Then we were out of the clouds and into a beautiful blue morning with a sunlit red desert below us. 'Shit,' said Sherling.

'Will they spot us?'

'They could. We've come in low. Fifteen hundred. We've just crossed the Texas border and nobody mentioned it. Not on the air. The weather's been bad here too. See the floodwater shining down there. Maybe it's too soon for them to put their blimps up.'

Feeling better now I said: 'Well, this is the United States, that's America down there. All they can do is to force us to land, or wait until we get down and pick us up.'

'With an immigrant without papers and a cargo of unlawful parrots,' he mentioned caustically.

'Then you flash your FBI credentials.'

'What FBI credentials? You know as well as I do that the Bureau would just disown me. "Bill who?" they'd say. "We don't have anybody of that name." The next thing you hear is the cell door clanging – behind you.'

Now he brought the plane down even lower. The land was still hilly and cleft, but there were no tall mountains. He was looking around, leaning forward, almost smelling the landscape. Eventually he smiled and said: 'There. We made it.'

I could not see anything, although he had nodded towards my side of the aircraft. He curved the plane over the red earth and dropped in a long approach until a scar in the desert came into view. He circled once again, then came in and landed bumpily on the ragged strip. He taxied to the shelter of some bulbous rocks, stopped, and turned off the engines. He sat back, exhausted and smiling. I clapped my hands. 'Bloody brilliant,' I said.

'I think so too,' he answered. The parrots all together seemed to realize that they were safe and stationary also, because they set up a collective screech from beyond the curtain. I pulled it aside, laughing, and came eye to eye with the big green bird occupying the nearest cage. Its vicious beak pushed itself into the gap, like a pair of wire cutters. Sherling had opened his door and I opened mine. The desert air was damp after the rain. We dropped down onto the red drying mud. A truck appeared around the corner of the boulders. There were two men aboard and, with scarcely a word, they began quickly unloading the crates of crying parrots from the plane and into their vehicle. A jeep then appeared with a young, effeminate man at the wheel. 'Brought some more tweetie-pies?' he called.

'Shut your mouth,' said Sherling tiredly. 'Let's get going.'

We travelled in the jeep following the truck. Sherling had waited until the final cage was carried from the resting plane, and insisted that the truck drove off first, with us close behind. 'Don't want them hijacked now,' he observed.

After half an hour we came to a small town. 'There's a Greyhound in an hour to Fort Worth,' said Sherling. He shook hands with me. 'You ought to be on it.'

'Thanks,' I said inadequately. 'For the lot.'

'That's okay. Make sure you tell them how good I was to you. Here's two thousand and five hundred dollars. I'm sending them the bill.'

I said: 'Two thousand five hundred – that's half a parrot. Thanks.'

The truck and the jeep drove away and I stood outside the downcast looking café that was also the bus terminal. Two small girls played with a doll in a pram. In exactly an hour the Greyhound appeared, lumbering up the street. I climbed aboard and settled myself tiredly in a rear seat. It took four hours to reach Forth Worth.

From there I got a flight to Washington, DC.

When I arrived it was snowing. It had been almost three months. I realized it was almost Christmas.

XIX

The black man was still haranguing the FBI building but had moved his pitch thirty feet so that he was positioned above a grating from which issued a skein of steam, an island in a street of snow.

'That's his winter quarters.' It was Fred Robinson's voice. He was just behind me. There was a quiet beam on his face and his step was jaunty. 'Great to see you again, Mike,' he said moving a book from below his armpit so that we could shake hands. My hand went out slowly, unbelievingly. 'How was Mexico. Good?'

'A good place to bloody die,' I said. He looked utterly unshocked. Surely, but *surely*, he knew. I realized I had raised my voice. The protesting black man stopped, looked towards us, and began protesting again. I dropped my tone but still gabbled. 'I was shot and thrown into a river and my body, in my London-made suit and with my passport in the pocket, was washed up a week later. It was in all the newspapers.' I regarded him truculently.

'No kidding,' he observed soberly. We were walking into the courtyard, the fountains draped with ice and snow but still gamely gushing. 'I'll get you identification,' he said as we went through the main doors. 'Then you must tell me about it. The beard's just great.'

Nothing had changed in the entrance lobby of the Bureau, not even the muzak. It seemed to be the same blank people sitting there waiting for attention. The redhead with the gun and the hips was behind the desk with two men. She took no more notice of me than she had previously. Ill-temperedly, I took the plastic oblong and, following Robinson through the turnstile, thrust it like a dagger into the required slot. As we walked through the corridors, Robinson said: 'I just took a vacation. That's why I didn't hear, maybe.'

We went into his office. There was a pile of documents and folders on his desk. He closed the door but people kept coming in and saying: 'Have a nice vacation, Fred?' and 'Everything okay, Fred?'

Caustically, I said: 'Have a nice vacation? Everything okay?'

His eyes drifted up. 'Sure,' he said. 'It's finished. Kaputt, man. I just feel good it's all over. Today I'm going to start looking around. I tried, she tried, everybody tried. What God hath put asunder, let no man try to bring together again. It don't work.'

He was sorting though the material on the desk. 'Huh, huh,' he said, opening a file and bringing out a pile of news cuttings clipped together. 'I guess this is your press coverage.' He hummed. 'Not bad.'

With patent patience I waited until he had gone through them. 'Nice picture of you,' he said holding up an American newspaper with my wedding picture. I said nothing. He read further and began to whistle. 'Wow,' he breathed. 'So you found Hine eh? And somebody found you.'

'I'm just flabbergasted you didn't know.'

'When I'm on vacation I never look at the papers,' he said. 'Or television. And especially on this vacation. It was just like our honeymoon. Once we knew the marriage was finished, we ended up having a good time.'

'Fred,' I said. 'Can we get back to my business? I

339

know I've got the answer – and it's not what we thought.'

'I never thought it was,' he said simply. 'You were sent to find Hine so that somebody could rub him out.'

'Jesus Christ, why didn't you tell me?'

'Look, Mike,' he said leaning wisely over the desk. 'This case is out of my hands. It's never been in them. I'm just an archivist here. Sure, I got interested, but the real motivators are people upstairs, the operatives, the bosses, get it? They make the decisions. They pay the money. They pull the strings.' His eyes went back to the newspaper clippings. 'Did they protect you?'

'Yes. The man saved my life.'

'Okay, so they did a good job then.'

A fat woman in unsuitable clothes and huge glasses came in and asked about his vacation. I felt like answering her myself. When she had gone I said: 'I've got to tell you what I think, Fred. It will shake you rigid. But I can't do it here. Can't we go somewhere quieter?'

For a moment he seemed doubtful. The building must have had a million rooms, and he seemed to be mentally ticking them off. 'I guess we could,' he said with eventual decisiveness. 'Let's go.'

He lifted the file from the desk. As we walked along the corridors he glanced at the cover and said: 'They even spelled your name wrong.' He showed me. It said: 'Michael Fontlater'.

The archivist shook his head. 'That's how files go missing. There must be a thousand files wandering around this building, lost, looking for a home. If they'd really rubbed you out in Mexico, this could have just been one of them, lost for years, nobody knowing anything about you or it.'

'That's very reassuring,' I grunted.

'I know, I know, but this is a big organization. When something gets out of line, it can just drift off into the unknown. It could be the next century before it turns up. A lot too late. What's important to you, and me too, Mike, is not always important to other people.'

'Even something like this?'

He shrugged: 'Even something like this. To a lot of folks in this building it's just a story. We hear a lot of stories.' He paused by a door and said: 'Here.'

It was unlocked. We entered a room that had a single oblong polished table at its centre with four chairs. Around the walls were ranged dark green metal filing cabinets. On top of one of these was a human hand and half an arm encased in a glass jar. 'They will leave these around,' muttered Robinson. He picked it up and placed it negligently in a cabinet drawer.

'This,' he said whimsically, 'is where you come if you need somebody to . . .'

'Lend a hand,' I finished sourly.

He reached into a drawer and withdrew a human female breast horizontally set like a blancmange in a jar. 'Or one of these,' he said. He put it away as I paled. 'Or maybe . . .' he retrieved a set of false teeth mounted like a necklace in a display box ' . . . these.' He glanced at the label. 'Richmond, Virginia, April 4th, 1921.' He shrugged. 'Get what I mean. About stories. We got plenty.'

Sombrely I sat at the table. 'Do you want to hear mine?' I asked.

'I certainly do,' he replied earnestly. He sat down opposite me and locked his hands on the table. 'I only said *other* people in this building would not be too interested. I'm different. This is one of the few opportunities I get of dealing with something that's not already ancient history.' He tapped the edges of his hands on the table. 'Go on, Mike, let's hear it.'

First I related chronologically everything that had occurred in Mexico. When I described, at the outset, my meeting with Cara at Mexico City Airport, he nodded and reached for the file. 'I think I got a glimpse of her,' he said. 'Just now.' He reached in the folder and took out a picture. I sat shocked and looked at it.

'Lucille Benedict,' he read. 'Alias Carol Van Dorn, Alias Maria Slessor . . . and a few more if you're interested.'

My eyes were still fixed on the picture. She was smiling her wistful smile at the camera. I could not believe what he was telling me. 'It's incredible,' I muttered. 'Just incredible.'

Robinson sniffed. 'It often is,' he agreed. 'She's been operating for five years. Was an actress in Spain.'

I felt myself nodding dumbly.

'Sexual blackmail, forgery, armed robbery . . . and then she went on to bigger stuff . . .' He glanced up from the paper. 'Want to hear it?'

'No thanks. She's stopped doing it now.'

He continued studying the dossier.

'She liked you, though.'

Angrily I stared at him. 'For God's sake . . .'

'Here, it says she sent her apologies for trying to kill you. If she had not liked you so much she would have got you.'

'When . . .? But how? She was dead. I saw her lying across the table. Sherling shot her.'

'Shot her maybe, but he didn't kill her. She lived two more days, even regained consciousness.'

My head went into my hands. 'I just can't take in all this,' I said. 'Go on telling me,' he suggested.

Hesitantly I returned to the story, describing how we discovered Hine in the Mexican town, how Sherling had interpolated himself, and the double shooting in the cantina. Then I described the fishing camp and the two men I had killed. He nodded at this, as if to approve. 'When you first kill some guy yourself,' he said quietly. 'That's when you know the business is serious.'

'Even if the FBI don't think so,' I retorted.

He held up his hands. 'The Bureau protected you, I got you the gun, remember. If it hadn't been for this guy, what's his name . . .? Sherling . . . you'd be just a mound of earth south of the border. All I said was that this is a big world in here, in this building, and worse things happen every day. It was serious for you, I know, it couldn't get more serious.'

'Sorry,' I nodded wearily. 'I'm in all sorts of pieces, that's all. I've been holed up, hiding, for weeks.'

'Sure, sure,' he nodded soothingly. 'But you got out, that's number one.'

Wanly I smiled. 'With a planeload of parrots,' I said.

'It's different,' he nodded seriously. 'Want some coffee?'

'Yes, thanks. I could do with some.' He got up and went out of the room. My eyes and my hand went towards the file containing her picture, but I pulled my hand back. He returned with two plastic cups.

'They relaxed the rules,' he said. 'At last. I'm permitted to buy you coffee. But still not lunch.'

He seemed concerned that the cups should not mark the polished table and took a sheet from the file, the sheet with Cara's details on it, and tore two squares from the bottom where it was clear of writing. He placed them carefully below the cups and replaced the sheet. I took a hot drink of the coffee. I said: 'But, I think I've

343

worked it out, the whole bloody plot, Fred. Nobody's going to believe this either. There's a few answers I need to get now. For a kick off, from Mr Brant Irving.'

Fred stopped the progress of his coffee cup to his mouth. 'You won't get any answers from him,' he said.

'I'll get them.'

'You won't. He took off in his boat, a few days before I went on leave, out into the ocean.'

'Christ.'

'The boat was washed up somewhere out there, Montauk, I think. All smashed up. His body was washed up two days later in the same area.

'Suicide,' I muttered.

'Shipwrecked,' he shrugged. 'Anyway, you're not going to get any help there.'

'A man called Harry Filling died like that a few years ago,' I said. 'Went out fishing and never came back. He was on the beach a few hours after Hine's party landed. He kept some of the stuff they brought ashore. Perhaps he knew too much.'

'Like Brant Irving, you think?' said Robinson.

'Brant knew a lot,' I said.

'Maybe he *found out* a lot,' pointed out Robinson. He leaned forward: 'Everyone still thinks you're dead, right? They read in the papers that this well-known British writer was involved in a shoot-up in some bar in Mexico. Two people die, one of them a man called Hine. The Brit escapes but then his body is found in a river a couple of hundred miles away. End of story. Whoever had something to hide must have been almighty relieved to read that information. Everything had gone to plan. If Irving was one of them, why go out in a storm in your boat and wreck it?'

Nodding I said: 'Yes, that could be right.'

'It narrows down the field,' he said.

'To Senator Sam Keenor.' I met his eyes.

'And his wife Madelaine,' he added.

Slowly I agreed: 'Yes . . . Madelaine.'

'You can certainly pick them,' he said. I looked at him sharply and he said: 'Okay, go on with the story . . .'

'Hine,' I said carefully. 'Just about the last words Hine said before Cara shot him were after I'd mentioned "Unter den Sternen".'

He tried to remember: 'What's that?'

'Under the stars,' I said. 'In the file, in his evidence to the FBI, Fleming the coastguard, the kid, remember?'

Robinson nodded. There was a touch of appreciation in the gesture. 'I remember,' he said. 'Go on.'

'Fleming said that when he met Hine and the other three Germans on the beach that night, he came through the fog with his torch, right?'

'Right.'

'And Hine said to him, according to the kid, his first words, "Under the stern" and Fleming thought he was referring to their supposed fishing boat which had gone aground. In fact Hine was saying "Unter den Sternen" – Under the Stars. Those were the last words Hine said to me before he was murdered, and he added: "It was our password".'

Slowly, Robinson said: 'Go on.'

'Fred, a *password* is something you say to *identify* yourself. Hine and the others were expecting to be *met* on the beach that night. It *never*, ever, seemed logical that after mounting an operation like that, risking a bloody submarine, all the preparations – the whole elaborate business – that the Germans would just hope for the best when their spies got ashore. It's inconceivable when you think it out. They had to *walk across the dunes*, they had to *get a*

345

bloody train to New York. That was their audacity paying off. But it was not *planned* like that, Fred. Hine was expecting a *contact*, someone or some people, were supposed to be on that lonely beach to meet him. "Unter den Sternen" was the password by which they would identify each other. *But the contact didn't arrive.* The coast-guard kid turned up instead. The man who was to conceal them and give them safe passage so that they could infiltrate quietly into the United States had taken fright, or for some other reason was not there. And the man we are talking about . . .'

'Is Senator Herbert Keenor,' recited Robinson.

A pink-faced, pink-haired woman came into the room. 'Hi, Fred,' she said genially. 'Had a good vacation?' She looked inquiringly around. 'What happened to my arm?' she asked. 'I could swear I left it . . .'

'It's in the drawer,' said Robinson. 'The vacation was good, thanks. I replaced the arm in case somebody took it. You can never tell.'

'You can't,' she agreed. She moved around the table and opened the green filing drawer. She took out the bottled forearm and hand like a housewife might take a joint of meat from the freezer. She tucked it under her own arm and prepared to leave. 'Haven't had a chance to talk since we were on the river boat,' she remarked to Robinson.

'Wow, yes,' he said flatly. 'The staffday on the Potomac. That was some day.'

'The singing captain,' she enthused. 'Remember the singing captain?' She looked towards the window brimming with grey sky. 'It seems so long ago when you look at the snow,' she added sadly. The dead limb remained trapped below her armpit.

As I was sitting there impatiently, half smiling, Robinson thought he ought to introduce us, although he did not use my name. 'This gentleman has just come back from Mexico,' he said. 'He got that beard there.'

'Really! Oh, how I'd just love to go to Mexico.' She looked challengingly at me. 'I bet you had a great time.'

'Oh, I did,' I nodded.

She made a move to the door. 'I must go,' she said. 'There's always something to do in this place.' She took the cased specimen in both hands and jovially waved it at us. 'Bye for now.'

When she had closed the door, Robinson looked slowly towards me and said: 'Herbert Forrest Keenor'.

'You've got some memory,' I observed wryly.

He said seriously: 'Do you *know* what you're saying?'

'I've thought it right through, Fred.'

'That's not the same as proving it right through.'

'Agreed. But just allow me to tell you how I've *thought* it through.' He nodded. I said: 'That night in 1942, the foggy night in June, Herbert Keenor had his rendezvous with the men coming from the submarine.'

'Why would he want to do that?'

'Because he was a Nazi sympathizer. A secret Nazi sympathizer. He believed they had to win. Perhaps he had visions of being President of a United States under Hitler. Who knows?'

'Some ambition.' He shifted uneasily.

'He was very ambitious. And getting nowhere in particular,' I said.

'We can check his political record anyway. It's here on file. It's okay to see it now he's dead. I can get it.' He moved to pick up a telephone.

'Can you get the records of two politicians called Fisher and Wale at the same time?' I asked.

'Who are they?' He paused before lifting the phone. 'Fisher and Wale?'

I said: 'You remember the first time we met, in the Smithsonian?'

'Sure. I went there to look for you.'

'That pre-war photograph, all the politicians . . .'

'Sure. Lined up. Smiling.'

'Right. Well, the two men on either side of Keenor were called Fisher and Wale. I remember them because of whales and fishing. The names stuck in my mind.'

'Sure. You're going to write a book about whales.'

'One day. Can you get their files?'

'If they've died. I'll try anyway.' He picked up the phone and made the request. 'We'll get them pretty soon,' he said. 'Filing is my department. I know how to make it work.' He regarded me steadily: 'Okay, suppose you're right. The spies arrive but Keenor, the contact man, doesn't.'

'Don't ask me why,' I said. 'I don't know. Maybe because the coastguards were unexpectedly called out that night on account of the fog. Maybe he just got cold feet. Something went wrong. It was fouled up. Hine and company were literally left high and dry.'

'But none of them, not even Hine, knew the identity of the contact?'

'No. If Hine had been aware of it, he would have certainly spilled the beans to the FBI when he gave himself up. In his statement at the trial he only said that his instructions were to work with US persons who would contact him.'

Robinson took out a pencil but only tapped it on the table. 'But later, years later maybe, he found out who that contact was.'

'He did. Years later,' I agreed. 'In fact only at the

start of this year. He had been bumming around in Germany, dabbling in antiques, trying to make a fortune but always failing. Then he raised some money and went to Paraguay, mainly, it seems, to try and start up some business, legal or otherwise, in shipping ancient artefacts, antiquities, out of the country.'

'You can get anything in or out of Paraguay,' nodded Robinson. 'It's like a sieve.'

'Okay. But while he was there he mixed with the many Germans who now live in Asuncion and other places nearby, some of them ageing ex-Nazis. They get together quite openly. They use the same German restaurants, cafés and clubs. He was soon nosing among them. And it was there that he met someone, a former officer in German Intelligence called Dieter Gottinger, who was involved in the Pastorius operation. And that man told him who his contact was to have been on the Long Island Beach – Herbert Keenor.'

Robinson transferred the pencil to tapping his nose. 'Do I hear the ugly word "blackmail" in the offing?' he suggested.

'You certainly do,' I said. 'Here, Hine realized, was a chance to make some real money. At the start he thought he could blackmail Herbert Keenor on account of Keenor's own reputation. But when he checked Keenor out he found something far, far better. Keenor's son, Sam, the apple of his eye, was now a famous politician, Mr Clean, a man with serious White House ambitions.'

'You think he was blackmailing Sam directly?'

'No, I don't. Sam knew nothing about it, at this stage. But Herbert Keenor was wide open for it, not only on his own behalf, but particularly on account of his son and his son's political ambitions. Hine probably wrote to Herbert Keenor first. Can't you see the old man coming face to face with the password again: "Unter den Sternen"? Then Hine followed it up with a visit. Hine made an unofficial journey to the United States last summer. He was smuggled in from Mexico. He went to Flagstaff.'

'The night Herbert Keenor died,' nodded Robinson. 'And at that point you were already involved.'

'Keenor contacted me through Madelaine, who may or may not have known about the blackmail situation, even if her husband didn't. I don't know. I'm inclined to think she didn't. Anyway she called me, making the excuse the need for me to see Susan our daughter, at Keenor's insistence. She also asked me to be nice, to co-operate, with the media should I be interviewed as the ex-husband of a Presidential-possible's wife. Perhaps she was unaware of the real reason. But, whatever, Herbert, having received the blackmail letter from Hine, realized that he would have to find this man. Hine did not give away the fact that he was in Mexico. The postmark was somewhere in the United States, Los Angeles, even Chicago. Hine could have arranged to have the letter sent from there. Perhaps there was more than one. All Keenor knew was that somewhere, and he believed somewhere in this country, there was a man who had discovered his forty-odd year old secret. This man was going to blackmail him or ruin his son's political career – but probably *both*.'

'Somehow,' nodded Robinson, 'he had to find him.'

'And that's where I came in. He knew that I had a reputation as an investigative journalist. I was a foreigner, I was discreet. I could work undercover. I was safe. So he set me on the trail to find Hine, under the pretence of assigning me to write a book or newspaper articles or whatever. He held enough dollars in front of my nose to make it tempting. He knew I could not refuse it.'

Robinson was animated. 'But shit, then *who* tried to kill you, who put the fucking ravens in your bed? There's no way you were going to find Hine if they'd killed you.'

'Nobody killed me,' I pointed out. 'Each time, remember, they missed me. Once the wrong room caught fire, once the go-go girl got shot.'

'But the other incidents happened after Herbert Keenor was dead.'

'Sam Keenor,' I said. 'Sam Keenor . . . and possibly Madelaine.'

'You like to give her the benefit of the doubt, don't you?'

'I suppose I do. But she's a born liar, Fred. Always was. She's a brilliant liar and because she can lie through her teeth, she's also a considerable actress. But she gets carried away. She overdoes it, and for no reason. She came to see me at Thoughtful Creek, the cabin there . . .'

His eyes only altered the merest shade. 'Go on,' he said.

'She lied about where she'd rented her car. She said it was Providence, Rhode Island, when it had a Massachusetts number plate. And when she came to Berlin, for God's sake, she said she caught a Lufthansa flight from Brussels. Lufthansa *don't fly to Berlin*, Fred. As the German national airline they're not *allowed* to fly there under the terms settled between the Four Powers at the end of the war. I know her of old, once she starts fabricating something, she doesn't know where to stop.'

'*When* did Sam Keenor know about the Hine business?'

'That I don't know. But I imagine it was after I had paid my first visit to Flagstaff. There was a gap of several days before the fire at New London. He had time to act. How he found out, I can't tell you, but he did.'

Robinson nodded: 'There were plenty of ears there. And he went crazy.'

'Wouldn't you? You've spent years working your ass off to become a future President. You've kept your nose clean, you've kissed a million babies and then you discover that your old man was a closet Nazi, helping saboteurs.'

'It's disappointing,' he said mildly. There was a knock on the door, and the girl who had spent four days with me in the archives came in holding three files. She showed no recognition, but handed the files to Robinson who signed for them. 'Keenor, Fisher and Wale,' he checked as he signed.

'That's Sheree from the basement,' I said when she had gone.

'Sure. She works with me now. She had trouble with her husband and her teeth.' He glanced up. 'I regret that she saw you. I'll tell her she didn't.' He picked up the files. 'Do you want to look at these now?'

'Let's leave them until last,' I suggested.

'Okay. Resume,' he said. 'So Keenor Junior is scared and mad.'

'So first he tries to frighten me off. The fire at the motel which accidentally kills an old lady. The bungled shooting in the go-go club. The people they used were not very efficient.'

He shrugged. 'Who is? In this very building, the FBI, there's mistakes made every day, ever hour, through incompetence. Don't tell me Scotland Yard don't make mistakes. Dumb mistakes.'

'They do, plenty,' I acknowledged. 'Anyway, these men were perhaps attempting to kill me and screwed it up, or trying to frighten me off. Unfortunately, an old lady and a young one got in the way. But then . . . then

Sam realizes. That sort of thing, *and* at the money I'm being paid, is only going to make me more determined to go on, to stick my neck out. Why not take advantage of the situation? After all, I'm the guy who is going to lead them to Hine. He still needs to find Hine, remember. So they let me go on, but they keep a check on me.'

'How did they do that? Keep check of your progress? Get to know exactly what you were doing?' he inquired with apparent innocence.

I sighed. 'Okay. It was Madelaine. She materialized at regular intervals and I told her everything. Just about everything.'

'She was there with her husband's connivance?'

'Maybe. Maybe not. She may have spared him the details. But it was the ideal way of keeping tabs on my progress. His career is more important to him than anything. Even his wife's virtue. There was no need to risk employing another agent, although there was always a back-up team – the people who deposited the ravens and dealt with Renate and Beckerman, for example. And, knowing Madelaine, the arrangement excited her. She always was one for a risk, an adventure. It would appeal.'

He kept his face sober. 'And Madelaine was the one who knew you well enough to know that the more difficult, dangerous, the situation got, the less likely you would be to lose interest.'

'After Renate Schmitt,' I said. 'She – they – knew there was no way I would turn back. It was handy eliminating people like Renate and Beckerman. First of all I would lead them to the intended victim, putting it on a plate for them. By eliminating those two they also got rid of two potential witnesses to the Hine business. They were people, they thought anyway, who knew

353

enough about it to prove dangerous to Sam Keenor in the future, if the matter of his father should ever be as much as whispered. And, as we've said, and they calculated, it made me determined to find Hine and his supposed Nazi group. The people I thought who were distributing bloody ravens. Believe me, Hine could not organize a piss-up in a brewery, let alone a group of killers.'

'Do you think Hine killed Herbert Keenor that night he came to visit him?'

'I doubt it. What's the point of killing the golden goose? Anyway, if you'd seen Hine, he was eighty and looked every day of it, he just couldn't have done it. He certainly went there that night but he wasn't there – he'd gone – when Keenor died, however he died. Perhaps Sam Keenor went there and was told by his father that Hine had been on a visit. Hine threatened him, named the blackmail price, and left him to think it over. He also told Herbert that if *anything* nasty happened to him – Hine – during the immediate future, that he had made arrangements for all to be revealed.'

'Sam Keenor was in New York,' pointed out Robinson.

'Less than a two-hour drive – and at night. Or he could have arranged it. Like he arranged other things.'

'Okay, so Sam and Madelaine let you go on the trail. They sit back and wait for you to trace Hine, which you do. Then they move in your lady friend, what was she calling herself . . .?'

'Cara,' I said dully. 'Cara Brown.'

'Sure, Cara. They attach her to you. She's a different calibre to the other operators. Except she still made one mistake. Her last one. She had orders to stay along with

354

you until you find Hine, and then murder Hine before he can say anything, and promptly murder you. Hine's dead, you're dead. Nobody knows anything.'

'No one would have known it was Sam Keenor pulling the strings, giving the orders.'

'No sir. Most certainly not,' he said emphatically. 'Keenor's wishes, his instructions, went down a line of command, way down until the people who organize such things, and live by them, knew what was required. They did not even need to know the reason. What about Irving?'

I shook my head. 'I can't imagine Irving being in on it. He would not have known. When he did find out – that's when he took his boat ride.'

Robinson opened the files on the desk. Expertly, he went through the index in each one. 'Herbert Keenor, nothing,' he said. 'Isolationist, that's all. But so were a lot of other people. Anti-British because of it. But so what? It didn't stop the Kennedy family. Nothing the least suspect as far as I can see.' He turned up the cover of the file as if to make sure it was the right one. 'A pretty poor dossier,' he grumbled. 'For that sort of guy.'

'Maybe something's missing,' I suggested. 'Taken out.'

He shrugged. 'We don't like to think so, but it could happen. Easily. Let's see Fisher and Mister Wale.' He tapped his fingers down the Fisher index and then went quickly to the second file. 'This is more like it,' he said. 'Both of German origin. Fisher's name once had a letter "c" in it, and Wale was called Walther. Both were admirers of Hitler. Both had dealings with the American Nazi Party, the Bund, although they did not officially belong to it. But even that was no crime at the time.' He handed me two photographs. 'Fisher,' he said, 'and Wale.'

He took Herbert Keenor's photograph out. It was Keenor as a young man. 'And young Keenor,' he said. 'Looks like Sam, doesn't he?'

'In the photograph we saw that day at the Smithsonian,' I said. 'Keenor had his arms about the shoulders of the two men next to him, Fisher and Wale.'

He stood up and folded the files. 'So?' he said. 'What does that prove, Michael? Maybe he was feeling faint, needed support.' Robinson rose and made to leave the room. 'How about a walk,' he suggested. 'A walk in the nice white snow.'

We went out of the building and into the street. Snow was falling and we pulled up our collars. 'That room isn't bugged like the interview rooms,' he said nodding over his shoulder. 'That's why I took us there. But you can't be sure.'

The black man was standing over his private steam and haranguing the FBI. Robinson said: 'Mike, you've got as much chance of anyone listening to that story as that poor bastard has of anybody listening to his. You can't prove a single thing. It would be easier to prove that you murdered two innocent fishermen in Mexico, if you get my drift.'

'What am I going to do?'

'Do nothing. Stay dead. If you're right and these people find out you're still around, they'll kill you for sure now. You know too many strong rumours.'

'So they get away with it.'

'Mike, rich and powerful people do get away with a lot of things. And especially in America.'

His black face peered through the dropping snowflakes. 'But surely,' I pleaded. '*Something* can be proved?'

'What something?' he asked. 'Who is going to prove it? One move from you now, I warned you, and you're a dead man. The way the cards are dealt, the way the dice roll, *they* always win.'

'What about Nixon?' I blurted. 'You couldn't be any more powerful than Nixon, and look what happened to him. Christ, he was demolished.'

'The President,' said Robinson thoughtfully, 'is the exception. When you get up there you're vulnerable. Presidents are vulnerable even to rumours. And they can't have people eliminated.' He turned to me and shook my hand. 'This snow's too white for me,' he said. 'I'm going back to the archives.'

XX

All through the journey to New York it snowed, the sky
bruised, the flat land a white-out; the lit buildings of the
nearing city reduced to a glimmer. When I got there I
bought an overcoat and a hunter's cap and rented a car.
My beard was thick.

I waited until the following day before driving out to
Long Island. The snow reached to the edge of the ocean,
the air was brittle and the sun reflected fiercely from the
white country. By the time I reached Flagstaff, an afternoon that was almost night had closed in. The sky
greyed then blackened, and a bitter wind blew from the
east. The house seemed like a haunted place now, dark,
with the drifts piled around it. The wind rattled a
guttering. Snow piled up against the tennis court. At first
the house appeared utterly hollow, empty, abandoned.
Then, as I trudged around its walls and windows, I saw,
within the pile, the smallest touch of light.

At the back of the building a door was open. It swung
restlessly. I walked into a rear hallway that led to a cold
room that was once the kitchen. There was just enough
of the afternoon left to see. After the kitchen came a
further door and a dark passage, which I recognized as
the main lobby of the house. The tremor of light was
coming from a door at the distant end, to the left; what
had been Herbert Keenor's gun room, his Armoury. I
knew who was in there.

The door was open. The room was naked, the shelves

like toothless mouths, every fitting removed, but there was a flickering wood fire in the grate and a sole candle on a table. A high-backed chair, which I recognized, was turned towards the meagre firelight. There was a thick log by the fender. I knocked at the open door. 'Lucette,' I said quietly.

When she turned the chair on its swivel, slowly towards me, I saw that she was pointing a gun. 'Lucette,' I repeated as calmly as I could. 'It's Michael Findlater.'

'Michael,' she said. She lowered the gun. It was the one that had killed Herbert Keenor. 'You've been away.'

'Travelling,' I answered. 'Can I come in?'

'Do,' she said. 'You are the only one who has been kind to me.'

'Thanks.' I walked towards her and shook her hand, which felt weak. Then I sat on the huge old log. 'Not the weather for tennis,' I said.

Her face was waxy in the uncertain flicker. Her eyes deeply rimmed. 'You couldn't get through the drifts,' she said.

'I saw.' I leaned a little forward. 'What are you doing here, Lucette?'

'Filling in the last few hours of this house,' she answered. 'Everything's gone, as you can see. I bought his chair, this chair, at the auction, although they would not have wanted me to have it. I was determined, and they weren't here to see. It was the third day they were selling things. Everything else has been taken away.' She gave a tight, crafty smile. 'But I have a key to a door.' She half held up the gun. 'And I kept this. Stolen, you could say. Technically I stole it. But nobody is going to have this.'

I said: 'It's very sad. Why don't you go back to your

359

home and take some time off? Then you can start again. You're a young woman.'

Lucette nodded: 'You can remember how he filled this place. Just by *being* here, Michael. With his ver resence. He was always larger than life, larger than all the pygmies. When he laughed it was a real laugh, not some snicker behind his hand. And his stories. Well, you know how he loved his stories.'

'Yes, I did not know him for long, but I realized that,' I said.

'You remember the story of the wedding party and the great fire?' she said. 'How they kept on dancing?'

'Yes, he told me that.'

'It was one of his favourites.'

She lifted up a plastic carrier bag which had been concealed around the far side of the chair. 'I kept some other things,' she said conspiratorially. 'I found them tucked away right in the cupboards at the bottom of the bookcases. They're nothing much, but they're from the time when we were . . . he was younger. Would you like to see what they are?'

On instinct my heart began to quicken. 'I would indeed,' I told her quietly. She was already reaching in the bag.

'Just photographs and things,' she said as she did so. 'I'm in some of them.' She glanced towards the candle. 'Will you be able to see?'

'I think so,' I said. It was all I could do to stop my hands going out to the bag. She had taken a few photograph folders out. She opened the first and passed it to me. 'That was his wedding day,' she said. 'I'm the first bridesmaid. See, that's me. That was the closest I had ever been to him up to then.'

It was a conventional wedding group. Keenor, as

handsome then as he was in old age, in frock coat with a smile and a laughing bride. Beside him was a thin ungainly girl. 'When did his wife die?' I asked.

'Years ago,' she said dismissively. 'She never made him happy. Never tried. Here are some others.'

She produced three more wedding pictures and then others taken at picnics and at Christmas. There were other groups of tennis parties. 'I'm there,' she pointed. 'I was eighteen then. And that's Herbert of course. It was when we were first partners.' She began to stuff the photographs away in the bag. 'There's a few others when he was young, when he was first in the Senate,' she said.

'Could I see them?'

She was grateful for my interest. 'Of course you can. I'm glad.' She took out a bundle of old photographs without protective folders. 'That's at some sort of summer camp,' she said. 'I can't guess where. He's got a beard. I never saw him before with a beard.'

Keenor was standing with a group of young men. Putting the picture close to the candlelight was sufficient to show me that he was flanked by Fisher and Wale. They were all in uniform, leather belts, stiff shirts, trousers tucked into high boots. I turned the photograph over. On the back was written: 'Bund, 1935.' Quickly and slyly I went on to the others. They were of no interest.

'Is that someone outside?' I said to her. 'Outside the window?'

She did not startle, but got up and walked towards the casement. As soon as she turned I pushed the camp photograph into my pocket. I returned the others to the bag. Something metallic shifted in there. 'It's nobody,' she said turning and coming back. 'Nobody comes here now. Maybe just a dog. They're having the carol singing around the flagmast tomorrow night. It's the last time of course. They will be coming.'

'Sam and Madelaine?' I said. 'Then Susan will be as well.'

'Senator and Mrs Keenor. I've now been told to call them that,' she said. She sat down again.

'Who told you?'

'They did. Ah, you put the photographs back, thank you. Nobody else would be interested, Michael.'

'Anything else?' I asked.

'No pictures.' She reached into the bag. 'There's just this. It's an old medallion – a sort of bracelet – of some kind. It looks like it's been buried or something for years and years. It's all green.'

I knew what it was before she had passed it to me, for I had seen its twin in the house of the old man, Zeb Smith, who took my cat. I rubbed my finger across the corroded cross.

'You can have that,' she offered suddenly. 'Take it. I only want the photographs. If it reminds you of the little time you spent here, then take it by all means.'

Closing my hand around it, I thanked her gravely. 'Lucette,' I said. 'I want to know if you can keep a secret?'

She seemed pleased. 'I've kept a few in my time, Michael, believe me.'

'Please don't tell anyone I came here today. Anyone. Or that you ever saw me. It's very important. I can't tell you why.'

She said: 'I don't need to know why. Nobody will ever know.' There was something going on in her face. 'And I will tell you a secret also,' she said at last. 'You may keep it or use it. I won't care.'

'What is it?' I moved a trifle towards her in the fire-light.

'That night,' she related. Her eyes drifted off as though she were recalling it for herself alone. 'That night when Herbert died.'

'Yes.'

'There was another thing. I told you I heard a car but when I heard the shot, I looked out and it had gone.'

'You told me.'

'Well, I put my robe on and hurried along the top landing, towards the main stairs. It was at the far end of the house, remember. When I reached your daughter's room . . . Susan's . . . I went in to see she was all right . . . she was at her window and looking out. Her room faced the back of the house, you understand. The way you came in tonight, through the kitchen. There is a back entrance and a path to a car park under the trees. When you go out you can see them. Deliveries always come in that way. Susan was looking out onto that path. She had not heard the gun; she was playing some pop music. But when I got there she said: "I have just seen Sam running down the path. I saw him come in and then I saw him run away. Why would he use that door? Why would he run like that?"'

Stunned I examined her face. 'You don't believe me,' she said.

'I do,' I said. 'I'm just . . .'

'It happened,' she said. 'She told me.'

'You never told anybody? You never told the police?'

She spread her hands in the uncertain light. 'How could I? Sam Keenor swore he was in New York, but that little girl Susan knew he was not. How could I drag her into it?' Her sad eyes came to me through the gloom.

'When the police were here,' she said, 'they asked Susan if she had heard anything. She shook her head. I was standing there. And at that moment she looked up at me and our eyes met, and I knew she would not tell. What could I do about that?'

It was very dark outside now.

Awkwardly, I stood up and shook her hand. She continued staring at the low fire. 'Will you be going to the carol singing tomorrow?' I asked.

She nodded. 'I'll be there,' she said. 'It always starts at seven. Mulled wine and cookies. It used to be wonderful.'

I drove back towards New York as far as Islip, checked into a motel, and sat there until the next evening. There was plenty of time to plan.

When it was dark that winter's eve, I returned to Flagstaff through newly-settled snow. My timing was good. Leaving the car near the gate, among many others parked along the white-banked verges of the road, I walked up the incline. The Stars and Stripes was illuminated, floodlit, although the pole was not. The flag looked as if it were floating in the purple of the night sky. People were singing.

Carefully I walked up the snowy incline. The house was on the top of the rise but invisible against the light that shone down on the circle of two hundred or more people. They were close together as if for warmth, wearing furs and hoods, heavy coats and thick boots. I had my long coat and my hunter's cap with ear muffs. Around my neck was a woollen scarf which I pulled up to my mouth as I walked. I felt as an assassin might feel approaching an unsuspecting group, his target a single person.

'As with gladness
Men of old,
Did the guiding star
Behold . . .'

They sang staunchly, as comfortably-fed people do at
such times. There was a man playing a small portable
harmonium, his head and shoulders moving to the solid
music. The collective breath of the singers rose up like a
halo. I moved to the edge of the crowd, singing behind
my scarf. You never forget the words of Christmas carols.

'As with joy
They hailed its light,
Leading onwards,
Beaming bright . . .'

There he was, the bastard. And there she was. No furs
for them. Furs could cost you votes. They had coats,
expensive and thick, and hoods. They sang close together;
him with his fervent mouth wide open, her forming the
words carefully. I searched for Susan. It was difficult
because of the mounds of clothing everyone wore. The
light was glaring and the vapour rising. Then I picked
her out, with a group of other young people. The others
were singing brightly, the boys loudly. Some of the girls
giggled as they sang. But my daughter's face was almost
hidden by the hood of her cloak. I could see her lips
moving only slightly as she looked down at her printed
sheet.

The carol came to a rousing end. The people shuffled
in the snow and pulled their clothes closer around them.
Sam Keenor called out: 'Okay, folks, one more carol
before we distribute the mulled wine and the other
goodies. There's coffee for those who can't take the

mulled wine this early in the evening.' Everyone laughed.

I was trying to see Madelaine. She raised her head to watch him with smiling approval as he made the announcement. Then she laughed at his joke. Her face looked dark and beautiful framed by the hood. Susan was standing quietly, still, while the youngsters about her pushed each other and laughed.

'The next carol,' Keenor called out, 'is "Silent Night".' There was a murmur of approval from the people as if he had composed it specially; a clearing of throats, a shuffling of song sheets. Feet stamped on the snow. 'It's a lovely carol, so let's sing it beautifully,' said Keenor. What an asshole. He stepped back and I saw Madelaine touch his arm and whisper something reassuring. The harmonium began to play.

> 'Silent night,
> Holy Night . . .'

At that moment my daughter saw me. She looked up and stared straight across the circle. The scarf had been around the lower part of my face, but it slipped as I started singing. It was only fractional, but her eyes came up at that moment and met mine. Her eyes opened as though they would burst, her hand came up as if to point. She was going to cry out. Firmly, with my eyes fixed to hers, I shook my head.

> 'All is calm,
> All is bright . . .'

It is possible that she, even then, when she checked herself, might not have been able to contain it further.

Her face had frozen, the cry temporarily trapped. Then someone shouted: 'Fire! Fire! The house is on fire!'

It was. A deep crimson glow was coming from the top of the rise. What had been an anonymous shape was now faintly outlined against the evening sky. Windows were squares of dull red. Smoke rose like dark trees. Everybody turned, the carol oddly enough still faltering on. 'Lucette,' I said to myself.

Typically, Sam Keenor was swift to take charge. 'Nobody moves!' he bellowed. Some people turned shocked faces towards him. 'Everybody stay here. The house is empty! There's nothing we can do!' He turned to a man at his side. 'Mr Blake, call the Fire Brigade.'

'I will, senator,' said the man almost proudly. He was portly, middle-aged, and he ambled off through the snow.

'Friends,' shouted Keenor. Susan's eyes were back on me now. But they were brimming with tears and smiles. Again I shook my head as a warning and smiled back. I blew her a secret kiss and she covertly returned it. Her face became radiant. Everyone else was watching the enormous burning of the house. Sam Keenor was urging them to carry on singing. 'My father,' he shouted, 'would have thought this was very poetic.' Like some prophet, his tall form outlined against the snow of the rising ground and the flames, which were turning the snow orange, he turned towards the house again. The fire was flying from the windows now. The timbers crackled in the crisp air. 'There's nothing we can do,' Keenor called again. 'Nothing, friends, nothing.' Christ, the bastard was enjoying this. 'It would be unnecessarily risking lives. The house is empty.'

It now, of course, also belonged to somebody else. I had to admire the way he boldly took in the situation and turned it to his own advantage. He had become an heroic figure, without moving anything but his mouth. 'Sing!' he called. 'Let's praise God! My father would want us to sing on!'

I was watching Susan and she was watching me. Only once did she glance around at the blazing building. Now I could see she had begun to cry. I wanted to go towards her. She wanted to come to me. 'Play, Mr Field!' ordered Keenor. The harmonium player obeyed and hesitantly at first, still looking up at the house, the singers sang:

> 'See yon Virgin,
> Mother and child . . .'

It was an amazing scene. Great cracks and flames issued from the mansion. The porch fell with a firework display of sparks, flames rose from the roof waving like red hands.

> 'Holy infant
> So tender and mild . . .'

With a last look towards Susan I turned away. She smiled through her tears as I did so. She was trying to sing. Some carollers had staunchly returned to their songsheets, like brave citizens in a war. Others could not take their eyes from the flames. They sang at random. As I went, my scarf back around my face, a loud and confused woman was singing the first verse again.

> 'Silent night,
> Holy night
> All is calm,
> All is bright . . .'

All was certainly bright. The snow was lit up for half a mile. The magnificent house blazed magnificently. Sparks and flames were high in the sky. Water began to cascade down the hill from the melting snow. The roof fell in with a huge, fiery sigh. I kept to the dark side of the park, below the trees, reached the road and went out. As I drove back to New York I was glad, beyond anything else, that my daughter had seen me and me her. Just that once. It was going to be a long wait, but I could wait. And she would know.

The early television news the following morning featured Senator Sam Keenor and his lovely weeping wife standing by the smoking skeleton of Flagstaff. They looked fraudulently sad and homeless. What remained of Lucette Harvey had been recovered from the flames.

That morning I flew from New York to Boston. The plan needed financing. In the First National Bank in Washington was now a considerable sum deposited regularly by Herbert Keenor's estate. That would have to remain untouched. Dead men do not make withdrawals.

The 1942 dollars given to me by Renate were in the Bank of America in Boston. They were still valid and nobody but me knew they were there. I went straight from the airport to the bank safe deposit. The dollars might still be legal currency but they were different. I saw that now. The notes were a distinctly darker green. I went to a teller and said I had found a hundred single dollars in a forgotten box.

'It's legal,' he said. 'But different.' He took a dollar note from his till, turned it over and read: 'In God We Trust'. Then he took one of my notes and reversed it. The words were absent.

I took five hundred dollars with me and left the rest in

the safe deposit. It was a setback but I could not risk any cash I used causing comment. I rented a car and drove down to New Bedford. It was a risk I had to take. From the bank there I withdrew all the money, sixteen thousand dollars, from the account I had opened when I first rented the house at Thoughtful Creek.

The following day I flew to Fort Worth and then made my way to the little town where I had boarded the Greyhound after Sherling had smuggled me in from Mexico. There I waited for a week before he turned up with another consignment of secret parrots. 'You're still here,' he said wryly. 'I thought you had things to do.'

'I missed the parrots,' I said.

With him I returned secretly to Mexico and over the next few weeks, by routes familiar to his bird-dealers, I progressed down through Central and South America and finally into Paraguay.

Paraguay is where I have lived for the past two and a half years. It is a country where you can easily assume another identity, obtain new papers; a good place for refuge or for waiting. I have made it my business to become a friend of Dieter Gottinger, formerly a Colonel in the *Abwehr*, the wartime German Intelligence. He still lives at Villarica. He is a jovial old man, very fit and keen on life. He was never, he says, a war criminal and I believe him.

I have never, of course, told him that I knew Peter Karl Hine, whom he first met at Quenz Lake at the training camp for spies. He has told me every detail of it, however, because I have been collaborating with him on his memoirs. 'It was crazy,' he said one day at the Villarica tennis club where he goes every day for lunch, and where we first met. 'This operation was the thought of a madman. We trained these men. They got their orders. Orders for New York. They set off in the U-boat. They had a navigation mark – a Stars and Stripes, the US flag itself flying on the shore, believe me, to direct them to the landing place. But then things went wrong.'

He has told me at great length and in detail during the course of our tape-recorded interviews of how things went wrong. At the time, he says, he did not know the identity of the contact who was supposed to meet the U-boat at Long Island, the man with the password 'Unter den Sternen', but that he discovered this man's identity by accident when they were busily burning the *Abwehr* files in Berlin at the end of the war, with the Russians advancing on the city. That was when he first saw the name Herbert Forrest Keenor.

It is going to be interesting reading, and with the dossier I have prepared on the events that were known to me personally, they will doubtless receive much attention at the time of the next US Presidential Election.

I keep in touch with political events in the United States through *Time* magazine and the newspapers. Sam Keenor is sweeping through the Primaries, and it seems nothing is going to stop him getting to the White House, with his lovely wife Madelaine.

Every week for three months before the Presidential Election, Sam Keenor will get a letter, each one containing a 1942 dark green dollar bill across which will be written 'Unter den Sternen'. They will be sent to him from different cities in the United States.

When he is nominated, as he most surely will be – that is when I shall come back from the dead. *Then* he will be vulnerable. That is when I shall nail the bastard. I only hope my wife Alice does not have to pay back the insurance money.

FOR THE BEST IN PAPERBACKS, LOOK FOR THE

In every corner of the world, on every subject under the sun, Penguin represents quality and variety – the very best in publishing today.

For complete information about books available from Penguin – including Puffins, Penguin Classics and Arkana – and how to order them, write to us at the appropriate address below. Please note that for copyright reasons the selection of books varies from country to country.

In the United Kingdom: Please write to *Dept E.P., Penguin Books Ltd, Harmondsworth, Middlesex, UB7 0DA*.

If you have any difficulty in obtaining a title, please send your order with the correct money, plus ten per cent for postage and packaging, to *PO Box No 11, West Drayton, Middlesex*

In the United States: Please write to *Dept BA, Penguin, 299 Murray Hill Parkway, East Rutherford, New Jersey 07073*

In Canada: Please write to *Penguin Books Canada Ltd, 2801 John Street, Markham, Ontario L3R 1B4*

In Australia: Please write to the *Marketing Department, Penguin Books Australia Ltd, P.O. Box 257, Ringwood, Victoria 3134*

In New Zealand: Please write to the *Marketing Department, Penguin Books (NZ) Ltd, Private Bag, Takapuna, Auckland 9*

In India: Please write to *Penguin Overseas Ltd, 706 Eros Apartments, 56 Nehru Place, New Delhi, 110019*

In the Netherlands: Please write to *Penguin Books Nederland B.V., Postbus 195, NL-1380AD Weesp*

In West Germany: Please write to *Penguin Books Ltd, Friedrichstrasse 10–12, D-6000 Frankfurt/Main 1*

In Spain: Please write to *Longman Penguin España, Calle San Nicolas 15, E–28013 Madrid*

In Italy: Please write to *Penguin Italia s.r.l., Via Como 4, I-20096 Pioltello (Milano)*

In France: Please write to *Penguin Books Ltd, 39 Rue de Montmorency, F-75003 Paris*

In Japan: Please write to *Longman Penguin Japan Co Ltd, Yamaguchi Building, 2-12-9 Kanda Jimbocho, Chiyoda-Ku, Tokyo 101*

A CHOICE OF PENGUIN FICTION

The Radiant Way Margaret Drabble

To Liz, Alix and Esther, fresh from Cambridge in the 1950s and among the most brilliant of their generation, the world offered its riches...'Shows a Dickensian desire to encompass the whole of contemporary British life ... Humane, intelligent, engrossing' – *Independent*

Summer's Lease John Mortimer

'It's high summer, high comedy too, when Molly drags her amiably bickering family to a rented Tuscan villa for the hols ... With a cosy fluency of wit, Mortimer charms us into his urbane tangle of clues...' – *Mail on Sunday*. 'Superb' – Ruth Rendell

Nice Work David Lodge

'The campus novel meets the industrial novel ... compulsive reading' – David Profumo in the *Daily Telegraph*. 'A work of immense intelligence, informative, disturbing and diverting ... one of the best novelists of his generation' – Anthony Burgess in the *Observer*

S. John Updike

'John Updike's very funny satire not only pierces the occluded hocus-pocus of Lego religion which exploits the gullible and self-deluded ... but probes more deeply and seriously the inadequacies on which superstitious skulduggery battens' – *The Times*

The Counterlife Philip Roth

'Roth has now surpassed himself' – *Washington Post*. 'A breathtaking *tour de force* of wit, wisdom, ingenuity and sharply-honed malice' – *The Times*

A CHOICE OF PENGUIN FICTION

The Clothes in the Wardrobe Alice Thomas Ellis

'Inspired malice … Alice Thomas Ellis only bothers with the things that really bother her. That's why her novel is short. That's why her novel is good' – Victoria Glendinning in *The Times*

Loving Attitudes Rachel Billington

Rachel Billington's bestselling novel of our search for love. 'A shrewd and compassionate book, an entertaining domestic comedy with an edge of believable tragedy' – *Evening Standard*

The Dearest and the Best Leslie Thomas

In the spring of 1940 the spectre of war turned into grim reality – and for all the inhabitants of the historic villages of the New Forest it was the beginning of the most bizarre, funny and tragic episode of their lives. 'Excellent' – *Sunday Times*

Only Children Alison Lurie

When the Hubbards and the Zimmerns go to visit Anna on her idyllic farm, it becomes increasingly difficult to tell who are the adults, and who the children. 'It demands to be read' – *Financial Times*

My Family and Other Animals Gerald Durrell

Gerald Durrell's famous account of his childhood years on Corfu and his development as a naturalist and zoologist is a true delight. Soaked in Greek sunshine, it is a 'bewitching book' – *Sunday Times*